D

"Forgive me if I do not feel married. Had I been given any other choice, I would not be."

"Nevertheless you are my wife."

Discard

Catherine's ire was ill suppressed as she ground out between clenched teeth, "And I chafe under it. This is not a proper marriage and I shall endeavor to keep myself apart from it. It is an arrangement, and most temporary."

"I think not." One dark eyebrow flickered upward in a measuring look. "You are a lovely and desirable young woman, Catherine. Why should I put myself through the expense of divorcing you?"

"Then as God is my witness I swear you will rue the day you married me. I will make you the coldest, most unwilling wife you can imagine...."

* * *

His Rebel Bride
Harlequin Historical #222—October 2007

HELEN DICKSON

was born and still lives in south Yorkshire—with her husband—on a busy arable farm, where she combines writing with keeping a chaotic farmhouse. An incurable romantic, she writes for pleasure, owing much of her inspiration to the beauty of the surrounding countryside. She enjoys reading and music. History has always captivated her, and she likes travel and visiting ancient buildings.

HIS REBEL BRIDE
Helen Dickson

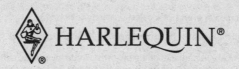

TORONTO • NEW YORK • LONDON
AMSTERDAM • PARIS • SYDNEY • HAMBURG
STOCKHOLM • ATHENS • TOKYO • MILAN • MADRID
PRAGUE • WARSAW • BUDAPEST • AUCKLAND

ISBN-13: 978-0-373-30531-5
ISBN-10: 0-373-30531-1

HIS REBEL BRIDE

First North American Publication 2007

www.eHarlequin.com

Printed in U.S.A.

**DON'T MISS THESE OTHER
NOVELS AVAILABLE NOW**

**#867 A WESTERN WINTER WONDERLAND—
CHERYL ST.JOHN, JENNA KERNAN, PAM CROOKS**
Love and family—the recipe for the perfect Christmas.
Three new novellas from three of your favorite authors!

#868 LORD LIBERTINE—GAIL RANSTROM
Andrew Hunter, cynical, disillusioned and dangerous, has
secrets to keep—and Isabella is determined to find them out!

#869 THE WARLORD'S MISTRESS—JULIET LANDON
Dania draws influential Roman officers to her House of Women
to learn their secrets, but one masterful warrior could all too
easily seduce her into his arms.

#870 THE HARLOT'S DAUGHTER—BLYTHE GIFFORD
Lady Solay was the most unmarriageable woman in England,
until the king commanded her to wed. Now the harlot's
daughter must find a way to be a modest wife!

**#221 AN INNOCENT COURTESAN—
ELIZABETH BEACON**
In making her escape from a forced marriage, Caro became
Cleo—an untouched courtesan. Amazingly, the husband who
ignored his plain bride is now pursuing *her*!

Chapter One

It was the year 1684 at the King's Head Tavern in Fleet Street that two men sat over a game of cards. Not an unusual occurrence, one might think, but not so for these two men. This was no ordinary game of cards.

Alone in a small room, they sat opposite each other at a liquor-soaked table, the flickering flames of the candles playing on chiselled features. The atmosphere was thick and tense as each man sat with bated breath, waiting for the turn of a card—a card that would decide the fate of one of them.

The older man, Henry Barrington, who sat so still he was like a figure carved in stone, had gambled and lost almost everything he owned to the other man, who watched him closely, quietly confident, and who had remained cool and perfectly calm throughout the two hours they had been playing.

Marcus Reresby had at last caught up with Henry Barrington at this tavern, which was used as a rendezvous, a rallying point for the political Green Ribbon Club, republicans and exclusionists alike. Marcus's deep hatred for this man, whom he knew to be in some way responsible for the cold-blooded murder of his father, was intense. In his search for proof of Barrington's guilt and the identity of his partner in crime, he had discovered that his father's death was directly connected to Barrington's involvement in a plot to murder King Charles and his brother James, the Duke of York.

When challenged, Barrington had arrogantly denied any part in the murder, but Marcus had proof of his guilt. He could see it in Barrington's eyes, and in something else. Marcus had realised that there was one thing Barrington was powerless to prevail against: fear. Barrington was afraid—primitively, abjectly afraid, and this feeling dominated any other feelings he might have. But who was he afraid of?

One way or another, Marcus would discover the truth, but meanwhile, knowing of Barrington's passion for gambling, to avenge his father's death he meant to deal Barrington a blow where it would hurt him most—his wealth. It was well known that Barrington was an extremely rich man, with considerable properties and shares in several trading companies. He relished what he had acquired and longed for more with an avarice that knew no bounds.

Henry Barrington had been educated for a legal career. He was a dangerously ambitious man, ruthless and unscrupulous, motivated by greed and ambition, but because of his controversial republican beliefs and connections among the Whig Party—those discontented with the present government, who used concerted efforts to exclude the Catholic Duke of York from the throne—he had been unable to achieve further advancement.

Sweat beaded Barrington's brow as he stared at the last card in his hand. Marcus Reresby was a strong aggressor and now Barrington found himself defenceless. Reresby had remained in control of the game throughout, calmly watching his victim, showing no sign of emotion other than impatience at Barrington's tardiness.

'You dawdle, Barrington,' Marcus uttered bitingly.

Barrington flung the card on to the table. His face was taut with anger and he had to fight the urge to reach out and throttle the man opposite, to wipe away the smug, satisfied smile that played on his lips. Placing his hands on the table, he half-rose out of his seat, determined to leave with as much dignity as he could muster.

'Wait.' Marcus's voice was razor sharp in the quiet of the room. 'We have not quite finished.'

Barrington remained still, eyeing his partner warily, wondering what new game he was playing.

'You have a daughter, Barrington,' Marcus said slowly, 'a daughter of divine beauty, by all accounts.' It was well known how much Barrington had worshipped his wife. After she had died, he had kept their only child, a daughter, at home. He was evidently protective of her and in no hurry to marry her off, and it was clear that he must care for her deeply. For Marcus to include the girl in his revenge would be to deal Barrington the final blow.

So, that was it, Barrington fumed inwardly. Not content with taking everything he owned, Reresby wanted his daughter also. 'What of her?'

Marcus's expression remained unchanged. 'I am interested to know what will become of her now she has no inheritance.'

'That is no concern of yours, Reresby.'

'Then I will make it mine,' Marcus drawled, stretching out his long booted legs.

'Explain what you mean by that.'

'I mean that I am feeling generous so I will give you one last chance to salvage something out of all you have lost. We cut the cards one more time, for your daughter's honour.'

Barrington's eyes narrowed. 'Are you suggesting that I should stake my daughter?'

'Exactly.' Marcus's voice was dangerously quiet. 'I said I

was feeling generous. If you draw the highest card, I will let you keep your property for as long as you live, but I will take your daughter as my mistress and keep her for as long as I choose.'

Barrington glared at him. 'Never,' he hissed. 'And why go to the trouble of ruining me only to hand it all back if I win?'

'I have not finished. If *I* have the highest card, you will sign a confession of treason, whereby I shall hand it over to one of the Secretaries of State and you will face the full rigour of the law.'

'Ah, so, that's your game. And my daughter?'

Marcus smiled. 'Will remain as chaste as she is now.'

A self-satisfied smile played on Marcus's lips, but his eyes lost none of their deadly glitter as he continued in a lazy, almost indifferent voice, 'Whichever card you draw you cannot win, but if you accept my wager and you draw the highest card, you have the opportunity to enjoy your property for as long as you live.'

A muscle twitched at the side of Barrington's mouth. 'While you make free with my daughter. Why should I accept your wager?'

'Because you are a gambling man, and it is rare for you to turn down a bet.'

Barrington loathed the thought of satisfying any part of Reresby's desires. Reresby had sprung a trap from which there was no escape—unless, he mused deviously, and not for the first time, he went to join his fellow conspirators in Holland. As a lesser member of the conspiracy, and now that his accomplice had permanently removed Reresby's father, the only positive witness who could testify against him—since to sustain a charge of treason it was necessary for the prosecution to produce two witnesses—he had considered himself safe from arrest.

Barrington stared down at the table, concealing his thoughts as he pondered on the options open to him. His opponent knew he wouldn't, couldn't afford to refuse his challenge, and this was one occasion he desperately wanted to win. The alternative was unthinkable. Although, he mused, thinking of his daughter, perhaps all was not lost and it might be possible for him to turn the tables on Reresby.

Ever since Catherine had been born, contrary to what everyone thought, he had been trying to forget that he had a daughter. He had been forever hounded by her presence. To others he always spoke of her with affection, and only those close to the girl knew the true nature of his feelings. Clearly Reresby thought he doted on her, otherwise he would never have included her in his revenge. Well, let him think that. It made it easier for him.

'You insult me, Reresby. My daughter is an innocent.'

'If you refuse the wager then you will face the consequences.'

'I fear you are being overzealous in your determination to bring me down,' Barrington said, lowering himself back into the chair, beginning to feel a little easier now he had something to barter. 'I have some conditions of my own.'

'Which are?'

'If I win, you will allow me to keep my property in my lifetime, and you will wed my daughter. You will not dishonour her by making her your mistress. As your wife she will not be destitute when I am gone.' Not once did he give a thought to his lovely Catherine's feelings, or to what she might say if she knew her future was about to depend on the turn of a card.

Marcus's look was scathing. 'What? And be burdened with her for the rest of my life? I think not, Barrington.'

'You might, when you hear what I have to say. On my terms, should you win, then I will tell you everything about your father's murder—including the name of the man who wielded the knife.'

Marcus became still. Barrington's words hung in the air between them. This was something he had not bargained on and was more than he could have hoped for. If he refused, Barrington would gain the upper hand. If he took the wager and lost, Barrington would escape ruin in his lifetime and Marcus would have to marry the daughter of one of his father's murderers. At first this was unthinkable, but on consideration, he knew he could not refuse the wager, even though it was heavily loaded. His chances of winning were even, and the desire to know at last the name of the man who had murdered his father was too great to resist. He nodded. 'Very well.'

'There is just one more thing, Reresby.' Marcus waited, watching him closely. 'If you win, I refuse to sign a confession of treason. I will tell you about your father's murder, and you will give me your word that you will not stand in my way when I leave England.'

'You have it. There is a chance that one of your fellow conspirators will betray you anyhow, so in the end you may have to forfeit your life. But I am a gentleman, Barrington, and like my father before me I honour the name I bear. I will keep my part of the bargain. I do not renege on my word. However, whatever the outcome of the final card, I shall keep what I have already won. All your wealth and properties belong to me, though I may allow you their use before your death. You agree?'

Barrington nodded. 'I shall extract from you one more proviso,' he said, 'that, should I draw the highest card, and after you wed my daughter, you will leave her with me to live out the rest of my life in peace, and only when I am dead will you claim what is yours.' For some reason unknown to him, he could not bear the thought of any form of intimacy between Catherine and Reresby. Perhaps it was the haunting memory of his wife, and that when they were reunited in the afterlife and he stood before her, he would be horribly punished for the coldness he had shown towards their daughter.

Marcus nodded. 'I agree.' He knew he would not have very long to wait for Barrington's demise. Barrington was an ill man, gaunt and with a liverish tinge to his flesh caused by a growth eating away at his insides. Whichever card Barrington drew he was already doomed.

Experiencing a feeling of heightened awareness, taking his eyes from his opponent, Marcus looked towards the door. He became very still, convinced in that animated, lingering moment that someone unseen observed the play. What he saw beyond the open door was a disappearing shadow and then nothing but the bleary ochre glow that seeped from the candles. Thinking no more of it, Marcus turned his attention on Barrington once more.

Slowly and with trembling fingers Henry Barrington reached out and cut the deck, turning it over. It was the queen of spades, a high card. The rope at Tyburn, which had begun to tighten about his neck earlier, began to slacken. Next it was Marcus's turn and Barrington waited, sweat oozing out of every pore in his body as he watched him reach out with slow deliberation. His eyes stared at the upturned card Marcus placed on the table.

It was the knave of hearts.

Marcus had lost.

Barrington smiled thinly at his opponent, smug in his triumph. 'The die is cast, Reresby. You cannot retreat. I think your pride and need to avenge the death of your father has led you into something you will bitterly regret.'

Marcus knew he was right.

Riverside House, the home of five generations of Barringtons, was beautifully situated upstream above Richmond on the banks of the River Thames. With gaunt old trees standing sentinel around the entrance, it was a graceful, impressive house built of red brick in the Dutch style. Inside it had a warm, comfortable feel to it, and Henry Barrington had spared no expense in the furnishing, with pieces collected from all over the world, colourful tapestries woven in Brussels and pictures painted by only the finest artists adorning the walls.

The night was black and the hour late when two carriages came to Riverside House. Seventeen-year-old Catherine was sound asleep, swallowed up in the warm comfort of her big four-poster bed. She was blissfully unaware of the dark-clad men striding quickly towards the house, the crunch of their boots striding over the frozen ground disturbing the silence of the night. Her maid, Alice Parks, shaking her, wakened her some time later.

'Catherine, wake up,' she whispered urgently.

Catherine's eyes opened and slowly, like a cat, she stretched her limbs full length in the bed. 'Alice! What is it? It's still the middle of the night,' she mumbled drowsily, turning over and pulling the covers over her head, wanting to be left alone to dream of her love, Harry Stapleton.

'Come, wake up,' Alice persisted, giving her another gentle shake. 'Your father is home and wishes to see you at once.'

At the mention of her father, Catherine came awake immediately. 'Father? But it's so late,' she said, sitting up straight and pushing the covers back.

'Be that as it may, he's home and in no mood to be kept waiting.' Alice held out Catherine's robe. 'You are to go to the chapel—and you should know that he is not alone.'

Without further questions Catherine thrust her arms into the loose-fitting sleeves of her robe, fumbling with the buttons as she slipped her feet into her soft slippers. Her young heart hammered in her breast as she sped along the length of the long gallery and slipped down the stairway that led to the chapel. On reaching the small chapel—draughty, and smelling dank and musty from disuse—she shivered when the cold air hit her. Partly hidden by a gilded rood-screen, she paused a moment to observe the scene. Shadows danced on the walls from lighted candles, casting a dull glow over the large box pews in the chancel and the raised pulpit.

Slowly she moved inside, aware of several people present, but overpowered by the strangeness of the occasion. She had eyes for no one other than her father. Contrary to this fact she had no desire to run to him, nor did her heart stir with the love and affection a daughter should feel for her father. Her father had been only an occasional figure in her life, stern, cold and remote. Not having seen him for several weeks, she observed how much thinner he was. His face was lean and gaunt, his nostrils pinched, and the eyes peering at her were dark and fathomless, like sunken caves.

The atmosphere inside the chapel was strangely charged. Baffled as to why all these men should be here at this time of night and why her presence was required, Catherine hovered on the perimeter of light, waiting for someone to say something to her.

Henry went to her, his face devoid of any warmth or affection. His gaze drifted over her, registering the startling changes that had altered her face from a girlish plainness into a young woman of exotic beauty. She had her mother's look about her now, and the memory twisted his heart. When his wife, Therese, had died, it had been the first time in his life that Henry had felt anything akin to grief over the loss of another human being. He held Catherine responsible for Therese's death, and he had coldly rejected all her attempts to become close. Reresby could have her. She was one possession he would not be sorry to dispense with.

'You sent for me, Father,' Catherine said softly.

'Yes. There is someone I want you to meet. It is late, I know, but he cannot stay long.'

Catherine turned to look as a figure emerged from the shadows. For a brief moment her vision seemed entirely filled by a tall man shrouded in black, a man, she realised, who was devilishly attractive, alive and virile in every fibre of his being. Immediately she was struck by the directness of his glance. The expression in his dark eyes was indefinable, and, as he continued to hold her gaze, she felt her cheeks grow hot beneath his scrutiny. She got the impression of great strength and formidable will power.

His hair was thick and a rich dark brown, ready to curl vigorously over the collar of his cloak. His nose was long and aquiline, his jaw firm and square. She stepped back when he bowed his head to her, his expression unsmiling, and then he turned away as though a few seconds' inspection was enough for a lifetime.

Catherine would have been surprised to learn that Marcus was not as indifferent to her as she thought. It was true what people said about her beauty. He saw for himself how lovely she was, thinking how pure and innocent she looked with her hair of sable blackness flowing down her back like the rippling mane of his own magnificent black stallion. Her nose was slim, fine-boned and ever so slightly pert, her face softly oval with gently rising cheekbones. Her lips were not the pouting rosebuds of the ladies of the King's Court, but soft, gently curving and expressive. He observed how her young breasts strained beneath the bodice of her robe and how her dark-fringed eyes—vibrant and green, seeming to illuminate the small chapel—were filled with a mixture of curiosity and alarm as she had tilted her head back to look up at him.

In the beginning Marcus had had no intention of involving the girl in his scheme of things—and now he had met her, he wondered at his own cruelty in doing so, for he'd certainly had no right, but once he had made the challenge and agreed to Barrington's insistence that he wed her, there had been no going back. And now here he was, having lost the wager and saddled with a bride he did not want any more than she wanted him.

His forbearance, never strong, which he had meant to keep in check this night, was beginning to wear thin. 'Come, Barrington,' he said. 'The hour is late. I must be away.'

Catherine jumped at the sound of his voice. It was deep and resonant and obviously used to giving commands and to being obeyed.

'Damn you, Reresby. Give me a moment,' Henry rasped.

Exasperated, Marcus slapped the palm of his hand with his gloves, melting into the shadows. 'Inform me when you're ready,' he growled over his shoulder.

Henry faced Catherine and did not flinch before the alarm mirrored in her eyes.

'Father, why did you ask me to come to the chapel?' It penetrated through a wave of alarm sweeping over her that there was something ominous in all this, something that did not make sense. 'Who is that man? What does he want?'

'You, my dear,' Henry replied coldly. 'You.'

Suspicious fear reared up like a sharp-clawed beast in Catherine's breast and her sudden wariness was evident in her tone. 'I do not understand. What have you done, Father? I ask you again, who is he?'

'His name is Marcus Reresby and the two of you are to be married this night.'

Catherine's heart contracted and for one dreadful moment she thought she was going to be sick. Her mind was reeling when she said, 'But I am to marry Harry Stapleton. You gave your consent. You said it was a good match.'

Henry's face tightened into lines of impatience and annoyance. 'Forget Stapleton. It is my wish that you wed Reresby instead.'

'But I am promised to Harry,' Catherine protested in defiance of her father's thunderous glower.

'Not any longer. You are very young, Catherine, and probably would not understand, but there are not only your selfish inclinations to consider in this matter. Let it be enough for now that, for reasons I do not have the time to enter in to, I want you to marry Reresby.'

'How can you expect that of me?' she cried in outrage. 'Surely I have a right to an explanation.'

'It's too late. Arrangements have been made. It is final, so prepare yourself.'

Catherine felt fear clutching at her heart, creeping through her body. Every vestige of colour drained from her face. Harry was the one she wanted, had taken for granted she would marry one day soon. She loved him with a young girl's intense passion and reverence. Harry was her first and last true love. He was her heart's joy and she would marry him—or no one.

She looked about her at the small gathering of people, recognising none, feeling like a hare cornered by the hounds in the hunt. What could she do? She saw Alice standing in the shadows, her eyes intent, her face set in anxious lines, her features revealing her concern as she waited to bear witness to this bizarre wedding. Catherine turned back to her father.

'I won't do it,' she insisted wildly. 'I cannot possibly marry a man who is a stranger to me.'

'It is of no consequence what you want. You will marry him, so let that be an end to it.'

Catherine's delicate brows snapped together. 'But why?' persisted the young woman who never questioned her father. Observing how her father's jaw tightened and how his cold eyes remained resolute, her stomach wrenched into sick knots at the thought of committing her entire life into the hands of a stranger. 'Father, I beg of you not to make me do this. I will do anything—anything to please you, but please do not ask this of me.' When he turned from her she reached out and gripped his arm, forcing him to look at her. 'Please,' she cried. 'It is Harry I love. Harry I wish to marry.'

Unmoved by her passionate plea, Henry shook her hand from his arm with such violence that she lost her balance and fell to her knees. 'Love!' he hissed at her. 'What has love to do with anything? Love is for fools. It is nothing but an unrealistic adoration that renders humans blind to life's unpleasant realities. It is wealth and power that protect them from life's hardships, not love. Now get up, and I order you to control yourself, Catherine.'

'Oh, Father,' she whispered brokenly. 'Do you really despise me this much that you will callously marry me to a man I have never met without consideration for my feelings?'

Coldly ignoring her, he strode to the altar where the minister was making preparations for the nuptials he was to perform.

The cold from the stone flags on the floor where Catherine knelt struck through her robe, but she was insensible to it. How long she knelt there she did not know, but she was brought back to reality when her small, icy hand was taken in a strong grasp and someone raised her to her feet. It was Marcus Reresby.

'Come, do not distress yourself so, Mistress Barrington,' he said gently, feeling her nerves stretched taut. He was not surprised when she angrily snatched her hand from his, and yet when he saw her eyes, expressive and alive, which were hurling scornful daggers at him, they were also glittering with bravely held tears. 'This will not take long. Allow me to soothe your fears. If it is of any consolation to you, I shall depart as soon as the ceremony is over. We may not meet again for some considerable time.'

Catherine gazed at him, searching his face. There was an oddly gentle look in his eyes—or was it pity? She had no way of knowing. Like a sleepwalker she allowed him to draw her towards the minister, a minister prepared to conduct this brief ceremony without asking awkward questions, a minister prepared to wave aside the required reading of banns for a substantial fee. She felt a constriction in her throat and swallowed, closing her mind to what was to come.

Facing the altar, Marcus turned his head slightly and glanced at the young woman at his side. She was standing with her head held proudly erect, her eyes not cast demurely down but ablaze with defiance. He felt a moment of admiration for her. The girl might justifiably be close to tears—humbled by her predicament and afraid for her future—yet her pride had come to the fore.

Catherine stood like a frozen statuette until the words prescribed by the Church were over and done with. All she could feel was the cold, a strange all-encompassing cold. For the time it took she let her mind slip away to a dark place where no one could reach her. Sudden, unexpected tears stung her eyelids when she thought of Harry and what his reaction would be when she told him she could no longer marry him. A sadness seemed to drag its way up from deep inside her, encompassing her with an unbearable sense of loss as her heart ached for the flame-haired youth to whom she had declared her love as he had declared his love for her, and she prayed he would be able to find it in his heart to forgive her.

The ceremony over, the minister stepped back. 'I wish you well. Go in peace.'

Momentarily blinded by a rush of tears, as she turned away, Catherine stumbled slightly on the hem of her robe. For the second time a supportive hand came to her aid and firm fingers gripped her arm as she regained her balance. Looking down, she saw they were long, lean and well manicured. Furious with herself that she should display such weakness, she shrank from him, snatching her arm back and pressing it to her side.

Marcus hid the flash of irritation her involuntary response stirred in him. Instead the corners of his mouth twitched in the ghost of a smile, but Catherine's eyes fell away without seeing it.

'As your husband,' he said, 'I feel that I must explain what is to happen—what is desired of you.'

With no anxious humility now the shock had left her, showing only haughty bravado, Catherine lifted her head imperiously, her small chin squared up to him in her proud challenge of his authority. Her eyes had turned to flint and her mouth hardened to an unsmiling resentment.

'What is desired of me? You need explain nothing to me, sir.'

Marcus lifted his shoulders in a casual manner. 'I do understand your reluctance to the marriage.'

His banal dismissal of what had just taken place provoked Catherine beyond the anger she felt toward her father. 'Forgive me if I do not feel married. Had I been given any other choice, I would not be.'

'Nevertheless you are my wife.' His voice was soft, though his smile was knowingly chiding.

Catherine's ire was ill suppressed as she ground out between clenched teeth, 'And I chafe under it. This is not a proper marriage and I shall endeavour to keep myself apart from it. It is an arrangement and most temporary.'

'I think not.' One dark eyebrow flickered upward in a measuring look. 'You are a lovely and desirable young woman, Catherine. Why should I put myself through the expense of divorcing you?'

'Then, as God is my witness, I swear you will rue the day you married me. I will make you the coldest, most unwilling wife you can imagine. I am yours in the eyes of man and God to do with as you will, but I make no secret of the fact that I love another and I will never be your wife in my heart—which is mine to give and mine to withhold.'

With a mocking smile lightly curving his lips, Marcus inclined his head briefly to indicate his acknowledgement of her statement. 'Then, my lady wife, I shall leave you in peace for the time it takes for your father to meet his maker.' He turned from her to hide a perplexing emotion he had felt when he had taken her hand in his as the priest had joined them. Not desire, not surprise that her hand should feel so soft, but a strange new impulse to protect.

It was clear to him that his new wife was quite different from her contemporaries. She was far too self-possessed, too self-assured. She would not play the coquette with him, as was customary with all the unattached young ladies he encountered. It was plain Catherine did not like him, that she resented him for preventing her marriage to Harry Stapleton—whoever that young man might be—and her reaction became a challenge.

Marcus had been blessed with more than his share of good looks, and since his early youth he had attracted the admiring glances of women of all ages—and more than one had told him he had that special charm women found irresistible. He was assured that, given time, Catherine would certainly not be any different.

On trembling limbs Catherine went to the door where she halted and turned to look back when she heard her father speak, but she was too far away to hear what was said.

'So, Reresby, I think we have concluded our business, have we not, to our mutual satisfaction—though 'tis a pity you never did find out the name of the man who murdered your father. Perhaps next time you will not be so hasty in making wagers when the stakes are set so high. Over-confidence often results in disappointment.'

'You really are about as despicable a specimen of the human race as my imagination can conjure, Barrington. I have let you off lightly. I should have run you through when I had the chance.'

Henry laughed, a nasty, rasping sound. 'You are right, Reresby. Under the circumstances you have indeed been generous. Had the situation been reversed, you would not have escaped with your life. Still, what do your think of my daughter? A comely wench, you must agree.' He chuckled, his words taunting. 'Think yourself fortunate that when I am dead you can drink your fill. I failed to warn you that Catherine does not lack spirit and will lead you a merry dance. I fear she will be a mightier foe than any you may encounter on the field of battle.'

'Catherine is indeed lovely, I grant you—in fact, I find it hard to believe she has any part of you. When I issued my challenge I proposed to take something from you that to any other man would be infinitely more precious than all his property and his life—but I was mistaken. It is rare indeed for a man to stake his own daughter's future on the turn of a card—indeed, most men would rot in hell first—yet that is what you did. May God forgive you, Barrington, for I doubt Catherine will.'

Henry shrugged. 'Catherine always was a drain on my resources, Reresby, and a thorn in my flesh. You were mistaken in your assumption that I cared that much for her.'

'As things have turned out, that is my misfortune. However, I shall continue to seek the man who wielded the knife that killed my father. The two of you were in it together, I know that. It is only a matter of time until I find him.'

Henry's smile was mocking. 'You believe that, do you? The man you seek is sitting tight. I have a warning for you, Reresby. You'd best have a care for yourself. The mood of the man you seek is dangerous, and whoever interferes with him and his plans risks his life.'

'I have no fear of a murderer.' Marcus looked away, pulling on his gloves as if he could no longer trust himself to speak, and then he said, 'I shall keep my part of the bargain and take satisfaction knowing how immense your suffering will be—

knowing all your accumulated, coveted wealth, mostly acquired by foul means, now belongs to me. You have nothing. You will not see me again in this life.' He turned and gave a curt bow in Catherine's direction before striding quickly out of the chapel.

Catherine returned to her bedchamber with a heavy heart. Her life as she had known it had come to an end, and from now until the man she had married this night returned, she would feel like a felon awaiting execution on Tyburn Tree. It was as though her world had split open and she had fallen into a place she did not recognise. Alone in her misery, she stood by her window and stared at the blackness beyond, unable to believe that when she had gone to bed life had held such promise. Now to have lost her darling Harry, to be trapped like this in a marriage to a total stranger—it was too much to bear.

Feeling a hardness around her finger, she raised her hand and looked at it. She had almost forgotten the wedding band Lord Reresby had given her. Her hand felt strange when she looked at it, as if it belonged to someone else. She remembered the moment he had placed it there, how her fist had been tightly clenched and how he'd had to prise it open to put the ring on her finger. His gaze had been hard and challenging, penetrating the depths of her own, and his hands had been firm and strong.

Irately Catherine wrenched the ring from her finger and dropped it in her trinket box, slamming the lid on the offending article. How she wished Marcus Reresby could be as easily got rid of.

Four days after suffering a stroke, King Charles II was dead and his brother, James II, the principal target of so much Whig plotting, succeeded him. James was as determined as ever to practise openly his Roman Catholic faith, although in an impromptu speech delivered before his Privy Council on the day his brother died, he assured it that he would govern according to the laws, announcing that he knew the principles of the Church of England were for monarchy and therefore he would always take care to defend and support it.

But it was soon evident that, although he would support and defend the Church of England, he would not prevent any other form of the Christian religion being practised—as had been the case in his brother's time of religious intolerance—including his own. It wasn't long after his accession that he began bestowing favours on his fellow Catholics, promoting them to offices of state, deeply offending his most powerful subjects and provoking concerted movements to overthrow him.

These seditious movements began to look for a successor. Some looked towards William of Orange, grandson of Charles I, and William's wife Mary, daughter of James, the present King. But others looked towards James, Duke of Monmouth, the handsome and charming bastard son of Charles II who had doted on and indulged him. The Duke of Monmouth was at present in exile in the Low Countries.

The world of politics seemed a million miles away from Riverside House. Other matters were concerning Catherine as she tried to come to terms with her predicament. Harry was oblivious to her marriage—it was as if by not telling him she could pretend the marriage had not taken place. She didn't want to talk about Marcus Reresby. Talking about him made him real. She could not bear to lose Harry. He would be devastated on learning she had wed another.

Almost as soon as Lord Reresby had left the house, Henry Barrington had fled to Holland where he lived for fourteen pain-filled months. His health had begun to deteriorate almost immediately. From letters sent to her from an acquaintance in Holland, Catherine was kept informed of his illness and how he suffered great pain. She felt nothing when she read the words. All the agony he was suffering now was like a salve to the mental torment he had made her suffer all her life. Even if he asked for her—which he never did—she would not go to him. Let him make his peace with God, not her. It was too late.

To add to her troubles, Harry was to leave for Brussels to join the Duke of Monmouth. Deprived for ever of her one true love, how would she survive?

Catherine looked at Alexander Soames sitting at the table, his elderly grey head bowed over her father's last will and testament. That he was not his usual calm self was evident. She knew instinctively that something was wrong. Mr Soames had been her father's legal adviser and a good friend to her for many years.

Mr Soames fixed his eyes on the papers in front of him. That Henry Barrington had not loved his daughter he had always known, but he had never fully realised the extent of his dislike until he had been summoned to the hall to draft out a new will fourteen months ago. How could Henry have gambled away his entire fortune, everything that had been this girl's birthright?

Raising his eyes, he looked at Catherine, perched stiffly on the edge of the chair opposite. She had backbone, did Henry's daughter, and she certainly knew how to conduct herself, he reflected silently. 'I wish I could spare you this, my dear, but unfortunately I can't. The fact is that your father was destitute. Everything he once owned already belongs to your husband, Lord Reresby.'

Catherine listened to what Mr Soames had to say, feeling as though she was frozen to the chair, every part of her set in a mould of ice. Fourteen months ago she had made a pact with herself not to think of Marcus Reresby, and now here he was, intruding like an uninvited guest. He hovered at the edges of her consciousness like a ghost in the gloom, when all she wanted was for him to be gone from her life, gone from her memory. She wondered why what Mr Soames disclosed did not surprise her. Despite her shock, she managed to make her voice sound calm.

'I see,' she said at length. 'Everything Lord Reresby has is his own—and that which should have come to me is now his, too.' Her soft lips twisted with irony. 'Lord Reresby has done well for himself. His circumstances must have improved considerably. Not only have I been robbed of my freedom, but also my inheritance. I think I have married a monster, Mr Soames. Who could blame me if I were to look elsewhere for affection?'

'Have a care, Catherine. If you were to do so, the consequences would be disastrous. Allow me to tell you what I know of Lord Reresby.'

'If you must,' she responded stiffly, unable to conceal the turbulent animosity she felt for the man she refused to consider her husband.

'Perhaps then you will not judge him so harshly. He is a military man, having distinguished himself in Scotland and Tangier. He is also well liked—a man of honour—'

'Honour? The man is beyond honour,' Catherine was quick to retort, making no effort to hide her scorn. 'There was nothing honourable in his dealings with me.'

'I understand that that is how it must seem to you, my dear. Lord Reresby is a man of great wealth in his own right—although there was a time when his family's fortunes suffered greatly when they supported the King during the Civil War. At the time of the Restoration, Lord Reresby's father's closeness both to Charles the First and his son played a great part in advancing the Reresby fortunes considerably. Your husband inherited Saxton Court, the Reresby estate in Somerset, on the death of his father.'

Unmoved by Mr Soames's account of Lord Reresby, Catherine rose and went to the window, staring out with unseeing eyes at the courtyard. 'How did this come about? Why did my father marry me to Lord Reresby?' She turned and looked at him. 'You know, don't you, Mr Soames? Tell me, and then I shall know what I have to face. And please do not try to spare my feelings, because you know as well as I how little he thought of me—so little as to marry me to a total stranger against my will—how unforgiving he was, and how he blamed me for the death of my mother until the day he died.'

Mr Soames nodded. She was right. Her mother had breathed her last the moment Catherine came into the world. This young woman had a right to know everything. Unfortunately he only knew what Henry had told him, and that wasn't the half of it. 'Your father lost his fortune to Lord Reresby in a card game. He gambled away everything he owned.'

'Everything?'

'Yes,' Mr Soames answered with a quiet finality that struck at Catherine's heart. 'Your father was a compulsive gambler—he never could resist the cards or the rattle of the dice, and the higher the stake the more exciting it became. It was at the tables where he acquired the greatest proportion of his wealth—he seldom lost. Reresby must be a clever man to have got the better of him.'

Catherine had to steel herself to ask the question uppermost in her mind, dreading what the answer would be. 'And what of me? Where do I fit in to all this?'

'I will try to explain as best I can, for I do not know all the facts. Your father told me that the game of cards was deliberately instigated by Lord Reresby with an aim to ruin him. Lord Reresby wanted to take revenge for some wrong Henry had done him. Your father was not a popular man, Catherine. Unable to achieve professional acclaim because of his extreme political beliefs, wealth became his god—a fact which you, of all people, are aware of. He believed power would come with wealth, that he could buy power. He had many enemies.'

'I've always known that. But tell me about the game of cards,' she asked, growing impatient to know all the facts. 'What do you know of that?'

'When your father had lost all his property, his fate—yours too, my dear—was to be determined on the turn of a card. If Lord Reresby drew the highest card, then he would extract a written confession from your father.'

A puzzled frown creased Catherine's brow. 'A confession? For what? Of what crime was he guilty?'

'High treason,' Mr Soames said quietly.

Horror filled Catherine's heart, for to accuse her father of high treason could only mean that he was guilty of some crime against the King, which was punishable by death.

'However,' Mr Soames went on, 'Henry refused the wager and made one of his own. He insisted that should he draw the highest card, he would keep his property for his lifetime and Lord Reresby would marry you instead of making you his mistress, which was what Lord Reresby originally intended.'

Catherine listened, caught in the grip of paralysing disbelief. 'Indeed. And if Lord Reresby drew the highest card? What then?'

'Unfortunately I was not made privy to that.'

'Are you telling me that my entire future was staked on the turn of a card?'

Mr Soames nodded.

'And who won this final wager?'

'Your father.'

Something cold clawed at Catherine's heart. What Mr Soames had divulged made her so angry she felt physically sick. Swallowing the lump of humiliation in her throat, in a voice shaking with fury, she said, 'Were there others present at that game of cards to witness my shame, of how I came to be Lord Reresby's wife, of how I was dragged from my bed in the middle of the night and forced into marriage—despite the fact that I was violently opposed to it?'

'I believe they were alone—and the shame is not yours, my dear.'

In humiliated outrage, fighting for control, she turned away, silently calling Marcus Reresby every terrible name she could think of. 'Lord Reresby is vile and I hate him. I hate him,' she hissed, with such conviction that Mr Soames could almost feel it. 'Had he realised how much my father despised me perhaps he would not have been so eager to involve me. But why go to all that trouble? If my father was guilty of some terrible crime, then why didn't Lord Reresby simply expose him?'

'The matter is extremely complex and I am certain there is more to it than I can tell you, but I am sure Lord Reresby knew what he was doing.'

'Of what treasonable offence was my father guilty?'

'I believe he was implicated in some way in a conspiracy to murder King Charles and his brother, then the Duke of York. You may have heard of it, for it was widely publicised at the time. The assassination was to take place after a visit to New-market when the brothers were en route from Newmarket to London, close to a house named The Rye, owned by an old Cromwellian.'

'Yes, I do know about it, and that, owing to a fire in the Earl of Sunderland's stables at Newmarket, half the town was burned down, which resulted in King Charles and his brother return-ing to London earlier than expected, whereby the conspirators were caught unprepared and the plot misfired. Some of the conspirators have been caught and executed, have they not?'

'They have. Others escaped abroad.'

'Then if, as you say, my father was implicated in the plot, I still do not understand why Lord Reresby did not expose him.'

'It is a mystery, I grant you. I still feel that your husband's revenge was of a personal nature. Perhaps you will discover the truth in time—when you know him better.'

'Damn Lord Reresby. I have no wish to know him better,' Catherine retorted vehemently, recoiling from the thought of committing her body, her entire life, into the hands of that man. In her mind he represented every cruelty that had been heaped on her throughout her life, every suffering and loss. 'I have nothing to give him. I will not be bound to him for all eternity— better that it were spent in purgatory.'

Her look became one of desperation, as though her senses had filled her with pain she could no longer stand. 'I simply cannot bear it. A marriage begun with a sham of a ceremony is doomed from the start. I want to be free of him—to have the marriage annulled, to divorce him—never to have to set eyes on him again.'

For a moment Mr Soames looked at her wordlessly, for what was there to say? There was nothing to be gained in comfort or pity. 'In the eyes of the church you are his wife,' he said quietly. 'There can be no question of a divorce, for it would require an Act of Parliament, and an annulment would be just as difficult to obtain as a divorce. But—just supposing the church did grant you an annulment, how would you live, Catherine? You have nothing of your own, only a few jewels you inherited from your mother and a small sum of money that is nowhere near enough to keep you for the rest of your life.'

When Catherine thought of this final insult to her pride, her heart pounded so hard she could scarcely breathe. There must be something she could do, somewhere she could go to escape Marcus Reresby. Then, as if by magic, the smiling face of Harry drifted before her mind's eye.

Harry. Harry was the one she loved with all her heart. Harry was the only son of a wealthy, respectable Protestant family who lived in Richmond. She suddenly remembered that he was to leave for The Hague this very day. In the merciless coldness of her mind and the goad of desperation, she knew Harry would provide her with a way of escape. She would go with him. They would be together after all. With nothing to lose and her mind made up, a curious sense of lightness, of freedom, pervaded her whole being, and she smiled at her own ingenuity.

'Alice,' she said when Mr Soames had departed and she had hastened to her bedchamber. 'Prepare me some clothes—just a few necessary articles of clothing suitable for a journey.'

Alice jerked her head towards her. 'What's this? A journey? And where to, might I ask?'

'Holland.'

Alice paused in what she was doing and stared at Catherine as though the girl had taken leave of her senses. 'You what? But—your husband will be arriving any day. Do you seek to provoke him?'

Catherine chafed at the reminder. 'What of it?'

'You wish to avoid him?'

A spark of resistance sprung to life in Catherine's heart. 'Exactly. I will not wait for Lord Reresby to come for me. I will not be his wife. I will not,' she reiterated adamantly. 'It is Harry I love. Harry I will have.' She went to her wardrobe and began pulling out several gowns, holding one of them against her that she had not yet worn. 'My father is dead, Alice, and suddenly my life has altered drastically. I am determined it will be for the better. I will take charge of my own life and choose its direction. There is no place in it for Lord Reresby. Harry is going to join the Duke of Monmouth in The Hague to offer his support to his cause. I am going with him.'

Alice's eyes revealed her disapproval and concern. She was the most sturdy and sceptical of women, and often severe on her charge. 'Nay, Catherine, you must not. Mark my words, no good will come of it. You are a married woman now. Your duty is to your husband.'

Catherine threw the gown on to the bed and stared at her old nurse. A rush of feelings rose in her chest. Alice had done so much for her. Deprived from birth of a mother's guidance and love, if not for Alice, her life would have been so much worse. 'Duty? I think not. I must go.' She went to Alice and hugged her. 'God bless you, Alice. I owe you so much. I fear I owe you a debt I can never repay.'

'You know that I love you like my own child, Catherine. You owe me nothing.' Alice smiled through her tears, holding Catherine at arm's length.

'Yes, I do, and please don't fret. I promise I will write just as soon as I arrive in Holland. Father stayed with Sir Percival Tippet and his wife until his death. They were always kind to me on the occasions we met and I know they will be glad to have me stay with them for a while. I hope you will join me there very soon.'

Alice stepped back, wiping her damp eyes on her apron. 'My beautiful Catherine. You always did have a penchant for not doing what is considered right. How will you travel?'

'On horseback.'

'And what shall I tell your husband when he comes?'

Catherine shrugged. 'The truth. I am sure he will make you tell him anyway, so you might as well.'

Alice was assailed by memories of the dark, sardonic man Catherine had married. Recalling how the candlelight had danced across his swarthy features, casting shadows that had made him look positively satanic, she thought there wasn't a woman in the whole of Christendom who would so blatantly defy and humiliate a man such as he.

'He will come after you, you know that.'

A chill crept up Catherine's spine as she imagined how angry Lord Reresby would be on finding her gone, but the alternative of facing him to suffer God knew what terrible fate was too repugnant to consider. Her eyes sparked and her jaw clenched wilfully.

'He can pursue me all he likes, and he probably will, just for the meanness of it, but Marcus Reresby can go to the devil for all I care.'

Chapter Two

'Where is my wife?' Marcus demanded of Alice on his arrival at Riverside House.

He had been in London when he had learned of the death of Henry Barrington, and he was quite astonished by how unmoved he felt. No feeling of guilt or remorse assailed him, and no ghost would rise up from the grave to haunt him. However, the bitterness Marcus had felt over the manner of his father's death eighteen months ago was as deep and strong in his blood as it had been at the time, and he would not rest until he had found the man who had conspired with Barrington to kill him.

At his first opportunity he had left London. Catherine would have matured into a woman now. She'd had plenty of time to come to terms with the idea of being his wife and resign herself to her responsibilities.

Marcus rose to his full six feet three inches. At first he was incredulous when Mistress Parks told him Catherine had left, and then his dark complexion turned darker. 'What manner of nonsense is this? If my wife isn't here, then where is she?'

Alice stepped back nervously from the furious blast of those dark eyes and repeated her words. 'Catherine has gone.'

'When?'

'Yesterday—noon.'

'Then perhaps you can tell me where I can find her. Come, I demand to know—and don't lie to me.'

Alice bristled at the suggestion that she would and drew herself up with all her dignity. 'It is not my way to lie, sir, and nor have I reason to. Catherine has gone to Holland—to The Hague.'

'The Hague?' Marcus's frown grew ominous, and the question blazed in his countenance. 'And why, pray, has she gone there? I take it she is not travelling alone, so who is accompanying her?' When Alice remained silent, uncomfortably avoiding his direct gaze, he said in a low, deadly voice, 'It's him, isn't it? She's gone with Harry Stapleton.'

Alice nodded. 'Yes.'

With a supreme effort, Marcus managed to keep his voice steady. 'Has she, by God? You must forgive my abruptness,' he said as patiently as possible, trying to stifle his agitation, 'but I thought Catherine understood that I would come for her as soon as I heard of her father's demise.'

'She did and I tried to prevent her from going with young Harry, emphasising the recklessness of her actions, but she was determined.' Alice clasped her hands at her waist, her misgivings and the unease that had attacked her when Catherine had told her she was to leave with Harry evident on her strained features. 'Lord Reresby, I have been Catherine's maid since she was a babe, and her mother's before that, and I must confess that for the first time I fear for her safety. You see, Harry has gone to offer his support to the Duke of Monmouth.'

Astounded by Alice's disclosure, Marcus stared at her, and then without a word he turned and paced back and forth. He had realised from the beginning that Catherine would never be a complaisant wife, and her fiery spirit would be compatible to his. He recalled how lovely she had looked: bravely, defiantly lovely. No matter how their marriage had come about she was his, she belonged to him, and no one interfered with anything that belonged to him. Harry Stapleton would regret ever being born if she wasn't physically untouched.

He could feel dark anger boiling up inside him, pounding in his temples. Never had he felt such rage. Always he dealt fairly with people, friends and servants alike, and he couldn't remember when his good nature had been so sorely tested as it was now. The idea of being defied and humiliated by a woman, particularly by his own wife, was unthinkable.

He ceased his pacing, coming to a halt in front of Alice. A muscle jerked ominously in his taut cheek. 'Your mistress has acted foolishly and wilfully. I shall leave immediately for The Hague and bring her back. My patience is not inexhaustible and she will very soon realise that her place is with me now and not running loose all over Europe with whomsoever takes her fancy.'

'A moment, my lord,' Alice said with caution. Suspecting Lord Reresby had a hot temper, she prayed Catherine's behaviour would not impel him into violent action and she would not be dragged back in humiliation.

Crossing to the door, he paused and looked back at her, impatient to be on his way and yet prepared to hear what she had to say.

'Without the guiding hand of her father, Catherine, in her gentle way, has always done exactly as she wanted. Her marriage to you was the one thing she was unable to do anything about. The situation was so sudden and so far beyond her experience that she felt quite helpless. It affected her deeply and she has tried to pretend it never happened. I beg of you not to deal too harshly with her when you find her.'

Alice's quiet, impassioned plea brought Lord Reresby's

black eyes to rest seriously on her. The thought came to her that
he looked very handsome, despite the mud on his clothes and
his wind-tangled hair. To anyone exposed to his anger he was
so very formidable, so intimidating, she thought, and she feared
for Catherine. And yet Catherine was a spitfire, and fully as arrogant as Lord Reresby. But the discomfort she would inevita-
bly be subjected to, should she continue to anger and defy her
husband, worried Alice. As if sensing her thoughts, at last Lord
Reresby smiled faintly and gave a nod of his head.

'I will heed your words, Mistress Parks. You may rest assured that I do not intend to terrorise her,' he promised gravely,
'only to make her see the error of her ways and to make it clear
that I expect better from her in the future. It is plain to me that
you care for Catherine a great deal, and if it is your wish to continue serving her then I will arrange for you to go to Saxton
Court. I do not know what will happen to Riverside House.
Until I have spoken to my wife, it is my intention to close it for
the time being.'

Oddly touched by something she saw in his eyes and heard
in his voice, Alice's anxiety for her young charge lessened.
'Thank you. I would like that. I have no wish to leave Catherine now.'

Despite his promise to Alice, as he rode back to London Marcus's anger increased. After years serving King and country, now
he had decided to retire from military life and spend his time at
Saxton Court with his wife and raising children, wasn't it time
for some peace and quiet in his life? By the time he reached London his anger was reduced to a state of deadly calm as he contemplated a variety of extremely gratifying ways of teaching this
outrageously wilful young woman a badly needed, unforgettable
lesson in how a wife should behave. He was remorseless and arrogant in his certainty that in the future she would obey him.

* * *

Marcus's enquiries had brought him to this large, fashionable house in The Hague, where a ball was being given by a wealthy political exile in honour of James Scott, the Duke of Monmouth. The majority of the guests were those who supported him in his desire to oust his uncle, King James, and to seize the English throne for himself.

The floor was full with dancers whirling and gliding around without the slightest effort to the music played enthusiastically by the orchestra. Marcus observed the undeniably handsome young duke dancing with his mistress, Lady Henrietta Wentworth. In appearance he had markedly Stuart looks, with that slight heaviness of chin and sensuality of mouth with which many of his family were endowed. Marcus walked slowly on the perimeter, looking on with cool disdain at the frenetic scene of gaiety—and then there she was.

He stopped, mesmerised by the picture his wife presented. When he looked at her it brought up some elusive emotion, the same feeling evoked by an exquisite work of art. She had a face that was full of contradictions, a face that was the most compelling he had ever seen.

Marcus was unprepared for the barb of resentment and jealousy that pricked him to a painful depth when a young man he assumed to be Harry Stapleton led her into the dance. With a toss of her head she followed him, her face rapt, frozen in perfect pleasure. Stapleton's eyes smiled into hers and never left her laughing face. She danced well and was as light on her feet as a lark. Harry Stapleton was a youth still, bright and beautiful in his masculine way. When he looked at Catherine she basked in his admiration and seemed to bloom as Marcus watched her. There was no denying the melting love in her eyes, and as she held Stapleton's hand it was as if she was his most treasured possession—which at that moment she was, for had she not left everything behind to come with him to Holland?

Marcus slowly began to pace once more, never taking his eyes from his wife. Despite his experience with women, Catherine was the most beautiful young woman he had ever set eyes on. Her long hair, caught back from her face in a gold band, shone like black silk in the bright candlelight. She was dressed in a gown of gold satin, the skirt overlaid with stiff gold lace. The bodice was low, revealing the soft, upward thrust of her breasts and the sheen of her skin. The becoming flesh had filled out in her transition to womanhood. She was completely female and womanly, sensual and beautiful, and she belonged to him.

When they had stood together in the chapel he had smelled a scent from her like roses, and when he had held her hand in his own, it had felt cool and fragile. Now she held that same hand out for Harry Stapleton to take and Marcus noticed that a ring with a green stone glittered on her finger. He looked at her face to see if the stone matched her eyes, but in the brightness and with her head half turned, he could not tell. Of her wedding band there was no sign.

Marcus continued to watch her dance with an air of polished graciousness and a lift of her proud head, noting the straightness of her elegant back. There was a certain air of sauciness about her—in the suggestion of the dimple in her cheek, the curl of her lips and the faint lift of one sleek black brow that seemed to say she found the occasion amusing and not to be taken seriously.

His contemplation of his young wife was interrupted when someone came to stand beside him.

'Why, Marcus!' Sir Roger Danby exclaimed when he came upon his brother-in-law idly contemplating the dancers. Pleasure creased his face. 'Surprised to see you. How long have you been at The Hague?'

Noticing for the first time the presence of his sister's husband, a wealthy cloth manufacturer also from Somerset, Marcus dragged his gaze away from his wife and clasped the other man's hand. 'Twenty-four hours, no more,' he replied with amiable cordiality. 'And you, Roger. What brings you here? I hardly expected to see you among this nest of malcontents.'

'I've been in Rotterdam on business. I return to England tomorrow—and I won't be sorry,' he added gravely. 'This place is nothing but a melting pot of political exiles—it resembles an ant heap with so many of them crawling all over the place. There's trouble brewing, mark my words.'

Marcus shrugged, his expression showing little interest. 'There has always been trouble and doubtless there always will be. My own reason for being in Holland has got nothing to do with politics, but I have to say the acts of these political exiles have made them irreconcilable enemies of King James.'

'Aye, that is so, Marcus, and since his brother King Charles was in excellent health prior to his death, suspicion has sprung up among the anti-Catholic fugitives eking out their days in Holland that he was poisoned by James. These men are desperate and eager to return to England with a Protestant king on the throne, and who better than King Charles's bastard son— if indeed he is illegitimate. Although I do not believe it myself, many believe that Charles was secretly married to Monmouth's mother, Lucy Walter, and therefore their offspring is legitimate and a true heir to the throne.'

'I too believe the allegations are false,' Marcus commented with disdain. 'In any case, indulged and spoiled as he has been all his life, Monmouth would not be an improvement. He is of an uncertain quantity—reckless and lacking in judgement, without the substance of his father or the constancy of his uncle the King. It is his Protestantism that appeals to the anti-Catholic backers in the succession stakes, and nothing more.'

'Nevertheless, Monmouth heeds these men and he is encouraged to do so by the Earl of Argyle, who is to return to the Western Highlands in an attempt to raise an opposition to King James while Monmouth invades England. Argyle is hot for revolt—in contrast to Monmouth, who has little stomach for it. He's acquired a taste for a retired life, and enjoys the delights of dallying with his mistress, Lady Henrietta Wentworth, who rashly believes his hopes. Despite the fact that he already has a wife—unhappy though his marriage may be—Lady Henrietta dreams of one day being Queen of England, and has sold her jewels to fund his cause. Monmouth has been encouraged by assurances from supporters in England, and is putting together an expeditionary force to invade.'

Marcus was frowning as he regarded the dancers. Sensing that he did not have the younger man's full attention, Roger fell silent. After a moment he remarked, 'So, Elizabeth informs me that very soon you will no longer be a military man, Marcus. What then? A gentleman's life at Saxton Court, or are you to be one of the smooth courtiers who surround King James?'

Marcus grimaced with distaste at the latter suggestion. 'Being at Court does not suit me. I have no taste for it. With all this talk of insurrection I cannot remain away from London and military matters for too long, but in truth I am weary of the army. As soon as I am able I fully intend returning to Saxton Court and familiarising myself with estate matters—which have been in the capable hands of Mr Fenton for the past couple of years. I've been away too long, Roger, far too long. I am impatient to settle down and turn my mind to the pleasurable matter of raising a family—and to seeing more of you and Elizabeth. How is my sister, by the way? I last saw her with your three offspring in London a month ago, on a visit to your mother.'

'Elizabeth is well, the children thriving. It will be good to see more of you when you take up permanent residence at Saxton Court. That great house needs a family living in it, Marcus. You get on well with Fenton?'

Marcus shrugged. 'I've had little to do with him. I do not dislike him. The truth is that I have no particular feeling for him at all. My father employed him—he came well recommended and seems to run Saxton Court like clockwork. I know from regular reports that the estate is prospering. I have no complaints.' There was a quizzical slant to Roger's lips, which prompted Marcus to add, 'Your thoughts appear to be unpleasant, Roger.'

Roger's face hardened quite dramatically as he eyed Marcus. With a strict military background and ruthless in his dealings with others, Marcus was sharp and brilliant in his ability to judge people and circumstances. He would set about any business that needed attending to with clear-cut strategy, sweeping aside difficulties that might have unnerved a lesser man. Roger wondered how he would deal with the likes of Fenton when he became better acquainted with him, because, as far as Roger was concerned, Jacob Fenton was as despicable a specimen of the human race as the imagination might conjure.

'To be frank, Marcus, I never did quite like the man. In fact, in all the years I knew your father, the first time I had to question his judgement was when he set him on. Mr Fenton is too ambitious for his own good—or for the good of Saxton Court. The servants murmur against him, and because of the trust your father placed in him, against *him*, also. Have a care, Marcus. Fenton needs watching.'

Unwilling to commit himself further and observing Marcus's hard mien as he watched one of the young ladies dancing, Roger wondered at his intensity, until he recognised her. 'You watch the Barrington girl with a good deal of interest, Marcus—but that is hardly surprising since you suspect her father of being behind the murder of your own.'

'It is more than a suspicion, Roger. I am certain of it.'

Roger's eyes were drawn to the gold ring on Marcus's finger. For a moment the young woman on Harry Stapleton's arm was forgotten. 'You wear your father's ring, I see. Tragic business, that,' he uttered softly. 'Tragic. Are you any closer to finding the man who murdered him?'

'No, but I will.'

Roger nodded, his expression sombre, for he knew the younger man would leave no stone unturned to find the man who had killed his father. He had known Marcus's father well. They had been good friends and he remembered the brutal manner of his death. He himself felt his loss deeply, but for Marcus and Elizabeth the murder had been shattering. Roger had not thought Marcus would wear a mental hair shirt, but he had been wrong. Would he never stop blaming himself? Upon learning of his father's murder, Marcus had suffered a shock of such magnitude that Roger knew a part of him would never get over it. He was racked with guilt because he had not been at home to help his father, and that his absence had contributed to his death.

'Barrington died recently—a rabid Protestant, as I recall, whose anti-papist views were as strong as anyone's and well known to most. His daughter is a lovely young thing—high-spirited, too. She arrived at The Hague with young Harry Stapleton recently. Raised a few eyebrows at the time—young lady travelling in the company of a young man alone. Quite unseemly, of course. I believe she is living at the home of an acquaintance of his in Rotterdam.'

Marcus nodded. 'Sir Percival Tippet and his wife. I called on them earlier and they told me she was here. Mistress Barrington is mistress no longer, Roger. She is Lady Reresby, my wife,' he revealed quietly.

Roger's eyes widened in amazement. 'Your wife? Good Lord! Is she, by God! And might I ask for how long?'

'A year last February.'

'That long? Strange choice of wife, Marcus—in fact, it would be funny if it were not so tragic. Good God! I shudder to think what Elizabeth will make of this. She doesn't know?'

'Not yet. I shall leave that to you—since you will no doubt see her before I do.'

'Do you mind me asking how marriage to Barrington's daughter came about?'

'The issue is complicated.'

'I seem to recall that Barrington was implicated in a treasonable act and branded a traitor, and the expectation of traitors is to be lodged in the Tower and duly executed.'

'True, Roger, but when I discovered Barrington to be behind my father's murder—because what he knew of Barrington's involvement in the plot to murder King Charles and his brother would have sent Barrington to the block—I dealt with it in my own way.'

'How? By marrying his daughter?'

'Not before I had ruined him. I then laid a final wager. If I won, he would confess his treason. If he won, I would let him enjoy his property for the rest of his life, but I would take his daughter as my mistress.'

Roger was surprised. This was not like Marcus. His tone was reproving when he spoke. 'I would not have expected such base behaviour from you, Marcus. 'Twas not an honourable act.'

'No, I agree, it wasn't. Barrington turned the tables, making a wager of his own. He told me that, if he lost, he would give me the name of my father's murderer. If he won, he insisted that I marry Catherine.'

'And being offered the name you wanted so badly, you gambled and lost.'

'That is obvious. I do not have the murderer's name and the lady is my wife.'

Roger shook his head slowly, unable to understand what had possessed his brother-in-law. 'You have a hard way of dealing with things, Marcus. Revenge is a poor master. Justice must be dealt with in a court of law.'

'I dare say you're right, but I did it my way, and,' Marcus murmured, looking at his wife as she tripped a circle round Harry Stapleton, 'no matter how much distaste we both feel for the marriage, we are bound to each other and will have to strive to make the best of things. I parted from Catherine after the ceremony and I have not set eyes on her since—until now.'

'Then you have some catching up to do. It will be amusing to see how people who know you will react when they find out—especially in the light of her behaviour with young Stapleton.'

'Only you and Elizabeth know of Barrington's involvement in Father's murder, thank God.'

'And you don't give a damn what people think, anyway.'

'Not in the least,' Marcus said, but in this case it was not the truth. Marcus was furious at the idea of being made to look like a public laughing stock who couldn't control his own wife.

'She does seem taken with Stapleton.'

Marcus absently took a step forward, a reluctant smile replacing his frown. 'Catherine is very young, very foolish and impressionable. In no way do I condone her behaviour in coming here to The Hague and I fully intend making her see her error in doing so. I am sure that when I take her to Saxton Court and keep her there, out of the public eye, I will succeed and that she will behave herself in the future.' Marcus spoke with supreme confidence.

'And if she imagines herself to be in love with young Stapleton,' Roger ventured, 'will you be assured that it is all in her imagination? For if not—then you have a battle on your hands. How will you deal with the young man?'

'I will hear him out and see how well he can defend himself.'

'If you're in a mood for it, Marcus, dine with me later, will you? I'll be glad of the company.'

Marcus smiled ruefully. 'Forgive me, Roger, but I have a wife to chastise. I have several choices on how to go about it, and right now they're all appealing.'

'Ah, well, some other time. I return to England tomorrow—and not a moment too soon. I am a Protestant and confess I too would be best pleased if a Protestant king sat on the throne, but I feel distinctly uneasy in this particular Protestant camp, and occasions such as this do little to ease my discomfort.'

'You leave tomorrow, you say.'

Roger nodded. 'I travel to Antwerp in the morning. There's a vessel leaving for Lyme. I intend being on it.'

'Indeed. Then we'll meet, Roger. I too intend leaving for England at the earliest opportunity. Tomorrow will be splendid.'

As she danced with her beloved Harry, Catherine was unaware of her glowing, happy face and the youthful, joyous movements of her body that had attracted her husband's attention. Since coming to The Hague, she had enjoyed the social life in which they had become involved, and on one occasion had driven out to the Dutch palace at Honselaarsdijk, where the prince and princess commonly kept open house.

Gazing at Harry, she thought how incredibly handsome he looked as he laughed at some remark made by a fellow who brushed past him. As he turned his attention back to her, his youthful face creased into a smile and his deep blue eyes softened with his love for her. As always he was charming and entertaining, and Catherine was scrupulously careful not to say anything about her married status that would jeopardise things between them. But the closeness they had shared for so many years was about to come to a shattering end.

She turned, and met the sardonically accusing dark eyes of

Lord Marcus Reresby—the epitome of her worst nightmare, the man with the power to blot all happiness from her future.

Her eyes became riveted in alarmed horror on the tall, daunting figure and she felt the world rock and tremble beneath her. Attired in a splendid midnight-blue loose-fitting surcoat over a long, beautifully embroidered dove-grey satin vest, with a cravat of delicate French lace at his throat, he was every inch the fashionable, expensively dressed gentleman, the sort she imagined graced the royal court.

He was just as she remembered him—darkly handsome, aggressively virile, stalking on the edge of the floor like a predator, a sinister, dangerous, malevolent spectre. There was an uncompromising authority about him, an arrogance in his stance and the firm set of his features that was not at all to her liking. He was looking straight at her, impaling her on his gaze, leaving her in no doubt that he intended to seek her out the moment she left the floor. The music faded in her ears and she felt the trembling begin in her suddenly weakened legs.

She felt sick with horror. She felt like a small bird snared by an eagle's sharp talons—tender bait for devouring. What was she going to do? How was she going to get out of here? she frantically asked herself, alternating between anger, despondent misery and desperation as she looked around for a safe place to conceal herself. The steps of the dance caused her to turn from him, and she could feel his eyes boring into her back, making it impossible for her to behave naturally with Harry.

Harry felt her standoffishness and frowned. 'Catherine, are you all right?'

She nodded. 'Oh, yes.' Without realising that she had done so, she grabbed his hand and looked towards the exit.

Harry was concerned. 'You don't seem to be.'

'It is nothing,' she hastened to assure him. 'It—it's just that all this dancing has made me overheated. Come, let's find some air.'

Together they left the dance floor, but if Catherine thought to escape her husband she was mistaken. His tall frame blocked her path to the exit. For Catherine it was like reliving a nightmare, and trying to escape it was pointless.

Resentful that he should have the effrontery to turn up at The Hague, with her head held high, as impressive as a tropical storm and a fierce challenging pride on her face, she walked towards him imperturbably, about to do battle, ready to do battle, ready for anything Marcus Reresby, her husband, would aim at her.

Tall and slender, Catherine waited for Marcus to speak to her, her very stance defiant, her exquisite features clouded with ill-disguised dislike.

Unsmiling, he looked at her seriously for a moment, one eyebrow lifted almost imperceptibly. Where she was concerned she had an aura of unattainability, which brought out the hunter in him—the conqueror. She stood straight and proud and unafraid. Her love for Stapleton shone from her eyes and Marcus recognised it and, for the moment, let it go. When the youth was no longer in the picture Catherine would be more malleable—the certainty of it was in her expressionless face.

'Catherine. I am relieved to have tracked you down at last—although I am most displeased at the lengths to which you have gone to avoid me. Was it your intention to provoke me, to try to make me dangle and dance to your tune?'

His words scraped at Catherine's lacerated nerves. His voice was clipped and cool, his stance relaxed, and yet there was an undeniable aura of forcefulness, of restrained power gathering force, waiting to be released on her.

'And do you expect me to fling myself into your arms and weep tears of joy on seeing you, to tell you how sorely I have missed you? I do not know you and I do not want to know you,' she replied tersely.

Something flickered in Marcus's dark eyes, but his expression remained the same. 'You will.' His gaze sliced to the bemused young man standing uneasily behind Catherine. He felt an instant antagonism as he looked into Harry Stapleton's brilliant blue eyes. He was too engaging, too closely linked to Catherine, upon whom his own desire was set. 'Come, Catherine. You forget your manners. Are you not going to introduce me to your friend?'

Catherine turned to Harry. She desperately wanted to take his hand, but she dare not show such intimacy before her husband. After the way she had behaved she had imagined Marcus Reresby would be icy, angry—anything but this cold self-possession. She was the one who was shaken and covered in confusion.

Reluctantly she yielded to the formalities. 'This—this is Harry Stapleton. Harry's family and my own have been friends for many years.'

Marcus fixed him with a hard stare. 'And I am Lord Reresby.'

Harry inclined his head politely, his face working with youthful emotion. 'I am happy to meet you, sir.'

'Catherine's husband,' Marcus stated flatly. 'I must thank you for taking care of my wife.'

Harry's colour disappeared, draining away in shock. 'I—I beg your pardon, sir?'

'Catherine is my wife—which is a fact I can see she has failed to disclose.' He gave Catherine a look of reproach. 'As a gentleman I disapprove of chastising a woman in public. I have never done so before, but I am your husband, madam, and demand your respect, to which I am entitled.'

Catherine looked at him with cold animosity, her eyes glowing like those of a spitting cat. 'How dare you speak to me of respect,' she was swift to reply, careful to keep her voice low so as not to draw the attention of those around them. 'I cannot remember you showing me respect when you married me.'

'Your opinion of me interests me not at all at present, Catherine, but I refuse to have everyone see my wife behaving disgracefully.'

Harry's voice came from his mouth in a delirium of pain as he stared at his love in disbelief. 'You are his wife? But—how can you be? Dear Lord, Catherine, tell me this is not true. Tell me you are not married to this man.'

Catherine could not speak. Her thoughts were spiralling away. Only her desperate hands clutching the folds of her gown and her eyes told Harry wordlessly that it was true and that she was crucified by it.

Harry's face changed from white shock to the red of anger. 'And you did not think to tell me—something as important as this? But why? Why, for God's sake? You know I love you. You have always been mine. You belong to me.'

'No, she does not,' Marcus said coldly. 'She belongs to me. We were married fourteen months ago.'

Harry was astounded. 'Fourteen months? When I was here—at The Hague?'

Catherine nodded. Shame and disappointment brought stinging tears to her eyes. 'Yes, and all that time I have tried to pretend it never happened. I—I have never wanted to marry anyone but you, Harry.'

'And I thought you were missing me—fretting.'

'I was, Harry. I swear I was, but I had no choice. They made me do it.'

'There is always a choice, Catherine. You could have said no.'

'I tried—truly I did. Do you think I would willingly commit my life to a complete stranger?'

Realising that she was beyond his reach, Harry struggled to hold on to his control.

Marcus tried to imagine how the young man felt, how deeply he must resent him, despise him, even, for taking his most precious thing. Before his eyes Marcus watched Harry Stapleton change from a happy, trusting youth to a man as he accepted the truth. The agony and the despair in his eyes matched those of the girl he loved. Marcus felt sorry for him.

Harry stared at Catherine with sick incredulity. He spoke to her slowly, with sadness coming through his anger. 'I would never have believed this of you, Catherine. You should not have deceived me. You should have told me. I really loved you. I trusted you against everything. How stupid does that make me?'

The look in his eyes tore Catherine to pieces. 'You are right. I have deceived you, which was wrong of me, I know and I am sorry. The only thing I can say in my defence is that I could not bear the thought of losing you. Please, Harry—'

Harry stepped back. For his own sake, the sooner he extricated himself from this nightmare situation the better. Catherine was lost to him, for ever out of his reach; no matter how much he loved her, he would not dare pursue a woman who was married to another man—a man as powerful as Lord Marcus Reresby, who happened to be an outstanding shot.

'No, Catherine, it is finished.' He looked at Marcus with politeness and an inbred courtesy, his face taking on a youthful dignity. 'I apologise, Lord Reresby. Catherine should have told me she was your wife.'

Marcus felt the first thread of respect for the young man, yet when he spoke his expression was mocking. 'I agree with you, although if I were you, sir, in the future, I would think twice before abducting another man's wife. However, you may rest easy. I am not after your scalp—as long as you realise that your friendship with my wife is over.'

'I do, sir. I was ignorant of the fact. I beg you to believe me when I say that had I known any of this I would not have brought her here. Please—excuse me.' Mortally wounded, without another word Harry turned and like a sleepwalker walked away. The music and the merrymaking all around him was a cruel mockery of his tragic plight. Before he left the room he looked back at Catherine before passing through a curtained recess, disappearing from her sight and her life.

The pain that pierced Catherine was almost unbearable— it was sharp, fierce, punishing. For a moment she was leaden, unaware of nothing except that Harry was gone and would not be coming back. But then his suffering scalded her and added further heat to her rage. Her chest heaving with indignation, she turned on her husband, her eyes shooting sparks of fire.

'Excuse me. I am leaving,' she told him as the viols struck up another dance.

Marcus's expression did not change. 'You will not leave without me. If you had the courage to come here in the first place, by God, madam, you will have the courage to stay or leave with your husband.'

Catherine glared at him, tempted to call him names that would have set his ears on fire, but, realizing it would serve no purpose, she refrained from doing so.

'Do you have contempt for women in general, or just me? Is it cruelty that makes you so obnoxious towards me, Lord Reresby, or are you naturally so?'

'I do not mean to be obnoxious and nor do I hold you in contempt. You are my wife, and no matter how repugnant that is to you, that is what you are and that is what you will stay. One more thing,' he said, taking her hand and glancing at her fingers. 'I see you have discarded your wedding band. You will retrieve it and wear it, and remove it at your peril.' Taking her elbow in a none too gentle grip, he said, 'Shall we go?'

Clenching her teeth, hating him, Catherine felt her self-control slip a notch as she let him guide her through the throng of chattering people. As she went she glimpsed the swift movements of heads turning away, and realised that a good many people had been observing their tête-à-tête.

In the darkness of the carriage travelling through the meandering streets of Rotterdam, settled in the seat opposite his wife, in the dim glow from the carriage lamps Marcus watched the changing expressions on her face.

Realising they were travelling in a different direction from the Tippets' house, Catherine's eyes shot to her husband in alarm. 'Where are you taking me? As I am sure you will know,' she said scathingly, 'I am staying with Sir Percival and Lady Tippet. They live some distance from here—in the other direction.'

'I know. I called on them earlier and instructed them to have your things packed and sent to the inn where we are to spend the night. We shall return to England tomorrow.'

Catherine was reluctant to dwell on how horrified Sir Percival and Lady Sarah must have been when Lord Reresby had turned up claiming to be her husband, and her blood boiled at the audacity of the man. Like everyone else, they had had no knowledge of her marriage. For reasons of his own, her father had chosen to keep it from his closest friends.

'Never. I will not go anywhere with you,' she fumed.

'Believe me, Catherine, you will,' Marcus said, continuing in that same deadly voice, continuing to be dispassionately immune to the wrathful expression on her lovely face. 'You will take up residence at Saxton Court very soon, where you will learn to behave like a good and dutiful wife.'

'Where you intend to keep me like a creature against my will.'

'With or without your will. It is clear to me that you have had more freedom than most—but you have gone too far with this madcap escapade of yours. I am well known in Somerset, Catherine. My family is old and respected, and you, besides being beautiful, which in itself gives rise to gossip, are my wife.

Now I have seen what you get up to, I will have none of it. There will be no more indiscretions. You will have a sense of dignity for my position and your own. From now on you will concern yourself with your new home, with household affairs—and myself, of course.'

Catherine looked at him coldly, her head held high, her eyes holding the darkness of a stormy day. 'You can go to the devil, Marcus Reresby. I dislike you intensely and I will never be a complaisant wife. I sorely wish I had never set eyes on you. You are arrogant and a bully, and I can see that my coming here with Harry has wounded your pride.'

'How observant of you,' Marcus drawled scathingly.

Catherine ignored his sarcasm. 'Let me point out that I am the innocent party in all this—not you. I did not ask for any of this. I am not afraid of you.'

'Then you should be.' Silkily he said, 'Listen to me very carefully, Catherine. I am treating you with more consideration than you have shown me when you took it into your head to come here alone with Harry Stapleton. Unfortunately, considering your close association with that young man, your reputation is not spotless and I have a great deal of interest in the repute which my wife bears. I cannot undo the fault you committed by coming here, but I can prevent you from committing new ones.'

'And how do you intend doing that, pray?'

As he spoke to her he measured his words with icy precision. 'I will, madam, believe me, in one way or another. My patience is tolerable but not endless. Do not try me too far.'

'Then I take it that you are unlikely to react reasonably to my suggestion for an annulment or the scandalous subject of a divorce.'

His eyes narrowed dangerously. 'You are right. I will not. You bear my name and I will not permit a breath of scandal to taint that name. It is a subject you will never raise again.'

Catherine shrugged and haughtily fixed her gaze out of the window. 'Pity. It's the only thing that will soften my attitude to you.'

For the remainder of the journey, Marcus avoided further conversation with her, sensing that Catherine would require a great deal of time and courtship to be lured into his arms and into his bed. Throughout his adult life he could not recall one woman he had wanted who hadn't been ready and eager to share his bed, but with Catherine it was different. Since she had such a low opinion of him she wouldn't be as easily coaxed, but already he was impatient to make her his wife in every way. He wanted Catherine, and he wanted her immediately, and he'd be damned if he'd take time courting her.

Chapter Three

The inn was crowded and noisy. In every smoke-filled room men and women were eating or drinking, transacting business or discussing the news of the day. They were shown into a cosy bedchamber, in which a fire burned bright. A four-poster bed with a canopy and faced bedspread of scarlet and gold dominated the room.

'Ah,' Marcus said on seeing baggage other than his own stacked on the floor. 'I see the Tippets have lost no time in having your things sent over.' From where he stood in the doorway, seeing Catherine's gaze sweep the room with unease, he said, 'I can see that something disturbs you.'

'You might say that.' She turned to look at him with contempt, not caring that her emotion showed plainly on her expressive face. 'It's the sleeping arrangements. Where are you to sleep?'

Closing the door, Marcus strode into the room and approached his wife in a misleadingly indolent manner. His dark eyes smiled, but his face gave nothing away of his thoughts. 'With you. In this bed. I thought you knew that.' To reinforce the point an almost lecherous smile touched his lips as his eyes swept the bed.

Energised by fear, Catherine faced up to him, an expression of indignation frozen on her face. 'Damn you,' she hissed. 'Have you not the decency to grant me time to come to terms with having a husband without forcing yourself on me?'

A ripple of something stirred in Marcus's breast and he marvelled at her courage. She might be stricken and feeling at her lowest ebb over the loss of Harry Stapleton, but this wilful young woman had certainly not parted from her temper. He felt a rush of blood through his veins and a hammering in his chest. Like a dangerous illness that desires a desperate remedy, he would make Catherine his wife and force her heart to forget Harry Stapleton before this night was out.

'Time? How much time do you need, Catherine?' he said mildly, his voice belying the need to ease the lusting ache that gnawed at the pit of his belly. 'You have had fourteen months to come to terms with our marriage.'

Marcus's nearness threatened to destroy Catherine's composure. A look had entered his eyes she did not recognise and she felt awkward. She swallowed, shrinking under his scrutiny. Anger had sustained her so far; now fear and something else, something she could not identify, began to nudge it aside. Struggling to steadfastly keep her thoughts on what was happening and aware that in her breast her heart was thumping far too fast for her to claim a mere tolerance of him, surreptitiously she stepped away to minimise contact.

'I do not see it as any kind of marriage.'

Marcus moved to stand behind her and ran his fingers down the shining darkness of her hair. 'Nevertheless that is what it is. Legal and binding in any court of law.'

'It was more an arrangement between you and my father, I'd say.'

'You are right,' Marcus admitted calmly. 'An arrangement I

am not ashamed to confess I entered into to destroy a man who was guilty of murder, treason and other assorted crimes. However, Catherine, despite the nature of that particular arrangement, I have a far better arrangement in mind, one that is much more in keeping with the whole idea of marriage. By any definition you are my wife.'

The heat of his stare lent the weight of truth to his words and something caught at Catherine's heart. For a moment she wavered, but, ashamed of her weakness, she met his stare squarely. 'Even though I love another?' she taunted coldly. 'Even though Harry's face, his smile, his voice took away the dreariness of my life, because what we had, our dreams, gave me hope and made everything bearable?'

'Yes. Our marriage is an inescapable fact.' His eyes looked directly into hers, leaving her in no doubt of his intention. 'Love me or hate me, Catherine, I am your husband and, be it duty or pleasure, before this night is out my will will be done.' Raising his hand, he touched her pale cheek gently with the tips of his fingers. 'Your father is dead and yet I see no sorrow or grief in your eyes. Not even the trace of a tear.'

Instinctively Catherine recoiled at his touch, which caused Marcus's jaw to tighten and his eyes to harden.

'I think I am right in assuming that you did not love your father.'

'I disliked him exceedingly—as much as he disliked me, and almost, if not more, than you did, it would seem.' Catherine said this without any hesitation and with such an intensity of feeling that Marcus could feel her hatred.

'It seems we have that in common, at least.'

'Then you can be sure it is the only thing,' she retorted scathingly.

'We shall see.'

'How could you despise him so much and yet sit down to a

game of cards with him? An immensely profitable game of cards,' Catherine stated meaningfully.

'So,' Marcus said, nodding slowly. 'He told you of that.'

'My father never told me anything.'

'Then who?'

'His lawyer. Not until he was dead was I told the sordid details of how I came to be your wife—how you intended using me as your mistress until you tired of me and how my father insisted on marriage instead. You could not have known then how much my father despised me, otherwise you would not have used me in your foul scheme.'

'Perhaps not—but it is done and there is no going back. Your father and I had an agreement, that once the marriage ceremony was over I would not see you again until after he was dead. I kept that agreement. However much you resent me and intend fighting me, Catherine, you are my wife—or are you going to tell me you did not know what was happening to you? That night, even though you were against it, you pledged yourself to me—or perhaps you don't remember.'

'I remember well enough,' she flared. 'I remember how I was bartered and sold like a piece of human merchandise. You and my father included me in a game in which I was not consulted. Tell me, Lord Reresby, when you played your tawdry, shameful game, did either of you give a thought to me and how I would feel having to tell the man I loved and hoped to marry that I could no longer be his wife because I had married someone else? Do you deem it right to force yourself on me, destroying any hope I had of wedding the man of my choice?'

Marcus remained silent, frustrated because he condemned his own actions and could not defend himself. From his own and Catherine's irate viewpoint, he had acted dishonourably.

'Do you wonder that I feel anger and resentment towards you?' she went on. 'How dared you treat me in such a fashion?

Put yourself in my place, my lord. Ask yourself how you would feel. And how do you expect me to live with you as your wife— to respect you as a wife should—after what you have done? I will tell you this,' she said, breathing deeply, 'that no matter what you expect of me, I despise you. I loathe you only a little less that I loathed my father, and I shall until the day I die.'

Marcus looked at her seriously, nodding slowly. 'We shall see,' he said quietly, seeing her stricken face and angry tears misting her eyes. He had caught the note of anguish in her voice, which tore at his heart. She was right and he was deeply sorry for the hurt he had caused her, but it was too late to change anything now. It would be a long time, if ever, he thought, feeling a pang of regret, that she would be able to trust him—but it would also be a long time before he would be able to forget that she was Henry Barrington's daughter. And yet he knew he must if they were to have any sort of life together as man and wife.

It was time for him to take control. Removing his jacket, he threw it onto the bed and seated himself before the fire. He leaned indolently back in his chair, and crossed his long legs at the ankles. 'I imagine you are now ready to explain your behaviour.'

The tone of his voice made Catherine's heart contract. No hint of softness showed in the marble severity of his face—no hint of anger, either, which was infinitely more disturbing. Fear stirred in her heart. After all, what did she know of this husband of hers? Was he a hard man, a violent man, who would beat her into submission? She forced herself to keep calm, not to appear ill at ease, not to show the unnerving effect being alone with him was having on her.

'Well?' he demanded impatiently. 'I should like to know precisely what has happened between the two of you. Your companion appeared to be a rather attentive young man, and as your husband I have to ask you just how far his attentions have gone.

And do not lie to me, Catherine. If there is nothing else, there has to be truth between us from the start.'

Understanding his meaning, Catherine felt the flush start somewhere deep down and rise upwards over her breast and face, and then rage, full-bodied and fortifying, propelled her forward to stand over him. 'Of all the loathsome, arrogant...' she erupted furiously. 'Harry and I have known each other since we were children, and his behaviour towards me has been impeccable.'

'Thank you for that edifying piece of information,' Marcus remarked coldly. 'And I am to believe that?'

'Believe what you like. I don't care, but I speak the truth.'

Marcus believed her, though as he continued to watch her, his face was set in lines of smiling challenge. Now was the time to let her know who was the master, his expression seemed to say. When they reached Saxton Court she would be mistress of both the house and servants, but as man and wife, what went on when they were alone in their bed was for him to decide.

'I shall soon discover that for myself. Now, take off your clothes and get into bed.'

Catherine's cheeks flamed suddenly as though he had hit her and she recoiled instantly. 'And what about my feelings? Do they count for nothing?'

'Your attitude suggests that I seek to force myself on an innocent, unprepared young woman,' Marcus remarked with a spasm of anger. 'You are my wife, and, by God, before we leave this place you will be my wife in truth.'

'Am I expected to be a servile creature, nothing more than a consenting slave to do your bidding? I will never love you—and you delude yourself if you think that. I know well that I must do my duty—but if you touch me now there will never be liking between us.'

As quick as a panther Marcus sprang from his chair and advanced towards her. Before she could protest he untied the ribbons holding her cloak and let the heavy folds fall to her feet. He gazed at her, standing straight and unflinching before him. The soft light fell on her lovely face and shoulders. Her face was pale under the heavy mantle of her midnight hair, and her eyes, blazing her defiance and as challenging as his own, were bright with bravely held tears. She looked so heartbreakingly lovely that Marcus longed to draw her into his arms, but to do so would earn him a harsh rebuff.

'Defy me one more time and I'll remove them myself. It is not my intention to make you dread this night, Catherine, but I consider it kinder to tell you how things will be than to let you wonder. We have to talk, you and I. There are many matters to be settled between us, but time for that later. Tonight I want us to set our differences aside and behave like any newly-wed couple.'

'Don't you lay a finger on me, Marcus Reresby,' Catherine warned, 'or I'll scream the place down.'

'And don't you threaten me, Catherine. You'll regret doing so. I'll touch you whenever and however I please, so let that be an end to it. Now get undressed.'

Catherine's soft lips tightened, and her eyes, glaring at him, blazing defiance, remained fixed on his as she began removing her clothes, her fingers fumbling with the difficult fastenings. When she came to the last piece of concealing clothing she cast it off and in one glorious gesture flung it to the floor. Breathing fast, she opened her arms wide, every curve and hollow and shining piece of flesh exposed for him to see.

'There. Is this what you want?'

Marcus, having watched her in mocking amusement, now froze in surprise and admiration for the amazing sight he beheld. She was beautiful, like a lovingly and delicately carved figurine, and yet as she squared her shoulders and shuddered at what was to come, he realised he'd hurt her and humiliated her, which brought a twinge of conscience. And yet even now her stubborn, unyielding pride refused to permit her to collapse at his feet. That indomitable spirit of hers remained unbroken, and for that he thanked God.

Without more ado she crossed to the bed, turned back the bed-spread and climbed in, where she lay staring up at the canopy, clutching the sheet under her chin, acutely aware of her naked-ness. She heard Marcus divesting himself of his clothes and re-fused to look at him. When he joined her and, intent on his purpose, drew her rigid figure into his arms, she did not flinch. She wanted him to take her swiftly, for the thing to be done.

And it was, for Marcus was of the same mind—determined to make her his, and quickly. There was an urgency about him, violent yet tender, and Catherine felt a sharp pain, just for a mo-ment, and when she would have cried out her mouth was stilled by his. When it was done and Marcus had rolled away, leaving her body trembling from the assault, she lay on her back in a state of confusion and frustration.

Knowing that she was irrevocably and eternally in love with Harry, she was ashamed that a man—yes, a man, she realised, not a boy—other than Harry had taken her virginity. Tears formed under her closed eyelids and slipped down her cheeks. Although it was not wrong to lie with one's husband, by doing so she felt that she had betrayed Harry.

The fire had died. In the darkness, leaning towards Cather-ine, his weight supported on one elbow, Marcus could not dis-tinguish her eyes, but her face was wet when he touched it. In response Catherine turned her back to him and curled up on her side. Miserably she tucked her head in her bent arms and sobbed. Putting his hand on her shoulder, Marcus gently tried to turn her toward him, but she shrugged his hand off.

'Please don't touch me,' she said in a suffocated voice. 'Please.'

After pulling the covers up to cover her, Marcus lay back. Something shattered inside him as he listened to her muffled sobs that seemed to go on for ever. He should not have done this to her. He should have shown patience, courted her, softened her, for no matter how impatient he had been to make her his wife, it would have been wise to do so. And now there was nothing he could do to atone for the act he had committed against her will.

At thirty-one years old Marcus was a man who knew his own mind, understood his motivations. He was a shrewd, rational man, highly disciplined, who prided himself on his inability to be swayed by emotion or flights of fancy. So what on earth was happening to him? Catherine had sparked feelings in him, feelings of protectiveness, and deeper, unfamiliar ones, too. Feelings he did not understand.

When at last she rolled on to her back and fell into an exhausted slumber, he leaned over her and tenderly brushed a damp strand of hair from her cheek, content to spend the rest of the night watching her sleep. Because he knew that until she welcomed him into her bed as her husband, this was the last time he would ever touch her.

The steady rain had dwindled into shreds of drifting, greyish mist by the time the carriage turned up the lane leading to the Reresby sprawling country estate. Catherine felt a palpably increasing aura of tension. She did not feel exactly enthralled by the prospect of their imminent arrival at her husband's home. She had enjoyed a relatively uneventful journey, though she found Marcus's stoic expression rather forbidding. She was careful to keep a guard on her tongue and held herself in reserve more than usual, and though she didn't ignore Marcus precisely, she seldom addressed him directly for fear she would reveal her emotions.

Catherine was a maid no longer. She was a woman now, Marcus Reresby's woman, but her heart remained unmoved and still belonged to Harry. The confusion her husband had created in her in their marriage bed that night at The Hague had evaporated with the dawn—until the next time, she thought as she looked at him. She remembered the unfamiliar, intimate things he had done to her, the feel of his long limbs pressed to hers, the feel of his mouth on her own, the strange joining of their bodies, and how it had left her confused, frustrated and curious about the act itself. Yet Marcus seemed to have easily dismissed what he had done to her that night, for three days had passed and he made no attempt to repeat it.

From Lyme Regis they had journeyed north towards Taunton, turning west before they reached the town. Travelling on top of the coach with the driver was Marcus's manservant, who went with him everywhere. He was a young, mild-mannered man named Dickon, with big laughing grey eyes and dark auburn hair. With his sunny, open disposition and constant chatter, he had eased Catherine's tension and kept her constantly entertained on board ship. She had been glad of his company.

As the carriage bumped along a winding stretch of road towards Saxton Court, a cluster of deer grazed under the dripping foliage of the trees. As the conveyance rumbled past, disturbed, they raised their heads to look at them before bounding away. Eventually the carriage passed through the archway of a battlemented gatehouse. A cobbled way led into the main court of the house, and the conveyance came to a halt before the towering edifice. Dickon leaped down to open the door. Marcus climbed out and held out his hand to his wife, but Catherine merely sat there, her gloved hands folded in her lap, her face set.

'Please get out, Catherine,' Marcus commanded her, a hard note in his voice. 'The servants are waiting to welcome you to Saxton Court—your home.'

'My home!' Catherine flashed him a quick look. 'I do not feel that Saxton Court is my home.'

'Nevertheless, Catherine, that is exactly what it is. As you see, the servants have gathered outside at some considerable discomfort to themselves.'

Still furious with him for refusing to take her to Riverside House, she was of a mind to defy him. But there was a look in his eyes that was suddenly intimidating, and then, too, she was conscious of the servants waiting in the damp conditions. Reluctantly, her face mutinous and gritting her teeth, she took his proffered hand and stepped to the ground. She knew she was looking her best. Beneath the fur-lined cloak resting on her shoulders her travelling clothes were of supple sapphire-coloured velvet. The open collar showed off her long graceful neck, its delicacy emphasised by a tiny pearl pendant.

With her hand on her husband's arm she allowed him to draw her forward. They moved down the line of the servants—a veritable army of clerks, housemaids, stable hands, gardeners, and all manner of estate workers, young and old. Every eye was drawn towards their new mistress. They were attracted by her beauty and enchanted by the spirit and animation evident in the way she moved and on her face. Almost instantly Catherine found herself consoled by the smiles and looks of admiration, and she knew that as Lady Reresby she would be treated with respect.

At the end of the line Marcus introduced her to Mrs Garfield, the housekeeper, standing respectfully to one side.

The older woman's face held a gentle kindness, and her grey eyes expressed complete admiration. She curtsied low to her new mistress as if she were of royal blood. 'Welcome to Saxton Court, my lady. I hope you'll be happy here.'

Catherine smiled wryly as she looked up at the great house towering over her. 'So do I, Mrs Garfield. So do I.'

Heads turned to watch as they climbed the wide stone steps between a double row of more servants and entered the house.

Catherine cast her eyes around the vaulted hall, seeing its towering walls hung with shields, swords and other trappings of ancient chivalry. A fire burned in a huge stone hearth, providing a welcoming warmth.

Marcus paused and looked around, noting with some satisfaction that the house was kept scrupulously clean. Light streaming through the long windows fell in bright shafts upon the polished oak floor and wall panelling, lighting upon the grand staircase. He could smell polish, and the sweet scent of fragrant blooms in several vases placed on tables. For a moment he was content to stand and gaze while the years slipped from him as if coaxed away by that sweet smell. Here, a lifetime ago, he had declared to his father his intention to become a military man. How disappointed his father had been, having hoped Marcus would take over the running of Saxton Court. With an effort he shrugged the memory aside. Now was not the time to dwell on what might have been.

Hearing footsteps coming slowly towards them, Catherine turned her head towards the sound. Her attention became focused on a figure clad entirely in black moving towards them with a stiff gait, casting a very long shadow across the floor.

'Ah, Fenton,' said Marcus. 'Come and meet my wife, Lady Reresby. Catherine, I would like to present Mr Jacob Fenton, my bailiff. Mr Fenton came to Saxton Court shortly before my father died.'

Allowing nothing of his thoughts to show, Fenton turned to Catherine, wearing a faintly superior, supercilious expression. A man in his fifties, there was nothing gentle looking about her husband's bailiff. His bearing and expression spoke of arrogance. He was a tall man, with dark brown hair drawn off his narrow face, and pale green predatory eyes. His chin was long and curved, a facial defect that did nothing to enhance his looks.

In Catherine's breast a ripple of something stirred. She didn't know what it was, but she knew that in some peculiar way it was important. Something about Mr Fenton was familiar, but she could not think what. She had never seen him before, so she could only surmise that he reminded her of someone else.

Fenton inclined his head slightly without taking his eyes off her face. 'At your service, Lady Reresby. Welcome to Saxton Court.'

'Thank you. I am pleased to make your acquaintance, Mr Fenton,' Catherine responded. 'But, do I know you?' she added uncertainly. 'Have we met?'

'No, Lady Reresby, we have not. I would remember. We were expecting you several days ago, Lord Reresby,' Fenton remarked to Marcus.

'Yes—unfortunately I was delayed—at The Hague of all places,' he replied drily, casting a meaningful look at his wife. 'And how has Saxton Court fared in my absence? From your reports everything appears to be satisfactory.'

For the next two minutes he questioned his bailiff about the estate.

For what seemed an eternity Catherine stood by his side perfectly still, waiting for the moment when Marcus would remember she was there. She felt as if there was a strange power emanating from him now, a force that seemed to communicate itself to Mr Fenton and diminish the man. When Marcus had finished discussing estate matters and he switched to something else, his voice began to scrape against her lacerated nerves, but she waited patiently for him to finish.

'I have noticed since our ship docked at Lyme that all is far from calm and peaceful in these parts. I have been at The Hague, where the exiled Duke of Monmouth resides. News will already have crossed the water that he is putting together an expeditionary force, its aim to wrest the English crown from James. You will be aware of this, Fenton?'

Mr Fenton smiled thinly. 'One would have to be deaf and blind not to be, Lord Reresby.'

'As yet it is unclear where Monmouth will land—Scotland to join Argyll, Ireland, Lancashire, where he has much support, or here in the West Country, which is the most fractious area of all.'

'I have seen no sign of anyone preparing for rebellion.'

'Have you not? Have local loyalists not been raiding conventicles, fining or imprisoning those who attend them, and searching private houses for weapons?'

'That is true. In the hope of securing religious freedom, one cannot ignore the fact that dissent is deeply rooted amongst many in these parts. But such determined repression by the loyalists merely serves to remove the Dissenters from under their eyes and forces them to seek spiritual consolation elsewhere.'

'Where they continue to plot and to pray for divine assistance for their cause,' Marcus remarked drily.

'I believe so.'

Marcus's mouth tightened as he took the measure of his bailiff. He caught the gleam in his eyes, a gleam that belied the controlled features. In the depths of those eyes he saw cold-hearted calculation, and it acted on Marcus like iced water. This man, he thought suddenly—wondering why he had not seen it before—could be dangerous. Fenton had an intelligent face, intelligent yet cunning, and a combination of these traits among men of Fenton's position was dangerous, especially with rebellion likely.

'And are any of these Dissenters to be found beneath my roof?' Marcus asked.

'There are some.'

'And you, Mr Fenton?' When he saw his bailiff hesitate, he said sharply, 'You have my permission to speak freely.'

'I am a king's man, Lord Reresby—a Protestant king's man.'

Marcus's brows rose. 'I see,' he said, his face hard and implacable. 'I gave you permission to speak freely—but you will not do so too freely, I hope. It is right that one should uphold a cause he believes in, but I expect you will do so quietly. While you remain in my employ I trust you will not constitute yourself as a member of the opposition.'

'By opposition you mean those who have a just purpose to oppose a king who stands for Catholicism and intolerance, those who wish to have a freely elected parliament? But no, I will not. My anti-papist and political views are as strong as anyone's and well known to most, but I am my own man, Lord Reresby, and not influenced by others.'

'I hope not, Mr Fenton. My days as a military man are at an end. I am heartily sick of battles, and should Monmouth decide to come to the western counties to raise the flag of rebellion— and I believe he will—there will be no blood shed at Saxton Court. The only blood that will be spilt will be if someone tries to take what is mine. I always take good care of what is mine.'

Marcus caught a sudden flash of anger in Fenton's eyes and the tightening of his lips. Not for the first time he wondered at Roger's words, and if his father had been misguided when he had brought Fenton into his employ. How much influence had he gained at Saxton Court? He would bear watching.

Catherine's patience was giving way to annoyance. The long journey of undiluted tension and anxiety was taking its toll. Obviously Marcus had forgotten all about her and considered her less important than Mr Fenton's view on Papism. 'Pardon me for interrupting, Marcus, but I am sure you can continue your discussion with Mr Fenton without me. I wish to rest and would be grateful if I could be shown to my chamber. It has been a long and exacting journey and I would appreciate some refreshment and some privacy.'

Marcus turned to her. 'By all means, Catherine.'

'You will excuse me, Mr Fenton.'

Although he had seemed unaware of Catherine as he answered her husband's questions, at that moment Fenton chose to meet her eye, before letting his gaze pass over her face. He seemed to be scrutinising her every feature, as if he could read there the answer to some question known only to himself. Catherine met his stare squarely. He stepped back, inclining his head slightly.

'Of course, Lady Reresby.'

Marcus turned to Mrs Garfield. 'Lady Reresby's apartments have been prepared?'

'Everything is in readiness, my lord.' She offered a tentative smile to her new mistress. 'I am sure you would like to freshen up before dinner.'

'Thank you. A bath wouldn't go amiss. We've been on the road so long.'

'I'll see to it, Lady Reresby. Shall I show you the way?'

'There is no need. I shall escort my wife myself,' Marcus said, turning to Fenton and excusing himself.

Catherine felt Fenton's eyes follow her across the hall. Not until they were climbing the stairs and out of earshot did she remark, 'I don't think much of your Mr Fenton. The man is far too bold for my liking. It cannot be easy for a man of such arrogant pride to assume the humble air of a servant.'

A frown settled between Marcus's brows. He too was uneasy about Fenton. His instinct told him that since his father's death and his own absenteeism, his bailiff had acquired too much influence at Saxton Court. The man must be put in his place and learn to know that from now on he, Marcus, was master of Saxton Court.

'Fenton has been in charge of the running of things for almost two years and does an excellent job. You are too hasty in your judgement, Catherine,' Marcus said sharply, not wishing to reveal his disquiet to his wife.

Catherine was not deceived. She turned and looked at him. 'Am I? I did not detect an easy comradeship between the two of you.'

'Perhaps that is because I have been absent too long and do not know my bailiff as well as I ought.'

'How long have you been away?'

'Close on eighteen months. I've kept meaning to come back, but the army always had urgent need of me elsewhere.'

'And now you have done with the army?'

'Almost—when this affair with Monmouth is settled.'

'When did you decide this?'

'I always intended to leave the army when your father died.' He fell silent for a moment, staring straight ahead, and then the tense muscles of his face relaxed and, looking at her wryly, he smiled. 'I began to look forward to settling down, to getting to know my wife, raising a family, eating good food, sleeping in a comfortable bed, and to running Saxton Court, which was what my father always wanted me to do.'

'Are you saying you will make Mr Fenton redundant?'

'Mr Fenton has always proved to be efficient and highly competent. I have no complaints so far, so it will be hard to dismiss him without good reason.'

They continued on up the long flight of stairs. In the gathering gloom candles provided the light and cast a soft sheen over polished wood. Marcus pointed out to Catherine the merits of her new home—several of which, with wide and fascinated eyes, Catherine had already noted. Where doors stood open she saw furnishings and decorations more grand than any she had seen before.

The long gallery, crossing the width of the house, was of tremendous proportions. Its floor was of polished oak and its walls supporting a huge vaulted ceiling of decorative plaster. Set in rows along the walls and giving the visitor the impression that he had stepped into the presence of gathered nobility were paintings of Marcus's ancestors—men and women who had coloured the exclusive world of Reresbys for generations, all housed in elaborately gilded frames.

'Well,' Marcus asked, 'what do you think of Saxton Court? Although, having grown up in the grandeur of Riverside House and surrounded by the trappings of wealth, perhaps my home does not impress you as much as it would some.'

Catherine's eyes were alight with interest as she gazed at the pictures and furniture that harmonised perfectly. Turning to look at her husband, she realised he was awaiting her reaction. There was expectant hope in the handsome face, and she could not deny him.

'On the contrary. I am impressed. It is very fine indeed,' she murmured. 'Few brides are presented with so much. Usually it is the groom who receives what his wife brings to him as a dowry—although, when I think about it, I come well provided. You have not done too badly out of marrying me, have you, Marcus?' Catherine could not resist the jibe.

Marcus scowled darkly, unable to hide his annoyance at her constant desire to provoke him. 'And I have told you that you may keep whatever you wish from your home, Catherine. You will find I am a generous man in that regard.'

She looked at him. 'Does that include Riverside House?'

'No. The house will be sold.'

'And I can well imagine just how eagerly you will claim the money from the sale of it.'

His eyes gleamed into hers. 'I have to protect my interests.'

Catherine studied him uncertainly. 'How old are you, Marcus? Thirty or a little more, I suspect. Why have you never married?'

'I am thirty-one, and I have never married because the army has been my life—and because I have not met a lady that was suitable.'

'And, yet, you married me. A highly unsuitable alliance, I would say; a marriage that hasn't a prayer for success.'

Marcus looked at her face turned to his, noting the softening that was currently replacing her normal hauteur. No man could not be moved by Catherine's beauty, and he was unable to believe this woman he had married could possess spirit to equal his own.

'You say that with so much conviction that I believe you are trying to convince yourself of it instead of your husband. I do not share your conviction,' he said, his mouth lifting in a slow, amused smile. 'You're not afraid of me, by any chance, are you, Catherine?'

Catherine intended treating him with cool hauteur, but his smile was so boyishly disarming that in spite of herself she smiled. 'No, you needn't think that—though your temper could do with some improvement. Must you look like some infernal thundercloud all the time?'

Marcus laughed at her, a deep, contagious laugh, and his eyes suddenly seemed to regard her with a bold, speculative gleam that Catherine found unsettling. 'I cannot help the way I look, and,' he said, on a softer note, 'I am more pleasing to look at than Harry Stapleton. You must allow me that.'

Catherine cast him a quick, sideways glance. This was the first time he had referred to Harry. She preferred not to think of him now. It hurt too much. 'You've conceit enough to make up for all the other qualities you lack,' she agreed, looking straight ahead, 'and I'll not deprive you of your handsome looks. Break as many hearts as you please, Marcus, but you'll not break mine.'

A slow smile touched his lips. 'A terrifying possibility, but I'll risk it,' he murmured.

'I suppose when you ruined my father and married me you considered it to be for my own good.'

'You know what happened. I don't need to defend myself.'

'I consider what you did to be a criminal act, so please don't portray yourself as some innocent.'

Marcus's eyes glowed in the warm light as he gave her a lazy smile. 'I never claimed to be an innocent, Catherine, but neither am I a black-hearted villain.'

'I would hardly expect you to admit it if you were.'

A crooked smile accompanied his reply. 'I am no saint—I admit that. I would like you to be more amiable towards me. I find you quite challenging. I would like to enjoy your company better, Catherine.'

'Why? Because you want to bring me to heel, and when you have done so, to trample me under your foot as you did my father?'

He arched a brow, amused. 'No, but I would like you to be less hostile towards me, less stubborn. Did anyone ever tell you that you have lovely eyes? And a lovely mouth as well.'

She looked away, staring fixedly at a point ahead of her. 'Please don't say those things. I am not interested. However,' she said as they left the gallery and proceeded along a narrow passageway, 'I believe you will live to see the day when you will rue that game of cards.'

'I don't agree. I live in hope that, given time, things will improve between us.'

'Nevertheless, what you did was hardly a gentlemanly act. If you had taken the time you would have learned I was betrothed and had no intention of shifting my affections to another.'

'I was aware of your options, and since no official betrothal had taken place, I came to the conclusion that I was probably your best choice.' The tantalising grin returned and grew wider when she gave him a doubtful stare. 'And if you could see past that pretty little nose of yours, you will see that I might have done you a favour.'

Catherine's expression was indignant as she looked ahead and tossed her head with a grand gesture. 'I was right. You are conceited.'

Marcus laughed outright. 'I admit it. So forget your girlhood suitor, Catherine, and face the truth of what you have.'

The chambers assigned to Catherine were situated in the right-hand wing of the house.

'Here are your apartments.' Marcus pushed open a large panelled door and bade her enter. 'You will find your maid in attendance.' A strange smile touched his lips, as if he were amused by some wry jest.

Catherine saw it and was puzzled by it as she went inside, wondering who had been assigned to serve as personal maid for the new mistress. How she missed Alice. She would see to it that the dear lady came to Saxton Court without delay. After all, since Marcus intended selling Riverside House and all its contents, apart from the items she wished to keep, Alice, with no family of her own, would have nowhere else to go. Besides, to live in a world without Alice was unthinkable.

While servants carried in her trunks, Catherine gazed around her with a kind of wonder. 'What a beautiful room,' she remarked, gazing round the panelled walls and up at the carved and embossed ceiling. A high four-poster bed with a tasselled canopy of ruby and gold and rich brocade draperies stood in the centre, and a cosy fire, burning to ward off the chill, cast a soft, intimate light over the room.

When the familiar figure of her maid emerged from an anteroom, Catherine stared, unable to believe what she was seeing. It was as if she had conjured Alice up from her imagination.

With tears of relief and happiness already forming in her eyes, she let out a cry of pleasure. 'Alice! Oh, Alice!' Immediately she went to her and, placing her arms around her, hugged her close. 'I had no idea you would be here. Oh, but this is truly wonderful and makes things a whole lot better. Now I shall not feel so alone.'

Catherine was so overwhelmed on seeing her beloved Alice that a small feeling of gratitude towards her husband stirred in her heart, for this had to be his doing. She turned and looked at him. 'Thank you so much, Marcus. You have no idea how much better it will be having Alice here with me.'

'I am happy to have done something that pleases you at last.'

Alice cupped Catherine's tearstained face in her palm. 'Lord Reresby arrived at Riverside House the day after you had left for The Hague. He asked me if I wanted to continue as your maid. When I said I did he had me brought here. So no more tears, Catherine. I am here now and, God willing, I'll be with you every day from now on.'

Watching the touching reunion of his wife with her maid, Marcus was glad he'd had the elderly woman brought to Saxton Court. He had need of her presence if he was to woo his wife. He was about to leave the room when Catherine stopped him.

'Marcus…'

'Yes?'

She crossed to him. Her dark eyes gazing directly into his, she asked quietly, 'Whereabouts in the house are your chambers?' The question was a perfectly natural one, but Catherine saw a spark ignite in his eyes.

'Right next to your own, Catherine. Where else? So, you see, I will not be far away. Don't you think I am looking forward to having you close to me again?—as it was between us at The Hague?'

The unexpected reference brought a flush to Catherine's cheeks. 'I—I thought you had forgotten that.'

A faint mocking smile touched his lips at her embarrassment. 'Why? Because I did not speak of it? It is still uppermost in my thoughts, Catherine. I keep the memory of that night hidden away in a corner of my heart. I am not insensitive to your feelings and will make no emotional demands on you. For now I shall ask nothing of you.'

An odd gleam hardened his eyes when her expression relaxed with the relief she was unable to conceal. Putting his hand under her chin, he jerked her face up to his. 'Until we know each other better I shall refrain from exercising my rights as a husband. But understand this, Catherine. I will not be a complaisant husband. You may keep your chaste sanctity for the time being. However, when you can look upon me as a wife should, marital relations will be renewed between us.' He grinned suddenly. 'They do say there is nothing like sharing a pillow to take away hostile feelings.'

The following morning bright sunlight filled the chamber when Alice drew back the heavy drapes. 'Come, Catherine, it's time to rise. Lord Reresby is expecting you to join him for breakfast,' she announced with gentle but unmistakable urgency. 'It is important that as Lady Reresby you look your best if you hope to win your husband's approval.'

Catherine struggled to sit up. Throwing off the covers, she looked crossly at Alice. The last thing she wanted was to win Marcus's approval—or anyone else's at Saxton Court for that matter. 'Alice, from the way you speak, anyone would think you like living here.'

'And would that be such a strange thing? I can see nothing wrong with it. Everyone here bears a fierce loyalty to the family and they've been kindly towards me.' She paused in what she was doing and looked into the wide accusing eyes. 'I know how much you miss Harry, Catherine, but if you're wise you will treat your husband with regard. He's an honourable man— a wealthy man—'

'I care nothing for his wealth. All I ever wanted was—' She bit her lip to stop the words, but Alice, sensitive to all Catherine's moods, knew what she had been about to say.

'What you feel for Harry will pass,' she encouraged her gently, 'and in the meantime, with everyone watching you, it's important to look your best lest one day you regret it.'

Chapter Four

During her first days at Saxton Court, Catherine's strong young body recovered from the journey from The Hague. The recovery of her spirits and acceptance of her situation would take longer. She was calm, doing her best to fight her way back to reality, the reality of the loss of her home and Harry—both of which no longer existed in her world. Yet common sense and a hard-headed practicality came to her aid. For better or for worse Marcus Reresby was her husband, Saxton Court her home, and she was the mistress of a vast estate where she would have many duties and social obligations to perform. Without realising it she slipped into the daily rhythm of her new life, and it wasn't long before the servants began to hold her in the same affection and respect as they did her husband.

Saxton Court stood in an isolated corner of Somerset, lying between the Quantock and Blackdown Hills. It was a fertile area of small fields, rich pastures, grazing sheep and cattle and cider orchards. May bloomed, and the sun turned the stone walls of Saxton Court into a warm gold. A two-hundred-foot paved terrace dropped away in steps to the immaculate gardens—the lush bright green lawns, the denser greens of topiary and gravelled walks. Built in Tudor times, the house had complete symmetry. Four storeys high with handsome windows and, at either end, two balancing wings, its grandeur reflected the prosperous conditions of the Reresbys, its elegance expressing the same power and pride Marcus possessed.

Catherine soon saw that the house was run efficiently and smoothly by the more than capable Mrs Garfield, who had been the housekeeper at Saxton Court for twenty years or more. She ruled the staff with a rod of iron, seeing that all work was done promptly, silently and efficiently. Despite this she was admired and respected by all, and she did her utmost to make it easy for Catherine to adjust to her new surroundings.

During the first two days, Catherine saw little of Marcus. Often she would glance out of a window and see him riding across the open green spaces with Mr Fenton. A cold shudder would pass through her whenever she set eyes on his bailiff, and no matter how often they met she found it increasingly difficult to hide her dislike. She would sometimes find his eyes watching her, almost speculatively, and there was an expression in them that she could not fathom. When he walked the passages of the great house with that steady gait, she froze as she waited and listened. He seemed to be able to move about at times with only the slightest whisper of movement—like a ghost or a shadow.

Her dislike, she suspected, was shared by the servants, including Mrs Garfield. The servants were always much too quiet when he was present in the house, warily keeping an eye out for him, and there was no mistaking a certain tension in the air, which relaxed the minute he left—Catherine was sure even the great house breathed a sigh of relief.

She explored the house and grounds and, accompanied by Alice and driven by the aged, talkative Archie Rumbold—a man who knew all there was to know about Taunton Deane—

took her carriage out several times to see the surrounding countryside. Wherever she went Catherine attracted a good deal of attention, for the news of her marriage to Lord Reresby had spread fast.

With a list of goods she wished to purchase, she visited nearby Taunton, a bustling, handsome town on the banks of the River Tone, with narrow streets, its castle very much its centre. The tower of St Mary Magdalene, its four stages rising skywards, its summit crowned by pinnacles and turrets, was soaring proof of the prosperity of this cloth town.

It was on this visit that she saw the unmistakable Mr Fenton. Unaware that he was being observed, she watched him stride towards the Red Lion tavern with a male companion. They were deep in conversation.

'Why, I believe that is Mr Fenton,' she said to Archie, who had climbed down from his coachman's perch to lend his assistance. Alice had turned away to inspect the contents of a shop window. 'Do you know the identity of his companion, Archie?'

Archie screwed his ancient eyes up and peered in the direction of Lord Reresby's bailiff. 'That be Esquire Trenchard— an important gentleman and a Whig. Member of Parliament once, he was.'

'A Dissenter?'

'Oh, aye, no secret 'bout that—no shame in it, either. Concerned himself in treasonable activities in the time of King Charles. Rumour has it that he's raised a troop of horse to fight King James should rebellion come about, but in spite of local loyalists and justices pokin' about and delving into people's affairs, nothing's been proved. William Savage—that be the landlord of the Red Lion over there—he's one of 'em. Free beer available to any man prepared to take up arms at a moment's notice.'

'Do you think the rumour about the troop of horse is true?'

Archie shrugged. 'Might be. Thing is, likely rebels know 'ow to keep their mouths shut.'

'Would you support a rising, Archie, should the Duke of Monmouth come to the West Country?'

Nodding his head slowly, Archie climbed back into his seat. 'Aye, I'd be behind it. I'm too old to fight, mind, but I can't speak for the rest of my generation. Where the young are concerned—well, some of 'em believe the cause their fathers and grandfathers fought for back in the forties and fifties and still dream about is a dead cause, and react against the piety and desperation that drove their elders, whilst others have been fed daily on stories of what happened.'

'Like bread and water.'

'Aye, you might say that, Lady Reresby. Back then Taunton was like an island of Parliamentary strength surrounded by Royalists. Its defiance at that time led to harsher persecution during the Restoration. It lost its charter when King Charles came to the throne, and singled it out as a centre of sedition, an' as I believe that's hardened the people's resolve enough to rebel.'

'So the people here were brought up in the shadow of events of forty years ago. Do you still sing the song that celebrates the relief of the Royalist siege here in Taunton?'

'Oh, aye. Our experience of the Civil War and of victory then will give plenty the inspiration to revolt, should young Monmouth come 'ere and raise his standard.'

Catherine looked towards the tavern door through which Mr Fenton and Esquire Trenchard had disappeared, wondering if they were already plotting insurrection over a mug of Mr Savage's free ale.

Marcus was in the hall when Catherine returned from her trip to Taunton. He told her he wished to speak to her, and Alice, who was carrying their purchases, excused herself.

Whenever Marcus addressed his wife he was always polite and considerate, his manner reserved, and Catherine had no way of knowing that this was to camouflage the warm tide of feelings he always experienced whenever they were together.

Since her arrival at Saxton Court, Marcus had kept his distance, watching her settle in under the capable wing of Mrs Garfield, giving her time to adjust to her new home and keeping callers at bay. He was rewarded daily when he saw how she began to relax, to move about the house with a newly acquired confidence.

However, he was not unaware that her presence was causing much talk and speculation among his wide circle of friends in the neighbourhood, and the time to introduce her to Elizabeth could not be put off any longer. Besides, he could not remain away from London for much longer, not with all this talk of insurrection.

That something was undoubtedly brewing here in the western counties was evident. Ever watchful, he observed how conversations were guarded and expressions closed. Letters that had been intercepted told of mounting unrest and possible rebellion. Conventicles were highly attended, where ministers preached of the revival of 'The Good Old Cause', of the time of the Commonwealth under Cromwell, rousing hope and expectations that the Duke of Monmouth might deliver them from the Papist King James before it was too late and the whole land was turned Catholic.

Marcus's good friend, Lord Stanhope, a deputy Lieutenant of the county's militia, had put him in the picture of how things were the day after he had arrived at Saxton Court, and he had soon seen for himself that there were many dangerous nonconformists, even in his own employ, who were active to bring about insurrection in the west. But they did not do it for their own gain, nor for a better standard of living, nor for greed or a fair share for all, but to defend the Protestant religion. For this Marcus had to respect them, for wasn't this what all true Englishmen adhered to? But still, believing in traditional hierarchy, he shared King Charles II's view, that it was right that his brother, James, should have succeeded him, and that he was the legitimate king.

'Really, Marcus,' Elizabeth had said, when her brother had told her she was to meet his wife, 'you are indeed asking a great deal of me, even though I am your most adoring sister and can usually refuse you nothing. Our father was murdered, and I cannot forget that your wife's father's hand was behind that foul deed. And now, not only do you ask me to forgive you for your marriage, but also to extend to her my hand of friendship. I declare, it is the outside of enough.'

Marcus understood in a measure what his marriage to Catherine had done to his sister, and it had tempered his manner and brought from him a soft plea. 'I am sorry, Elizabeth. I did wrong, but, if you can find it in your heart to forgive me and face up to it, we'll weather this together. I hope you won't take against Catherine because of who she is.'

'How can you ask that of me?' Elizabeth had fumed indignantly. 'She is *his* daughter, and because of who she is she does not deserve the benevolence one would ordinarily extend to a relative.'

'You mustn't vilify Catherine, Elizabeth. None of this is her fault. She didn't want to marry me—she tried very hard not to. She's stubborn and headstrong, and she's also young and emotional.' His lips had curved slightly when he recalled how challenging his young wife could be. 'Her nature is singularly impulsive and passionate—passion is characteristic of girls her age, I suppose. She's a fine young woman, and entirely innocent. You may not believe it, but she suffered, too, being Henry Barrington's daughter.'

'How so?' Elizabeth had sounded unconvinced.

'Her mother died giving birth to her. Barrington blamed Catherine for her death and rejected her all her life. She knows nothing of the events surrounding our father's death and the part Barrington played in his murder. I am sure she will be devastated when she finds out.'

'You aim to tell her?'

'Of course. I must.'

'And you expect me to accept her.'

'I ask this of you in the confident belief that Catherine will prove herself to be worthy of the name she now bears. I know you are bound to resent her. I only pray it won't be permanent.'

'You will not cure me of it, but I will try my best to abide by Barrington's daughter—your wife—my sister-in-law. Else it will make matters between us impossible, and I would not wish that.'

Despite Elizabeth's heated declarations, Marcus knew that with Roger's help his sister could be persuaded to relent, but her attitude mattered to him, and he had remained concerned for Catherine's sake.

'You have been out,' Marcus now remarked, moving slowly towards his wife. His expression was soft as he let his admiring glance rove over her restless figure. Beneath her bonnet her dark hair was blown into untidy wisps. Her face was pink from her ride in the carriage, and the tip of her nose was red. How he longed to kiss those cheeks and that small, pert nose, but, knowing her reaction would be to draw back, he restrained himself.

Peeling off her gloves, Catherine caught his eyes. He was standing less than a yard from her, his tall, broad-shouldered form almost blocking out the light from the high window behind him. With his mud-splashed boots he looked as if he had spent the day in the open, and had merely removed his hat and unfastened his shirt at his throat. His black brows were lifted slightly in inquiry, his gaze unwavering on her face. The scent that clung pleasantly to him stirred her awareness and roused feelings she could not even explain to herself. Feeling strangely vulnerable and angered by the weakness, her voice was sharper than she intended when she spoke.

'Alice and I have been into Taunton, to purchase a few items I have need of. What is it you wish to say to me?'

'That I have decided it is high time I presented you as my wife. Your arrival has created a frenzy in the neighbourhood.'

Catherine glanced at him sharply. 'Why? Because of who I am? Unless you have spoken of the circumstances that led to our marriage, I cannot imagine why I should be of interest—apart from being the wife of the illustrious Lord Reresby,' she argued. 'Besides, I do not relish being the prime target of anyone's curiosity.'

Marcus's jaw tensed. 'Any member of my family is a target of curiosity. However, I am not in the habit of bending local ears with matters personal to me,' he assured her. 'I would like you to meet some friends of mine—George and Margaret Stanhope. They live at Burton Grange, not far from here. I assure you they are exceptional people. They are old friends of my family and I greatly savour their friendship. George is a deputy Lieutenant of the county militia. You'll like him.'

'And his wife?'

'Warm, witty, honest and sincere, utterly devoted to George, and with a strong belief in friendship. There—is also someone else I want you to meet, and that is…'

When he hesitated, Catherine met his gaze directly. 'You were about to say?'

'My sister, Elizabeth, and her husband Roger.'

Catherine lifted a wondering brow. This was the first hint she'd had of Marcus having any living kin. 'Your sister?'

He nodded. 'She is married to Sir Roger Danby and has produced three children—two sons and a daughter. She is a highly intelligent and discerning woman, slightly older than me.'

'You—you have a sister, and you never thought to tell me?'

'Forgive me. I've been meaning to, but I wanted to give you time to settle down, to adjust to your new surroundings, without adding further complications.'

Catherine stiffened, eyeing her husband with the wary disbelief of an innocent who is suddenly and unaccountably confronted with a threat they neither understand nor deserve. 'Complications? You consider your sister a complication? Why, is she some kind of ogre?'

Marcus cocked an eyebrow, amused by the idea of his sister being depicted as an ogre. 'No, far from it. Elizabeth is a good wife and mother. She is also staunch and true, and extremely fond of me.'

'And is the reason why we have not already met because she will not approve of your choice of wife?'

'Elizabeth is fully aware of the enmity that existed between your father and me, and in truth she cannot for the life of her understand why I married you. She feels resentment, which I can understand, but I do believe that when she meets you and gets to know you she will like you.'

Pride swept away Catherine's surprise at his revelation, bringing her chin high and making her eyes suddenly defiant. 'Is that so? Well, what is more important to me, Marcus, is will I like her? Taking the circumstances into account, of course she could not possibly think I am suitable for you. And I am not at all certain how well she will be suited to me. If she doesn't want me in the family, then any cordiality she extends to me will be a pretence.'

'Elizabeth is not a hypocrite.' Marcus was swift to defend his sister. 'Pretence is not part of her nature.'

'That's a relief to know. At least we will know where we stand with each other. I hope you told her that I was a most unwilling bride, that the last thing in the world I wanted was to be married to you, and how I was manipulated by two unscrupulous men for their own ends.'

'To hell with how it came about,' Marcus snapped angrily. 'Elizabeth is fully aware of the circumstances surrounding my marriage to you, and you will be gratified to know that she fiercely disapproves of my behaviour and has berated me most severely.'

'And no doubt in your autocratic arrogance you felt you were being unjustly vilified,' Catherine retorted coldly, her cheeks flushed, her eyes the cloudy dark green of a stormy day. The fragile unity they had shared since she had come to Saxton Court began to slide down the slippery slope of clashed wills.

'Stop it, Catherine. Anyone would think you were being asked to live like…like a—'

'Like a what, Marcus? A creature that is being kept against its will? For that is exactly what I am.'

Marcus stepped close, and Catherine almost retreated from those suddenly fierce brown eyes. But she steeled herself and held her ground before his glare. 'I suggest you put aside this damned silly notion and enjoy what luxuries I have to offer. You are here because you are my wife.'

'I am here because I had no other choice.'

'If you cannot accept this marriage, then I order you to behave as if you do for the sake of appearances.' He raked her with a brazen stare. 'That shouldn't be too difficult for you, my dear.'

Catherine held her tongue, not in acquiescence, but, since she was determined not to give way to her emotions, she considered it prudent to remain silent. 'When am I to meet your sister?' she said finally.

'Tomorrow evening.'

Catherine's smile was ironic. 'As soon as that.'

'It's just a friendly get-together for family and my two closest friends.'

'Then I shall have to prepare myself and be on my very best behaviour so as not to embarrass you. I shall hold my head high and be as gracious and charming as I can be, and if your sister and your friends don't like me then they can all go to the devil for all I care.'

With a toss of her head, Catherine stalked towards the stairs. As she went, Marcus scanned her trim and shapely figure before he halted her. 'It is my desire that you wear a gown appropriate for the occasion. After all, the event will be a form of celebration.'

Icy green eyes cut back at him. 'Celebration?' she repeated coldly.

'Since becoming my wife it will be our first entertainment together,' he drawled leisurely. 'Is that not cause enough to celebrate?'

'For you, maybe, but not for me.'

Nothing had prepared Marcus for the sight of his wife when she presented herself to him in the hall the next evening, for the apparition that moved towards him wiped his mind clear of anything but sheer appreciation. He felt the full weight of her beauty; to his supreme gratification, she was wearing a charming creation of sage green velvet, tasteful and demure, that bared her shoulders and the twin soft mounds of her bosoms sublimely. Her heavy black hair, drawn from her face by a jewelled band, fell free over her shoulders and down her back, and round her swan-like neck a thin band of diamonds seemed to vibrate with shimmering life.

'I trust my gown meets with your approval,' she quipped.

Marcus tilted his head to one side, crossing his arms over

his chest and studying her with arrowed eyes. 'You look very lovely,' he remarked, looking positively dazzling himself in black knee breeches and frock coat and a dove grey satin vest. Delicate lace cascaded from his throat and spilled over his wrists, and his stockings were of fine white silk. His dark brown hair gleamed in the candlelight, and his dark eyes were calm. It was hard to believe that this was the man of yesterday.

'Nervous?' he asked.

'Terrified,' she confessed.

'Don't be.'

Sir Roger and Elizabeth arrived only minutes before the Stanhopes. Catherine urged Marcus forward to meet his sister. Marcus would have taken her with him, but she stood quietly back by the hearth, hoping that a moment alone with his sister would break the ice—and praying to the Lord to get her through the evening unscathed.

When Marcus greeted his sister, kissing her cheek affectionately, and she returned his kiss, he sighed with relief. He could see that Elizabeth's ideas had been moderated by her husband's arguments since he had last spoken to her, but even so, knowing her moods as well as his own, he could see that she was not prepared to capitulate entirely in her attitude towards Catherine. As she looked across the hall, her eyes coming to rest on the still figure of his wife, it was obvious that her manner was aloof and there were many reservations in the formal welcome with which she was prepared to greet her sister-in-law.

As Marcus held out his hand to her, Catherine walked towards them, the graceful folds of her gown swaying elegantly.

Elizabeth looked appraisingly at Henry Barrington's daughter, who was surveying her with eyes of vibrant green. She was momentarily taken aback by the sheer magnetism of her presence and her beauty—it was a dangerous beauty, and it was easy to see how she had managed to captivate her brother. The force of her personality burned through her eyes, and she could see that this was no easily manipulated female. For Marcus's sake, Elizabeth wanted to believe Catherine would be worthy of the name she bore, yet in her heart of hearts she wondered if such beauty could ever be without guile.

Subjecting Elizabeth to the same appraisal she was giving her, Catherine saw there was an acute, penetrating look that she would come to know so well. It did not hold one, or question or accuse. Rather it seemed to penetrate the very centre of one's being, and see all that was there, tolerantly and with surprise.

Catherine had somehow expected Marcus's sister to be a tall woman—perhaps because Marcus was tall—but instead she saw someone about the same height as herself. At thirty-four Elizabeth was extremely attractive. She had auburn hair, and arched eyebrows over warm, lively brown eyes, which seemed by contrast to make the pale texture of her skin even whiter than nature intended.

'Elizabeth, may I present Catherine, my wife?' Marcus frowned as his sister's gaze fastened on Catherine and she subjected her to an intent, lengthy inspection before she spoke.

'Welcome to the family,' she said with polite reserve, looking as if she were trying to smile when she didn't want to. And then, as if she belatedly thought of it, she held out her hands and said, 'I am happy to meet you at last, Catherine.'

Something about that forced cheer in Elizabeth's voice set off alarm bells in Catherine's brain, and she felt her hands tremble as she held them out to her sister-in-law. 'Thank you. I regret that I cannot say the same.' She cast Marcus a look of reproach. 'I thought perhaps it must be a habit with Marcus to spring surprises on people, for until yesterday I had no idea whatsoever that he had any siblings.'

'Now, is that not like my brother,' Elizabeth remarked drily.

'Always inconsiderate to another's feelings and, what is more, always springing surprises when one least expects it. I was severely annoyed with him when my husband returned to Somerset, and told me he had met up with Marcus at The Hague. Imagine my shock upon being informed that my brother had been married for months and never a word to me. I was most displeased.'

Catherine saw the frown between Marcus's eyes and the sudden tightening of his lips and knew that he was put out by his sister's rebuke. Her chest tightened with anxiety and irrational foreboding. There was something behind Elizabeth's remark that only Marcus would understand. Something was odd, dreadfully odd, and she felt as if she wanted to flee from the house with its tension and undercurrents.

'It was indeed inconsiderate,' Catherine managed to say. 'And had I been in your place, Lady Danby, I should have been just as angry as you were.'

'We are sisters-in-law, Catherine. My name is Elizabeth.' She turned to the man hovering beside her. 'May I present Roger, my husband.'

Roger affected a courtly bow. 'Welcome to Saxton Court, Catherine,' he said, smiling warmly. 'I trust Somerset is to your liking.'

Catherine took an instant liking to him. His voice was deep and quiet and somehow quite different from what Catherine had expected, following her strained introduction to his wife. 'I like it very well, at least what I have seen of it.'

At that moment they were interrupted by the arrival of Lord and Lady Stanhope.

'Lady Reresby, how lovely to meet you at last,' Margaret Stanhope said, smiling widely as she swept across the hall.

The gentle smooth tone of her voice and the radiance of her smile were such that Catherine began to relax. In her late forties, Margaret Stanhope was a small, trim woman with glossy brown hair peppered with grey. Her gaze was frank and open, and her eyes, a startling blue and wide apart, were kind.

'Please call me Catherine, and, if I may, I will call you Margaret.'

'I should be delighted, my dear—and this is my husband, George,' she said, drawing a foxy-looking man forward. With his stout figure and once-red hair turning white, George Stanhope gave the physical impression of age, yet his pleasant pink face, bright grey eyes, bushy red eyebrows and ready smile were the epitome of youth.

George smiled broadly. 'The pleasure is all mine. I cannot tell you how delighted I am to join such gracious company. At last I have the honour of meeting you after hearing Marcus sing your praises from the moment you arrived in Somerset.'

Catherine was not immune to the gallantry of Lord Stanhope, and she was astonished by his remark. Meeting her husband's eyes, which rested on her as boldly as ever, she raised questioning brows, wondering what she had done to deserve his acclaim. Slipping her arm through George's, she took the initiative as hostess.

'Lord Stanhope, would you be so kind as to escort me into the dining parlour? I believe the food is ready to be served.'

'I'd be honoured, my dear—and George will do.'

George led her to her place at the far end of the table from Marcus, leaving the two of them separated from the other by the length of it.

'You are very lovely, my dear,' George proclaimed, pulling out her chair. 'As lovely as my Margaret.'

'Nay, George,' Margaret laughed chidingly as she followed her husband on Roger's arm. 'Your memory deceives you. I never looked as lovely as Catherine.'

'You did to me, my love,' he said, looking back at his wife, 'and oft was the time I had to fight off smitten swains.' His eyes twinkled down at Catherine. 'Your face would slight the beauty of a lily in full bloom, my dear.'

'And are you familiar with lilies, sir?' Catherine questioned.

Her light laughter threaded through Marcus's head, weaving a spell. His gaze fell upon his wife as she slipped into her chair, and he was relieved to see that George's compliments had put her at ease.

'I have some prime blooms in my garden at Burton Grange,' George answered as he seated himself. 'I shall see to it personally that some are delivered to Saxton Court when they flower later in the year.'

'Why, thank you. You are most kind.' Catherine glanced at his wife. 'Is your husband always so charming, Margaret?'

'Always,' Margaret admitted, giving her spouse a fond look. 'You must forgive him, my dear. You'll get used to him in time. George never can resist complimenting a beautiful woman on her looks, but he is utterly devoted to me and never strays.'

'I wouldn't dare—and nor would I want to,' he chuckled good-humouredly. At that moment he really did look most endearing, like a naughty, overgrown boy. It was difficult to believe he was a deputy Lieutenant of the county's militia, with orders to disarm all dangerous and suspected Dissenters in Somerset.

'Why the frown, Elizabeth?' Marcus asked lightly, giving his sister an amused look as she became seated. 'Your thoughts appear to be mightily unpleasant. Are you wondering where Mr Fenton is, by any chance?' Elizabeth's feelings towards his bailiff were well known to him.

Elizabeth glanced at him sharply. 'You know I seldom think about Mr Fenton if it can be avoided. However, since you mention it, where does the man skulk?'

'Fenton doesn't skulk.'

'Yes, he does. The man's a menace. Where is he, by the way?'

'He's taken a few days off to visit his brother in Bath. I expect him back tonight.'

Catherine frowned, puzzled as to how Mr Fenton could possibly be in Bath when she had seen him in Taunton only yesterday.

Elizabeth shot Catherine a hard look. 'What do you think to my brother's bailiff, Catherine? You must have had time to form an opinion of him.'

'I—I haven't—I mean, I don't often see him, so I don't really know him all that well.'

'Undoubtedly that's a blessing. I cannot like the man.'

'I mean no disrespect, Marcus, but Elizabeth has a point,' Roger said. 'You know what I think where Fenton is concerned, and I cannot for the life of me understand why your father employed him in the first place.'

'Having run Sir John Mortimer's estate in Surrey efficiently for a number of years, he came well recommended. Sir John spoke highly of him and was sorry when he left.'

'Then why did he?' Elizabeth asked.

'To seek a position closer to his family in Devon.'

'Has Mr Fenton never married?' Catherine enquired.

'Not to my knowledge,' Marcus replied. 'What you seem to forget, Elizabeth, is that Father was not the man he used to be. He always prided himself on being able to manage Saxton Court, but gradually it became too much for him. Whatever Mr Fenton's political and religious beliefs might be, he has done a great deal for this place. And I would add that, among certain people in the neighbourhood, he is well respected.'

'Not by many,' Elizabeth countered. 'Please, do not be deceived. I find him extremely offensive. Beneath the surface your Mr Fenton is quite ruthless.'

There was the faintest edge to Elizabeth's voice, an edge of wry rebuke for her brother that Catherine recognised. 'What do you know of him?' she asked, taking a sip of her wine.

Elizabeth looked at her. 'Before he became the most influential member of staff?'

'If you like.'

'Since Father's death and Marcus's long absence, Mr Fenton has enjoyed tremendous influence at Saxton Court—indeed he lives in high style. His father was a gentleman from some place in Devon—somewhat impoverished, as I understand. Being the youngest of four sons denied him the hope of an inheritance. He had to make his own living. Father was in London when they met. I'm not at all sure how Father came to offer him the position of bailiff, but he did and that was that. I confess that at the time I was relieved he had someone to take over the burden of running the estate. With Father's full trust and authority behind him, and his own competence, within no time at all Mr Fenton has successfully carved himself a niche at Saxton Court.'

'And when Father was killed he continued to run things with my full approval,' Marcus remarked, 'and he will continue to do so until I have just cause for complaint and until I have done with the army.'

'In which time he will become more powerful, his competence only exceeded by his malice and ambition,' Elizabeth argued calmly. 'I find his presence here suspicious. Given his extreme political views and this being a hotbed of dissent, I believe he sought to use Father and his position at Saxton Court to establish a niche here in the West Country, should there be insurrection.'

'Really?' Marcus's dark eyes were hard as they looked at his sister. 'Surely you must see that it puts Father in a very poor light, implying that he was unable to judge a man's character for himself.'

'No—no, I don't. I would not be so disloyal, but perhaps there were things I could see in Mr Fenton that he could not.'

'Such as?'

'Mr Fenton is not your ordinary, hard-working man. There is an aura about him. An aura that is threatening and dangerous. The workers on the estate go in fear of him. He is fond of hunting and he's got himself a pack of hounds to specialise in tracking down creatures other than foxes.'

Marcus's eyes narrowed. 'Are you saying those who live and work on my estate are ill treated?'

'In truth I don't know. I have no proof, but I suspect he metes out his own kind of punishment on those who fall foul of him.'

'You always did have a wild imagination, Elizabeth. I know well that it is your custom to make mountains out of molehills. I am astonished that my bailiff is worth such concentrated attention, and I do wish you wouldn't attack the man,' Marcus chided, concealing the disquiet his sister's accusations regarding his bailiff had stirred. 'You know I disapprove.'

'And you know that I would never do anything to upset you. But I am uneasy about the way he runs Saxton Court—and I dare say it would well survive without him.'

'And I say he stays for the time being.' Suddenly Marcus smiled. 'Calm yourself, Elizabeth,' he said, spinning the wine around in its goblet, first one way and then the other, as he looked thoughtfully at his wife. 'I shall be finished with the army in a matter of weeks. Then we shall see.'

As dinner progressed topics were discussed, from the latest fashions and affairs at Court to the weather. Marcus was unusually quiet. His eyes flicked constantly from his wife to his sister, anxiously waiting to see if they were warming to each other. Halfway through the delicious meal and several glasses of wine, Margaret could no longer resist broaching a subject that piqued her curiosity.

'Marcus, we know very little about Catherine—how you met and how you came to marry her. It's all very intriguing, you know.'

Over the clutter of dishes filled with meats, vegetables, fruits and sauces, Catherine saw the tenseness in her husband's face and manner. She also saw that Elizabeth, who had become conspicuously quiet, was watching her closely. It was humiliating enough for Catherine that Marcus's sister should know the sordid circumstances of their marriage, and she would not give anyone else more meat to chew. She experienced a brief surge of irritation that Margaret should raise the matter, but forced it down as she realised the question was asked in all innocence.

'Marcus and I met through my father,' she explained. 'His military duties kept us apart—until recently, when my father died.'

'And you were at The Hague, I believe?' Margaret said.

'Yes. It is no secret that my father was a political exile.'

'And you went over there to be with him?'

'Catherine's father suffered ill health, Margaret,' Marcus was quick to reply, saving his wife the embarrassment of having to invent a lie, for the truth was known only to himself, his sister and his brother-in-law, and none of them wished it to go further. Margaret was a very dear friend, though something of a gossip. In no time at all the whole county would have him down as a cuckold. 'It is only natural that he would want his daughter with him.'

'But of course. Still, I believe most of the exiled nonconformists settled in the Low Countries have little to do and allow the wildest conjectures to flourish. Did you see the Duke of Monmouth, my dear,' Margaret asked excitedly, 'and is he really as handsome as they say he is?'

'I—did see him. He is an impressive figure, noble and military in his bearing, gracious and charming, and, yes, he is very handsome.'

'It is obvious that you express an interest in Monmouth,' Elizabeth commented, 'for you to defend him so passionately. If he should come to these parts to aid his victory, do you intend to clasp your hands in pious prayer, or sing his praises in support?'

Catherine met her gaze squarely. 'Both. You can be assured that I will not forget my place, but I am of the opinion that one must follow the dictates of one's conscience. Were I a man, I would do whatever was in my power to aid the Duke's cause. He has right on his side, after all.'

Catherine's imprudent remark caused Marcus's jaw to clench in a tight line of rage. However, thirty-one years of strict adherence to certain rules of etiquette could not be disregarded, and he only looked, albeit with stern disapproval, at his wife.

'Monmouth is a man of many moods, weak and easily led,' he stated coldly. 'I fail to understand why a man blessed by birth and the love of his father ever drifted into opposition to the Court. Why, also, has he made an enemy of his uncle James, who will prove ruthless in his retribution should Monmouth come to England to try and take the throne? James Scott, Duke of Monmouth, would fare better to forget his treasonable ideas, to remain in the Low Countries hunting and making love to his mistress and other frivolous pursuits.'

Catherine glared at him. 'England founders beneath James and you know it. As a Catholic king he cannot last. A returning Protestant king would surely be welcomed and we could all look forward to better times. The nation loves Monmouth. James would make papists of us all, and he is in danger of doing so should Parliament let him have his way. Already people murmur under his tyranny.'

'Even so, James was the due, legal successor to King Charles—our sovereign. Do you think that taking up arms against him is the answer?' Elizabeth retorted.

'Catherine, this is not a subject to be discussed at table,' Marcus remonstrated sharply.

Catherine met his eyes, eyes that gave nothing away but saw everything. His words told her to be silent, but she had gone too far to be curbed. 'When might it be discussed, Marcus? When the Duke of Monmouth arrives on our doorstep?' Her artless comment drew uneasy smiles from Elizabeth and Roger, and an appalled look from George, but when Marcus's expression didn't change in the slightest, Catherine felt a prickle of foreboding.

'Why, do I detect a malcontent, Marcus, here at Saxton Court?' George said with quiet irony. 'Your own wife, Marcus?'

Catherine looked at him. 'Please do not mock me, George. I am not a rebel. I have no weapon. I have only my heart, which seems rare enough these days in England. I am an English woman and in favour of a Protestant king. The Duke of Monmouth's cause is most passionately my own—with respect, sir,' she added, inclining her head gracefully.

A mildly tolerant smile touched Marcus's handsome visage, but the glint in the dark eyes was hard as steel. His gaze did a sweep of his guests, noting the cold glint that had appeared in George's eyes as he seemed to study Catherine in a new light. Despite his stirring unease, he managed to laugh lightly.

'Who can blame you, George, for thinking we have a Radical in our midst?' His eyes fastened on his wife. 'My wife has clearly spent too long at The Hague in the company of Dissenters. Have a care, Catherine. George has orders to arrest anyone expressing such extreme views. Ladies are no exception.'

'And what a delightful prisoner she would make, eh, George?' Roger said jovially in an attempt to lighten the atmosphere around the table. 'However, Monmouth is like a piece on a crowded chessboard, as yet with no more value than a pawn.'

Catherine jerked her head round to him, not yet ready to let the subject that had attracted her beloved Harry to The Hague drop. 'You forget that pawns may advance to the final square of the game and be transformed,' she remarked.

Roger smiled at her indulgently. 'True, my dear, but there are many powerful pieces on a chessboard—Prince William of Orange, for one, himself half a Stuart, King James's nephew and husband of his eldest daughter, Mary. Unlike Monmouth, William has a legitimate claim to the English throne, and a popular one, since he is a Protestant. Should Monmouth cross over to England and attempt to usurp his uncle with a rebellion, it will lead to his downfall, mark my words.'

'A rebellion is nothing without rebels,' Catherine countered. 'And it is no secret that there are many in these parts who would support him in a Protestant rising—should he decide to come to the West Country, in a place where he was received like a prince five years ago, greeted by country folk and fêted by gentlemen, where people have been long known for their independence and their attachment to liberty—or their rebelliousness, as you will. When I came to Somerset, I believed I would find myself among friends.'

'Be assured that you will have friends in abundance, my dear Catherine,' Roger said smilingly, 'but you must realise that many of those that choose to follow Monmouth have a low opinion of him and have no wish to see him made King. They would prefer to have a man made of sterner stuff and they follow Monmouth only because of the lack of any alternative leader attuned to their cause. I have to say that his supporters are more selfish than wise.'

'Catherine,' Marcus said when his wife opened her mouth to argue the point with Roger, 'we are supposed to be celebrating our marriage—and your new life at Saxton Court. Can we not be united in peace and harmony? Let there be no more talk of Monmouth. Time enough for that later, should he decide to raise his standard here in the west.' He saw her colour rising, but his dark eyes flashed his wife a warning that she would be ill served to cross him.

For a moment Catherine floundered beneath this monumental slap to her dignity, and did her best to hide her chagrin that Marcus had reminded her of the reason for this get-together. She glanced at him scathingly, noting how his hand flexed on his goblet of wine, and she knew he was wishing that her neck and not his goblet were in his grip.

It was Margaret who brought back gaiety to the feast, and although the rest of the evening swept past in a relaxed and congenial atmosphere, there wasn't a moment when Catherine did not feel her husband's eyes resting heavily on her.

It was not until they left the dining parlour that Elizabeth steered Catherine to one side, out of earshot of Margaret, who had disappeared to the ladies' retiring room, and the gentlemen, who had hung back to drink their port.

Replete with food and wine and having mellowed a little, Catherine was happy to have a moment alone with her sister-in-law. Elizabeth had looked out of sorts all evening, and Catherine had the sense to realise that this was probably because she was a standing reminder of the wrong her father had committed to her family—whatever that might be—that had brought all this about. Whatever the breach, and sick at the idea of Elizabeth disliking and resenting her, Catherine wanted to repair it, and was vain and young enough to suppose that with good will she could do so, until she heard what Elizabeth had to say.

'I advise you not to continue in this vein, Catherine, lest Marcus becomes angry. He has such a violent temper. You would do well not to aggravate him with talk of Monmouth. Do not make free with such matters.'

Meeting her sister-in-law's eyes, Catherine felt the first flash of genuine anger. 'I might be Marcus's wife, but I will not become humble before him. I am not some trained underling to do as she is told. I have thoughts and opinions of my own. I shall not indulge him,' she said coldly.

The thought of Catherine indulging anybody, even Marcus, brought a reluctant smile to Elizabeth's lips. The girl was much too high-spirited to be servile, and fully as arrogant as Marcus. The two of them would be a combustible combination. 'I can see you lack meekness and docility—and a respect for authority, Catherine. Nevertheless, you will do well not to provoke him.'

'Then he should not speak slightingly of the Duke of Monmouth. Treasonable ideas, indeed! I fail to see what is treasonable about wanting a Protestant king to rule England.'

Elizabeth peered closely at Catherine's face. 'There you go again, unaware of the harm you do Marcus and yourself by being so outspoken. My goodness. I am concerned for you, since you are now part of the family. You're as ignorant about such matters as a child, aren't you? What did you expect from Marcus? His support? He is a soldier, who has sworn loyalty to King and country. If he should utter one word in favour of Monmouth and his cause, then it will be seen as a treasonable act and the consequences would be dire. Do you understand, Catherine?'

Catherine looked into her eyes and suddenly felt herself startlingly weak and naive. 'I only said what is true.'

'Only as you see it. I am telling you to be careful. Listen to me, Catherine. I am going to talk to you as I would to any member of my family who is about to bring the name into disrepute, and I will not waste time dancing around in circles that go nowhere. These are dangerous times—particularly in Somerset, which is a hotbed of dissent. The loyalty and secrecy of the rebels make it difficult for the Government to learn what is going on. You speak dangerous words. Your opinions are your own affair, but be quiet about Monmouth and his cause. Keep your lips sealed. Someone might hear you. Start listening instead.'

Catherine was vexed, more with herself than anyone else. She did not want to be open and obvious, like a child. Such had been her stupidity that night, and there is nothing like chastisement for making one realise one's mistake.

'You are right, and, yes, I am young,' she said simply. 'Perhaps I have spent too long at The Hague among political exiles, but I do understand what you are saying and will curb my tongue in future.' She met Elizabeth's gaze squarely. 'I know what you must think of me. My marriage to Marcus must be a terrible disappointment for you, and your contempt for me must bite deep—and perhaps with good reason. However, I make no excuses for who I am. I had no part in the hurt my father inflicted upon your family, which is still a mystery to me, and I tried very hard not to marry Marcus.'

Elizabeth's misgivings were etched in the troubled frown on her forehead. 'I cannot forget for a moment that you are the daughter of that scoundrel, Henry Barrington, but for the sake of my brother's happiness I must accept the situation.' Unexpectedly Elizabeth smiled, and the warmth of it began to melt the icy misery in Catherine's heart. 'What a difficult situation this must be for you.'

Catherine found herself smiling back. 'Yes, isn't it? But I thank you for making it easier.'

'You have courage, Catherine, which is something I admire. You are going to need a great deal of it married to Marcus.'

For the first time Catherine began to warm to Elizabeth. Her husband's sister was as unpredictable as he was—one minute cool and distant, the next friendly and kind. 'What did my father do to your family that was so terrible?'

A hard, remembering look came over Elizabeth's face. 'That is for my brother to tell you. What I will say is that it was very wrong of Marcus to make you a part of it.'

Chapter Five

After saying goodnight to their guests, when Marcus went to speak to Mr Fenton about an estate matter, Catherine escaped to her chamber. In a state of jarring tension, with a feeling of dread she waited for the inevitable moment when Marcus would seek her out. She didn't have long to wait. He entered without knocking and closed the door behind him with an ominous thud. She turned, seeing the explosion of her husband in her room. The room, which had been calm, with Catherine seated at her dressing table brushing out her hair, and Alice and a young maid turning down the bed, was suddenly alive with Marcus's handsome, virile presence.

'Perhaps I am mistaken, Marcus, but I did not hear you knock,' Catherine rebuked with a hard note in her clear voice.

Her tone suggested he had committed a grave error. His mouth tightened. 'Possibly because I didn't knock.'

'Your visit is inconvenient. I am tired and wish to prepare for bed.'

'Then don't let me stop you,' he said shortly. He glanced at Alice. 'Have you finished with your mistress?' he enquired.

Alice looked at him and smiled. 'We have, sir.' She indicated the other girl. 'Martha and I were about to depart.'

'Good. Then I bid you a pleasant night.'

Alone with her husband, Catherine's lips tightened. 'It was for me to dismiss Alice, not you.'

'Then why did you not do so?'

'I did not wish to.' Her face mutinous, she continued to brush her hair. 'Well? What have you come for, Marcus—to give me a lecture for transgression and a punishment to fit the offence?'

Slowly Marcus came to stand over her, stern as a guard. He stared at her for a long moment. 'What the devil did you think you were doing? What have you to say for yourself, Catherine?'

Catherine looked at him through the mirror, steeling herself for what was to come, enduring the icy blast of his glare.

When she didn't reply he bent his head down to hers, meeting the gaze of the tempestuous young woman, her face both delicate and animated, with her stormy eyes and soft pink lips. 'Have you lost your tongue?' He spoke sharply, his breath warm on her cheek. 'When I address you, I expect an answer.'

'Then don't be giving me that frosty look,' she replied with infuriating calm and no hint of apology. ''Tis cold enough without that. And if you have come here to berate me you can save your breath. Your sister has already given me a tongue lashing for my remarks over supper.'

Marcus's sleek black brows snapped together. 'Has she, indeed? That comes as no surprise. Such outbursts are intolerable and unacceptable. How dare you embarrass me, my family and my friends in such an appalling manner? I will not abide such insolence. And don't insult my intelligence by telling me you didn't know what you were saying.'

'Do you think I would speak out on such a matter if I didn't? And you're scarcely in a position to lecture me on manners, my lord. Your behaviour has been anything but that which befits a gentleman,' Catherine accused him with blazing sarcasm.

'Damn you! You seem determined to push me to my limit.'

Drawing himself up to his full height, Marcus folded his arms across his chest and regarded her with anger and a terrifying firmness. 'Being the daughter of Barrington, who was party to plots subversive to the throne, plots ill-conceived and destructive to the peace of the realm, it is hardly surprising that you hold such extreme views, but your position in the community forbids you to speak out on such seditious matters.'

'Who is to say what is seditious and what is not?' Catherine countered furiously, getting to her feet. 'And how dare you presume to believe yourself to be entirely right? And, pray, where am I at fault in expressing my opinion?'

'Be damned to your opinions,' Marcus snapped. 'What is so fine about them that you must be for ever parading them?'

'I find the reprimand about my behaviour and what I said unjust, infuriating and hypocritical, since I am certain that everyone present—including you—must agree with me.'

'Don't insult my intelligence by telling me you didn't know what you were saying.'

Catherine glared at him with stubborn, unyielding pride. 'Of course I knew. Not content with forcing me into marriage, now you must turn preacher and impose your views on me. Like it or not, Marcus, I will not change.'

'Good God, Catherine, you know George's position. To openly speak against the King in support of Monmouth could bring about your arrest. George is as cunning and wily as a fox—such is the curse of red hair, so do not be deceived by his flattery. He has been empowered to search for arms and to try to discover who is actually involved in the proposed insurrection here in Somerset. So far the results of such enquiries have been discouraging—until tonight. With such radical views as you expressed and fresh from that hotbed of rebellious malcontents at The Hague, you're in deep water here. Being my wife will not save you. George would be failing in his duty if he were to let it go.'

His words were distinct and dangerous. Catherine had to summon all her patience to stop herself bursting out in a fury. Marcus's inquisitorial, aggressive manner angered her beyond belief. Still bruised by Elizabeth's chastisement and with Marcus's condemnation coming so close on its heels, all her grievances were renewed. Contrary to the warmer feelings she had begun to experience for her husband of late, at that moment she hated him with such virulence that she was capable of committing cold-blooded murder.

'I resent it as a personal insult that anyone should associate me with sedition and anarchy. I have committed no crime that I can be charged with, nor have I any intention of committing one.'

Anger was pouring through Marcus's veins like acid. 'From now on you will apply discretion and forethought. Never again speak in front of others as you have tonight.'

Catherine stared at him with hard eyes. 'I shall speak in any manner I choose.' Despite her arrogant words, Catherine felt a spark of fear at the look in her husband's eyes.

'By my faith, Catherine, how dare you?' His soft voice was infinitely more intimidating than a raised one. 'You will do as I say.'

With an imperious lift of her chin, Catherine said, 'By your faith, Marcus? What faith? The same faith as your King?'

'Be silent.'

'I will not be silent.'

'I am Protestant and you damned well know it.'

'How can that be, when you have given your loyalty to a Catholic King? I have been too carefully reared a Protestant to think well of that.'

'My loyalty is to England, so let that be an end to the matter. You are Lady Reresby—little though I can believe it at this moment. I would have you act the part. You will compose yourself, and call upon your dignity. The sooner you accept your position the better it will be for us all. You will be accountable to me for your actions. Is that understood?'

Catherine didn't even recoil from the blazing violence. Fury rose up like flames licking inside her, her face as uncompromisingly challenging as his. 'You can go to hell, Marcus Reresby, and the sooner the better. I own no man my superior—and least of all you. Ever since I was little I have been accountable to no one for my actions—not even to my father. And you're no better than he was. You married me for your own purposes, with no more compunction than you would have married a cow.'

'Your scoundrel of a father was equally to blame,' Marcus stated cruelly.

Catherine's pupils had dilated till her eyes seemed as black as his. 'I do blame him. I wasn't offered a choice because it's clear women don't have choices. Men make choices for them. You had better get used to the fact that I love Harry, I shall never love anyone else that way, and I will not be accountable to you for what I do.'

'Yes, you will. Someone should have taught you some sense and beat that wilful pride out of you years ago,' Marcus fumed, anger pouring through his veins like acid at her taunting mention of Harry Stapleton. He chose to ignore it, but his fury made him carelessly cruel. 'Defy me at your peril.'

To her consternation and fury, all of a sudden Catherine felt infuriatingly close to tears. Rather than let him see her flagging courage and refusing to be humbled, she raised her chin and assumed an expression of remote indifference. 'And if I do?' she ground out in a low voice.

In the face of her defiance, Marcus moved closer and leaned forward until brown eyes stared into green from little more than a foot apart. His eyes were hard, yet when it came his voice was soft and slow, his words careful and distinct.

'Defy me and you will rue the day. Heed me and heed me well, Catherine. As my wife you will conduct yourself with proper decorum and never discredit the name you now bear. I have never been an abuser of women, but if you tempt me enough, I might change my mind. I become very unreasonable when I am angry.'

'You are a loathsome, overbearing, despicable monster, Marcus Reresby—'

'Yes, I think I have the picture,' he drawled.

'Then I needn't go on—but how I wish I'd never come here. I wish I'd never met you. I want to be free of you. I didn't want any of this. I didn't ask for it.' She breathed as if she couldn't inhale enough air. 'Don't you understand that I hate you?'

Marcus looked at the proud beauty that was glaring at him like an enraged angel of retribution and realized that she was on the brink of tears. He felt a twinge of conscience, which he quickly thrust away. 'I know you do,' he said coldly. 'And you will hate me a good deal more before I'm finished with you.'

To Catherine's utter disbelief, he lifted his brows and gazed at her with enigmatic dark eyes and an impassive expression for several endless, uneasy moments. Her brushed hair lay on her shoulders like a gleaming black cape. His cool gaze warmed as it rested on her. She was wearing a white linen shift. The candlelight behind her exposed the shadowy outline of her limbs through the thin material. She was very lovely, this obstinate, spirited young woman he had married. So lovely, in fact, he could almost forgive her for her outspokenness in front of their guests.

'Do you know, Catherine, you are one of the very few women who does not like me? The majority of your contemporaries usually find me quite charming. I might even say that some have a great affection for me.'

'Perhaps that is because they have not had the pleasure of

being married to you. Given the choice, any woman would be stupid to attach herself to the likes of you.'

With an amused quirk to his lips, standing straight, Marcus stepped back. 'Nevertheless, many have tried.' He moved away from her. 'Goodnight, Catherine. I trust such an outburst will not occur again.'

Marcus seemed to hesitate, then he turned on his heel and left the room, his face set in such lines of implacability that left Catherine feeling thoroughly chastened, stupid, and what little fight she had left within her drained away.

Marcus's fury died the moment he left Catherine's chamber. He could not find words to describe his defiant young wife. He was enraged by her attitude, yet at the same time he could not help but admire her courage. She had spirit—too much damned spirit, he thought. He didn't know another woman who would stand up to his wrath as she did. She had stood up to him on the night he'd married her, and then angered him by running off to The Hague with young Stapleton.

Catherine lived in his house, ate at his table, he had made love to her, yet he did not know her. She wasn't a woman he could wrap around his finger and charm with that usually irresistible smile. With her back straight, head held high, her hair hanging to her waist in a black sheath and her eyes flashing a desperate green, she would face up to him. He was intrigued by her eyes, for they would glow with the fervour of her belief that one day she would be reunited with Harry Stapleton, and at others they were quiet, looking inward and sad, and it mattered to him.

Folding his arms across his chest, he propped a shoulder against the window and stared out into the dark, thinking about everything she had said, how vehemently she had expressed her hatred of himself. For a long time he stood there, knowing he must try and make amends for all the wrongs he caused her, before her hurt really did harden into hatred.

The following morning, the desire to atone for his sharp words and win her forgiveness prompted him to go and look for her. He found her along one of the passages leading to the kitchens talking to Mrs Garfield. With some concern he saw dark smudges beneath her eyes. *This is not good*, he thought, despairing. *We can't go on behaving like enemies*. So he smiled at her, well aware of the effect his smile had on females of all ages.

Looking towards him as he approached, booted and spurred and carrying his large cavalier hat, Catherine observed that he was dressed for riding. She stood stony-faced, waiting for him to speak. Considering their bitter altercation of last night, he seemed surprisingly cheerful and at ease.

Marcus's gaze rested warmly on his wife. 'I've come to rescue you from household duties, Catherine. Mrs Garfield won't mind if I whisk you away on what I hope will be a more pleasurable pursuit.'

Immediately Mrs Garfield disappeared down the passage, leaving them alone.

'What you consider pleasurable might not appeal to me, Marcus.'

Determined not to be deterred, he said, 'I thought you might like a change of scene. It's about time I showed you something of the estate before I leave tomorrow.'

'Tomorrow?' Catherine uttered quickly, experiencing a sharp stab of something she did not understand. 'You are going to London?'

'I cannot delay any longer. Now—you do ride, I take it?' His suggestion obviously appealed to her, for a smile broke out on her lovely lips.

'Of course I do. I learned to ride almost before I could walk.'

Seeing the ice melt briefly—she had smiled with genuine feeling that lit up her eyes—he knew that he had reached her at last. 'Good, then off you go and change—and hurry, for I've a surprise for you. A pleasant one, I hope,' he said with a merry twinkle in his eyes. 'I'll be at the stables.'

As though she had wings on her heels, Catherine flew up the stairs, only to come to a halt on encountering Mr Fenton coming down. She watched him approach her, doing her best to conceal her dislike of him. On reaching her, he stood before her in a deferential attitude. Instinctively she took a step to one side as she fought to hold his impenetrable stare, determined that she would not be driven over by her husband's bailiff. He didn't like her—it was apparent in his demeanour, and the way he looked her up and down as if she were something unpleasant that had entered the house.

'Good morning, Mr Fenton,' she said, sounding more cordial than she felt. 'I am in rather a hurry, so if you will be so kind as to step aside. My husband is to show me more of his estate before he leaves for London and I do not want to keep him waiting.'

'He goes tomorrow, I understand,' Fenton stated smugly, a sharp gleam in his eyes.

'That is so—although he must feel reassured knowing Saxton Court will be managed efficiently in your capable hands while he is away.'

'I do my best. He has never had cause for complaint in the past—let us hope he won't in the future.'

The hint of sarcasm in his tone was not lost on Catherine or the hidden meaning behind his words.

'I have no wish to make you my enemy, Mr Fenton.'

'Enemy?' His smile was blatantly smug. 'After airing your views so vociferously—and courageously, I might add—in front of your guests last night? Yes,' he said at her look of enquiry, 'servants do talk. So how can you even think such a thing? Why, I am your ally, not your enemy. Do we not both desire the same thing?'

'For the Duke of Monmouth to lay claim to the throne?'

'Not quite, but it would be a start. And with such influential people as yourself behind the cause, how can we fail?'

Catherine's head lifted, her eyes flashing with indignation. 'I do not care for your words, Mr Fenton.' Colour flared into her face. 'Is it for such as you to tell me what to do?'

'Aye, madam, when the Protestant cause is at stake.'

She stared at him in genuine amazement. 'You are impertinent, Mr Fenton.'

'I wish to make quite sure you understand me. As you know, many in these parts speak their discontent. Some are even beginning to utter the name of Monmouth. Hearing them, those who have held their peace from fear or prudence—or apathy—are beginning to find their voices. The atmosphere is changing, becoming charged, expectant. I hold Monmouth in esteem because he is a Protestant. But not even he would I allow to lead me from the path of my sworn duty. I have no wish to see any king in England. I care nothing for kings and princes, for royalty and its selfish pleasures.'

'I am all puzzlement, Mr Fenton. What is it you do want?' Catherine asked, reining in her temper with some considerable effort.

He speared her with a look. 'I am for the return of a Republican state. I would not let any man, be it the King or Monmouth, stand in the way of that. Without men such as Cromwell and Ireton to lead us, I will support Monmouth. If he is made King, his claim to the throne is so weak that he will be easily controlled.'

'Then I fear you will be disappointed, Mr Fenton, and a very unhappy Republican. I am too young to remember life under the Commonwealth, but I know of it and would not want it to return. So you see, Mr Fenton, you and I are different in that. Something must be done about the desperate state England finds herself in, I agree. And you, I suppose, would like to constitute yourself leader of the opposition?'

'If by opposition, Lady Reresby, you mean those who have the courage and the purity of purpose to oppose the king, then the answer is yes, right willingly. True Republicans are few in England as a whole, but they will be well represented in the rebel army, should it come to that.'

His face was hard as flint. He would have his own way, it said, and this woman who was nothing to him would be swept away like so much discarded chaff if she opposed him.

'You are shocked, I see,' said Fenton, his eyes expressing the fire within him.

Catherine favoured him with a freezing glance. 'I know that should rebellion come about, the motivations of those who follow Monmouth are wide-ranging and extreme. You are a dangerous man, Mr Fenton. I do not like your purpose and I cannot help but wonder what you are doing in my husband's employ. He shall hear of this conversation, naturally.'

Unmoved, Fenton shrugged his shoulders. 'As you will.'

Let her tell her husband, it mattered not to him. He was satisfied with the impression he had made. He did not fear Reresby, and he could manage his wife. It was for the sake of England that he was here in the west. Was he not a Republican of the most freezing, implacable zeal? During the Civil War he had followed the Republican cause. The Commonwealth under Cromwell had suited him. On the death of Cromwell, when the English had seemed to run out of ideas and had no wish to return to the Puritan drabness of Cromwell's rule, they had fallen back on the idea of monarchy. Fenton had been unable to accept the restoration of Charles II, and he truly believed that royalty in England was only for the present. Anything that had happened once could happen again, and if he could be instrumental in bringing it about then he would do it. And so he had prowled and paced through those years, mixing, for ever watchful, looking around him to see if there were someone more worth talking to, more profitable, more use—which was when he had met Henry Barrington.

Now he turned his gaze on that man's daughter and smiled. 'There have been many who have aired their views, madam,' he said, not caring that his tone was openly menacing, 'who have paid with their heads for far less offence than you gave to his Majesty last night.'

'I am no traitor, Mr Fenton.'

'That is not for me to say. I would say, however, that by your own words you have so branded yourself.'

'You will do well to remember, Mr Fenton, that I am not unprotected. And with such radical views as your own, I advise you to have a care for your own head.'

Fenton smiled thinly and bowed before her, and there was mockery in his deep obeisance. 'I managed to hold on to it during the Commonwealth while others were losing theirs. However, I will consider your advice.'

'If you will excuse me,' Catherine said as calmly as she could. 'I have to change. I have kept my husband waiting long enough.'

Catherine swept past Fenton and carried on up the stairs. It was clear in his manner towards her that he would not take kindly to any interference or criticism from her while Marcus was away, for if she did then there was no doubt that their mutual dislike would break into open conflict. Fenton saw her as a threat to the power that was his when left alone to play Lord of the Manor, enjoying all the privileges that went with it.

'Dear me,' Alice murmured on seeing Catherine's troubled

features. 'You look as though you've lost a penny and found a farthing.'

'Perhaps that's because I've just encountered Mr Fenton. I cannot like him, Alice. He is a ruthless, unlikable man. In truth there is something nasty and pantherish about him. He puzzles me. He is out of the ordinary, a man who goes his own way regardless. He is also a confessed nonconformist—a true Republican. I have a feeling that he's plotting something?'

'Plotting, is it? Who is to say he is plotting anything? Still, these are times of plots and counterplots, of rumour and innuendo, I suppose.'

'Whenever I think of Mr Fenton, I experience a feeling of familiarity and a sense of having seen him before.'

'But how can that be?'

'I really don't know. Although I cannot remember seeing him before, when we first met and he looked at me, as soon as I discerned cold recognition in those pale eyes in that stone face, I knew I must have at some time. And yet, rarely leaving the confines of my home, where visitors were a rarity, as you well know, Alice, we can't have met. Yet I cannot rid myself of the feeling that I have seen him before, and if so when—and where?'

'Have you mentioned this to your husband?'

'No.'

'Why ever not?'

'Because Mr Fenton's position at Saxton Court is a special one, and it is not for me to interfere in his concerns.'

Pulling on her gloves, her riding crop tucked underneath her arm, Mr Fenton forgotten for the time being, Catherine arrived at the stables looking extremely fetching in her deep blue riding gown with a matching wide-brimmed plumed hat set at a rakish angle on her glossy curls. Picking up her skirts she crossed the cobbled yard. The sight of the horses' heads peering out over the stable doors with their ears pricked forward and their soft whickering never failed to excite and cheer her. Breathing deeply, she inhaled the familiar smells. She always found the smell of leather and saddle soap, warm hay and horses an intensely masculine and restful smell, a smell that brought back childhood memories of riding with Harry.

The yard was a hive of industry. The stable hands, having spent the morning riding out, were leading mounts back to their stalls for grooming.

Catherine's experienced eye told her that some of the big hunters, full of fire and blood, could readily gallop and jump, their main priority being to follow the hounds. A notable horsewoman, the sight of these magnificent beasts gladdened her heart. Horses had been a part of her life from early childhood, and she looked at them appreciatively. She admired them for their superb noble beauty and understood them. Unable to resist reaching out and stroking the neck of a big chestnut closest to her, she experienced a feeling of absolute joy when it nuzzled her arm.

Having watched her enter the yard, Marcus observed the rapture illuminated on her face. He moved to stand beside her. 'I can see that you like horses, which pleases me, since I also have an abiding passion for these noble beasts.'

'I do,' she replied, laughing delightedly when the chestnut reared and tossed its head, snorting and blowing with pleasure. 'I loved to ride from an early age, and I do believe several horses I saw being led into the stalls were thoroughbreds.'

'True. I had some of them sent down here from London— a couple of Arab mares from King Charles's own stable.'

'Will you race them?' Catherine asked with interest.

'I'd like to, when I have the time. Possessing some prime horseflesh—some of the finest in Somerset—I pride myself on my stables, although George would disagree with that. He's a keen racing man, and considers his to be the best,' Marcus joked good-humouredly.

'They would have to be quite exceptional to compete with these.'

'Come over here. I have something to show you I think you'll like.'

Marcus took her arm and guided her across the yard to where a young tousle-haired boy with a smattering of ginger freckles over his face emerged from the stalls leading a beautiful, silky smooth bay mare with the queenliest neck Catherine had ever seen. A star blaze between its eyes and three white socks made it quite distinguishable from any other horse.

Catherine's face lit up with joy as Marcus drew her towards it. Reaching out, she fondled its neck. Marcus watched her with interest. It gave him immense satisfaction to see the glow of pleasure on her face, and for the first time since she had come to Saxton Court he felt it was real, and not the polite façade she usually adopted.

'She's beautiful,' Catherine murmured. 'What's her name?'

'She is your horse,' Marcus told her. 'Name her what you will.'

Catherine jerked her head round to face him with wide-eyed astonishment. 'Mine? But—oh! I—I don't know what to say. Thank you. It's the most wonderful gift anyone has ever given me.' Falling silent, she appraised the horse. 'I have always believed a name to be about the most personal thing one can give a person or an animal, so it's worth thinking about. I shall choose her name with care.'

Slapping the horse's flank appreciatively, a half-smile curving his lips, Marcus's passion for horses shone in his eyes. 'She is a beauty, isn't she?'

'It's a pity you are not as gifted at choosing a wife as you are at selecting horses,' Catherine quipped on a teasing note, unable to resist the taunt.

A mildly tolerantly smile touched Marcus's handsome visage, but the glint in the dark eyes was as hard as steel. 'That remains to be seen. Saddle her up, Bobby.' His gaze rested on Catherine's enraptured face. 'The best way of getting to know each other is to ride her.'

When the horse was saddled, Marcus locked his hands together to accept Catherine's slender booted foot and was amazed at the agility she displayed as she sprang into the saddle.

With Marcus mounted on Lightning, his large, beautifully muscled gleaming black stallion, together they rode out of the stable yard, through the tall double gates and into the park. The mare was so quick to the touch of the crop that Catherine only had to think of a canter and she responded. With a watchful Marcus by her side she rode over the green turf, breathing deeply, exhilarating in the wonderful fresh breeze on her face and the strong spirited mount beneath her. Overwhelmed by her husband's generosity, she was unable to deny the warm gratitude she felt towards him for his gift.

At last, with Marcus's permission, she gave her horse its head, gently cracking her silky flanks with her crop. The horse gave a delighted squeal and broke into a brisk gallop, deftly clearing a shallow ditch.

Marcus rode beside her with unconcealed admiration. Her horsemanship was faultless. He noted her straight back and proud set of her head as she handled her horse superbly, especially when they soared effortless over a low hedge.

After a time Catherine slowed down, restraining herself and her horse and eventually pulling her to a halt. Laughing breathlessly, her colour high and her eyes alight, she leaned forward and gave the mare an appreciative pat.

'You like her?'

Catherine met his gaze warmly. 'She's truly wonderful. I cannot thank you enough.'

'Have you thought of a name for her?'

'Yes, I have. She reminds me of a dancer, so I shall call her Melody.'

Marcus considered the word and then nodded and smiled his approval.

They rode slowly along a narrow path by a broad stream that fed the lake, the peace disturbed only by the water, which rippled and foamed over rocks. The lake was ahead of them, its waters still and gleaming through the contrasting foliage of the trees. Leaving the path, they threaded their way through them, the ground carpeted with a mass of vivid bluebells, their scent intoxicating. Eventually they emerged into the open, disturbing ducks and other birds, which noisily took flight in alarm. Huge willows trembled and trailed along the water's edge.

Dismounting, Marcus went towards Catherine. Holding out his arms, he spanned her waist, supporting her while she jumped lightly to the ground. The horses moved away, their bridles jingling as they snorted in eagerness, lowering their heads and beginning to crop the sweet, juicy grass.

'Let's walk a while,' Marcus said.

They strolled by the side of the lake where the water lapped the stones a few feet away, quiet for a time, content to bask in the tranquillity that surrounded them. Where a rocky promontory jutted out into the water, in a clump of reeds a heron stood absolutely motionless. Catherine came under the spell of the lake, feeling the peace and enchantment reach her innermost being, appeasing the constraint she always felt whenever she was in her husband's company.

Glancing at his profile as he gazed wistfully towards the house in the distance, she thought how remote he was and how much there was to him that she didn't know. She was surprised to find at that moment how much she wanted to know. It filled her with a warm glow and a shameless longing to reach out and touch him, to push back the wayward lock of hair that dipped over his brow, to be close to him.

Often when she lay awake at night she tried to understand the turbulent, consuming emotions he awoke in her. He broke into her thoughts against her will, and whether it was their closeness of that one night he had lain with her, the feel of his hands, his skin touching hers, his smile, she did not know, but something inside her responded to him. The very thought of him was an irritant and a stimulant at the same time. She realised that her dislike and attraction ran close together—the line between them was very thin.

Suddenly she found the unease of being near him replaced by a stirring anticipation, an uncharacteristic desire to talk. When she stopped walking he did likewise, looking down at her enquiringly.

'Marcus, there is something I must say. I—I want to apologise for being so outspoken last night and for the embarrassment I caused you and those present. I was carried away—arrogant and extremely offensive and very rude. What I said was imprudent and unjust. I am very sorry and I ask your forgiveness.'

There was no doubting the sincerity of her tone. Of all the things she could have said, that was what Marcus least expected, and the most he wanted to hear. 'Granted,' he said gently, his eyes locked on hers.

'Thank you,' she said simply. 'No doubt George thinks I'm some kind of ranting fanatic.' She looked up at him, mischief dancing in her eyes. 'You don't really think he'll have me arrested, do you?'

Marcus grinned. 'He wouldn't dare—not if he values my friendship,' he said as they resumed their steady walk.

'What are you thinking?' Catherine ventured presently, breaking in upon his thoughts.

Marcus was smiling, a quiet, secretive smile as he looked with longing at the calm waters. 'That the more I am away from Saxton Court then the more I miss it. I hanker after having the time to hunt again on my land, and to catch fish here in the lake.'

'You like fishing?'

He nodded. Picking up a handful of stones, as a small boy would do he started to throw them, one by one, into the water, the ripples he created widening until they travelled out of sight and the surface of the lake returned to its mirror-like calm.

'When I was a boy I could often be found out on the lake in a boat with rod and line, sometimes with my father, who taught me how to fish. Afterwards we would cook our catch here on the bank over an open fire. I remember how good it smelled, how the air never failed to give me an appetite so that the fish always tasted doubly delicious. You know, Catherine, the lake is positively teeming with fish.' He paused and looked down to where she stood by his side, her face upturned to his. 'Have you ever been fishing?'

'No—never.'

'Then when I am done with the army I shall teach you and we shall cook what we catch here on an open fire, as I used to.'

'Yes,' Catherine murmured, meeting his gaze, trying to imagine him as a boy eagerly cooking his fish over an open fire. 'I would like that. But why do you spend so much time away, feeling as you do for Saxton Court? I find it strange for an only son of an esteemed family, with an estate as grand as this, to make the regular army his life. Did your father never try to dissuade you, fearful lest you were killed?'

'I could as easily be killed falling from my horse in the hunt.'

'I suppose so.'

'My father understood my desire for a military career, for

he himself commanded a troop of horse during the Civil War. However, it was not a situation he sought. It was forced on him by circumstance. He fully expected me to take over the running of Saxton Court in time.' He smiled. 'He was disappointed when I told him I wanted to be a soldier, but he understood my need to rebel a little—slip the traces, test myself in the world. Then I would return home. He gave me his blessing.'

'He must have been very understanding.'

A soft, remembering look came over Marcus's face as he spoke of his father. 'He was. There was no one finer. Should anything happen to me then Elizabeth's sons would inherit Saxton Court. However,' he said, gently tipping her chin up, forcing her to meet his gaze, 'things have changed with my marriage to you. Our marriage is highly irregular, I know, but I grow impatient to begin performing my husbandly duties, Catherine. I hope for sons of my own one day. Will you give the matter some thought?'

The quietly spoken words carried a wealth of meaning, and the intimate implications of how that would come about made Catherine's face burn. She tried to ignore the intensity of his steady gaze, but she could not sustain her animosity when she was in such beautiful surroundings and her husband was behaving in this odd, almost tender fashion.

'Very well. I—I shall consider it while you are away.'

'You do that,' he urged.

They walked on a bit further. Coming to a patch of soft grass, Marcus sat on it. Patting the space beside him, he invited Catherine to do the same.

'When are you going to tell me what my father did to make you hate him enough to ruin him?' she asked suddenly, tucking her feet beneath her skirts and sitting sideways to face him. 'I need to know, because only then shall I be able to understand why I am here now.'

Leaning his back against the trunk of a stout tree, Marcus drew one knee up against his chest and draped his arm across it. He looked at her hard, considering her words, seeing the unmistakable desperate need to know everything there was to know in her eyes.

'I intended to tell you. It is right that you should know. I am not saying that what I did to your father was right, but maybe then you will understand why I did what I did.'

As they faced each other, for the moment all the rancour and animosity between them was gone. A deep silence fell between them as Marcus contemplated her serious face for a moment before beginning.

'There is no easy way to tell you, Catherine. The reason I despised your father was because he was directly responsible for the murder of my own.'

Catherine stared at him in stunned disbelief. The shock his statement caused her was visible in her eyes as she stared at him wordlessly, trying to digest what he'd said. Her voice was strained when she finally spoke.

'Murder? No, that cannot be. My father was many things, Marcus—but to stoop to murder…Surely not. Did—did you have proof of this?'

He nodded. 'Following extensive enquiries I tracked down an associate of his, a weak and frightened man who, when promised he would be dealt with leniently, surrendered everything he knew.'

'How did your father die—and where?'

'In his house in London. His own dagger was thrust into his heart.'

'But I—I don't understand. Why would my father want to have him killed?'

'As you are aware, your father held extreme radical views. He was a Republican who wanted to see the return of the Commonwealth. During the reign of King Charles he used concerted efforts to exclude his brother James, then the Duke of York and a Catholic, from the succession. He conspired to have my father killed to prevent him betraying him.'

'I recall Mr Soames—my father's lawyer—telling me when he came to Riverside House to read the will that my father was involved in a plot to assassinate King Charles and the Duke of York. The plot misfired and the conspirators who were caught were executed.'

'That is correct. My own father's death was directly connected to Barrington's involvement in the conspiracy, which was to take place at The Rye House as the King and his brother returned from Newmarket. You see, my father was a Justice of the Peace, and he had papers in his possession incriminating your father and one other. And so your father and this other man arranged to have him removed—permanently. In doing so his fellow conspirator removed the only witness who could testify against him. You see, to sustain a charge of treason, it is necessary for the prosecutors to produce two witnesses,' he explained. 'The papers would have been damning proof, but they disappeared.'

'And the man who killed your father?'

His face hardened. 'I am still searching.'

'Are you any closer to finding him?'

'No. But I will.'

'I wish I could be of help, but like everything else, my father was always careful to keep that part of his life from me. I remember the men who came to the house—always at night— those who opposed the King, Whig lords, old Republicans from Cromwell's time, spies, informers, men who loved the taste of conspiracy as others love fine brandy. There would be candlelight conferences and debates, smoking and drinking long into the night. I would crouch on the stairs and watch them from the dark of the upper floor, hidden from view by the sturdy banisters.'

Marcus's expression softened. 'Poor Catherine. What a strange childhood you must have had—without a mother and living with a man of Barrington's ilk. Between your father and me, you haven't been very lucky in your men, have you?'

'No,' she said, averting her gaze. 'I haven't.'

'With hindsight I know that what I did, to exact my own personal revenge, was wrong and I have no excuse. I should have handed him over to the authorities to be tried along with his fellow conspirators. But at the time making him pay for the suffering he had caused my father, myself and my sister was paramount. My deepest regret is that I involved you. It was unworthy of me and you did not deserve it. In the beginning I thought I could strike at Barrington through you, but I now know that I should not have made you the instrument of my vengeance.'

'No, that was quite wrong of you. It seems I am the one who will have to pay for that wretched card game for the rest of my life.'

'Do not let it stand between us, Catherine. Until this matter of Monmouth is cleared up, military matters will keep me from home, so you will be spared my presence for the time being. No doubt you will consider my absence as something of a respite. But the time is fast approaching for my retirement.' A sudden frown creased his brow. 'There is something I wanted to talk to you about.'

'Is it important?'

'It's about Monmouth and the unrest in these parts, where people are most warmly affected by him.'

'You're really worried about it, aren't you, Marcus?'

'Extremely so. If I thought rebellion was to occur in some other part of England then it would be a different matter, but here in Somerset we'll be in the thick of it. These western counties have been like a powder keg waiting to explode for years now. The very fact of their successful defiance during the Civil War led to harsher persecution in the Restoration period and thus hardened their resolve to rebel. And in truth, because of the vindictiveness of the loyalist justices towards the Dissenters, which cannot be matched elsewhere, it is not difficult to understand why the men of these counties should be so ready to emulate their fathers and again rise up to disperse the cavaliers—so to speak.'

'But there may be no rebellion. You don't know anything for certain.'

Marcus looked past her to watch the sunlight dance on the water's surface, his expression grave. 'I know enough. From what we have been told by the King's messengers who pass frequently between London and The Hague, preparations are already under way. I saw it for myself, don't forget, when I was over there. My greatest fear is that Monmouth will decide to embark on his mission to dispose James of his throne when Parliament is in session.'

'Why? What difference will that make?'

'Many of the Lord Lieutenants and their deputies will be up in London then, which will prevent the militia being raised against him. As a deputy Lieutenant, George is to travel to London shortly. He is worried because many of the militia incline to Monmouth. Without their officers there will be wholesale defections to the rebels.'

'I can see why you are concerned. Does the Duke of Monmouth have many officers—experienced officers to train an army?'

'Officers are his most urgent need. There are plenty of old Cromwellians in England and Holland who would dearly like to strike at the crown, but they're too long in the tooth now.

They may prove invaluable for training, but would hardly do for company and troop officers. There are some officers, dismissed from English and Dutch regiments for sympathising with Monmouth, who have gone over to him, but on the whole they're a pretty scratch lot. There will be old men and good men waiting to join Monmouth, but they are not quite the same as the disciplined soldiers in the royal army.'

'But surely if it is known that Monmouth is planning to embark on such a mission as to incite rebellion here in England, then he can be stopped. Can he not be prevented from landing?'

'It's not that simple. He does run the risk of being picked up, for we do have several small ships of the Royal Navy patrolling the Channel, and he will need to go to great expense to charter a vessel large enough to get through, but I fear that this is precisely what he will do. The only consolation of him doing this is that it will drain his funds considerably, limiting him in the purchase of arms.'

A softness came into Marcus's eyes as again he fastened them on Catherine's face. 'My immediate worry is that without my presence at Saxton Court you will be relatively alone, Catherine. I know many who work both in the house and on the estate sympathise and may leave to join Monmouth. I have instructed Mr Fenton to take the utmost care of you, to see you come to no harm.'

Catherine grimaced with distaste. 'Mr Fenton is himself a sympathiser whose mind runs on insurrection. Can you be sure he won't desert his post?'

'I sincerely hope not. He gave me his word.'

'To the limit of his restraint. If he is pressed beyond that, you may find yourself without your steward. He despises kings and princes and as a Republican wants to see England return to life as it was in Cromwell's time.'

'To want such a thing the man must either be a dangerous villain or a dangerous fool.'

'Dangerous villain is how I would describe your Mr Fenton. I cannot pretend to like him, Marcus, and I do not think he likes me overmuch either.'

'Then you must try to set your differences aside. Catherine, the situation is more serious than many people realise so I beg you to be cautious and vigilant, for these are dangerous times. If anything you should say against the King should fall upon the wrong ears, then it could mean disaster for all at Saxton Court. Please remember that I am an officer in the King's army. It would not do if my wife was suspected of having inclinations towards Monmouth.'

'Please don't worry, Marcus. I promise I will be careful.'

'It there is rebellion and Monmouth is defeated—as I am certain he will be—then there will be dire consequences for any who support him.' Marcus leaned forward, looking earnestly into her eyes. 'If I ask for nothing else, I ask for your support—your loyalty—in this.'

A tremor ran through Catherine at his nearness. 'Then you have it,' she said without hesitation. 'I will never again speak as I did last night. I give you my word.'

Marcus stared at her, looking startled and pleased and dubious, half-expecting her to return to the attack. 'You do?'

She nodded. 'Although you must understand that I was brought up to uphold the Protestant religion, to abhor papism.'

'I don't like a Catholic King on the throne any more than you do, but to oppose him at this time is tantamount to signing one's own death warrant. I'm a Protestant, and I'm also a realist, and not a man to support a rebellion doomed to failure. Bide your time—that is my advice. James will not reign for long, but Monmouth is not the solution. He is too weak, too indecisive. I believe it will come in James's daughter, Mary, and her husband, William.'

He got to his feet and extended his hands to her, but she ignored them and rose unassisted. His dark eyes on her face became searching. Just when she had begun to thaw a little, just when she had ceased to treat him as the dangerous alien creature who had invaded her life, he was going away. She waited for him to speak, unaware of the struggle that was taking place inside him when he looked down into her wide green eyes and hauntingly beautiful face framed by her black hair.

'I do want to make you happy, Catherine,' he said at length, 'in spite of yourself if need be. When this is over and I leave the army, is there a future for us together?'

'In all honesty, Marcus, I don't know. Ours is not a marriage like others and I cannot readily forgive you for the manner in which you made me your wife. However, I am slowly becoming reconciled to the fact that that is how things are and I shall use the time you are away getting used to the situation. I ask you to be patient with me. I do promise to think seriously about us, for I have no wish to live the rest of my life in bitterness.'

As they rode away from the lake, both accepted that there was a change in their attitude to each other, but when Marcus, astride his mount, rode away from Saxton Court the following day in his buff coat of leather and long jackboots, his sword by his side, Catherine was unprepared for the strange mixture of emotions that filled her and the heavy sadness in her heart.

Chapter Six

Catherine emerged from the wood into a small clearing. The open ground was filled with silent people, men, women and children milling in panic. The faces were stamped with expressions ranging from fear and shock to outright anger. She paused for a moment, assessing the event. A chill raced down her spine.

The wretched figure of a man was being dragged moaning and stumbling towards the trunk of a stout tree. His hands had been forced behind his back and tied. Fiercely excited, yapping hounds circled him, and the gaping wounds on his legs told Catherine that they had already had their taste of blood.

'Mercy! Don't kill me!' the man cried out, his eyes darting about in terror.

A woman ran out from the crowd and threw herself at Fenton's feet in desperation. 'Let him go! He is my father. For the love of God, let him go!' she pleaded tearfully.

Fenton's eyes were merciless as he watched one of his henchmen, a brutal-faced man with a whip in his hand, roughly push her aside.

Losing awareness of the crowd, an anger sweeping through her veins as she recalled how Elizabeth had staunchly condemned Fenton's behaviour and now was discovering at first hand the truth of it, Catherine urged her mount forward until she was within two yards of her husband's bailiff.

'Mr Fenton, what are you doing?'

At the sharp, commanding sound of Catherine's voice, heads turned and all eyes became fixed on her. Taken unawares, perhaps by the tone of her voice, Fenton looked up. His eyes became narrowed on her, his body stiff with defiance.

'I would have thought that was perfectly obvious—although perhaps your question has to do with the reasons why I am doing it.'

'My question was plain enough. I'll let you judge the manner in which you choose to answer it.'

'It's nothing to bother you with, Lady Reresby,' Fenton answered, inclining his head slightly in mock respect. 'Flogging a man is a nasty, messy business, so I would advise you to ride on by. Go back to your business of running the house, and leave me to mine.'

Catherine was incensed by his calculating rudeness. 'I do not like your tone, Mr Fenton. You are being deliberately uncivil.' She looked down at the drooping figure that was about to be flogged. The miserable wretch was in a state of abject terror and shaking in every limb. 'What is this man's crime that he deserves to be beaten? What has he done?' she commanded.

'He was caught poaching, my lady.'

'Poaching?' Catherine glared at him. 'And for that you would beat him?'

'Poachers and their kind are not welcome. Flogging is the usual punishment for such a crime—well deserved, too.'

'I think not, Mr Fenton. Do you so far forget yourself as to put yourself in my husband's place? By what right do you set yourself up as judge? I believe it is for the local magistrate to mete out punishment. I command you to release this man at once. Judging by the state of him, your hounds have inflicted punishment enough.'

The bailiff's lean cruel features were drained of colour, and the smile on his lips had faded, as if he no longer considered it worthwhile to maintain the fiction. Catherine knew the man before her was her implacable enemy. His thin face was taut and a fierce hatred for her burned in his eyes, making her realise that this incident had turned into a battle between their two selves—a battle of wits, which she must win at all costs if she wished for the respect of the people around her. She kept her icy gaze locked on his relentlessly, and he was the first to turn away.

He strode towards the poacher. 'You're fortunate that the lady has a gentle heart, thief,' he growled, making an angry gesture to the man holding him. 'Cut his bonds and let him go. Get out of my sight.'

'Take him home and tend his wounds,' Catherine said softly to the woman who had pleaded for his release.

'Thank you, my lady,' the woman said, with gratitude burning in her eyes. 'May God bless you.'

Silence reigned as these two people shuffled away. Slowly the crowd dispersed. Catherine looked at Fenton, now mounted on his horse.

'I do not wish to bandy words with you, Mr Fenton. As my husband's bailiff you are in charge of the administration of the estate, so it will be run in a proper manner while he is away. I do not wish to hear of any more atrocities carried out by you. Is that understood?'

Enraged to find himself being made to look a fool by this slip of a girl, Fenton nudged his mount closer to her. 'Perfectly, my lady,' he sneered. 'I must say that I am surprised at the ease and speed with which you have slipped into the role of wife of a King's man—a man who will take up arms against those who will rise to destroy for ever the hated regime of popery and arbitrary government. You've got high-minded since you married his lordship. Your father would have been disappointed in you. Most disappointed.'

Catherine could not have been more thoroughly stunned had one of the surrounding ancient trees fallen on her head. She stared at Fenton as if she had begun to doubt her sanity.

'My father? You—you knew my father?'

He nodded. 'I knew him well.'

'But how?'

His curled smile was sinister. 'We belonged to the same club.'

Fenton inclined his head slightly in mock obeisance, but his malevolent smile froze Catherine to the core of her very soul.

Satisfied that his words had had their desired effect, without more ado he turned from her. There were obscenities on his tongue that he silenced, and a seething madness filled his brain as he jerked his horse and galloped away, followed by his men and yelping hounds. All vestiges of self-restraint had been stripped from him and he vowed, with a terrible hatred, to make Barrington's daughter pay for this. How dare she undermine his authority in front of the peasants and his own men? By God, he swore that by the time he was done, he would make her wish she had never been born.

Riding slowly back to the house, Catherine did some thinking. Images drifted across her mind like fragmented clouds being blown across the sky. She saw images of the faces of the men who had come to Riverside House to see her father—meetings, clandestine meetings after dark stretching into the early hours…meetings of Republicans.

Had Fenton been one of them? Was that why he seemed so familiar to her?

* * *

On the last day of May, the Admiralty of Amsterdam cleared all three of the Duke of Monmouth's ships ready to sail from the island of Texel at the mouth of the Zuider Zee.

Amsterdam was traditionally Republican and thus had a natural antipathy to King James, both as a king and as a Papist. The Dutch, eager to assist those who fought for a Protestant cause, would do nothing to hinder the rebels. Many went out of their way to help them, giving them money, selling them arms, and providing shelter.

Monmouth was assured of strong support in England, and a strong ally of his, the Duke of Argyle, had set off to rally Scotland to the cause, to stir up rebellion and push out the King's forces. He knew that he could raise an army and march towards London unopposed, together with eighty officers and men. So he landed at Lyme Regis in Dorset on the eleventh of June to the rallying cry of 'Monmouth, Monmouth. God save the Protestant religion!' At Lyme, the Duke of Monmouth denounced his uncle, King James, as a usurper and murderer of his father, Charles II, and declared himself Charles II's legitimate son.

People from the middle ranks of society—those engaged in industry and commerce—exultant that their beloved Duke had come to liberate England from the Papist tyranny of his uncle James, flocked to his side. Over one hundred men from the small town of Colyton alone went to swell the ranks.

The West Country militia managed to prevent large numbers from joining the rebel army and contained the rebellion, but there were many in the militia who were Protestant themselves, who sympathised with the rebels and did little oppose them— some even going over to the rebels. However, a large number of the gentry, even the ones sympathetic to Monmouth, were not prepared to risk their necks.

Monmouth's plans, formulated in Holland, had echoed

across the water, giving the English government time to consider counter-measures. Once it was known that the Duke had landed, an Act was rushed through Parliament condemning him to death for high treason and a reward of five thousand pounds offered for his capture.

News of the Duke of Monmouth's landing, his capture of Axminster and his progress northward, gathering strength on the way, spread like wildfire. It was a tense time, with the whole county full of confusion and disorder. It was an anxious period for Catherine, Saxton Court being so close to Taunton, where Monmouth was welcomed with jubilation amid the pealing of church bells and proclaimed king at the Market Cross.

To add to her anxiety, many of Saxton Court's labourers left to join Monmouth's army, among whom there was an element who, under the pretence of zeal for their country and common cause, in truth saw it as an opportunity to rob and pillage whatever they could lay their hands on.

It was men such as these that Catherine bravely faced when they arrived at Saxton Court. The intruders were aware that it was the property of Lord Reresby, who, having signed allegiance to King James, had been proclaimed an enemy and a traitor to the cause.

Twilight had fallen and the candles had been lit. Because she was to dine alone, a table had been laid in a small parlour. It was warmer than the huge dining room and curtains could be drawn to shut out the drafts. This was why she did not see the moving shapes of men approaching the house. It was Mrs Garfield who came rushing in to tell her that some men were trying to force their way inside. There was complete mayhem in the hall. Above the noise of barking dogs and shrieking servants running to and fro were the thunderous hails of blows on the main door.

'Open the door,' Catherine instructed Mrs Garfield. 'We must see what they want.'

Catherine faced the formidable men who piled in wielding pistols and swords. She had no idea where Fenton was: in fact, so many men had left to join Monmouth that there were only women in the house. Never before had she so much missed Marcus's cool mind and authority.

The man in front of the rest—middle-aged, paunchy, smelling of sweat and obviously the leader—lumbered towards where she bravely stood in the centre of the hall. Others crowded in behind him. Catherine's body was frozen in shock, but with great effort she tried to appear calm. Beside her, Mrs Garfield was silent. These men certainly didn't resemble soldiers.

'My goodness. What are we to do? What do you think they want, my lady?' Mrs Garfield whispered, her voice trembling fearfully.

'No doubt we shall soon find out,' Catherine replied, steeling herself for what was to come, her hands clenched in the folds of her skirt to keep them from trembling. 'Try to stay calm. There is nothing to be gained by antagonising them. Who are you?' she demanded.

With just six feet between them, the man with the paunch leered at her. 'Sam Becket's the name—from Axminster born and bred. And what do we have here?' he jeeringly questioned. 'How nice to meet you. You must be Lady Reresby. You're too finely dressed to be a kitchen maid.'

'What do you want?' Catherine demanded, trembling but trying not to show it. 'I am Lady Reresby and you have no business here.'

'Those are the words of a malignant,' Becket sneered. He turned to the men. 'Search the house. A house such as this must have arms by the cartload.' He looked at Catherine. 'Any weapons we find I sequester in the name of the Duke of Monmouth. We seize what can be found from any source available.'

'*Steal* is the word I would use to describe what you are doing. How dare you? I demand that you leave this house immediately.'

'Cease your tongue. We're the ones dishin' out the orders. Stand aside, Lady Reresby. I'll not ask again.'

'Then I must advise you to be careful,' she said sarcastically, realising that old arms, from sporting guns to old matchlocks, were already being pounced upon in the Reresby armoury. 'The majority of what you have there are likely to be more dangerous to the user than to the enemy.'

After that everything was a complete chaotic nightmare. Footsteps pounded through the house. There was a crash as furniture was overturned and objects hit the floor. Martha, the young maid who assisted Alice with her duties, a short, rosy-cheeked girl, began weeping hysterically. There was a roaring in Catherine's ears. At that moment any sympathy she had felt for the Duke of Monmouth's cause vanished. It was replaced by a deep and abiding anger.

Looking around in desperation, her gaze was drawn to an ancient broadsword hanging above the fireplace that had so far escaped notice. The sight of it gave her hope. Dashing towards it, she wrenched it from its peg. Unconscious of its weight, her graceful fingers trained to etiquette now gripped the hilt of the ancient sword, as one might cling to a log in the middle of a raging current.

The weeping Martha started to scream.

'Silence the wench.' The order was shouted from Becket. The maid was slapped hard twice across the face. The vicious blows sent her to the floor with a groan of agony and blood pouring from her cut lip.

The sounds of the house being ransacked faded to dull confusion as something in Catherine's mind snapped. On seeing one of her maids treated so brutally, her anger came hot and strong. The greed she saw in the men's eyes as they carried off arms and valuables alike triggered her instincts for survival. When Becket raised his hand to silence the maid, who continued to wail, with a cry of fury she crossed the intervening space between them.

'You'll not touch her again,' she cried and raised the sword like a talisman, her anger so powerful and consuming it took over her mind. She lunged straight for his heart, but anticipating the danger he sidestepped and the blade sank into his shoulder. Catherine felt the metal grate on bone. Becket howled and reeled backwards, clutching the wound, his blood gushing through his fingers.

'She's struck me, the stupid bitch,' he shouted, his face twisting with pain and fear. 'Get the sword, for God's sake.'

Catherine sprang away and, her sword raised on guard, she crouched, awaiting the attack. It did not come. 'Get out,' she hissed. 'You have what you came for, now get out.'

A couple of men advanced towards her, but the injured man ordered them back. 'Leave it. Get me out of here. A physician—I must get to a physician before I bleed to death.'

Catherine and the terrified servants watched them go, relieved that the incident was over. After the mayhem Saxton Court was oddly quiet. Only the quiet weeping of the injured maid broke the silence.

Her dazed mind veering away from the horror of what had occurred, Catherine put the sword down and turned to Mrs Garfield. 'Please tend to Martha, Mrs Garfield, while I see what damage has been done and what has been taken.'

It was shortly afterwards that Archie came to tell her that most of the horses had been taken, including her own precious Melody. Only half a dozen coach horses grazing in the paddock had been missed.

Outraged that the rebels had dared to steal her most treasured possession, a fervent glitter brightened Catherine's eyes. 'I must find Melody. I shall go into Taunton first thing, before the Duke of Monmouth moves out and takes my horse with him. I shall procure an interview with the Duke himself if necessary—although my sympathies where Monmouth is concerned are beginning to wane in the wake of so much wanton pillaging. Melody was a gift to me from Marcus. I will get her back.'

Gazing at the people filling Taunton's streets the following morning, Catherine likened it to a holiday crowd buoyed up with excessive optimism and merriment. It was thickest around in the centre and around the taverns, and washed up against the castle walls. The crowd was made up mainly of Monmouth's followers—an ill-assorted collection of troops, all occupations represented, their arms as diverse as their uniforms and in a similarly poor condition.

They presented a bizarre spectacle. Some wore the red coats and white kersey breeches of the New Model Army, a sight not seen since Cromwell's time, reminding one of glories past. Others wore purple coats faced with scarlet, which had been made in Holland for the rebellion, but most of the rebels wore sensible clothing typical of the Dissenting artisan class from which they sprang.

Seated with Alice in the carriage behind Archie, Catherine had an excellent view of the scene, and she wondered how on earth she was going to find her horse in all this mayhem. She would go directly to the Duke himself, and lodge a complaint against the disgraceful treatment they had received at Saxton Court.

The carriage made slow progress through the jostling crowd. Approaching the Castle Inn, where Monmouth's officers could be heard roistering, some fortified with cider and spilling out onto the street, her eyes were drawn to a young man about to enter. She stiffened. No, it could not be. Her eyes must be playing tricks with her mind. She looked closer and her heart contracted. There could be no mistake. No one else she knew had hair that colour. Falling somewhere between red and gold, it glowed like a flame in the drab light. Clad in stout buff leather coat, belonging to an elite troop of Monmouth's cavalry, it was Harry, and no phantom conjured up by a fevered imagination.

Ignoring Alice's protests, she was scrambling out of the carriage and shoving her way through the throng towards him. Harry turned on hearing her call his name. His eyes widened in recognition and warmth kindled in their depths, striking like a flaming arrow at her heart. She stared into his face, the one she knew by heart. It was the same, but different, having aged in the short time they had been apart. His eyes were the same— as blue as she remembered, but sad now, brooding and withdrawn. There was also a settled air of strength and purpose about him that had not been there before.

Taking her hand, he drew her closer to the wall of the inn. 'Catherine. Confound it! What the devil are you doing here?'

'This is where I live, Harry. Saxton Court, my husband's estate, is close by.'

Harry's mouth set in a grim line. 'Of course. How remiss of me. I should have known. I would have thought your husband would be with you, guarding you against the rebel army.'

'Marcus has gone to join his regiment in London,' she hurried to explain. 'The Royal Dragoons.'

'Indeed? A troop of John Churchill's own regiment. I am impressed. 'Tis a little ironic to think they are on their way with the regular troops to fight Monmouth, to reinforce the militia and destroy us. Originally the Royal Dragoons were Monmouth's Horse under his own command in the service of France and later Tangier—crack troops who can fight equally as well on foot or on horseback. We will fight hard before we admit defeat. Are you in Taunton unescorted?'

'Alice came with me. I have come to look for my horse. Last night some of the rebels came to the house to seize arms. Not only did they ransack the house, taking with them what weapons they could find and certain items of value, but the horses, too. To steal arms is one thing, but to take the horses…'

'Battles are won by cavalry and guns, Catherine, and Monmouth's army is deficient in both. We have sufficient muskets to arm a quarter of the infantry—the rest of the men will have to fend for themselves. A third of an army usually consists of mounted men. Monmouth's army falls short of this, reflecting the fact that not many real countrymen have joined him. Weavers and shoemakers cannot afford a horse. It was fortunate that I was with the Duke when he landed and managed to procure a horse quickly.'

'I knew you would be with Monmouth, Harry, but I never thought to see you.'

Harry's expression softened once more. 'I'm glad we've met. I keep thinking back to that last night we were together at The Hague. You were so magnificent—when you cared.'

'Oh, Harry, please don't. I've always cared for you, you know that.'

'You were beautiful, so proud.' His eyes hardened. 'What you did hurt me deeply. Didn't you think I deserved an explanation? If you had told me, maybe I could have accepted it.' She stared at him and seemed confused, which heightened his anger. 'How do you think I felt?'

'Harry—I am so, so sorry. The last thing I wanted was to cause you pain. I feel dreadful about what I've done to you.'

'You said you had no choice. How did you come to marry Reresby, Catherine?'

'It was decided between my father and Marcus,' she said, lowering her head, too humiliated to tell Harry the sordid details. 'It happened. There was nothing I could do. It's no use going over it now. It's past.'

'I know marriages in eminent families are made for many reasons—financial or political, or to fuse two families together to make them more powerful. I had hoped that between us it would be different.'

'I always thought it would be. I hoped…Children are brought up to do their duty with no room for sentiment—but I did fight it, Harry. I swear I did.'

'Would you come away with me, Catherine, if I asked you to?'

She stared at him hard. 'Leave Marcus? No. You know I cannot.' Her voice was no more than a whisper. 'Not any more.'

'Can you tell me why?'

'I do not know. Something in me—in Marcus—prevents me.'

'I see. You will remain with him?'

'I must. If I am to be content in the future, I have to commit myself to him and our lives together. Besides, adultery is a sin so dreadful that I would hate myself.'

'And hate me?' His voice was low.

Catherine stared at him, her heart turning over with pity for him. 'Hate you? I could never hate you—my dearest friend.'

Harry's lips twisted with scorn. 'Friend? Is that all I am to you now?'

'It is a large word, Harry. Please don't torture me with these questions.'

He drew back. 'Will *he* give you up?'

'No. I—I do not take my vows lightly. I am firmly bound by my word.'

'You thought little of your vows when you went with me to The Hague,' Harry reminded her harshly.

'I make no excuses for the way I behaved. I was foolish—I did not know Marcus then.'

'I always thought that you and I were meant for each other. I loved you and you led me to believe you loved me.'

'I do love you, Harry. You have always known that.'

'But not as much as you used to. You've changed, Catherine. I can see it in your eyes when you look at me. Are you in love with your husband?'

'I—I can't explain what I feel,' she said, though she dared not look at him. She was unable to push away the memory of that moment by the lake, before Marcus had gone away, when he had told her he wanted to make her happy and asked her if there was a future for them together—when he had stared down into her eyes and her emotions had raged a terrible war. 'Since he went away I think of him a great deal—and I would certainly have been glad of his presence last night to deal with the rebels.'

'Does he treat you well? Is—is he…?'

She raised her eyes to his. 'Marcus is good to me,' she answered softly. 'He demands his own way in most things, but he does not ill treat me. I have everything I need. I am not unhappy.'

'He is a very fortunate man.'

His voice was soft, and those blue eyes holding Catherine's, still full of yesterdays, conveyed far more than words.

'How I would like to seem proud and arrogant and indifferent, to show you I don't give a damn that you are married to someone else, that you don't mean a thing to me. But I'm not that good an actor.'

Harry's pain almost overwhelmed her and she moved towards him to comfort him, but stepped back again, aware that she must not. Her heart ached with the desolation of it and with her loss, the loss of Harry and her girlhood dream. Her love had grown up, leaving him behind, and there could be no room for any other man in her life but her husband. Her eyes shone with tears, but she remained composed.

'You will get over me, Harry. You will. You must not think of me now, and when this is over make a new life for yourself. But for the time being Monmouth needs you and you have a rebellion to fight. I know how close the Protestant cause is to your heart, and I know you will prove your worth.'

Catherine saw his expression relax a little and his eyes became animated, which she knew had nothing to do with her. He had withdrawn from the intimacy of moments earlier. With a single-mindedness she was glad to see, she realised that his thoughts were again upon his purpose in coming to England.

He smiled. 'You are right, Catherine,' he said, taking her hand and pressing it to his lips. 'As always. Now, tell me about this horse you're looking for. If I come across it, I promise to see it gets back to you.'

From inside the Castle Inn Mr Fenton peered out of a window, his eyes fixed on Lady Reresby and Harry Stapleton. The anger he felt over his last encounter with her ladyship still smouldered inside him. Even the raid he had instigated on Saxton Court by whispering in Becket's ear about the arms kept inside the house, the home of a King's man, had not diminished it.

Damn the bitch! he thought. Damn her for her arrogance and for making him look a fool. He had almost revealed overmuch of his association with her father there and then that day in the wood—thank God an inborn caution had stopped him from saying more. Because of his close connection with her father, Henry Barrington—a man he'd despised despite being of the same political bent—he knew that it had been intended that Catherine would wed Harry Stapleton, and now, seeing them together and the intimacy that still existed between the two of them, he would not restrain the impulse to drag her indiscretion into the clear light of day when he next saw her husband.

* * *

After three days in Taunton spent in pointless ceremonies—
three days during which the royal reinforcements marched fifty
miles closer to the West Country—the Duke of Monmouth left
Taunton, deciding to maintain the momentum of rebellion by
marching on towards Bristol.

Fearing another raid on the house, Catherine was glad that
they had moved on. Marcus had been away from Saxton Court
for four weeks. She thought of what Harry had said, that Marcus might have been sent to the West Country with John
Churchill. She prayed this would be so. In the wake of the
rebels' raid on the house and her encounter with Harry—and
Mr Fenton's long absences from the estate, which made her
wonder if he was about to desert like the rest of the men—she
felt perilously close to tears.

She tried to convince herself that this aching misery she felt
was merely because of all that had happened, but her lonely de-
jection sprang from something much deeper. She was missing
Marcus. She thought of him often, and wondered how he was
faring, wherever he happened to be. He had stressed the danger of his task, and that it involved risks.

What did she know about him, really? He had started out as
her enemy, and had turned out to be a man of honour and a no-
bleman, different to any she had known before. She knew that
his mother had died when he was ten years old, and that his father had been murdered—and that her own father had played
a major part in his death.

She knew so little about her husband, and yet he seemed to
have become important to her. Was she about to surrender to
this battle of wills that had raged between them from the moment they had set eyes on each other? When he returned would
it be a beginning for them? Would she be willing to become a
proper wife to him, to share his bed? Surprised at the tears that

misted her eyes, she blinked them back and prepared to endure another evening alone.

When Marcus did unexpectedly arrive, he surprised her by his sudden appearance in the small parlour. She was seated at the table about to eat when he walked in. Her heart gave a traitorous leap at the sight of him and she found herself drawn by an irresistible impulse to where he stood. He was bareheaded, and his dark hair was rough and tousled. The features were the same, a little more sharply defined, perhaps, and he held his head in just the same old arrogant way. Looking slightly travel weary, he had hooked his leather jerkin over his shoulder, for the evening was warm.

'Very cosy,' he said. 'Do you mind if I join you?'

'Marcus!' Catherine stood up. The awareness of his presence in the candlelit room was enough to unravel her composure. Why hadn't he sent word for her to expect him, so that she would have been prepared? 'This is a surprise. Welcome home.'

Tossing his jerkin into a chair, he moved further into the room, his eyes never leaving hers. 'Am I truly welcome, Catherine?' he asked.

'But of course,' she replied evenly, knowing the answer he wanted, yet giving him a different one. 'Why would you not be, in your own home? We—we weren't expecting you.'

'I'm here with Lord Churchill—although I've resigned my post with the Dragoons. Until this business with Monmouth is settled I'm still with the army, and because I'm from these parts I've been sent at the head of a small patrol to reconnoitre the area. I was concerned as to how you fare here at Saxton Court—being so close to the rebel army.' He regarded her for a long moment. 'But first, how are you, Catherine?'

The way he was looking at her brought a rush of heat to Catherine's cheeks, and suddenly she was unable to hold his appraising stare. 'I—I am well.'

'I'm sorry. I didn't mean to frighten you by arriving unexpectedly. I hope you're not lonely in the house all by yourself.'

'You didn't frighten me. Not really,' she assured him. She felt safe again, now he was home. 'And I'm not lonely. This house is so big—there's so much going on all the time, so many noises—so many echoes.' She lowered her eyes in self-conscious confusion and finally in a rush of an apology, she added, 'I'm glad you're home, even if it is just for a short time. But—you must be hungry. As you can see, there isn't enough food for two, so I'll go and instruct one of the servants to have some extra brought in.'

She made a move towards the door, but he reached out and gently took her arm. 'There's no need. I've already done so.' Marcus was hungry, and the thought of dining with his wife in the intimate confines of this small parlour held some appeal.

Catherine gazed at the hand on her arm. There was something so masculine in the strength of that hand that her heartbeat quickened. He released her and she looked quickly away. There were times when Marcus was too attractive for her peace of mind.

Choosing a comfortable seat near the hearth, Marcus stretched his long booted legs out in front of him. He looked at Catherine, at the tumbling mass of black hair. Beneath its fullness, dark-fringed green eyes glowed with their own light, the colour in their depths changing like a newly hewn gemstone.

He found himself much enamoured with this young wife of his, who had entered his life with reluctance. There was more woman in her than he had at first realised, and it was not the calculated femininity of all the other women he had known, but an easy, natural thing that would never fail to stir his ardour.

He gestured to the chair opposite. 'Come and sit down.' When she was settled, he said, 'Tell me what has been happening in my absence. According to Mrs Garfield, most of the labourers on the estate have gone to join Monmouth.'

'Unfortunately that is so.'

Marcus raised his brows in mock surprise. 'Unfortunately? Knowing all too well where your sympathies lay, Catherine, I find that a strange word for you to use. Has something happened to change your opinion?'

Catherine shifted uneasily. 'I confess that I am confused. I don't know what to think any more. I must apologise if you find anything amiss in the house. We…had unwelcome visitors recently—some of Monmouth's recruits. They ransacked the house in their search for weapons, emptying the gunroom and taking whatever else they found of use, along with a few valuables— I've compiled a list. They—they also took the horses, apart from half a dozen coach horses that were in the paddock at the time. I'm sorry, Marcus. There was nothing I could do to stop them.'

Appalled, Marcus slowly rose from his chair. As she spoke a dark rage filled him that his wife should have been subjected to this. 'Those damned rebels came here—forced entry into this house?' Suddenly his look became anxious. 'Did they hurt you, Catherine?'

Catherine was touched by his concern for her safety—she could not recall Harry reacting in the same way when she had told him of the raid on Saxton Court. 'No, I am perfectly well. In fact, I injured one of them.'

'How?'

'With that old sword you keep hanging over the fireplace in the hall. One of the rebels abused one of the maids, and when she became hysterical the man leading them ordered someone to silence her. When he was about to do it himself I—I—'

'Ran him through?' he asked incredulously.

'Something like that. I had no time to take in the full enormity of my action or the danger to myself. It—it was quite dreadful. But I didn't kill him,' she was quick to explain.

'I wouldn't be too sure about that, Madam Warrior,' Marcus remarked, chuckling softly, full of admiration and not at all shocked by her actions. 'That broadsword was a rusty old weapon and hasn't been used for decades.'

'It was needs must, Marcus. I'm no mouse to scurry for cover behind a curtain when trouble arrives. Women are more resourceful than men give us credit for. When threatened, any one of us will kill to defend family and home. I did not trouble myself to consider that the man might get blood poisoning. In fact, he was a bit of a coward really. When I thought the rebels would turn on me, he demanded to be taken to a physician right away, frightened by his own blood. Beneath all his bluster the man was a weak fool. May God help Monmouth if he has to depend on men such as that.'

Her eyes blazed with passion and Marcus was touched by their fire. He lowered his gaze to her hands resting in her lap. Small and slender, they gave the impression of fragility, yet at a time of desperation they had become strong enough to wield a broadsword and strike a man.

'You're a strange woman, Catherine. Just when I think I'm getting to know you, some new trait appears.' He smiled and his expression softened with his humour. 'Nature made a sad mistake when it made you a woman. You would have done better as a youth.'

'A youth?'

'You are incorrigible and have the recklessness of a young man. To raise a sword to an opponent takes courage—and strength. How does the maid fare?'

'She was more frightened than hurt. I gave her into the care of Alice, who lavished on her the attention she normally reserves for me.'

'And Fenton? Where was he while you were being abused?'

'I don't know. I have no need of his guardianship. I see little of him these days.'

'Are you saying that he left you to the mercy of those blasted rebels?'

Catherine merely nodded and did not confide her nagging suspicion that Mr Fenton might have been behind the raid in the first place, to get back at her for reprimanding him for his conduct in the woods. There was no evidence of this and without proof she did not wish to openly accuse and make matters worse.

Marcus shook his head impatiently. 'It was dangerous folly. Fenton knows the rebels are ill armed and look for weapons where they can—and where better than a house whose owner fights for the King? He cannot be permitted to get away with this—he's supposed to be the strong arm on the estate in my absence.' His anger rose at Fenton, though before he had left Saxton Court he had felt none, for, where his duties were concerned, Fenton had proved his worth many times.

At that moment Marcus seemed to Catherine to be the embodiment of unquestioned authority as he stood there, his dark head thrown back, his eyes stern. 'Perhaps it is I who have been lax for not seeking Mr Fenton out and making sure he did what he is paid to do,' she ventured.

'Nonsense! You have not been here long enough and are far too young to have learned the arts of running Saxton Court. If Fenton cannot be found, I shall leave a man here to guard you. I can well imagine the fear and distress this must have caused you. Knowing that in my own and Fenton's absence everyone would be looking to you, you would have to appear strong and in control. You did well, Catherine. You showed spirit and I am proud of you, but it would displease me to have your life so imperilled again.'

It was the closest Marcus had come to expressing feelings

for her, and Catherine could not prevent the flush heating her cheeks.

The door opened and more food was brought in. Alone again, Marcus rose. 'Come, we can talk while we eat.' He grinned almost boyishly. 'My backbone has been rubbing against my stomach since leaving London.'

The food was accepted with ravenous appreciation. Marcus ate heartily while Catherine toyed with her food. When he was finished eating, Marcus settled back in his seat, fingering his wine goblet. He tried to think of the rest of his journey when he left Saxton Court, but in his state of sated relaxation he was more inclined to dwell on his dinner companion.

'So tell me, Catherine, apart from beating off marauders and protecting young maids, what else have you been up to in my absence?'

'I've found plenty to occupy my time. Elizabeth and Margaret are frequent visitors. They have been most kind—making sure I don't get bored on my own, and introducing me to more people in the neighbourhood.'

'I am relieved to know you are getting on with Elizabeth. With all that is between us I do know it can't be easy for either of you.'

'It is important that we try to get along, and I do like your sister. Although there must be times when you regret your impulsive action and married me, Marcus.'

He lifted a brow and regarded her with some amusement. 'Sometimes I do wonder what kind of wild and unprincipled creature I made my wife.'

'You could have married any one of the beautiful, unattached ladies who grace the court.'

Marcus's lips curved in a half-smile. 'It is strange, but despite the unconventional beginnings to our marriage, I have no regrets. You are more beautiful than any of the dull creatures who preen and saunter about King James's Court.'

Catherine smiled. 'And you, my lord, are a flatterer.'

''Tis not flattery.' Marcus's face was serious. ''Tis the truth.'

Catherine met his gaze. A heavy lock of dark hair dipped over his brow and the candlelight softened his angular features. There was an intensity in his eyes as he gave her a long, silent look. Catherine was beginning to find in him a sensitivity that made him capable of perceiving her need for understanding. Was it possible that, after all the rancour and the arguments, she could believe that he cared for her—that she had come to care for him?

'This was my mother's favourite room,' he told her softly, letting his gaze drift. 'You obviously like it.'

'Yes. When I'm alone I always dine in here.'

'I cannot blame you,' he murmured, draping his arm across the back of his chair, watching her, relaxed and indulgent. 'It's cosier.'

Cosier. Avoiding his eyes, Catherine picked up her glass and drank some wine. By Marcus's definition, she knew perfectly well that cosier meant more inducive to intimacy. She knew it, just as clearly as she knew that the situation between them had altered. Marcus knew it, too. There was a new softness in his eyes when he looked at her and a smiling tenderness in his voice. A warmness grew within her that was nothing to do with the fire burning in the hearth. Surrendering to the compulsive urge to leave the table, she rose.

Marcus watched her return to the chair by the fire, her movements graceful and uncertain, like a nervous fawn. Firelight gleamed on her hair and her sooty lashes cast fan-like shadows on her smooth cheeks. As he looked at her now, despite the fact that he had made her his wife in the true sense on that one night they had lain together at The Hague, he marvelled anew at the strange aura of innocence about her. Since he had met her she had opposed, defied and challenged him, and yet for all her dauntless courage she was amazingly shy.

'Marcus, there is something I must discuss with you—it concerns Mr Fenton.'

'Apart from not being here when he was most needed, what else has my bailiff been up to in my absence that has set you on edge?' he asked, getting up and sitting opposite her.

'He has a tendency to overstep himself.'

'Yes, I know, but he does his job well.'

'Too well sometimes,' Catherine retorted scornfully. 'As well you know, Mr Fenton made a disagreeable impression on me from the start, and my opinion of him has not improved.'

'Why should you be so serious and troubled over Fenton, who is of such little importance?'

'Unimportant? Marcus, I fail to understand how, when everyone who is familiar with that man speaks nothing but ill of him, you go around as if you are wearing blinkers,' Catherine admonished sharply. 'Your own sister cannot abide him and makes no secret of the fact. I've had an uncomfortable feeling about him from the moment I first set eyes on him.'

Marcus frowned. 'Tell me.'

'Do you recall the evening before you went away, the first time I met Elizabeth?'

He nodded, recalling the evening in question and the unpleasant scene that followed. 'What of it?'

'You mentioned that Mr Fenton was in Bath visiting his brother.'

'I remember.' His look had become wary.

'Well, I saw him in Taunton that very day, so he couldn't possibly have been in Bath.'

'Was he alone?'

'No. He was with a man by the name of Trenchard.'

'I know him well—a Whig country gentleman and former Member of Parliament for Taunton. A staunch Republican, he was involved with The Rye House Plotters. He is a marked man and fled the country before Monmouth's arrival so he cannot be charged with complicity in his rebellion. I know Fenton is acquainted with him, and just how well I now intend to find out. How do you know it was Trenchard?'

'Archie told me. They were deep in conversation and disappeared into the Red Lion tavern. There's also something else.'

'Oh?'

Catherine fixed him with a level gaze. 'He knew my father. Did you know?'

Something quickened in Marcus's eyes and his expression hardened. 'No, I confess I did not. How well did he know him?'

'I don't know. When I asked him, he said they belonged to the same club.'

Marcus's eyes narrowed as he considered her words. 'The same club? Now I wonder, I really do, what he meant by that.'

'I was confused at the time. I thought perhaps a club in London—a Republican club, since my father was a Republican too. That was the last time I saw Mr Fenton. I don't know where he spends his time. I half-expect him to leave to join Monmouth.'

'Fenton is not a young man. Perhaps he's no stomach for a fight.'

'I disagree. When it comes to dealing with those weaker than himself, he is quite ruthless. I—I discovered him in the woods one day about to flog an old man he had caught poaching. Sadly, the poor man had already been savagely mauled by Fenton's hounds.'

Grim-faced, Marcus rose. Catherine shrank before the murderous look in those dark eyes fixed on her.

'So, Elizabeth was right all along when she accused me of being too trusting, too generous, where Fenton is concerned. I am beginning to see Fenton for the scheming, manipulative opportunist he is, and understand how my father was tricked into employing him. This is unacceptable. There is a matter of justice here. Whatever the man has done, I cannot permit Fenton to take it upon himself to administer punishment. Go on, Catherine. I want to know everything. I am beginning to realise that where my bailiff is concerned there are no surprises.'

Marcus was standing beside the high-backed chair, his tall figure dominating Catherine as she sat, his eyes fixed compellingly on her features as she described the scene that had taken place that day she had come upon him in the woods. All trace of softness had vanished from his expression. As she spoke Catherine was able to follow the swift succession of emotions reflected on her husband's face—surprise, fury, indignation and contempt. He did not utter a single word until she came to the end, and even then he remained where he was for a moment, rigid as steel, watching her in silence.

Forced to admit the truth to himself about his bailiff, a man he had trusted because he believed his father had considered him right for the position, and refusing to doubt his father's judgement, Marcus realised at last that he had fallen victim to a man who had blithely incurred his anger, mocked him behind his back, and flatly refused to yield to his authority.

'What will you do now?' Catherine asked quietly.

'Get rid of him. Were it not for this damned rebellion I'd personally investigate this matter—and no doubt there are others— and call him to task for his crimes. After all you have told me, I wouldn't be surprised to find he was behind the raid on Saxton Court.'

'I have wondered that myself.'

Snatching up his jerkin, Marcus turned to the door. 'Marcus, wait,' Catherine cried, getting to her feet and following him. 'Where are you going?'

'To deal with Fenton. I can't leave things like this.'

She shook her head. 'But you said you didn't have much time. Will—will you be back?'

He paused and looked at her. Was he mistaken or was she sorry to see him go? 'Do you want me to?'

'Yes. Yes, I do.'

Marcus stepped closer. 'Do you have any idea how much I have wanted to hear you say that?' he said with tender solemnity.

Catherine's delicately shaped eyebrows lifted in mute question. The intensity of his dark eyes held her transfixed. The potency of his gaze was intoxicating, setting her body aflame until her entire being glowed.

'My hands have ached to touch you,' he went on. 'At times the temptation almost proved too hard to resist.'

'When—when I spoke my vows, I did so with the full knowledge and determination not to see them out. There was bound to be a barrier between us. Remember that I saw you first as an enemy.'

There was something in his eyes like an involuntary tenderness. 'Then we will have to rectify that, won't we? And now? How do you see me now, Catherine?'

'As—as a friend. A husband.'

Marcus nodded slowly as his lips curved in a seductive smile. 'Husband? Now, that we *can* talk about. Are you willing to carry out your commitments as my wife in full?'

A lump of nameless emotion constricted Catherine's throat. Although she had not forgotten all the valid grievances she had against him, she nodded and answered truthfully, 'I—I believe I am. Once I despised you for causes that were justified, but the sting has been taken out of my ire by slow degrees. My resentment and my fears were difficult for me—but I think that perhaps both will cease to be the obstacles that keep us apart.'

'I am glad to hear it, although your resentment was understandable. When I married you it was nothing less than an act of outrage on my part—an act of selfish revenge. When I brought you to Saxton Court, in the beginning my objective was to show you every civility in my power in the hope of obtaining your forgiveness and to lessen your ill opinion of me. 'Tis painful for me to wait, but I will endure anything, knowing there is hope.'

Catherine's cheeks grew flushed beneath his unwavering regard. Raising his hand, he gently traced the curve of her cheek with his fingertips. 'I'll be back as soon as I can.'

Alone, Catherine stood motionless, staring at the closed door through which she had watched her husband disappear. Perhaps it was the tone of his voice and all that it implied, or perhaps it was the combination of tenderness and solemnity in his dark eyes as they had gazed into hers, but, whatever the cause, her heart had doubled its pace in anticipation of what was to happen when he returned.

Chapter Seven

Leaving the half dozen men he had with him to partake of rest and what refreshment Saxton Court had to offer, Marcus set off for Burton Grange for an audience with George Stanhope. As deputy Lieutenant of the county's militia, if Fenton had been actively involved in aiding Monmouth and was guilty of gross misconduct towards the workers at Saxton Court, George would know about it.

'We've had our eyes on Fenton for a while, Marcus,' George informed him gravely. 'I tend to agree with Elizabeth, that coming into your father's service was a guise that helped to lead suspicion away from him. I have evidence that he has been assisting John Trenchard in drawing a large number of West Country men into Monmouth's faction for some time. He hasn't taken up arms himself—whether he will or not remains to be seen, but I will tell you now that he is a marked man.'

'I understand that Trenchard left the country before Monmouth landed.'

'He did. Like yourself, Marcus, I have known John Trenchard for a long time, and he has a much clearer view of the realities of English politics than the supporters of Monmouth.

Maybe your bailiff shares his views—along with the clearest-sighted gentry, since few have rallied to Monmouth's standard—and they are for the Princess and Prince of Orange to succeed James, because they see the line of succession clearer that way. If so, Mr Fenton may desert his post as your bailiff and follow Trenchard across the water to bide his time.'

'If he isn't arrested before he does. There is another serious matter that troubles me, George, concerning Fenton. The estate seems to have prospered while I've been away, so I cannot fault him on that, but my wife came upon him one day when he was about to inflict a flogging on a man caught poaching. I find that kind of thing unacceptable and will not tolerate such misconduct from anyone—and certainly not from my bailiff, who should know better.'

'As you say, Fenton is your bailiff, Marcus, and far be it from me to interfere. It's up to you how Saxton Court is run. However, my enquiries have uncovered an unsavoury side to his character. He has cruel tendencies. It would appear that he uses excessive brutality to estate workers who do wrong—however minor the crime. He believes in discipline, and he is of the opinion that the only way to discipline those subservient to himself is by instilling fear into their very souls—by showing no mercy to those who would challenge the lawful commands of their betters.'

Grim-faced, Marcus turned abruptly and strode across the hall towards the door. 'This cannot be overlooked. When I find him I will deal with him.'

George frowned, bringing up a worry that had been plaguing him since the night he had dined at Saxton Court and met Marcus's wife for the first time. 'And your wife? Still a Monmouth sympathiser, is she?'

'She did not give succour to the enemy, if that is what you think.' Marcus laughed softly when he saw a polite objection spring to his lips. 'Worry not, George, you will be as relieved as I to know that Catherine has little sympathy for Monmouth following the raid on Saxton Court. It was fortunate no one was injured—apart from one of the rebels when my wife courageously saw him off with a broadsword.'

George watched his eyes soften when he mentioned his wife's name and the subtle trace of pleasure and admiration that threaded his voice when he spoke of her courage. 'I heard about that, Marcus. Dreadful business, but Saxton Court wasn't the only house the rebels plundered for weapons before moving on.' George followed Marcus out into the night air and watched him mount. 'Where to now in such a hurry?'

'Taunton. My intuition tells me that is where I will find my bailiff.'

'The taverns will be a good place to start. I wish you luck.'

As he rode off, Marcus thought long and hard about Fenton, and tried to imagine how his mind worked. He had not become his father's bailiff by chance. Quick wits and tact had formed a large part of his usefulness. How blind, how stupid he, Marcus, had been where Fenton was concerned. Why had he not listened to Elizabeth? Why had he not taken the time to see for himself how the estate was being run in his absence? Was it possible that Fenton was behind the raid at Saxton Court as an act of vengeance to get back at Catherine for chastising him when he had been about to flog a man? And how well had Fenton known Henry Barrington? Had Fenton been involved in The Rye House Plot?

All these questions plagued Marcus as he rode into Taunton. Just what had he stumbled upon? What unspeakably cruel quirk of fate had impelled his father to take Fenton into his employ? How cruelly ironic.

Inquiries in the taverns gave him the information that Fenton had been seen supping in the Castle Inn earlier. The taproom was crowded and smoky. Fenton was there, seated at a table in a corner. There was a stir among those present, men turning from their drinks. Fenton looked up and saw him. He rose slowly as his employer advanced towards his table.

Marcus's features were grim as he fixed his eyes on his bailiff. All the subtle indications that an unusually unpleasant confrontation was evidently about to occur were there. Positioned at the same table, four of Fenton's friends were sitting with rigidity, their faces watchful, alert, tense, as if they, too, sensed something seriously amiss in this unexpected and unprecedented appearance of Lord Reresby.

'A word outside, if you please, Mr Fenton.' Marcus turned and went out, confident that Fenton would follow. He didn't have long to wait. Fenton sauntered out, his eyes hooded and wary in the orange glow seeping from the inn. Marcus studied him from his superior height with a cold and barely contained anger. 'I arrived at Saxton Court tonight to discover you have been neglecting your duties.'

'You find fault with the work I do for you, Lord Reresby?' His stance was insolent, his look resentful.

'Not with your work—although my wife would disagree with me.' He narrowed his eyes. 'In truth she has never liked you, Fenton, and in her opinion there are men of far better character who would do the job just as well.'

Fenton felt besieged. Reresby's seeking him out wasn't random. That bitch of a wife of his had orchestrated it. Unconsciously, his hand went to the hilt of his sword. 'I have always been aware of Lady Reresby's opinion of me, which disappoints me somewhat, since her father and I were—acquainted.'

'So my wife informs me, but it makes no difference. In my absence I left my wife and the servants in my household in your protection. Where were you when Monmouth's rebels came to call? Because you are of their persuasion, did you intentionally make yourself scarce for fear of being branded a traitor to their cause? Good God, man, my wife could have been assaulted and killed. What were you thinking of?'

Fenton shrugged, resentment creeping into his voice. 'Lady Reresby did well enough without me. She managed to fend them off admirably—even wounding one, almost fatally, I hear.'

'Damn you, Fenton, that is not the point. You make your living from Saxton Court. You are in a position of trust. Your responsibility is to me and mine, not your own selfishness.'

Fenton met the hard, dark eyes. Devoid of warmth, they probed him. Inwardly he seethed, his fury rising. 'When I came to Saxton Court I swore no allegiance to your father or his kin. I have done what I was paid to do and have done it well. Your father had no complaints.'

'That remains to be seen. My father, God rest his soul, was too fond and too forgiving. He did not see you for what you are.' Marcus studied the older man closely. He had noted how Fenton's hand had moved to the hilt of his sword, how he fondled it, suggesting both a familiarity with the weapon and a liking for it.

'I think I have your measure now, Fenton. I know of your close association with John Trenchard, and I have concluded that you ingratiated yourself to my father and secured the position of bailiff at Saxton Court for your own means. You came to the western counties for one purpose and one purpose only— to support a rebellion. Joining forces with Trenchard, you have drawn a large contingent of men into Monmouth's faction. But no matter how many men you recruit, you cannot hold out against King James.'

'You think not?' Fenton replied, making no attempt to deny the accusations. 'Monmouth's army does not lack courage, and is sending a hornet of fear amongst those who oppose him.

There has been wholesale flight of the militia, some leaving their old officers and joining this new company. Monmouth is confident he will succeed.'

'He's a little premature in his confidence. What hope is there? Monmouth's treasure chest is empty. Aye, some of his men are equipped with swords and guns, but his raw recruits have nothing but the tools of their trade—pitchforks, scythes, hatchets and knives. Pray God for Monmouth's sake they know how to use them if put to the test. Food is in short supply. Your resistance is weak. The King's forces are united and will advance and break it as surely as he has broken all defiance in London and is bound to defeat Argyll's rebellion in the north. So what now, Fenton? What will you do? Do you fail to support the rebellion after all, and, like Trenchard, is it your intention to vacate these shores for a safer place?'

Fenton's eyes flashed. 'What I do is for my conscience to decide.'

'Is it your conscience, Fenton, or is that you lack the courage for a fight? There is another matter I wish to raise with you. My wife claims that you abuse your position, that you take it upon yourself to act as judge, jury and executioner should any man transgress—poachers seem to be a speciality of yours—and yes, she has told me about that disgraceful episode when she came upon you in the woods. That sort of behaviour cannot be tolerated. Your actions have crossed the line of acceptability. What have you to say? I have no doubt your version will vary from hers, but I would like to hear it all the same.'

'Do you always believe what your wife tells you, Lord Reresby?' Fenton sneered.

Marcus's anger could no longer be held in check, and his words issued forth like lashes from a whip. 'Do you challenge the accuracy of my wife's account? At a time when the whole of the western counties are filled with strife, you flog a man for poaching! How many others have there been? I wonder.'

Fenton smiled with ironic amusement. 'I see nothing wrong with my methods in keeping order. I admit it. I've flogged poachers and thieves on more than one occasion, and you've commended my ability to keep things running smoothly in your absence.'

'Had I been familiar with your *methods*, Mr Fenton, I would have flogged you myself.'

'I'll see you in hell first.' Fenton's eyes were cold and unemotional, and his expression was contemptuous.

Marcus thrust his face close. 'That you will, Fenton. That you will. I know what you are—and among your other crimes I suspect you were behind the assault on my home and my wife. By your own actions you leave me with no choice but to relieve you of your position as my bailiff. I no longer have any use for you. I have terminated it on the grounds of moral inaptitude. You are at liberty to leave at once. I don't give a damn where you go, so long as I never see you in the vicinity of Saxton Court again.'

'The pleasure will be all mine.' Fenton's tone was sarcastic. More than caution now, more than anger, he felt hatred. It was in his heart and on his face. He knew Reresby could see it and he didn't care. 'My work in the western counties is done anyway. But there is one thing you should know before I go. While you have been hellbent on destroying the rebels, your wife has been carrying on an intrigue with one of them, right here in Taunton.'

Marcus fixed him with a fierce gaze. What he said distracted him. The words Fenton now spoke were loud, clear and horrifying. He answered him without thinking, his habitual self-possession deserting him. 'You're lying.'

Fenton favoured Marcus with a mocking grin. 'Lying, am

I? I think not, and your wife can hardly accuse me of lying. Stapleton is with Monmouth—Harry Stapleton. I saw him and your wife together with my own eyes—still familiar, they are—extremely so. 'Tis obvious the flame still burns between them. Why don't you go home and ask her? I knew Henry Barrington, your wife's father, well, but I did not like him. The man was spineless—a coward, who nearly did for us both. We were of the same persuasion, but I despised him. I hold no loyalty to his daughter.'

'Clearly.'

'I understand the fair Catherine and Harry were to wed—until you came along.'

For the briefest moment Marcus did not react as he attempted to control his emotions, then a red rage, clouding his vision, seized him. 'Shut your mouth. You overstep yourself.'

Fenton smiled, a sneering expression that twisted his features. 'Since I have been banished from your employ, I can speak my mind. Now your rival has reappeared on the scene, your wife may be finding her cold, empty bed somewhat lonely. Perhaps she can coax him into a little flirtation.' He gave a harsh, vindictive laugh. 'Following her lack of subtlety when she was at The Hague with Stapleton whilst married to you, her reputation is not spotless. It is, in fact, very much befouled, which is probably the reason you avoid her chamber on a night.'

Marcus's face had taken on a grey tinge. Even his eyes, strangely emptied of expression, seemed to have lost their colour. 'What did you say? You insolent dog,' he said through gritted teeth.

'Why, it is common talk among the servants that you seem to fill such a negligible part of her life.'

'You will do well to govern your tongue, Fenton,' Marcus hissed, trying to control his raging ire. 'I will not hear my wife so maliciously maligned.'

'You are strangely fastidious concerning a woman who is more than generous with her favours.'

Marcus's look was deadly. 'You are impertinent. Your duties at Saxton Court did not require you to interfere in my relationship with my wife. What interests me now is just how well you knew Barrington?' he said, changing tack, yet determined to attend to Catherine's infidelity later. 'Friendly enough to have been involved with him in that malicious plot to murder King Charles and his brother?'

'Why do you want to know—so that you can pursue the charge of treason—as you do your father's murderer?' Noting how Marcus's face stiffened, an indication that his barb had hit its mark, Fenton let his smile broaden, but smiles were not becoming to that sallow face. 'The Rye House Plot is in the past now, Reresby, and the vultures have found some other man's liver to tear out and chew.'

'Aye, Monmouth's—who was also party to that particular plot. Where my father is concerned, I do still pursue his murderer, and I shall continue to do so until I find the man responsible.'

In the gloom, Fenton's eyes glittered with malice. 'And when you do?'

'I shall make it my business to see him hanged.' Marcus's fists clenched in a visible effort not to drive them into Fenton's arrogant face. 'A word of advice, Fenton. Go now before I give way to my inclinations. Put as much distance between yourself and Saxton Court as you possibly can. If I ever see you on my estate again or even smell the sour scent of you, I'll hunt you down like the filth you are and leave your carcase to rot.'

'You haven't heard the last of me,' Fenton said in calm, measured tones. 'Nobody does this to me and gets away with it. I'd advise you to watch your rear, Lord Reresby, because one of these days you too may find a slither of cold steel between your ribs.'

Fenton turned abruptly. Instead of returning to his friends inside the tavern, he disappeared into the dark.

What Fenton had divulged had destroyed any pleasure Marcus might have had in the forthcoming night. It seemed to him that all the malice surrounding Fenton had been concentrated in that one pair of eyes. Fenton! The thought of the man nagged at him increasingly as he mounted his horse. He should have known that Fenton was a man to be reckoned with. The man hated him, and that hatred had reached out to strike him like a physical blow. Also his parting words troubled him—that he too might feel the slither of cold steel between his ribs. To whom had he referred? His father?

All at once the issues connected. Turning his head, he looked back in the direction Fenton had taken. He was beginning to feel the creeping onset of something sinister in all this, the onset of a deep suspicion that Fenton might have been connected with his father's murder. There was undoubtedly a dreadful truth at the base of it all.

Marcus was overcome by the turmoil of his feelings, made up of a combination of relief and at the same time a kind of horror, mingled with surprise that he might have employed and just been talking to the man who had murdered his father and let him go. Frustrated that this might indeed be so, he allowed his rage to recede and a calmness to envelop him. Turning his horse, instead of heading for Saxton Court, he rode instead to his sister's house. When he arrived Roger received him in the hall.

'Marcus! What can I do for you at this late hour?' he said, strolling into the salon to pour them both a drink.

'I apologise for disturbing you, Roger—and please don't disturb Elizabeth, it is you I've come to see,' Marcus said, giving him a brief account of what he was doing in Somerset. 'I understand that you are to leave for London shortly.'

'The day after tomorrow. It is high time we paid my mother

a visit—and what with all this upheaval, I shall feel better when Elizabeth and the children are removed from it. We shall return at some uncertain future date. Is there anything I might do for you?'

'Aye, there is something you might consider doing for me, Roger.'

'Yes?' Roger asked, handing him a brandy. 'Anything you request.'

'Will you play the spy for me?' Marcus said grimly. 'Investigator, if you like.'

'Spy?' Roger echoed, surprise on his face. Of all the requests his brother-in-law might have made, this was the least expected. 'On whom?'

'Fenton.'

'Fenton? Good Lord, I am surprised! I thought he would have joined Monmouth by now.' Roger's expression became anxious. 'Has something happened?'

'I have banished him from Saxton Court. I was deceived— as was my father. The soul that animates Mr Fenton is a chilling quagmire of deceit and wickedness. Not until tonight did I discover how much. He said something that makes me suspect he may know something about Father's murder and I want him watched.'

'Are you certain of this?'

'Not entirely. I need more proof. I need unassailable evidence, and that will be hard to attain without your help. Fenton was a close associate of Henry Barrington. Eventually I think he will join Trenchard abroad, but first I think he will make for London to liaise with his cronies there. I wish to know his whereabouts and his companions and what he was doing at the time of the murder. Should he go abroad without going to London, see what you can uncover anyway.'

'And if he was the man who wielded the knife? What then?'

'Unlike my dealings with Barrington, where Fenton is concerned I will do things differently. I want him to stand trial and will not cheat the hangman of his pleasure. But if his judges do not send him to his death, then I swear that I will kill him myself, if I die in the attempt.'

Roger swallowed a large draught of brandy, taking a moment to digest what Marcus had said. 'So be it,' he said at length. 'Knowing how important it is to both you and Elizabeth that your father's murderer is caught, I shall infiltrate Republican clubs and their meeting places where I can.' He exhaled noisily. 'Spy! Who would have thought it? I suppose it will enable me to find out many things, hear many secrets which may be of interest to you.'

'I am obliged, Roger, but proceed with caution. If danger threatens, then step back. I would appreciate Elizabeth knowing nothing about any of this.'

'No, I shan't say a word—keep it to ourselves for now, eh?'

'Write to me, Roger. That is all I ask of you.'

Roger nodded. 'I will abide by your wishes.'

'Thank you.' His face now held a most unpleasant expression. Marcus knew that if the information Roger sent him was as he thought, then he would destroy Fenton, and it would be a day to avidly welcome.

Not until he was heading for Saxton Court did Marcus turn his thoughts to his wife. He was seething inside. He was furious with Catherine for going into Taunton when the town was full of rebels, and angry with himself for not being at home to exercise some control over her.

It came as no surprise to learn that Stapleton was with Monmouth, but that Catherine had liaised with him was not to be borne. If what Fenton had told him was true, then Catherine had played him for a fool. The barbs of jealousy were sharp and pricked him to a painful depth. He felt a rush of bitterness, a bitterness that increased as he realised how much he had come to care for her. No matter what she had done or might do, nothing would ever change that. Ironic indeed to know that he could care so deeply for a woman he had taken unwillingly for a wife.

For weeks he had anticipated not only the delights of her supple young body, but this time he had hoped to court her, to win her love. Even more than this, he had hoped to bring her to a complete understanding not only of himself, but of their lives together.

Catherine was in her room. Alice hovered. Marcus scarcely noticed when she left. His attention was all on his wife.

Self-consciously pulling her robe tighter about her narrow waist, Catherine shivered and wondered why Marcus did not speak. Why did he stand there motionless, his dark eyes narrowed as he studied her with unnerving intensity? His body was tense, the muscles in his neck corded, and, looking at him closely, she was appalled by the anger and naked pain she saw in his face. She searched his forbidding countenance for some sign that he cared for her. But there was none. She put out a hand nervously.

'Marcus? Is—is something wrong?' What had she done, she wondered, to make him look at her like that? Marcus stood before her, yet somehow it was as if he had removed himself a great distance. His eyes were remote.

Turning from her he moved towards the hearth. 'The entire western counties are in upheaval, with God knows how many unsavoury characters roaming all over the place, and far from staying at home like any decent, respectable woman, you flaunt yourself in a town seething with rebels.'

'I did not flaunt myself,' Catherine flung back at him, her cheeks flaming with indignation at being spoken to so harshly.

She knew he was referring to her visit to Taunton to enquire after her horse. He half-turned and looked at her, and she almost withered before the blast of those cold dark eyes. His face might have been carved out of stone, and there was a saturnine twist to his mouth. 'Why, to hear you anyone would think I'd gone there to prostitute myself.'

Marcus looked at her with obvious displeasure. 'Catherine, have you no shame?' he rebuked coldly. 'I know why you went there. While you were obliged to marry me and fought against it, I conceded that you had right on your side, and I admired you for it—and was ashamed of my own behaviour. However, it is done and there is no going back. You are my wife and bear my name, and I demand that you at least show some respect for that name.'

'And how have I failed to respect it?'

'By seeing and speaking to Harry Stapleton.'

'Harry? Why—yes, I have seen him.' Utterly perplexed, Catherine stared at her husband's rigid features. 'Marcus, do you have a problem with that?'

'As a matter of fact I do, Catherine. Why did you not tell me you had been into Taunton?'

'Why? Because it slipped my mind.'

He began striding up and down the room, his hands clasped behind his back. Catherine forced herself to keep calm. Above all she must not let him see the small nagging fear within her or the unnerving effect his anger tended to have on her. Suddenly he came to a halt across the room and pierced her with his gaze.

'You went into a town heaving with undisciplined rebel soldiers, you saw a man you were once almost betrothed to, a man you swore you would love for ever, and you are telling me that it slipped your mind?'

The gentle drift of happiness Catherine had felt since his departure earlier shattered away and her heart, that which had been stirred and beat faster in sweet anticipation of the night to come, hardened and her face turned mutinous.

'As a matter of fact, it did. Oh, a plague on you, Marcus,' she cried, tossing her head in frustration. 'Am I to be condemned out of hand? And what right have you to look at me like that? One would think me to be guilty of murder. I cannot for the life of me imagine why you are making such a fuss.'

'Can you not?' he remarked in a contemptuous drawl. 'It doesn't take much imagination to guess what you went for.'

The insinuation stung Catherine at a moment when she was most vulnerable. No hint of softness or affection showed in the marble severity of his face. 'If you believe I made an assignation with Harry, then you are wrong, Marcus. After the raid I was angry. I went to look for the horses—for *my* horse—your gift to me. And, yes, I knew Harry would be with Monmouth, but it never entered my head that we would meet. I was so incensed by what had happened here that I never gave Harry a second thought. I encountered him quite by chance.'

'Indeed. It is the intriguing parts of what happened between the two of you when you did meet that interests me. Did he take you in his arms? Did he declare his undying love for you? What?'

Stung by the contempt in his voice, Catherine stared at him white-faced. Her green eyes met his, flashing a greater defiance than she knew. 'You are in error, Marcus. I am a married woman. Harry would not have taken me in his arms—it is I who would have taken him in mine.'

Marcus's face grew so deathly pale that Catherine found herself exulting unashamedly in her power to hurt him. Disregarding the menacing look he gave her, she stood her ground as he bore down on her, eyeing her relentlessly.

'Do you dare to tell me you would do that?'

'Why not?' she flared angrily. 'You want the truth. I have

told it to you. Harry was an important part of my life for a long time—he was my life. Nothing can erase that. He has done me no harm, it is you that harmed him, and harmed me, too,' she reminded him, her voice like steel, knowing how aggravated he would be by this. Her face was set in stiff lines of her unsparing will, that which had brought her from the pain of losing Harry into this man's life. 'And, yes, Marcus, I would have taken him in my arms—to comfort a man in his grief who finds the woman he loves, only to realise she is lost to him for ever.'

Marcus wanted to ask her if she was still in love with Harry Stapleton, but he dare not, for he feared the answer, yet in her eyes he saw something move and glow a little, and a small flame of triumph licked about his heart. He desperately wanted to feel her need for him, to hear his name on his lips, to know she was his. Only his. To know Harry Stapleton meant nothing to her. Turning from her, he strode towards the door.

'Marcus, where are you going?' Catherine asked in alarm. She didn't want him to go. She didn't want to be left alone.

'I have a duty to my men.'

All that existed in Catherine's world just then was the presence of this man and his dark eyes upon her, but he was drawing back. Why this particular moment was the right one for them to be together, she was never to know, or even what it was that made her rush to seize it. But some instinct, perhaps an expression that seemed to linger on his face sometimes, something she was aware of but reluctant to test for fear of rejection, made her bold. Quickly she moved towards him, her senses dominated by his closeness.

'Earlier we planned the evening quite differently. Please, Marcus, will you stay—or return when you've spoken to your men?' There was a slight stiffening to his figure at her presumption. Her heart lurched, fearing that she might have caused affront. But affront or not, she was intent on making him stay.

'That remains to be seen. I suppose it's not outside the realms of possibility.'

'Then shall I go to your room, or shall I await your pleasure in mine? You—do still want to stay?' Her stance was brazen, the smile on her lips enticing and assured of a willing conquest.

'That was before I rode into Taunton and met Fenton—who told me of your meeting with Stapleton.'

'He saw us together?'

Marcus nodded.

'Forget Harry, Marcus.'

'Forget him? How can I?' he said, his voice strained. 'He stands between us. He always will.'

Catherine could see that his words had sprung from a bitter, yet reassuring jealousy. Tilting her head to one side, she laughed softly. Amusement twinkled in her eyes, brightening them to a dazzling brilliance. 'Why, Marcus, I do believe you're jealous.'

His eyes narrowed. 'Should I be?'

She sauntered closer, and with her hands on her hips regarded him sternly. 'No, and you can glower all you like, but you won't impress me with your ill humour.'

A half-frown, half-smile crossed his face. 'No?' He eyed her warily.

'I have no knowledge where your duties call you at such a late hour, Marcus, but right now don't you have a duty to your wife?'

His brow raised in question. 'How am I to resist so much temptation?'

'Do you want to resist it?' Without thinking, she lifted her hand and touched his cheek.

Marcus tried without complete success to ignore the tender innocence of her touch. 'I could be persuaded. Are you willing to surrender, unconditionally giving up the battle of wills that has waged between us since we met?'

She smiled impishly. 'Well—not quite that. I do have my pride to consider.'

'To the devil with your pride. Is it in your mind to be reasonable about our marriage, and henceforth share my bed?' he queried.

'Me? Reasonable? Why, Marcus, I am never unreasonable. I accept our marriage as any wife might. I have no right to deny you any longer. In fact, I shall play the loving wife to such perfection that it will confuse you into playing the role of adoring husband.'

Marcus felt the heat flame in his belly as he gazed down into the warm green orbs. It was easy to become mesmerised in their clear depths. 'That will not be difficult. I well recall the one and only time I enacted that role. It was an experience I would rather forget. I know that particular aspect of our marriage can be improved, and I look forward to working on it.'

Catherine blushed, remembering that other night with embarrassing clarity. Their coupling had been brief and without passion, leaving her confused and curious, for she was certain there was more to what went on between a husband and wife than what she had experienced with Marcus. He reached out a hand and untied the silken fasteners at her neck, plucking them free. Catherine's breath caught in her throat as he parted her robe and slid his hands inside and round her waist, drawing her close.

'You wish to please me?' he murmured.

'As best I can.'

'Never fear, Catherine. I have a thing or two to teach you in the way of pleasing me.'

'You would have me do that?' she asked sweetly. The heat of his gaze set her blood on fire and struck sparks along her flesh.

''Tis my fondest dream.'

Her mouth curved in a sublime smile while her eyes grew dark, the pupils dilating to obliterate the green—promising Marcus more than he had ever expected. 'What about your men?'

'With full bellies and a warm hay loft,' he breathed, his eyes lowered and focused on her moist, softly parted lips, 'they'll believe they are in heaven and feel relieved they haven't to ride towards Bridgwater until morning.'

Catherine sighed. The smell of him, of leather and the outdoors and the faint, seductive scent of sandalwood he always used, filled her senses, and before she knew what he was about, lost in the excitement of her, Marcus lowered his head and his lips took hers in a deep and tender kiss. Her body responded— he was aware of it, and he deepened his kiss. With a long, shuddering sigh their bodies fused together. Her arms slipped and twined around his neck like the tendrils of ivy, drawing him into herself.

The ecstasy of their union brought Catherine a wondrous awe. She had nothing but the memory of the last time with which to compare this sweet agony of passion and the merging of herself into another. This time it was so very different. She was surprised, and slightly shocked, by how much she enjoyed making love with Marcus, by the fierce, darkly unravelling sensations and the sheer wantonness of her responses. It was as if he knew her body absolutely, every piece of flesh, every curve and hollow and every movement of it, as if he had been intimate with it always. Floating in a sea of mindless pleasure, she gave herself willingly, supplicant to his mastery.

To Marcus his wife was erotic, beautiful and tender. She was a woman he didn't know, a creature he never dreamed existed. There was no need for reticence. They came together naked and unashamed. Never had he felt so much contentment. No woman had given him so much pleasure.

That night seemed to be a new beginning for them both. Afterwards they lay peacefully together, listening to each other breathe, until they slept.

* * *

The grey light of dawn crept in past the heavily draped windows, and distant sounds of the great house awakening could be heard. Marcus stirred at last. Opening his eyes, he brought the room into focus, and pleasure filled him when he felt the woman move in his arms. The snowy whiteness of her shoulders and half the smooth globes of her breasts showed above the covers. Her black hair was strewn over the pillows and across his chest like liquid jet. Her eyes were closed, the sweeping lashes making faint purple shadows on her cheeks. A slight half-smile played across her sensual lips.

He did not move. He made no sound. He lay there with his breath caught in his chest, afraid to break the magic of the moment. It was a picture of her that captured the deep womanly essence and true soul of her, and Marcus knew it was a picture he would remember as long as he lived. At length, very quietly, without waking her, he got out of bed, pouring water out of a pitcher into a bowl to wash, but the noise made her stir.

Catherine woke, berating herself for sleeping so long. Half-opening her eyes, she felt drowsy, disoriented, tired enough from the night's emotion and exertions to feel light-headed. Feeling happy, languidly she stretched beneath the sheets, her body tingling and aching from so much loving.

Hearing splashing noises, she turned on to her side and propped her head on her hand to watch her husband as he washed, marvelling at the flexing muscles across his shoulders and back and how his dark brown hair, shot through with golden lights, fell in soft waves to his shoulders. It was time for him to leave and she dreaded the moment.

''Tis well past dawn,' she murmured, glancing towards the light. Rain rattled on the windowpanes and the sky was dark and oppressive.

'So it is,' he answered raising his head, droplets of water running down his face, which he wiped away with a towel. 'I must be away shortly, Catherine.'

'I know. I'm afraid,' she murmured. 'I wish you didn't have to leave. The thought plagues me that there will be a battle, that you will have to fight and may be wounded.'

'By the grace of God, Catherine, I will prove myself better than my enemies.' Thrusting his arms into the sleeves of his shirt and then his jerkin, he sat on the bed and gathered her to him.

'Promise me you will do nothing foolhardy,' she said, linking her fingers through his.

'You have my word, my love. Now we have begun married life, I have a fancy to see where it will lead.' He squeezed her hand with a tenacity that revealed his intent as strong as his word. 'Though it be from hell itself, I will come back.' He had no way of knowing, when he spoke, how much truth there was in his words. 'I'm worried about you at Saxton Court at this time—the raid proves how vulnerable you are.'

'But the rebels have moved on. I doubt they will trouble us again.'

'I know, but that does not ease my worry. Roger is taking Elizabeth and the children to London until all this is over. I would feel easier if you went with them.'

Catherine stiffened and pulled away from him. 'You mean you wish me to live in London with Elizabeth?'

'A temporary measure, that's all.'

'Then I refuse,' she said staunchly. 'I will not go. My place is here. I insist on it.'

'Catherine, I want you to go for your own good.'

'What do you mean for my own good? I am not alone here.'

'You have the servants, the kitchen boys and women. But Thomas the head gardener is old—and so is Archie, and neither would be much use at fighting. All the real fighting men have joined Monmouth.'

'Just what kind of nonsense is this, Marcus? And what of the servants left with no one to guide them should anything happen? In your absence I withstood the rebels and I will do so again if I have to. I will not forsake those who depend on us from any danger. I am not leaving Saxton Court, and that is final.'

Marcus knew by the set of her jaw and the flash of her eyes that she meant exactly what she said. He raised an eyebrow with amused admiration. 'I know you have courage, but I didn't know your wits were addled. However, you have proved that when faced with the gravest danger you will not be daunted. So, very well, Catherine. Have it your own way,' he conceded. 'I'm only thankful that Monmouth will be halfway to Bristol by now, so hopefully the danger is past.'

'Thank you, Marcus. I'm glad you see it my way. Now,' she said, settling herself against him once more, 'tell me about your encounter with Mr Fenton. You said you saw him in Taunton.'

'I did. Fenton is no longer employed by me.'

The harshness of his voice told Catherine that whatever had befallen him in Taunton had angered him. 'Why?'

'Because of what you told me—and Roger. I called on him when I left here. Fenton's life has been one long litany of deceit and intrigue. Arrogance and insolence are the keystones of his personality, and he has too much confidence in his own opinions.'

'Has he joined Monmouth?'

'No. He'll more than likely go to London or to Holland. You were right, Catherine. Fenton did know your father, but they were not friends. They were of the same persuasion, but Fenton made no secret of his dislike for your father. I suspect he may also know something about my own father's murder.'

Catherine saw that a new expression had crept into his eyes. It was an unsettling mixture of sorrow and rage. 'Do you think Fenton could have been responsible for his death?'

'The thought has crossed my mind. He's capable—there's no doubt about that. But, if he was responsible, I don't suppose he would confess to it. I also doubt that he would kill a man to protect another.'

'Unless Fenton was involved in the same plot to murder King Charles and his brother, and your father discovered this and would have exposed him.'

'Maybe you're right. My intuition tells me he knows more about this issue, but intuition is only a feeling.'

'If Fenton goes to Holland, it will be difficult to find him.'

'If he is the murderer, there will be no hiding place.' Marcus sighed, shifting his position. 'And now, if I am to join Churchill, I must leave.'

'How long will you be gone?'

'There's no knowing.' His eyes travelled downward, following the contours of her body beneath the sheet draped around her. He wanted her again, but there wasn't time.

'I shall miss you, Marcus.' The regret in her eyes was sincere. She pressed his hand to her lips. 'Please come back.'

A single tear formed on her lashes. He bent his head and kissed it away. 'A tear, Catherine? What is it that makes you weep?'

For a long moment she did not answer, and after swallowing with difficulty, turning her head away, she whispered hesitantly, 'Because—because it would be so easy to fall in love with you.'

'And would that be so very foolish?'

Catherine shook her head slowly. Marcus had made long and lingering love to her, with an exquisite, restrained gentleness. He had called her his love, but he had not told her that he loved her, and more than anything she wanted to hear him say it.

Marcus knew what she wanted, just as he knew it was folly to think the words, let alone say them, at this time. He gazed down at her. Ever since he had brought her to Saxton Court he had been tormented by her elusiveness. She fascinated and intrigued him. The joy he had felt at finally conquering her had been equalled by the pleasure she had given him.

Reaching out, he turned her face to his, wanting to see her eyes. 'Look at me, Catherine.' When she raised her eyes to his they had brightened with a luminous intensity. 'Our marriage, what we have, is special to me. You are truly my wife and desire can only heighten what we have. I've wanted you for so long, but your heart was held by Harry Stapleton. I've bided my time, discovering a patience I did not believe I possessed. Night after night I've wanted to come to you.'

'Then why didn't you?'

'I wanted you to be ready, Catherine, to want me.'

'Then as you say, our marriage is special. What happened between us last night will be repeated.'

Marcus tightened his arms about her and smoothed the tendrils of her hair back from her face. 'I know. I don't want to lose you now that I have found you.'

'I fear there may be a vicious battle ahead,' she murmured. 'Please take care. There's danger—I feel it, like the blackness of the sky.'

'The rain will soon pass, Catherine, and then the sun will shine. Already 'tis easing. Come—smile, my love,' he said, standing up and drawing her up beside him, reluctant to leave her yet knowing he must. 'I'd not take the memory of a dismal face away with me.'

With an effort she obeyed and he took her in his arms once more. His kiss was one of finality, but before he could release her, the oppression in Catherine's breast sharpened to panic and she threw her arms around his neck, pressing her face to his chest.

'Goodbye, Marcus. God keep you safe.'

From the window she watched him ride away with Dickon

and his men. He spurred his horse, riding north towards Bristol, Monmouth's immediate destination. The rain continued to fall.

Alice had gone to bed worried about Catherine, but when she entered her room carrying a tray laden with poached eggs and gammon, her worries faded. Still in her nightclothes, Catherine was seated at the dressing table, gazing at her reflection and coiling a tendril of her hair round her finger. There was a subtle change in her, and Alice laid the reason for her dreamy state to her husband's visit.

'My, you're looking in fine spirits this morning.'

So lost was Catherine in her reflections that she hadn't noticed that Alice had entered the room. The smile still in her eyes, she turned, still feeling the effects of Marcus's lovemaking. 'And so I am, Alice,' she replied, sending her a reassuring smile. 'So I am.'

Chapter Eight

Monmouth's army of ill-assorted troops was worryingly short of experienced soldiers. At Bridgwater, ten miles north of Taunton, he was received even more enthusiastically than at Taunton, and by the time his troops left, they were boasting that, within a week, King James would have been ousted and James Scott, Duke of Monmouth, would be enthroned.

They could afford to boast for now. So far they had only been tested by county militia of doubtful allegiance, but the regular army, arriving in the western counties in significant numbers, was drawing closer each day, outnumbering the rebels. There was no organisation in the rebel army, and the weapons and armour Monmouth had brought from Holland were never distributed. Also, there were hardly any officers.

Lord John Churchill, originally the commander of the King's forces sent to combat Monmouth's rebellion, had been superseded in command by the Earl of Feversham. With twenty-five years of loyal service behind him, the King thought Feversham to be more suitable to the appointment. Many of those who considered Churchill to be the better soldier believed he was superseded and made second in command because he was a West

Country man and former friend of Monmouth's and therefore not to be completely trusted, despite the fact that most officers in the regular army were former friends of Monmouth.

With Churchill's troops snapping at his heels, Monmouth marched his army through the rain towards Bristol. No man dare straggle or wander far for food lest they were picked up by the royal troops. Being constantly harried by the enemy, tired and footsore, the nerves of the rebel army began to fray and Monmouth's confidence to flag. If he could only take Bristol, where he could replenish his empty coffers from its overflowing customs house, it would be a tremendous psychological boost to his troops and encourage others to join him.

But Monmouth failed to take Bristol. Had he displayed resolution and moved more quickly, he might well have captured England's second largest city before the King's army had assembled there in sufficient strength, but he failed to seize the moment—finding the strategically vital bridge at Keynsham, halfway between Bristol and Bath, undamaged despite the King's instructions to Feversham to destroy it. Instead Monmouth decided to wait until darkness before he attacked Bristol, but torrential rain began to fall, turning the roads to quagmires of mud, and the rebel army was forced to move back to Keynsham to seek shelter.

From that moment on, wet and dispirited, the rebel army fell into decline. Doubts were beginning to grow about Monmouth's leadership. He abandoned Bristol and moved south to Philip's Norton, where they were attacked and managed to beat off the regular army. As the rain continued to pour down, Monmouth continued south.

Worse was to come. Still no forces came from Wiltshire as had been promised, and the Londoners were notably silent. At Frome he heard of the complete collapse of Argyll's rebellion in Scotland, and the King's free pardon to all rebels who laid

down their arms. It had a devastating effect on Monmouth. Many
of his ragged men took the pardon and deserted him in increasing numbers, and, having lost his resolve, Monmouth would
have done so, too, had he been included in the King's offer.

Methodical movements were made by both sides. Monmouth marched his troops from Frome to Shepton Mallet to
Wells, and from there back to Bridgwater. Feversham reached
the village of Weston Zoyland, just to the east of Sedgemoor
with its treacherous dykes. Monmouth planned to take them unawares. About eleven o'clock on the night of the fifth of July
the rebel forces, approaching four thousand in number, silently
moved out of Bridgwater along the Bristol road, and galloped
across the flat and misty moor to within a mile of the King's
army. They were brought to a halt before a black ribbon of
water, the Bussex Rhine, one of the dykes criss-crossing the
moor. Hampered and casting about for a way across, the rebels
found themselves fighting the royal guards.

The battle that followed lasted for about an hour and a half.
Unable to come to grips with the King's seasoned and practised
troops, Monmouth's army blundered in disorder and were cut
to pieces. The rebels who were left took flight, their army dispersed. Monmouth fled with the rest of them.

At Saxton Court, every day Catherine waited for news about
what was happening. The conflict between the rebel army and
the King's troops was the main topic of every conversation
among the servants. She listened to the rumours. It was said
there had been a battle at Sedgemoor near Bridgwater. It was
said the Duke of Monmouth's army had been defeated and was
scattered, and that Monmouth had taken flight and was in hiding. But it was only rumour.

And then Margaret Stanhope confirmed the rumour when
she came to call on her. Catherine was half-heartedly arrang-

ing flowers in the window. When Margaret came into the room, relieved to see a friendly face, she let them fall from her hands and rushed towards her.

'Margaret! Oh, thank you for coming to see me. If only you knew how good it is to see someone other than the servants. In the light of that awful time when the rebels came, Marcus has told me not to venture far from the house.'

'Marcus was right, Catherine. It's not safe to wander from home at this time.'

'Then, in God's name, tell me what is happening,' Catherine demanded, pulling Margaret down beside her on the sofa. 'We may as well be on a desert island for all the news we hear at Saxton Court. It's at times like these I feel so useless being a woman. What news have you?' she asked anxiously, her gaze searching Margaret's face.

Margaret lost no time in telling her of the battle that had been fought at Sedgemoor a week ago. 'Monmouth attacked, hoping to surprise the King's troops in their beds, but things did not go as planned. The fighting was heavy and confused. George says it was such a close-run thing, where a rebel victory of appalling magnitude was only prevented by a miracle.'

Catherine was deadly still, her face white. 'And what about Marcus? Does George know where he is? You don't think he's dead, do you, Margaret?' she asked in no more than a whisper.

Seeing tears in Catherine's eyes, Margaret was quick to reassure her. 'If he is, then George would know. I'm sorry,' she said gently, 'there isn't anything more I can say, but I'm sure he's safe. Marcus was with Lord Churchill during the battle.'

'Are—are there many dead?'

'Well over a thousand—perhaps the final figure will be closer to two. George says that with experienced men, Monmouth might have won the day, because of his surprise attack and that his force outnumbered the King's, but the fighting was so confused, and his unskilled troops fired without coordination.'

Catherine allowed her mind to wander as Margaret carried on talking. What about Harry? she wondered. What had become of him? Was he lying wounded somewhere? Did he need help? *Please God, don't let him be dead. Oh, sweet Jesus, not Harry—so brave and true. He can't be dead.* Suddenly understanding that this might be so, she became conscious of both outrage and a wave of bitter grief.

Noticing Catherine's sudden pallor and believing it to be on account of Marcus, Margaret placed a comforting hand on her arm. 'Of course you must be worried about Marcus.'

'Yes—I am.' Catherine's voice trembled. It was unsettling that she could care for two men at the same time, but in many ways she cared for them differently. She had loved Harry with all the passion and innocence of her youth, and he was an important part of her past, but Marcus was her future. He made her feel very much his wife and undeniably a woman.

'Marcus is a survivor, Catherine, as indestructible as the earth itself. I'm sure he'll be all right.'

'Were—were many prisoners taken?'

Margaret nodded. 'Many of those who managed to escape are in hiding—anywhere they can find shelter. Apparently the area around Sedgemoor was the scene of terrible atrocities. George spared me the details, but he did say that some captives are in prison houses—some were hanged immediately after the battle,' she finished quietly.

'And Monmouth?'

'He escaped, but he was found half starved and dressed in peasant clothes hiding in a ditch three days later. He has been taken to London.'

'Then the rebellion really is over. King James will show no

mercy for Monmouth. How terrible that it should have ended like this.'

'The royal army, with Feversham and Churchill, set off for London soon after the battle.'

'Then is there no holding force to sort out the aftermath of Sedgemoor?'

'Not everyone has gone. There is still business to be done. A Captain Kirke, in command of two Tangier regiments of infantry together with cavalry and dragoons, has taken charge to round up the rebels.'

'And what is he like, this Captain Kirke? Is he a fair man? Will he be merciful in his treatment of the rebels?'

'It would appear not. He's a tough man, who commands equally tough men. He is also one of the cruellest, most dissolute officers in the British army by all accounts—a man who commanded the garrison at Tangier, where Marcus served for a time, so he will know Captain Kirke. The barbarism with which he conducted the arbitrary spate of executions there outraged and sickened most decent people. It is an example of what the people of the western counties can expect. Indeed, already there is much injustice and brutality being done, and general condemnation of his treatment of prisoners—although most people are too afraid to speak out. Three days after the battle I watched prisoners manacled together and carts full of wounded, being escorted into Taunton by Captain Kirke. It was a pitiful sight.'

'Then may God help Monmouth's rebels,' Catherine said quietly.

'George and I are so worried about you being here alone, Catherine. Will you not come and stay with us at Burton Grange, at least until Marcus comes home? We'd love to have you.'

'I am touched by your concern, Margaret, but please don't worry. Since Marcus and Captain Kirke both fought for the

King, I don't think Captain Kirke and his soldiers will bother us at Saxton Court. Besides, now Monmouth has been defeated, Marcus will soon be home.'

'I have been thinking,' Margaret said, 'about what you said about the Duke of Monmouth—on the night we dined with you here. You spoke with such fervour about his cause.'

Although Catherine smiled, she managed to look contrite. 'I am mortified every time I remember how outspoken I was.'

'Monmouth's defeat must have come as a terrible disappointment to you.'

'In truth, Margaret, I don't know what I feel—immense sadness for the huge loss of life, of course.'

'And blood so needlessly spilt.'

'I wouldn't say that. I still believe everything I said that night and will continue to hope for a Protestant King on England's throne—but please don't quote me to George.' She gave her a winsome smile. 'He may come and arrest me. But really, Margaret, my behaviour was outrageous and tactless. I quite forgot my manners. I was very silly. What must you have thought of me? Perhaps I should blame the wine for loosening my tongue and making me lose my inhibitions.' She looked down at her hands and breathed a ragged sigh when she recalled how severely Marcus has admonished her over it. 'Marcus was extremely angry with me afterwards, and with just cause. He spoke to me like an adult does to a foolish child that needs chastising.'

'I can see how much you care for him, Catherine,' Margaret said softly.

'Everything is made worse because I am missing him so acutely.'

'I do so hope you hear news of him soon.'

Catherine nodded solemnly. 'I hope so too. I just want him to come home. These past days I've missed him more than I would have believed possible.'

There was also another reason why she wanted Marcus to come home. The nausea and tiredness she had begun to feel of late were hard to shake off some days, and she now knew she could not put them down to her anxiety about her husband and the strain of trying to run Saxton Court. It was Alice who, four weeks after their departure from The Hague, had reminded her that her monthly flux was two weeks late, yet it hadn't occurred to Catherine that she might be with child. After their brief coupling, she did not believe she would have fallen pregnant the first time.

However, under the watchful eye of Alice, when she missed her next monthly flux and started experiencing occasional bouts of queasiness and tiredness, she was left in no doubt. Alice was quietly delighted, and Catherine excited. When, with a fond, conspiratorial look in her eyes as she embroidered a gown for the baby, Alice asked when she intended telling his lordship, she had replied, 'Soon, Alice, when I think the time is right.' For now she would hug her secret close.

Remembering the way Marcus had made love to her before he had gone away, she wanted him more than anything she had wanted in her life. She was glad she was his wife in more than name. She had been unable to withstand his ardour, and he had brought her to that moment of pure ecstasy, knowing full well what he was doing to her, and how she would for ever hunger for that same devastating rapture. She wanted him to fill her days with happiness and her nights with pleasure, until he loved her as much as she loved him.

Loved him? She frowned at the thought, and then sighed, admitting the truth to herself. She was in love with her husband, the man she had infuriated, mocked and refused to yield to from the day she had first set eyes on him. So what now that she knew that she loved him? Now his smile and the tender look in his fathomless dark eyes warmed her heart, and she could not imagine her life without him.

Having waved goodbye to Margaret and wishing to escape the confines of the house and think about what Margaret had told her, Catherine went into the gardens. Despite a change in the weather and the sun's warmth, a cold numb feeling remained with her as she unthinkingly wandered towards the woods, where the smell of damp undergrowth was oppressive. Reluctant to return to the house, she wanted to walk and walk for ever, glad to be alone with her thoughts and hoping that Mother Nature would soothe away her melancholy.

Where could Marcus be at that moment? she wondered. She felt that he was safe—she would surely know if he had come to harm. Margaret had said he was as indestructible as the earth, and she believed he was. She firmly believed that luck and divine protection would be with him wherever he went. She had to believe that. It was all that she had to hold on to, for to lose Marcus now would be too terrible to contemplate. But Harry. Dear Harry. He was without Marcus's experience, impulsive and tender-hearted—not indestructible.

Lost in these thoughts, she had walked further than she intended and did not notice what was going on around her. She failed to hear the dull thud of approaching hoofbeats, of a horse being ridden slowly through the undergrowth, and she did not stir from her reverie till horse and rider appeared in front of her. The rider's clothes were bloodstained and so thick with dust that his face was indistinguishable. His head was drooping with exhaustion and he was slumped in the saddle barely conscious. It was only when she saw his red hair that she recognised Harry with a shock of surprise. Snorting loudly, the horse came towards her trustingly.

With a frightening cry, reaching out, Catherine leapt towards Harry, and as she did so he fell forward and toppled wearily from the saddle. The effort sapped the last of his waning strength and he fell to his knees.

'Harry! Oh, Harry, you are hurt!'

Catherine reached his side and fell on her knees beside him, racked with her own emotion. As she looked down at the pain-filled face, for an anxious moment she steeled herself against panic. His skin was dry and stretched like parchment across his cheekbones. She laid her palms on either side of his face as a tear ran down her cheek, dripping on her dress. She wiped her wet face resolutely, for this was Harry, her love, and it did no good to weep for him when he had need of her help.

'What has happened to you? What have they done?'

Somehow Harry managed to draw his head back and look at her. His face was haggard, his eyes bleak and sunken with pain. 'I found your horse, Catherine. Remember? I promised I would bring her back if I found her. She was running loose on the battlefield—Sedgemoor.'

For the first time Catherine looked at her horse. Tears started to her eyes once more when she recognised her beloved Melody. The mare was weary and one of her front legs had a gash on it, but otherwise she seemed all right. Seeming to sense she was on familiar ground and that sweet fresh hay and oats were not far away, Melody walked off in the direction of the stables.

'A musket shot got me in the side,' Harry gasped. 'Thanks to your horse—my own horse was shot from under me—after the battle I managed to increase the distance between myself and my pursuers.'

Catherine was about to stand up when she heard voices, male voices. Three of them. The voices were low, the words indistinct. She felt a tug on her sleeve. 'Catherine,' Harry started to say. She clapped a hand over his mouth, her expression urging him to be quiet. *Please don't come closer*, she begged as she heard them approach. *Go away. Please go away.* Her silent pleas were ignored, for the voices came closer, she could hear them quite clearly now.

'This is where Lord Reresby lives,' one of the men said. 'Military man—with Churchill. No sign of any rebels hereabouts.'

Shoving Harry down into the undergrowth and holding a finger to her lips for him to be quiet, Catherine stood up and walked forward to meet the three mounted men splashing along the muddy road that led to Taunton. They carried themselves proudly, with the air of professional soldiers. Panic threatened, but she steeled herself against it, knowing it would do neither of them any good if she broke beneath the terror that bound her chest tightly. When the riders were close they paused, eyeing her suspiciously.

'Can I help you, gentlemen? I'm Lady Reresby of Saxton Court.'

One of the men rode forward, inclining his head with a modicum of respect. 'Captain Simmons of the King's army,' he said by way of introduction. 'We're rounding up rebels who fled the battlefield at Sedgemoor.'

'As far south as this?'

''Tis only ten miles or so, Lady Reresby. Intent on escaping across the Channel, some of them will be trying to make for the coast. Have you seen any strangers, anyone asking for food and shelter?'

'No, no one. What will happen to the rebels if they are caught?'

'There's severe punishment in store for men in arms, those who levied war against the King. Any who proclaimed Monmouth King may be hanged without bringing them to a formal trial. Examples will be made.'

'I see,' Catherine said stiffly. 'Then I will not hinder you in your search any longer. Good day.'

With tremendous relief she watched them ride on, and not until they were out of sight did she deem it safe to return to Harry. Turning from the road, she paused, her gaze drawn to the wood where she thought she saw something move. Her heart pounding, she stood perfectly still, her eyes fixed on the trees. The depth of darkness was impenetrable, then a gentle breeze stirred, moving the tall grass and swaying the boughs. She turned away, telling herself that her heightened senses were making her imagine things. But as she returned to the place where she had left Harry, she did not see the black horse, and on his back a shadowed being, calmly observing her every move.

'They've gone, Harry,' Catherine said, kneeling beside him. 'It's safe, but not for long. We have to find somewhere to hide you, and then I'll take a look at your wound.'

'You can't, Catherine. It's too dangerous for you. I must be on my way.'

'And just how far do you think you'll get in your condition, and with the King's soldiers swarming all over the county? I can't take you to the house—the servants will talk, but I must hide you somewhere. The stables are close by. I think that's the best place for now. Can you stand? Here, I will help you. We must hurry before someone else comes this way.'

With Catherine's hands under both his arms, aware of the need for urgency, Harry stumbled to his feet, and with her support they managed to make it into the stable yard. They paused, and holding the swaying Harry, Catherine glanced around. A creaking sound of an opening door came from the direction of one of the stalls. Glancing towards it, Catherine saw a man emerge from the doorway. She expelled a sigh of relief when she saw it was Archie. At least he could be trusted.

Being shortsighted, Archie craned his neck to see who it was that stood in the yard. 'That you, Lady Reresby?'

'Yes, Archie. Please help me. Hurry. This gentleman is hurt. I must get him inside—out of sight.'

Archie came quickly. The limp figure covered in blood told its own story. He asked no questions and took most of Harry's weight.

'Where to, my lady? The big house?'

'No, it's too dangerous. No one must know he's here, Archie, and I cannot depend on the servants to remain silent. I'll hide him in the stables for now.'

Without reservation or objection, Archie helped Catherine support the wounded rebel and between them they managed to get him inside. Propping Harry against one of the wooden stalls that had once held some of Marcus's finest horses, Catherine's eyes darted to a low door in the corner.

She went and peered into the dark hole. 'What's in there?'

'Nothing but straw and rubbish. Used to hold tack until the old master had the new tack room built across the yard.'

'It will have to do for now. At least it smells dry.'

'Aye, but there's no window in there.'

'All the better. If we can get him inside we'll hide the doorway as best we can.'

Together they hoisted Harry into the small, dark room, not big enough to stable a pony. Harry slumped down onto the straw on the floor. Breathing hard, his head thrown back and his eyes closed, he yielded to his tenuous grasp on consciousness, to the peace and security of the stable, however temporary.

Archie produced a lantern and set it on a box, its yellowish glow making long eerie shadows on the walls festooned with years-old cobwebs. Catherine unfastened Harry's coat and pulled the blood-soaked shirt free of his breeches, rolling it up to reveal a gaping hole in his side where the musket shot lay embedded. Blood oozed slowly from the wound. Her hands shook as she ripped a length of cloth from her petticoat and bound him tightly with Archie's help.

'It's not satisfactory, but it will have to do for now,' she said, sitting back on her heels and surveying her work with a critical eye.

'The wound's not too serious,' Archie pronounced. 'I've

seen worse. The shot's in a fleshy part—not close enough to have damaged one of his organs. I'd say he's suffering from loss of blood and exhaustion more than anything. When the shot's out and he's slept off his fatigue, he'll be better.'

'I hope so, Archie. I'll fetch Alice. Her knowledge of such things is far superior to mine. She'll give him the necessary medicine to combat any infection and aid his recovery. I'll also get some food and blankets. Lord knows when he last ate.'

Archie looked at her gravely. ''Tis not my place to tell you what to do, my lady, but he's a rebel soldier. You have to think of the consequences—to you, to all of us at Saxton Court, if the young gentleman is found. 'Tis a dangerous thing you are doin' hidin' him.'

'This whole situation is dangerous, Archie. The young gentleman is known to me. His name is Harry Stapleton. He is a dear friend whom I have known my entire life. I cannot leave him to die in a ditch and nor can I let him be taken. If he is found, I will take full responsibility and insist you had no knowledge of his presence.'

'What of Lord Reresby? He'll be home now the battle's over and won. He's eyes like a hawk, has his lordship. You'll not hide a rebel from him—he'll smell him. Before long the entire western counties will be crawling with fleeing rebels and King's soldiers trying to flush them out. It'll be a cat-and-mouse existence for months till they're all rounded up. Mark my words, my lady, they'll leave no stone unturned. They'll be sending out patrols right and left, and 'twill fall hard on you—on all of us—should it be discovered we're harbouring a fugitive.'

Catherine was unable to stop the shudder that gripped her body. 'I know. I also know there are people in the house who have no sympathy for the rebels. If a price is put upon their heads and they find out about Harry, they will lose no time in informing on him.' Leaning over Harry's prostrate form, she rested a hand on his unshaven cheek. 'Harry, can you hear me?' He nodded, his eyes flickering open before closing again. 'I'm going to leave you now, but I'll be back soon. I promise.'

Helping Archie to drag old cartwheels and fencing and anything else that could be found to cover the low portal, Catherine lost no time in returning to the house in search of Alice. Her heart pounded with urgency of what she must do for Harry—Harry, with whom she had laughed and loved. Harry, whom she had shared sweet, wonderful memories for as long as she could remember. No one would hurt him. She would not let them. She could not bear to lose him again. She would fight to the bitter end to save him. And so she became focused on making him safe, to restoring him to health whatever the cost, and the fact that she was another man's wife did not trouble her then.

Running up the steps, she entered the hall just as someone came down the stairs. It was Marcus, pulling off his riding gloves and flexing his fingers as if they were stiff. Absolutely taken by surprise, Catherine stared at her husband in disbelief. There was no denying the reality of that achingly familiar face. Joy exploded in her heart, obliterating all memory of that past hour she had spent with Harry. Marcus was alive and the sight of his handsome face almost sent her to her knees. He came slowly down the stairs, a faint smile lingering on his lips, and it seemed to Catherine as if his eyes never left hers.

Mentally she reached out to touch his beloved face, but then she remembered Harry, and her entire expression froze. For a moment she was thrown into such a panic she could not think coherently. She wanted to turn to run from the house, and yet she was unable to move.

'Marcus! What are you doing here?'

In the light that slanted through the high windows, Marcus's eager expression changed as her words sliced through him. Disappointed and offended by her tone, he said with bitter sarcasm, 'If I had any hope that you might be pleased to see me, that response would have taught me.'

'I—I fail to see why. You appear without warning, and then you are surprised when I ask you what you are doing here.'

'I apologise if I surprised you,' he replied sardonically. 'Next time I will give you fair warning.' He frowned. What was wrong? She hadn't been like this when he had ridden away to battle and she had shown such tender concern for his safety. He sensed that all was not well with her and in the hope of finding out what it was he made an effort to overcome his ill temper.

'There has been a battle, Catherine, a hard-fought battle. Is this how to greet a returning warrior? You are supposed to tell me how sorely you've missed me, fling yourself into my arms and weep tears of joy at my safe return.'

Catherine could see his hands were clenched, as if he were holding himself in check. She could see the harshness in his taut features and sighed with helpless understanding. She was shocked to see how strained he looked. His look of exhaustion was real, as if he, too, had gone through a great ordeal since she had last seen him. She gave a faint smile, guilt-ridden and ashamed of her ill-chosen remarks, though she made no move to go to him.

'You are right to reproach me, Marcus. I have missed you, truly. I am so sorry, and of course I am relieved to have you return home safely. Just because we have been apart does not mean you were absent from my thoughts.'

'Unfortunately the same cannot be said for Dickon.'

'Why, what has happened? He—he is dead?'

Marcus nodded. 'At Sedgemoor. He didn't fight in the battle, but his horse was startled by the noise of the guns. He fell from his horse and tripped over the sword he was carrying. There was nothing anyone could do.'

Through Catherine's mind flickered memories of Dickon, with his dark auburn hair, sunny open features and large grey eyes. Sadness at his loss filled her heart. 'I'm so sorry, Marcus. He will be missed. You were fond of him, I know.'

'Dickon was a fine young man. He served me well. I could trust him with my life.'

'Have you notified his family?'

'Not yet. I shall notify them, of course, but I intend to deliver his personal possessions to them myself. It's the least I can do.'

'Please express my condolences, Marcus.' It was then that Catherine remembered her appearance. Her hair must be untidy. With shaking fingers she smoothed it into place. Marcus advanced towards her, calm, unperturbed and unaware of the tumult raging within her breast.

'I have been home some considerable time. Where have you been? I was about to come and look for you.'

'I—I was in the garden—now the weather has taken a turn for the better,' she explained breathlessly. 'I quite forgot the time.'

As she spoke his eyes dropped to the skirts of her gown. Catherine instinctively looked, too, and as she did so felt, with a sudden stab of horror, as if the ground had opened to swallow her. For on the pale blue of her gown below her knee, was a large smear of blood—Harry's blood.

Slowly Marcus raised his eyes to hers. 'You have blood on your gown,' he said quietly. 'Are you hurt?'

'Blood? I—I—' Wildly she tried to think of some excuse, some reason why it should be there, and said the first thing that came into her head. 'Why, the most marvellous, strangest thing has happened. It is from Melody,' she said, seizing on this as if it were manna from heaven.

'But your horse was stolen.'

'Yes, but she came back—just now. She has a gash on her shinbone. Archie is tending to it.'

He raised a quizzical brow. 'How curious. Did Melody not have a rider?'

'No—no, she must have found her own way back.' Catherine struggled with a feeling of her own guilt. She was shocked that she could lie so blatantly. Marcus was her husband and she loved him, and yet at that moment she felt totally isolated from such emotions.

'What's wrong, Catherine?' Marcus asked quietly. 'Has my wife gone cold on me so soon?'

Catherine felt the sting of tears behind her eyes. 'No, of course not.'

He tipped his finger under chin. 'There's something troubling you,' he insisted. 'Are you going to tell me what it is? What secrets are you harbouring?'

'Secrets?'

'Yours, Catherine.'

His quiet, polite calm so unnerved her that she stammered, 'I—I don't have secrets.' Even as she said the words she felt the colour rush to her cheeks.

Marcus dropped his hand and took a step back. 'You had best go and change your gown. If the blood dries, then it will be ruined.'

'Yes—yes, I will. It is one of my favourites.'

He moved closer once more, and, seeing the fear in her eyes stopped short only inches in front of her. 'Catherine, what is it?' he asked.

It was his voice that made Catherine want to cry, that softly deep voice, and his face, that severe, handsome face she had come to adore. In that moment of weakness there came the temptation, so powerful as to be irresistible, to give in, to tell him everything. She needed him so much, his strength and his warmth, but she could not. She was too fearful of what he might do on finding his rival ensconced in his stables. She could not be certain how he would react.

'Are you feeling unwell?' he asked, frowning and studying her pale face and strained features.

Grasping the excuse he'd offered, she nodded hastily. 'I—I haven't been feeling too well of late. I—have a headache,' she said now in reply to his question, feeling the guilt of deception when the baby fluttered inside her. 'I don't seem to be able to shake it off.'

'Then I insist you see a physician to take a look at you. Although I suppose that without Fenton and with more responsibility thrust on you, it's understandable. You've been working too hard,' Marcus said with a worried frown. 'Now I am home I shall see to it that you get more rest.'

'Now you are home? Why, what do you mean, Marcus? Are you not returning to the army?'

He noted the panic that leapt in her eyes and was puzzled by it. 'No. My time is finished. I am home to protect Saxton Court from rampaging troops. There is much to be done here. So you see, the army's loss is your gain, my love—and besides, I have a desire to spend more time with my wife. Now away with you and change your gown.'

Catherine burst into her bedchamber. 'Alice, you've got to help me.'

'Why, what ails you, Catherine? It's not good for the baby to be getting so upset. And, goodness, will you just look at your gown?'

'I know, but never mind that now.' Grasping Alice's hand, Catherine pulled her down on to the bed and gave her a hurried account of all that had occurred since Margaret had left.

Alice looked at her, appalled. 'Harry? Harry Stapleton is here?'

'Yes, Alice, he is a fugitive. I can't let him be taken. Please, I am begging you to take a look at his wound. I dare not leave the house. Marcus is home and he mustn't suspect a thing.'

'Catherine, you have to tell him. You cannot keep something as important as this from your husband. It isn't right.'

'I can't tell him.'

'Don't you trust him?'

'Yes, of course I do, but under the circumstances I believe it is expedient not to say anything for the time being. It's better to be safe and not raise undue suspicion until Harry is well enough to go on his way—hoping the hue and cry will have died down by then.' Gone was her youthful candour, her adherence to the absolutes of right and wrong. She was too desperate to save Harry's life without involving her husband.

'How bad is Harry?' Alice asked as she hurriedly began putting everything she might need into a basket.

'He's been shot. The musket ball is still in his side. He's lost a lot of blood and he's exhausted. Take some food as well, Alice.'

'I'll see to it. Now, get yourself out of that dress and go back to your husband,' Alice ordered, not wasting another moment on enquiries.

Marcus watched Catherine climb the stairs before walking slowly to the fire. He looked into the flames with deep concentration. His wife was behaving extremely oddly. He sensed danger. What was going on?

Some time later, out of curiosity he left the house and went to the stables, just in time to see a woman hurrying away in the opposite direction. She was clad in a black robe and carrying a basket, and he recognised her as Alice. His puzzlement deepened. What was Alice doing at the stables? His suspicions roused, he was determined to get to the bottom of it.

The light was beginning to fade as he stood thoughtfully surveying the stables. For a moment he could imagine how they had once look, filled with some of the finest bloodstock in Somerset. When an owl flew out of a barn and screeched as it flew into the woods beyond, his vision faded. Since the horses had been stolen he had wondered despairingly a thousand times what had become of them. Had they been slain at Sedgemoor? He almost dreaded to discover the truth.

He noted that now only one of the stalls was occupied. It was Catherine's horse, Melody, its head looking out over the top of the stable door. So she had told the truth about that. Archie, bringing fresh water, placed the pail on the ground and stroked the horse's neck.

Marcus crossed towards him. If Archie was surprised to see him he didn't show it. 'How is the horse, Archie?'

'Welcome home, Lord Reresby. Glad to see you're none the worse after Sedgemoor—though the same can't be said about the rebels who took up arms against the King.' He looked at Melody. 'Wherever the horse has been for the past weeks, she appears to be in good condition, apart from a nasty gash to her front leg. She isn't lame, thank the Lord. I've cleaned it and bound it, so it should be all right.'

'My wife tells me the horse wandered home by herself.'

'It seems like that,' Archie replied truthfully, for the horse had been riderless when he'd found her. 'Pity she didn't bring the rest of them back with her.'

'Yes, a pity. Thank you, Archie.'

Marcus strode away, pausing and looking around in the gathering gloom in frustration. Everything looked as it should be, but somehow it wasn't, and Catherine knew why. The silence was ominous, the shadows concealing. It was this that roused a feeling of anger in him. He frowned and made his way back to the house.

* * *

Catherine had changed into a gown of russet and gold and draped a thin shawl casually over her shoulders, which partly covered the low, square-cut bodice that revealed a display of tantalising flesh. As she gazed into the fire and felt its warmth on her face, her thoughts turned to the child she was to bear. Now that Marcus was home she would have to tell him of his impending fatherhood. How would he react when she told him? she wondered. Would he be happy about being a father? She hoped so. She wanted so much to see his white smile gleaming in his swarthy face, to see his dark eyes flash with joy.

Smiling softly, she turned around when he stalked into the parlour. The smile on her lips faded as she beheld the hardness of his taut jaw and the cold glitter in his eyes. Her instinct told her that now was not the moment to tell him about the child.

'Is—something wrong, Marcus?'

'Wrong?' he repeated cynically.

Catherine's mouth went dry and her heart began to beat in heavy, terrifying dread as she sensed that Marcus had withdrawn from her. 'Why,' she asked cautiously, 'are you looking at me like that?'

'Suppose you tell me why,' he countered, pacing the room with frustrated strides. 'I have just seen Alice coming from the stables. Perhaps you can tell me her reason for being there. It cannot be that she has an interest in horses, since they have been stolen. Perhaps she went to see Melody to welcome her back— or then she might have developed a penchant for stable hands, for Archie, even, but somehow I don't think so, do you, Catherine?' He stopped pacing just inches from her and looked at her, his eyes like dagger thrusts. 'Tell me. And lie to me just one more time,' he said silkily, 'and you will wish you hadn't.'

Her heart and mind ravaged by divided loyalty, Catherine knew she would be unable to keep Harry's presence at Saxton

Court from him. Deciding it was time to be honest with him she dredged up her courage and said quietly, 'You—you aren't going to like what I have to tell you.'

'Try me,' he said in clipped tones.

'All right. Melody didn't return alone. She—she was brought back—by one of Monmouth's soldiers.'

Marcus's brows snapped together. 'Do you possibly think you could be a bit more specific?'

'The—the soldier was Harry.'

For a fraction of a second Marcus froze in total disbelief, unable to decipher what she had said and send the message to his stunned brain. Moving away from her, he turned and stared at her, his eyes darkening until they were almost black, his scorching anger burning a flame in the centre of each one.

Belatedly registering the thunderous expression on his face, Catherine jerked her gaze from his and stared at his shoulder. Never in all her life had she witnessed such controlled, menacing fury. 'I'm so sorry, Marcus,' she whispered. 'I—I wanted to tell you—but—but I couldn't.'

She braced herself for a verbal blasting, and after an ominous silence, he said, 'Harry Stapleton. And where is he now, Catherine?' His voice had a dangerous edge.

'He—he's injured. I—I hid him in the stables—in the old tack room. I sent Alice to tend his wound.'

Marcus strode back to her, bringing his snarling anger with him until they were face to face, but Catherine did not step back. 'And is Archie party to this subterfuge?'

She nodded.

'You idiot! You are playing with fire. Have you any idea of the enormity of what you have done? There will be no room for mercy—not for fugitives or those who harbour them—in the aftermath of Sedgemoor. Stapleton came over with Monmouth. He played a key part in the rebellion and will be high on the wanted list. The reward offered for the captive of such a prominent man will ensure that he is hunted down.'

'Please allow him to stay here until the period of search and watchfulness is past. He is in no condition to go anywhere until he has recovered from his wound. Marcus—I am begging you.'

His eyes sliced through her. 'It galls me beyond measure to have him at Saxton Court. I do not want him here. I do not want him in my house, in my stables, or anywhere on my property. And I do not want him talking to my wife. Why did he come here, if not to see you?'

The tone, aggressive and deliberately offensive, would normally have provoked Catherine to an equally stinging reply. But she knew if she wanted to help Harry she must cast off her pride and humble herself. 'He came to bring me back my horse,' she answered quietly.

'And how did he acquire your horse? I know they were in short supply in Monmouth's army.' His eyes hardened. 'Did you give it to him?'

Catherine stared at him, offended and hurt that he should think she would do such a thing. 'No, of course I didn't. Melody was your gift to me. I would never part with her willingly. She was stolen along with the rest of the horses. When I saw Harry in Taunton I told him about the theft and he said he would keep a look-out for her. He recognised her at Sedgemoor from the description I gave him. I never thought I would see her again and I'm so grateful to him for bringing her back.'

'Stapleton must have been a fool to come here. With the cavalry hot on his heels he must have known the danger—that he was placing all our lives in jeopardy by coming here.'

Catherine's eyes were filled with misery. She saw the savage, scorching fury that was emanating from her husband. His handsome jaw was taut with rage, his mouth drawn in a ruthless, forbidding line. 'He is wounded, Marcus. He could go no further. Have you no pity?'

'For him? None whatsoever. I am sure his feelings for you have not changed, but your circumstances have. You are my wife not only in name but in fact—as I am sure you will recall,' he ground out, his tone heavy with sarcasm. 'You may be acting from a feeling of pity in nursing him and keeping him hidden from the King's troops, but I cannot condone it. Until yesterday I was a soldier. I fought for the King. Harry Stapleton is a traitor and will suffer a traitor's death if he is caught.'

The thought that Marcus would hand Harry over to the soldiers made Catherine feel violently ill. Pleadingly, she placed her hand on his arm. 'It takes time to get used to losing what Harry and I once had, but my feelings have changed. I do still love him—only differently,' she said quietly. 'What I feel for you has much to do with that. But I do care for him—I care very much what happens to him.'

Feeling wrath that was beyond anything he had ever felt in his life, Marcus shrugged her hand away with distaste. 'This is not the time to demonstrate your affection. You will have to control your passions until I have decided what to do about Stapleton, and until I see fit to receive them.'

Catherine looked at him, numb with anguish. 'What are you going to do?'

'What do you expect me to do? Lower the drawbridge and invite him into the house—into a feather bed where my dear, devoted wife can coddle him and nurse him back to health?'

Catherine recoiled, his wrath, and his failure to understand how difficult this situation was for her, incurring her own. 'I'll do anything you ask of me, Marcus, but I hope you won't deal harshly with Harry. Please be patient until he's well, and it's safe for him to leave.'

'He can stay where he is for now—until I decide what is to

be done. As for you, Catherine, you will not leave the house under any circumstance without my permission. Is that clear?'

'No, Marcus, it is not,' she burst out, her temper rising at his injustice. She faced him without flinching. No doubt he was fearless in battle, his courage equalled only by his temper, which when roused was blistering in its fury. She saw it now, blazing red hot in his eyes. 'You are unreasonable and mistrustful and I am sorry I told you about Harry.'

Marcus smiled sardonically. 'That's more like the Catherine I have come to know,' he commented imperturbably. 'I am aware of what you think of me—and unreasonable and mistrustful I am not. You are in deep water here, my dear, and no display of fireworks will get you out of it. You are harbouring a traitor, and I'd be failing in my duty if I did not hand him over.'

'Duty!' She almost spat the word at him. 'You don't know the meaning of the word.'

'I assure you I do. I also know the meaning of pleasure, and your fury brings it to my recollection.'

Before Catherine could divine his intention and step out of his reach, Marcus moved fast. His strong hands drew her to his hard chest, and his lips were on hers before she knew what was happening. For a moment she swayed in his embrace, blood pounding in her ears, hating him and hating her treacherous body for responding eagerly to his touch.

Raising his head, he laughed softly, triumphantly, and released her. 'What a pity we have no time to indulge our appetites further. Grim duty calls...No, Catherine.' His voice cracked like a whiplash when she looked towards the door. 'You will remain here.' Turning from her, he crossed the room.

'Marcus.'

He paused and looked back at her. 'Well?'

'Devil take it!' she fumed, sweeping across the carpet towards him. 'You act as though I betrayed your trust. I did not ask for any of this. I did not invite Harry to come here, but now he is I cannot, will not, turn him away. You are being unfair. Can you really ask me to betray the trust of the man who sincerely loved me and wanted to make me happy? He is relying on me. I cannot deny him this one last service. It is important to me.'

'At what cost, Catherine?'

His dark eyes seemed to withdraw more deeply beneath the black brows and Catherine's heart was wrung as she read the huge disappointment in them, and the underlying jealousy of Harry that still persisted. 'All I can ask is for you to help me in this. I cannot do it alone. Afterwards we will be together. I shall be all yours, heart and soul. I will do whatever you want—but please grant me this one thing.'

Her eyes blazed with passion and Marcus was touched by their fire. 'And I cannot see how it can be done. What about our marriage and the damage this will do? You are pledged to me, not Harry Stapleton.'

Poised and composed, she raised her head. 'I hold loyalty and honour to my friends higher than any marriage contract. You took from Harry something he held dear. There comes a time when we must all pay for our mistakes. You now have the chance to redeem yourself, to do something for Harry in return.'

Marcus's eyes narrowed dangerously. 'I do not like ultimatums, Catherine.'

'It isn't one. As your wife I am appealing to you to give Harry's plight some thought. I was beginning to know you as being a man of honour, a man to be trusted.'

'I am not perfect. None of us are.'

'Nevertheless, I cannot believe you would hand a man who fought for what he thought was right over to the infamous Captain Kirke to be hanged.'

'Don't bet on it, Catherine.'

The finality of these words to Catherine acted like acid on a burn. 'Then why go to all that trouble?' she flared, her heart shrieking her resentment. 'Why wait? You have a sword. Do it yourself. Go and kill him now and be done with it. It won't take a minute.'

Marcus looked down at her with the furious impatience of an adult about to chastise a naughty child. 'Don't be ridiculous.' His gaze froze on the tantalising flesh swelling over her bodice. 'And cover yourself.'

Self-consciously, Catherine rapidly drew her shawl over her chest.

'Thank you,' he drawled. 'I do not care to have you display yourself to everyone who may care to look—or should I place the fault with your gown? In the future when we have guests, whether they be invited or not, I insist that you select what you wear with more care. Such sights will be reserved for me and my pleasure.' He smiled. 'My generosity in that regard is limited. I will not tolerate the thought of another man having what I have claimed for myself.'

'You mean Harry.'

'Any man, Catherine. And one thing more. Always tell me the truth because, if you don't, I will know.'

Marcus looked at her in silence, and then, without uttering another word, strode from the room. Catherine watched him go, her heart and mind empty. Something told her that things could never be the same again between them. She experienced a piercing stab of regret for the night before he had gone away when all their quarrels had been dissolved at last in kisses. From now on there would be a bitter taste of loneliness and renunciation.

Chapter Nine

Intending to go and see Harry Stapleton, and in no mood to be charitable or accommodating, Marcus paused on the terrace, putting off the moment, and stared into the darkness beyond, deeply affected by his conversation with his wife. The thought of having to deny her was becoming a growing torment. He knew that for her sake he must try to do what he could to save Stapleton's life, for there would never be any happiness between them if he refused her this. A familiar ache appeared to strike at his heart. He didn't want to lose Catherine, so what was to be done? Maybe she was right. He had inadvertently destroyed Harry Stapleton's future and perhaps it was time to make amends for the wrongs he had done. His lips twisted in a cynical smile. Amends! Hadn't that something to do with a repentant conscience—a conscience which was becoming a great deal more inconvenient than he would ever have thought possible?

The shadowy outline of a tall man clad in a long cloak and standing, feet planted wide, at the other end of the terrace cleared his mind of all else. Darkness shrouded the land, and there was little light from the house to identify the man. Marcus advanced steadily towards him. When he was close enough, as he recognised his visitor, his clear dark features were set as hard as the granite of the Cornish cliffs, and as dangerous as those rocks that appear innocent above the water, but in the hidden depths lie in wait to crush a vessel unfortunate enough to sail too close.

The two men were only six feet apart. Fenton had come unnoticed. He was smiling, but the eyes that rested on Marcus were hard as stone.

'I'm genuinely astonished, Fenton,' Marcus remarked, his voice pure venom. 'I doubt you've come to pay your respects. I never imagined you would have the audacity to linger in these parts, let alone come here. I though you'd be on your horse and away to Lyme or some other port. To what do I owe this dubious pleasure?'

'You owe me money,' Fenton uttered, quite matter of factly.

'You've been paid what you are owed.'

'Not quite. I thought I'd come to settle with you on a personal basis.'

'You come armed, I see,' Marcus remarked, seeing the glint of steel protruding from Fenton's cloak at waist height. 'Just to bolster one's courage, 'tis wise to carry a pistol to defend oneself, I always think,' he drawled sarcastically.

'It is a precaution I considered necessary—in view of our last encounter.' Fenton stepped closer, seeming to be sure of himself. 'I'm sorry if I delay you.'

'Delay me?' Marcus's voice was carefully controlled.

'You were about to check on the rebel your wife has concealed in the stable, were you not?' He smiled thinly. 'I came across him on the Bridgwater to Taunton road. I suspected he might make for here, so I followed him and observed how tenderly your wife received him.'

Marcus read the mockery on Fenton's face, but the steadiness of his gaze did not falter. 'Must I remind you that you too are a fugitive,' he countered sardonically. 'I credited you with more sense. I thought you'd be well away from here while you had the chance. Already it is almost impossible to stir with the whole county seething with militia men and Captain Kirke's troops searching for fugitives.'

'In which case we may as well talk business.'

Marcus arched a brow, his lips twisting with distaste. 'Business? With you? I think not.'

Fenton shrugged. 'I see you still bear some prejudice against me.'

'What I feel is neither here nor there. However, I will say that, where you are concerned, I have not changed my mind.'

'As you so rightly say,' Fenton agreed smoothly, 'it is neither here nor there.'

'Enough,' Marcus said coldly. 'What do you want?'

'Thirty thousand pounds.' He gave a twisted smile. 'I have expensive tastes.'

The sum was astronomical, but Marcus's expression didn't alter. Pure greed glittered in Fenton's eyes, almost as brightly as the moon glinting on the barrel of his pistol, and for a naked moment his smile betrayed the workings of his grasping mind.

'And I have a feeling this is going to cost you a good deal more,' Marcus said.

'Call it compensation for my dismissal if you like.'

'You can go to the devil, Fenton. What is to prevent me from handing you over to the authorities?'

'This pistol—and your wife. For one thing, it will do no good to denounce me, for should I release the name of the fugitive who is dear to your wife's heart—and whom, I might add, has a fifty-pound reward on his head—she will be arrested for harbouring a fugitive. Another thing is that she is Henry Barrington's daughter, and I am certain the King would like to hear what I have to say—should I decide to turn King's evidence, that is. He is relentless where those who concocted The Rye House Plot, those who conspired to kill himself and his brother, are concerned. I doubt she will be granted clemency. Being Barrington's daughter will not stand in her favour.'

The sneering tones of Fenton acted as a goad to Marcus's thoughts. 'You want me to pay for your silence.'

'Something like that.'

'I doubt the King would be interested in my wife since she was not directly involved in the plot and her father is deceased. You should worry about your own skin, Fenton. You may not have taken up arms, but it is no secret that you were active in the planning of James Scott's rebellion. While we speak, the constables of each parish in the area of the rebellion have been ordered to produce a list of all those suspected of being involved. Your name is certain to be included.'

Fenton smiled ironically. 'Lists? I think we both know that many of the parish authorities compiling the lists are open to corruption, and the scope for error and dishonesty is enormous. What a chance to settle old scores, to write down the name of an enemy, to leave off other names—for love or money.'

'In your case money, which you hope to obtain from me, so that when your name is left off the list you will not be defined in official eyes as a traitor. Who do you intend to bribe, Fenton—Captain Kirke?'

'I think we both know what Captain Kirke is capable of. I have heard that he fought many a bloody skirmish in the Moroccan hinterland, in which every form of atrocity was casually perpetrated. As commander of operations here in the western counties, he will rule as despotically as he did in Tangier—already he has put to death close on one hundred captured rebels since Sedgemoor. You must have seen for yourself some of the victims at Taunton he has strung up from the signpost of the White Hart Inn. By the time he's finished he'll become the most ardently reviled man in the British army.'

Marcus knew this to be true. He'd had dealings with Captain Kirke in Tangier, an English possession relinquished in the reign of Charles II. Kirke's taste for plunder and violence had known no bounds, and he could not abide the man. It was a heavy irony that Kirke's regimental flag bore the emblem of the paschal lamb, for the men under his command—thugs who raped, pillaged and bullied—were known as Kirke's Lambs.

'Kirke will exact satisfaction from the local populace by waging a campaign of terror and extortion—how else is a serving officer to make money out of a rebellion that yields so little worthwhile plunder? He can be bought, for the right price.'

'You're right,' Marcus agreed, 'but not with my money.'

'It may not come to that—if I escape safely. Come now, be sensible, Reresby, and be satisfied with your own power and what you have—Saxton Court, where prosperity abounds and your peasants are content, and your beautiful wife. It would be foolish to throw it all away for the sake of a few thousand pounds. I know your wealth is considerable—I have made it my business to find out. Your father's loyalty to Charles the First throughout the Civil War paid off. The Reresby fortunes were greatly advanced after the restoration of Charles the Second.'

'And you will not get a penny piece, Fenton. I will not fill the pockets of the man I suspect of killing my father. He showed you every favour, and you exploited that favour to the full. If I find proof that you had a hand in his death I will kill you. There will be no hiding place. I shall hound you to hell like the scum you are and show you no mercy. Take heed. I don't make empty threats.'

Fenton stepped back and raised his gun in salute. 'Spoken like a true Reresby.' He spoke the name with contempt.

Marcus took a step towards him, fixing him with his fathomless black eyes. His hand shot out and he grasped the pistol, flinging it aside. 'Don't bait me, Fenton. I am only inches from murder.'

Fenton, a man who could kill a man without a dent to his conscience, was surprised to feel a chill go down his spine.

'Marcus.'

Marcus turned in the direction of his wife's voice. She emerged from the opposite end of the terrace and walked quickly towards him. Her face was strained and pale in the dim light.

'Who were you talking to? Who was that?'

Marcus spun round to where Fenton had stood. He had left as quickly as he had appeared, and retrieved his pistol. The man was as slippery as an eel.

'Marcus, I—I wanted to say—'

'Not now,' he snapped curtly, not feeling entirely safe with Fenton loitering in the dark with a pistol pointing at him. And with fugitives all over the place and soldiers in hot pursuit, how many other pairs of eyes were out there, watching from the darkness? 'Come back inside the house.'

Marcus marched her with unseemly haste back along the terrace and into the house, not stopping until they reached the privacy of the dining room, neither of them speaking a word until the door was closed.

Catherine's frayed nerves stretched taut as she faced her husband. The hard, stubborn line that had settled disquietingly between his black brows earlier was still there. Aware of his still smouldering anger, she said, 'Please don't look at me like that, Marcus. I know you're angry, but you shouldn't be.' Reaching out, she placed her hand on his arm, trying somehow to gentle him.

The gesture failed. Marcus jerked his arm away. 'Do not try to distract me. It will not work.'

'I realise,' she began again, 'that you must despise me for what I've done.'

'Not quite, but close,' he bit back. 'This is not a game we're playing, Catherine.'

'I'm not playing games,' she whispered bravely, her voice trembling with emotion while she tried to think of how to begin to diffuse his wrath. She was stung by Marcus's tone, especially as she was beginning to feel slightly guiltier and a trifle less nostalgic about Harry, who she was beginning to see as a source of discord between Marcus and herself. 'If I wanted to play games with you, I would not have told you about Harry. Who— who were you talking to?'

'No one important,' he snapped, 'and the next time I tell you not to leave the house, you will do as I say.'

'It was Fenton, wasn't it?' she persisted, ignoring his chastisement. The dark look Marcus gave her confirmed it. 'What did he want—and why did you hurry me inside?'

'Because he was carrying a pistol and would probably have shot one of us or both if he had a mind to.'

'Have—have you seen Harry?'

'I have not yet had that pleasure.'

'I've just seen Alice. She said we're not to worry. His wound is superficial—though he is exhausted. Even without the tisane she's given him, he'll sleep the night through.'

'Thank you for that edifying piece of information, Catherine. No doubt I shall sleep better myself tonight knowing Stapleton is warm and snug in my stable. What made you come looking for me?' Pouring himself a brandy he drank slowly, watching her over the glass.

Marcus's scathing sarcasm sliced into Catherine's highly sensitised emotions like a knife. It was not so long ago when they had been ready to melt together in the same fusion of joy, and now a curtain of incomprehension had fallen coldly into place between them. 'I—I just want to say I'm sorry. Please forgive me. I spoke hastily earlier. Only—please try and understand what Harry's safety means to me.'

His eyes became twin black daggers that impaled her. 'I do understand, Catherine. Oh, I do, and you are right, none of it is your fault. You have nothing to reproach yourself with. I accept full responsibility. What I did to both you and Stapleton was reprehensible and I should repent of my past actions.'

'Repent? That word sounds strange coming from you,' she said with a nervous little smile, thinking his mood was beginning to improve, but the quelling look he threw her told her it wasn't and wiped the smile from her lips.

'I don't see why. It is the correct word in the circumstances,' he said, his voice coldly formal.

There was a long silence. It took all Catherine's courage to break it, certainly to pose the question. 'So, will you help Harry? Please, Marcus, it will mean so much to me.'

He banged his empty glass down on the table. 'I don't please, but I suppose I must—out of some kind of distorted duty.' His lips twisted with ironic amusement. 'No doubt you look upon the situation as you would a pleasant comedy—my sins have come home to roost and I must make amends,' he hissed in self-mockery. 'At last the time has come to stone the husband who wronged his wife and her lover.'

Catherine stiffened. He was being deliberately cruel. 'You don't have to sound so melodramatic about it, Marcus. Harry was not my lover.'

'No, maybe not, but it is amusing, is it not, with the husband ending up looking like a damned fool. How does it feel, Catherine, to have your husband stand by you and promise to do everything in his power to save Stapleton's hide?'

The hope that leapt in her heart became mirrored in her eyes. 'You will?'

It was the first time that Marcus hadn't paused to consider Saxton Court before making his decision. 'You have my word that I will do everything I can to aid his escape.'

Catherine found it difficult to believe that Marcus had capitulated. He certainly didn't look happy about it. It was some small victory, but she doubted whether he would grant her the opportunity of winning any more. He had relented, but at what cost to his pride? Pride, that terrible, unapproachable masculine pride, was still uppermost in his posture and in the hard, cold way he was looking at her. Instinct told her that while ever Harry was at Saxton Court, Marcus would avoid her like the plague.

'It is a great favour I am asking of you. I realise that.'

'You're right, it is, but there is no way out of this for either of us now.'

'Why, what do you mean?'

'Fenton saw Stapleton come here, he saw you hide him, and has threatened to expose him if I refuse to pay him for his silence.'

Catherine's eyes widened with horror. 'Pay him? You—you mean he is demanding money?'

'Thirty thousand pounds.'

'Thirty thousand pounds?' Catherine repeated, aghast. 'But that is an enormous sum! It is also blackmail—and Fenton is as much a fugitive as Harry.'

'Try telling that to our Mr Fenton. Fenton is a wanted man, and if he is apprehended he will require the means to bribe his way out of it and live in comfort on the Continent—hence the thirty thousand pounds. Without the money he will lose no time in telling his captors of Stapleton's whereabouts.'

Catherine paled. 'What will you do?'

'What matters is that Stapleton is here. Because I care greatly about what may happen to us all if he is found, I cannot for the moment do anything about it. However, he cannot remain where he is. He'll have to be moved.'

'Where to?'

'Leave that to me.'

'And Mr Fenton? Are you going to give him the money?'

'No, I'm not. He will not get a penny out of me.'

'If—if Harry is discovered, can you not use your influence? You know Captain Kirke. Perhaps you will be able to persuade him to be lenient.'

'What touching faith you have in me, Catherine. Kirke and I are old acquaintances, I grant you, but it is difficult to look on him without contempt. He is brutal and dishonest—and would find a soul mate in Fenton if they weren't on opposite sides. I have no influence whatsoever. Now, if you don't mind, I will go and take a look at our fugitive.'

Catherine moved closer to him. 'Can—can I come with you?'

'You dare to ask me that? No, Catherine, you cannot. You will not go near him. Is that clear?'

Marcus's voice rose, and he took a menacing step towards her. Catherine shrank away, for there was a look on his face that said he was driven to the end. Much as she would have liked to see Harry, she raised no objection to this. She was just enormously grateful to Marcus for taking charge of the situation.

'Very well. I—I'm sorry for placing you in this awful predicament, Marcus—and thank you for your co-operation. It means a great deal to me, truly.'

Thinking wildly for some way to reach him before he took irrevocable steps to banish her from his heart and mind, she stretched out a hand to him in a gesture of mute appeal, letting it fall to her side when her touching move got nothing from him but a blast of contempt from his eyes. Then he turned and strode to the door and went out, the noise of it closing echoing in the depths of Catherine's heart.

* * *

When Mr Fenton slipped away from Marcus, his face was devoid of emotion. Inwardly he seethed. Reresby was right. He had inveigled himself into his household, and safe in the knowledge that Marcus Reresby was away on the King's business and determined to profit from his exalted position at Saxton Court, he had made himself invaluable to the old Lord Reresby. And then, when he was out of the way, his son had returned home and brought havoc to his life.

As he urged his horse on, his eyes held a feral glitter in their depths. If Reresby did not give him the money, his own impatience would turn to vindictiveness. And only he knew just how malicious that vindictiveness might be. His thoughts were bent upon revenge. But the revenge he set his heart upon was halted when he heard a jangle of harness and stamp of horses' hooves. His hatred of Marcus Reresby was fierce and powerful, but it wasn't powerful enough to keep him from what happened next. Before he knew what was happening, soldiers appeared out of the darkness and he was surrounded.

On entering Harry's hiding place, Marcus took random stock of the shadowy old tack room in the light of a lantern Archie had left hanging from a hook on an overhead beam. There was a platter of uneaten food and a jug of water on an overturned box. Old bridles and ropes hung on the walls festooned with cobwebs. The fugitive was sleeping like the proverbial babe, his head pillowed on a mound of straw and snoring softly. Marcus left him to his slumber, deciding to return the following morning.

Harry was sitting hunched on the straw, his arms wrapped about his knees, his head bent in thought. His head came up when Marcus entered, his body tense, alert. Seeing who it was, clutching his injured side and clenching his teeth when a wrenching pain shot through him, he scrambled to his feet, his look wary.

Leaning against the wooden doorframe with his arms folded, Marcus calmly studied him in silence. The lantern threw a yellow flicker upward, carving the young man's face from the shadows behind. Marcus had to admit that Harry Stapleton was well made—long legs and good breadth about the shoulders, and he'd have a fair reach with a sword.

'I am sorry to disappoint you,' Marcus said at length. 'No doubt you were expecting my wife, but I have forbidden her to visit you. You will understand why.'

'Yes, of course,' Harry was quick to answer, with politeness and an inbred courtesy that he always directed towards those of Lord Reresby's station, and those older than himself. 'I am sorry to have put you in this predicament, sir. It was not my intention to put Catherine in any danger—'

'I am glad to hear it.'

'But when I found her horse I knew I had to bring it back to her. When I saw her in Taunton, she was clearly distressed that it had been stolen. I give you my word that I shall leave at the earliest opportunity and no one will be any the wiser.'

Marcus nodded slightly. He could see regret in Harry's eyes quite clearly. The man was genuinely worried that he had endangered Catherine's life by coming here.

'Your injury—does it pain you?'

'Not much. 'Tis superficial and will soon heal, thanks to Alice's ministerings.' He smiled broadly. 'She always was good at making things better.'

Marcus's heart was struck by a dart of jealousy, the more painful for being unexpected. Was he always to be reminded of what Harry Stapleton had been to Catherine? 'I apologise for the accommodation not being up to much,' he said, shrugging himself away from the door and moving closer to Harry.

'Beggars can't be choosers. As things are, I am grateful for whatever I can get. I implore you, sir, as soon as you feel it is safe for me to do so, let me be on my way.'

'And have my wife reproach me for it for the rest of our lives? No, I think not. But be assured that the sooner you are recovered and it is indeed safe for you to leave and find your way to the Continent, where, God willing, you will find yourself a wife and stop hankering after mine, the better I shall feel.'

To be taunted over losing Catherine to Lord Reresby brought all the bitterness and loss Harry had suffered because of this man to erupt like a vicious strength. His anger showed in his heightened colour and the stiff set of his shoulders.

'I dare say that you are stronger than me, with the added advantage of more years and experience of close fighting as a professional soldier. Nevertheless I would challenge you, sir, for that remark, but that it would be folly for me to do so now, weak and wounded as I am.' Harry was tempted to add that his body was soaked with sweat in the hot and airless confined space he was forced to hide in, and itching from the dust and bits of chaff from the straw trapped inside his shirt and rubbing on his skin, but he would not give Reresby the satisfaction to gloat on his discomfort.

'I am no stranger to a fight,' he went on, his voice having become dangerously hard, which surprised Marcus. The cub had teeth, when pricked by the spur. 'God knows I have good reason to despise you, but after escaping the hell of Sedgemoor, I am not about to jeopardise my life by attacking you.'

'That is wise. I have no quarrel with you, and I thank you for returning my wife's horse.'

Harry took a step forward, and not for the first time, Marcus felt a thread of respect for him.

'I am entirely at your mercy, Lord Reresby. Will you hand me over to Captain Kirke?'

'No—not out of any regard towards you, you understand, but because I have promised my wife that I will not do so.'

'You will help me? The decision is yours, sir, not Catherine's.'

Marcus studied him in thoughtful silence. After a long considering look, he nodded. 'Still, it will be for my wife's sake, and also because obligation compels me to help you. I did wrong by you when I married Catherine, for which I ask your pardon.'

'Catherine is your wife. I don't know if I will ever forgive you for taking her from me, but I have accepted that I have lost her. The time when everything might have been possible between us has gone. When we met in Taunton I knew it was finished, and so did she,' he said, the words hurting his throat with the pain of speaking them. He had loved Catherine for so long, and now—now she was gone from him, and the weight of her loss lay heavy on his heart. Suddenly he smiled with a cynicism way beyond his years. 'But fear not, I will survive it.'

Marcus knew he would. With the steel-tempered strength of generations of well-bred gentlemen behind him, and a cause he would continue to fight for despite Monmouth's capture, Harry Stapleton would not fail.

'I can offer reward for any assistance you may give—when I reach Holland.'

'That will not be necessary,' Marcus said in a cold voice. 'I want no reward for such service.'

'I meant no offence to you, sir.'

'None taken,' Marcus answered shortly.

'Have you any news concerning the Duke of Monmouth and his whereabouts?'

'Monmouth has been captured and taken to London. Are you not aware of that?'

Harry's expression didn't change for a moment, then the words fell into place. 'No, I am not. That it should have come to this,' he said softly, deeply affected by this news. 'May God show him mercy, for his uncle the King will not. What a mockery it all seems now. We came to England with our hopes high, convinced that God was on our side—and what has happened? The Londoners stayed at home and Argyll was defeated in Scotland.' He sighed, shaking his head wearily. 'I fought for Monmouth and my own ideals at Sedgemoor. No matter what happens now, I do not regret having done so, and while there is breath in my body I shall continue to fight until a Protestant King sits on England's throne.'

Marcus was suddenly struck by Harry's youth, his vulnerability and his courage. His strength of purpose was evident in the set of his unshaven face, and he could see it in his eyes how proud he was to have stood firm by his convictions, to have fought for what he believed was right. Nothing could divert him from his cause. Marcus was almost overwhelmed by an unexpected feeling of admiration, which replaced some of the resentment he had long harboured for the young man, and with the admiration came guilt and something else he could not ignore, for the loyalty, determination and courage of Harry Stapleton—indeed, of the whole rank and file of Monmouth's army—made him feel ashamed.

This young man had fought for what he, Marcus, believed in—to set a Protestant King on the English throne. But he had preferred to step back and wait until his own analysis had worked itself out, believing that the time was not right for rebellion, that illegitimate Monmouth wasn't the right man to be King, and because he would rather the Princess and Prince of Orange succeed. He didn't feel very proud of himself as he turned and moved towards the door.

'I'll leave you to rest. It isn't safe for you to remain here. After dark I will have you moved to a safer and more comfortable place.'

'Thank you. I appreciate all you are doing for me.'

A slight hesitation in Marcus's step showed the words had been heard. He turned and glanced back. 'Call it the tribute of a repentant conscience.'

Any hope that lingered in the hearts of those in the West Country faithful to Monmouth died when news reached them of his execution. On the fifteenth of July, just nine days after the Battle of Sedgemoor, he was beheaded on Tower Hill. Seldom can an execution have been as badly botched. After five blows with the axe, with Monmouth still alive, Jack Ketch, the executioner, had to take a knife to complete his work.

Harry's new hiding place was in a shallow cave under a rocky overhang in the sunken water garden at Saxton Court. It was walled in along the front by several boulders, trailing ivy and brambles and beech trunks, stout enough to deter even the most resolute searching soldier. It was dry, cool and shadowy, smelling sweetly of undergrowth and the scent of flowers wafting in from the garden.

Marcus informed Harry that it had been used successfully several times as a hiding place for escaping Royalists during the Civil War.

Over the following days, Catherine rarely came into contact with Marcus, and when they did meet he was coolly aloof. Mealtimes, when he condescended to join her, were tense, joyless affairs. She continued to endure his coldness, while her mind whirled with questions about what was happening to Harry that only he could answer. How long would this interminable situation go on, assuming there would be an end to it eventually? It was a tense and difficult time, and it was imperative that no one at Saxton Court, apart from themselves, Alice and Archie, knew of Harry's presence.

Occasionally Marcus told Catherine of Harry's progress and

that he was recovering well. Aware of the dangers his presence at Saxton Court posed to them all, he was impatient to leave and try his chances on the road. There was an organised non-conformist underground movement for the purpose of aiding fugitives to escape to friendly Exmoor, where guides could be found to take them across the moor by hidden ways to seek passage in small boats from Ilfracombe or Lynmouth, or the ports of South Devon, Dorset and Hampshire, which offered a quicker passage to Holland.

Harry asked Marcus to try and get in touch with the organisation to help him reach the coast, but having fought on the opposite side at Sedgemoor, Marcus knew his chances of doing this were negligible.

Soldiers, armed and alert, patrolled the roads in the search for rebels. Many were lying low, hiding until the intense period of search and watchfulness had passed. The West Country was a paradise for the fugitives, where woods of beech and oak, bracken, gorse and heather provided marvellous great sunken ditches covered by undergrowth.

Afraid of what Fenton might do next and not knowing if Marcus had seen him since the night he had come demanding money, Catherine was living on a knife-edge. The fear lingered uncomfortably. Thankfully the days, stretching into weeks, passed without incident, until the beginning of August, when a long line of soldiers rode up to the house.

Catherine joined Marcus on the steps in front and watched them ride closer. A grim-faced George Stanhope rode behind the leader.

'What the devil does Kirke want?' Marcus muttered.

The name of the officer left in command to deal with the rebels caused Catherine's stomach to contract with foreboding. The horrifying menace that had hung over Saxton Court since Harry had appeared seemed to have come home to roost. She read disaster in the set of his face, and she was sure that his eyes held a threat. Glancing at Marcus, she saw that his features were perfectly bland, but he was physically tense, as though he knew that an unusually unpleasant confrontation was about to occur. She heard him utter something under his breath that she recognised as a vicious obscenity, but then he was moving down the steps to greet his visitors with no hesitation in his manner.

'Ah, Reresby,' Captain Kirke said pleasantly. Much in the manner of a flamboyant officer, he swung off his still-prancing horse and came to stand in front of them, arrogance in his stance. 'It is a pleasure to be renewing our acquaintance.' He smiled, but the smile didn't reach his eyes. 'I heard you'd done with the army and hoped to find you at home.'

'Captain Kirke,' Marcus said in tones of mild surprise, as one might greet a casual acquaintance. His gaze flicked to George, whose usually good-humoured face remained expressionless. He fixed his attention once more on the captain. Kirke had always been difficult to deal with, but he had been adroitly managed by Marcus when they had been together in Tangiers. 'I hadn't thought to see you here. What can I do for you?'

'I regret to say this is not a social call. I'm here in a professional capacity. I have your bailiff locked up in Taunton gaol.'

Captain Kirke's proclamation hit Marcus like a thunderbolt, but his expression remained impassive. 'If you are referring to Mr Fenton, Captain, he is no longer my bailiff. I dismissed him from his post several weeks ago.'

'Yes, that is what I have been told. However, he has made serious allegations that I cannot ignore.'

'Allegations?'

'Aye, that you are harbouring one of the rebels here at Saxton Court—and maybe more than one.'

'I am as amazed as much as I am intrigued,' Marcus replied coolly. 'Are you quite certain your information is correct? All this talk about concealing rebels…' He shook his head in smiling disbelief. 'I would not cast doubts on your information—only on your informant. It is nothing but the fictitious, vindictive ramblings of a man set on revenge.'

Kirke raised a quizzical brow. 'Really? And why should Mr Fenton wish to be revenged, sir?'

'I refused to give him money to aid his escape—and this is his way of hitting back. I confess I find it all very surprising. Come now, Captain—with my long service towards King and country? Are you forgetting that I fought against Monmouth at Sedgemoor—and have we not fought side by side in past battles?'

'We have, indeed, but then it's amazing the lengths one will go to to placate one's wife.' His eyes, cool and derisive, shifted from Marcus and settled on Catherine's taut features. If he had hoped to see a flicker of emotion pass across her face, he was disappointed. He smiled and bowed his head slightly. 'You are Lady Reresby?'

Catherine had listened with mounting alarm to the stiff exchanges between Marcus and Captain Kirke, but now at the mention of her own name her fears took on a new edge. However, it was with dignity and a fair assumption of icy civility that she replied.

'I am Lady Catherine Reresby, and I have never had the need to placate my husband, sir. He is no callow youth I can lead about on a string and expect him to obey my whim.' With a soft, wistful smile, she moved closer to her husband's side. 'If you know him well, Captain Kirke, you will agree with me.'

Captain Kirke could find no answer to her words. At least, not one he wished to entertain. 'You husband is his own man, I grant you.' His eyes were as cold as the waters in a West Country dyke in midwinter as they remain fixed on Catherine. 'The man I seek is Harry Stapleton, who sailed from Holland with Monmouth and has been by his side throughout. My informant stated that Stapleton would be found at Saxton Court—and that because you were once his mistress, you would do everything in your power to shield him and aid his escape.'

Rage, hot and furious, flared in Catherine, but before she could say a word in her defence, Marcus had stepped forward. His eyes glittered at the offensiveness of the captain's remark. The muscles of his jaw were taut with a rage barely under control, his voice hard and his eyes ice cold.

'Let that be enough, Captain. Do what you came to do, since the word of my disgraced bailiff is enough to make you invade a respectable household, but do not insult my wife.'

Unperturbed, Captain Kirke shrugged, having grown accustomed to the disdain the West Country folk bore him and his soldiers. 'I was not insulting your wife. I was merely repeating what I have been told.'

'If you believe everything you are told, I am sorry for you, Captain,' Marcus said with biting contempt. 'For myself it makes no difference, but let me advise you to behave more courteously towards my wife, unless you wish me to register a complaint against you.'

'There will be no need for that.' Captain Kirke looked at Catherine. 'If I have made a mistake I apologise, Lady Reresby.'

'Thank you.'

'Stapleton was your betrothed, I am told. You were close.'

Shock drained the blood from Catherine's cheeks as she realised the implication of the captain's words and sensed an underlying threat. 'No, sir, he was not,' she told him bravely. 'We knew each other, but we were not betrothed.' She stepped closer to her husband. His shirt was open at the neck, and she could see the corded muscles of his throat and the pulse that was beating furiously there.

'Stapleton is not here,' Marcus said shortly, fighting to keep his voice neutral. Whatever past conflicts lay between himself and Captain Kirke, the last thing he wanted now was trouble.

'We'll take a look,' said one of the soldiers behind Kirke, enthusiastically jumping from his mount, but his leader stopped him with a gesture.

'Now who would be doubting the word of a gentleman like Lord Reresby?' he said. 'But I don't suppose there's any harm in looking around now, is there?'

'Be my guest,' Marcus offered through gritted teeth, 'but I wonder at the sheer extravagance that could employ such a large contingent of soldiers to check on one house for one rebel.'

'It is necessary with a house and grounds of this size.'

'You will be wasting your time. You will not find Stapleton here—or any other rebel, come to that.'

'Nevertheless, my job is to round them up. Harbouring a rebel is itself high treason, and it is important that people here in the West Country realise just how dreadful the consequences of such behaviour is likely to be. I have a duty to investigate, you understand.' Turning to his men, his voice rang out in tones of authority for them to get on with the search and to leave no stone unturned.

Catherine released a sigh of relief when he went with them, noticing that he made straight for the stables. Clearly Mr Fenton had told him where to look. Overcome by a fit of trembling, she closed her eyes. Though she was thinking and functioning, she was still in shock.

'I don't like Captain Kirke,' she uttered in a low voice.

'You are not alone in that,' George murmured, having dismounted and come to stand beside them.

Marcus looked down at his wife. He hadn't missed the flare of temper in her eyes, or the fright when Kirke had addressed her. Even though she had borne his insult with a touching dignity that had earned his admiration, her fear had been almost palpable. Sensing her distress was almost more than he could bear, arousing in him a sudden need to protect. Taking her hand, he drew her to his side and looked at George Stanhope.

'I am surprised to see you here with Kirke, George,' he remarked.

'Under ordinary circumstances I would not be—I abhor the man. He is a conceited braggart who has little regard for honour or human life.'

Marcus's mouth twisted, and presently he said under his breath, 'You forget that I know him, George—I know Kirke better than most.'

'Then you will know that I am right. When I heard he was coming here, I took the opportunity to accompany him so I could warn you.'

'There are enough soldiers to search the whole of Somerset,' Catherine whispered. 'I am baffled as to why. Something else is afoot. I can feel it.'

Marcus frowned. 'You look concerned, George. What is it you have to warn us against?'

'I neither know nor care whether Stapleton is here or not, that is your affair. My anxiety is for your wife—and it has increased considerably since Mr Fenton was apprehended. He was always suspected of being involved in The Rye House Plot and successfully evaded the clutches of the Government in the summer of '83. All four of the leading Republicans in that plot have been active in the planning of this rebellion in Holland and have escaped from Sedgemoor. Kirke has been trying to persuade Fenton to turn King's evidence, promising him a pardon if he informs on his fellow rebels.'

'And has he?' Catherine asked quietly.

'No.' He looked at the young woman's ashen face. 'But he has divulged information that may be dangerous for you, Catherine—about your father. I have not been made privy to that information, but I know it is of a serious nature.'

'How serious?' Marcus asked.

'Serious enough for me to advise you to leave Saxton Court as quickly as possible. While Kirke is in Somerset, go to London, anywhere, just as long as you leave. It matters not one iota that Catherine is your wife, Marcus. I fear Kirke may take her to Taunton for questioning.'

Catherine felt cold and sick and a terrible panic, and for the first time a sense of fear for herself. A feeling of genuine terror jarred through her. She looked blindly at her husband, groping for his arm and gripping it as though to steady herself. 'No—it's not possible!' she uttered in a breathless whisper. 'He wouldn't.'

The words were barely audible, but the horror in them was unmistakable and it shocked Marcus into putting his arm about her trembling shoulders and drawing her close.

'Don't underestimate him, Catherine,' George remarked sharply. 'Kirke is not a man to be trifled with.'

'But what can Mr Fenton have told him? I have done nothing wrong.'

'The mere fact that you are Henry Barrington's daughter—a staunch Republican who was constantly scheming to topple the King, a man whose very name is anathema to any royalist as fervent as Captain Kirke—and also your close association with Harry Stapleton are enough. You are involved by association.'

'Was the information extracted from Fenton under torture?' Marcus asked.

'No. It was freely given.'

'Which proves my point. It is all part of Fenton's revenge. But what would Kirke hope to achieve by arresting Catherine?'

'It will give him considerable satisfaction. Not only is your wife Barrington's daughter, she is also one of the few persons of quality he suspects of assisting one of Monmouth's rebels, and therefore ripe to be made an example of. Nothing will bring the gravity of the crime against the King home more quickly than the arrest of a lady of quality.'

Marcus's eyes were bitter. 'And with Fenton's vindictiveness, and Kirke's zeal, my wife's fate is sealed.'

'I believe the normal punishment for a woman convicted of high treason and found guilty is to be burned at the stake,' Catherine whispered, unable to keep her voice from trembling.

Marcus's arm tightened around her. 'Fear not, Catherine. It will not come to that.' Seeing some of the soldiers returning from the stables, he gripped George's arm in a gesture of gratitude. 'I appreciate the risk you have taken by making me aware of this, George,' he said in a low voice. 'I shall take heed.'

'Do so—and quickly.' His face hard, George strode off to join Captain Kirke.

Catherine stepped away from Marcus, seeing his stony profile and eyes that stared straight ahead. 'I'm afraid,' she said quietly. 'This place is a terrible one to be at this time. It's impossible to go anywhere—with soldiers crawling all over the countryside like ants in their search for rebels. Taunton—if the servants' gossip is true, and I believe it is now that I have met the infamous Captain Kirke—resembles a charnel house, and smallpox is rife among the prisoners. I fear what he will do, and I fear for Harry. What is to become of him? How can he possibly escape? I can think of little else but his mortal danger.'

The catch in her voice was so touching and tragic that Marcus was moved in spite of himself. He felt the weight of her misery, and if any tiniest bit of anger remained because of her continuing devotion to Harry, it immediately vanished at the sight of her tear-bright eyes. Unable to keep her at arm's length a moment longer, once again he gathered her to him like an infant, stroking her hair, thinking how well her body fitted into his arms.

'It's all right,' he soothed. 'We'll think of something. George is right. We will have to think about leaving Saxton Court.'

The soldiers searched the house and grounds thoroughly but were unable to locate any concealed fugitives. Not until Captain Kirke was mounting his horse did Marcus enquire, 'What will happen to Fenton?'

'There are serious charges against him. He was one of the men responsible for planning the rebellion and raising men to fight for Monmouth. He will not be left in prison to await his fate for long. There is no need for a trial. He will hang.'

As Kirke was about to ride away he turned to Marcus once again, delivering his parting salvo with a smirk and a fervent gleam in his eyes. 'Oh, and one more thing, Lord Reresby. You may not yet know it, but a cavalcade of lawyers, judges and their attendants, led by the Lord Chief Justice, Lord Jeffreys, is on its way to the West Country to dispense the King's justice. Lord Jeffreys has been given a special commission to try the rebels at the next assizes. I have rounded up sufficient to keep him and his helpers busy for months. The trials will begin in Dorchester.'

Even when Captain Kirke and his soldiers had ridden away, Marcus's expression did not ease. His face was drawn tight at what Kirke had disclosed.

'What do you know of Lord Jeffreys, Marcus? Is he a fair man.'

'Intensely loyal to his Majesty, Lord Jeffreys vents his rage on all who seek to disturb the security of the monarchy. He has no love for Dissenters or rebels. The news of his appointment will do little to cheer the prisoners in the gaols awaiting their fate. With over a thousand awaiting trial, his task will be formidable.'

'Thank God they didn't find Harry,' Catherine whispered, her face white and set. 'If they had, I'm certain Captain Kirke would have had him flogged and hanged before the day is out.'

At the fear clouding her eyes, Marcus reached out and took her hands, finding them cold and trembling. 'Everything will be all right. He is safe for the moment, and so are you, but for how long? It is wise to be careful.'

Dropping her hands, he stared rigidly at the backs of the departing soldiers. Catherine watched as he lifted one hand and massaged the taut muscles in his neck, his expression becoming darker and more ominous as his mind went over what had just occurred. He was deeply troubled, Catherine could see that, and naturally so, all things considered. Weren't things difficult enough between them, without the added responsibility of hiding a rebel on his property and the possibility of having his wife arrested? In a desperate attempt to make things right between them, she moved closer to his side.

'I'm sorry about all this, Marcus. If I could spirit Harry away, believe me, I would.'

He turned his head and looked down at her, barely unconcealed doubt clouding his dark eyes. 'Would you, Catherine? Would you really?'

'Yes. Yes, I would. There was a time, not so long ago, when I could never have imagined being close to any other man but Harry. But times and emotions change—and they have changed me. When will you realise that I no longer love him? Haven't you felt, during that last night we spent together, that I belong to you?'

Marcus's shoulders stiffened and his jaw hardened as he coldly rejected the memory. 'I would be grateful not to be reminded of that occasion just now, Catherine.'

'Why not? Are you ashamed of the way you behaved? Be honest with me, Marcus. I'm not ashamed. I was glad it happened, and it was in the hope of every night to be like that one that I was glad when your time with the army was at an end.' She slipped an arm around his neck and pressed against him, distracted by her emotions, and longing to communicate this torment that possessed her to him.

Marcus tried hard to shove her away with hands that secretly asked nothing better than to hold her. She had taken the first step toward a reconciliation, and she expected him to take the next one, which, while ever Harry Stapleton remained at Saxton Court, he found difficult. He was ashamed of his own discomfort, for he could not shake off his remorse at having destroyed what had existed between Harry and Catherine. He also suspected that deep down Catherine still harboured tender thoughts for him, that she still wanted him, and he could not bear to imagine forcing himself on her while she was thinking of someone else.

'Please listen to me,' she pleaded fervently, gripping his arm. 'I find it hard to see myself as I used to be—living my life believing Harry would be a part of it for ever. That was another lifetime. Then I was somebody else. Having discovered this life with you here at Saxton Court, I cannot conceive of anything different. But now, suddenly, with this awful rebellion, my life is different, cruelly so. I want to help Harry, there is no question of that, but I also want you.'

Gazing down at her upturned face, Marcus caught her shoulders in a hard grip. 'I am touched by what you say, Catherine, and more than anything I want to believe you. In the beginning I did wonder how you could ever respect me as a wife should— a man who had sworn vengeance on your father, and yet when I made love to you and felt your response, I hoped you had forgotten my legitimate feud in the passion I aroused in you.'

'During the time I have been at Saxton Court, I have gained a deeper understanding of why you married me. My attitude to you has gradually become more sympathetic and my thoughts more favourable towards you, Marcus. Not only that, I can forgive the implacable hatred you felt for my father. Perhaps, in your place, I would have felt the same. But I really don't understand you sometimes. In the short time I have known you, you have gone from enemy to friend, to loving husband, and then to someone indifferent.'

His dark eyes slid over her face, trapping her in their burning gaze. 'What man could be indifferent to you? One must either love you to distraction or want to strangle you.'

'And what would you like to do to me, Marcus? Tell me.'

The sudden noise of a carriage coming up the drive interrupted them. Catherine would never know what he would have said. As abruptly as he had caught her to him, he pushed her away.

Chapter Ten

In no mood for company, Marcus was about to turn away as the heavy coach lumbered up the drive. However, when it came to a halt, he was pleasantly surprised when Roger emerged. 'Roger! I thought you were still in London. Is Elizabeth with you?'

'No. She's content to remain in London while all this upheaval is going on.'

'You're right, it's the best place for her at this time. She is well, I hope?'

'Aye, she is, and the children. I'm relieved that you survived Sedgemoor, Marcus. We heard about it in London—dreadful business.'

Marcus nodded. 'Sadly Dickon didn't make it.'

'Then I'm sorry to hear it,' Roger said with sympathy. 'Fine young man. Gave you loyal service.'

Putting on a bright smile, Catherine faced Roger, prepared to play the congenial hostess with guileless warmth despite her inner torment. 'It's good to see you, Roger. You will share a meal with us?'

Affecting a fine, courtly bow, Roger took her hand and bent over it. 'Thank you, my dear, I accept gladly.' He studied her face. 'It's good to see you, too, Catherine—although I have to say you are looking somewhat peaky. Why don't you join Elizabeth in London? The city's a suitable haven from these worrying times—put some colour back into your cheeks.'

'I'm fine, Roger, truly.' Catherine had already decided not to mention George's warning. She'd leave that to Marcus, when he had decided what they must do for the best.

'Well, if you say so. I came down here to check on the house—make sure it hasn't been broken into in our absence—and to see you, Marcus.' His pleasant countenance became set in sober lines. 'I have news, and I wanted to tell you myself.'

Marcus nodded, his expression serious, knowing why he had come. 'Come inside.'

'I passed a troop of horse on the road. I saw George was with them. Trouble?'

'You might say that. They're searching for rebels—one in particular.'

'Anyone I know?'

'Harry,' Catherine said softly, closing the door of the salon. 'Harry Stapleton.'

The name stopped Roger in his tracks. He stared at Catherine in astonishment. 'Young Stapleton? Is he here?' He held up his hand to stop her words. 'No, do not tell me anything you would rather not,' he said quickly.

'It makes no matter. I know I can trust you. Stapleton is here,' Marcus divulged quietly. 'The soldiers' search revealed nothing, so he remains safe and secure for now. The same cannot be said of Fenton. He is in Taunton gaol.'

'Is he, indeed?' Roger muttered, sitting in the chair indicated by Marcus, his eyebrows drawn together in a frown. 'Well, I am hardly surprised. He's been discussing rebellion ever since James became King—and before that.'

'Tell me.' Marcus handed Roger a much-needed brandy.

After taking a healthy draught, Roger glanced to where Catherine perched uneasily on the edge of her chair facing them both.

'It's all right, Roger. Feel free to speak in front of Catherine.' Meeting his wife's questioning look, Marcus explained, 'I asked Roger to make certain enquiries regarding Fenton while he was in London, to see if he could find out what he was doing around the time my father was murdered. I'm hoping you have been successful, Roger.'

Roger's expression became grave. 'I have discovered enough to see Mr Fenton hanged.'

'Nothing would please me more,' Marcus agreed. 'Please continue, George.'

'As a committed Republican, twenty-five years of monarchy has not changed Mr Fenton's nature. The man's been plotting against successive governments since the Commonwealth. In my opinion, Mr Fenton is a fanatic dedicated to the destruction of the monarchy. He is a quietly active and extremely rebellious subject—but despite this, he is clever, and no one has ever been able to lay anything on him. In fact, Marcus, your Mr Fenton seems to have led a charmed life.'

'Until now, it would seem,' Marcus commented drily.

'I'm only surprised he didn't leave Somerset when he had the chance. He always distrusted Monmouth, suspecting him of double-dealing after The Rye House Plot, and also suspecting him of seeking his uncle's crown—an ambition which, of course, is anathema to the committed Republican. He did not think the time was right for a rebellion, but when it went ahead, he was willing enough to be in the thick of the scheming.'

'You said you have news, Roger. How close was Henry Barrington to Fenton?'

'They were both members of a movement to overthrow the King—though I believe their association was often volatile.

When your father appointed Mr Fenton as his bailiff, he became concerned that he spent some considerable time in the company of John Trenchard—as you know, he was the man charged by The Rye House Plotters to raise the men of the West Country to join Monmouth.'

Marcus nodded slowly. 'I am aware of that. He left the country before the rebellion.'

'Thwarted in their attempts to discover either arms or rebels, the local loyalists redoubled their persecution of the Dissenters. As a Justice of the Peace, and ably assisted by paid informers, your father raided conventicles, fining or imprisoning those they found attending them. Mr Fenton was at one such meeting. You can imagine your father's shock and his feeling of betrayal by a man he himself had placed in a position of trust on his estate. What happened afterwards is not known exactly, only that your father immediately left for London and Mr Fenton went home to his family—or so it was thought at the time.'

'That was what he told everyone and no one, including myself, had any reason to doubt him.'

'Why should you? Being away from home for such long periods, you didn't know the man from Adam. However, I have it on good authority from a man by the name of Albert Watkins, also a Republican and an acquaintance of Mr Fenton—although he had nothing but ill to say of him—that Mr Fenton did not visit his home and went instead to Riverside House to meet with Henry Barrington.' He paused and glanced at Catherine. 'I'm sorry, my dear, but this will be painful for you, I know.'

'My father was a man of considerable intelligence and strong character, and a man of that stamp is wholly committed to his beliefs, even if those beliefs go against the general rule of things. No matter what his feelings were for me, I always admired him for that. I am aware that he was involved in The Rye House Plot to murder King Charles and his brother—and probably others before that, so nothing you say will surprise me. I want a Protestant King as much as anyone else, but I cannot condone the murdering of a Catholic King. There has to be another less brutal way to depose a monarch. Whatever crime my father committed I want to know about it, so pray continue, Roger.'

'Well, if you say so. Fenton and Barrington went to London together and arrived at your father's house in Westminster late one night, Marcus.'

'And Mr Watkins? Did he meet with Fenton at this time?'

'At the King's Head Tavern in Fleet Street, where Fenton dropped in before leaving for Somerset.'

Marcus's face darkened and his voice lost its warmth. 'It was at the King's Head where I fleeced Barrington of everything he owned. I recall how uneasy he was, and I also recall seeing a shadowy figure hovering briefly in the doorway. I am beginning to suspect that it was Fenton who bore witness to events that night, and that Barrington was aware of his presence, but dare not speak out for fear of meeting the same fate as my father. Do you know why Fenton went to Riverside House instead of going directly to London?'

'Your father had written evidence—manuscripts and letters— sent to Fenton from a fellow conspirator in Holland, and found at Fenton's meeting place when it was searched. Upon examination they were found to contain several treasonable passages concerning The Rye House Plot that would prove valid in a court of law. The Government may have suspected Fenton as being involved in that particular plot, but your father clearly did not, otherwise he would never have employed him in the first place.'

'From my own enquiries made after my father was killed, I knew of these papers' existence and that they incriminated Barrington,' Marcus told him. 'The other name remained a mystery to me until now. You have done well, Roger.'

'Those letters were clear proof that Fenton and Henry Barrington were two of the perpetrators in The Rye House Plot who had not been apprehended and were still at liberty in England. At the time Barrington was arrested on suspicion of being connected, but he managed to talk his way out of trouble, assuring his interrogators that the names of leading Republicans written in his pocket book were for remembrance of business he had to do and meant nothing more. A witness did come forward when the plot was discovered to speak against Barrington, but his testimony was weak and thrown out. As you know, the prosecution must produce two witnesses to sustain a charge of treason.

'Your father seized upon what he had found, to be employed, in effect, as a second witness, and he was taking his evidence to the King. However, we must not forget that his grievance was with Fenton and not Barrington, but he must have known that he, too, would be arrested. Sadly your father was killed before he could present his evidence, and as far as I know no trace of any incriminating manuscripts or letters was found.'

'Fenton will have found and destroyed them.'

'Afterwards he returned to Saxton Court and calmly resumed his position as bailiff as if nothing untoward had happened. If your father had dismissed him from his post before leaving for London no one knew of it. The fact that there was no trace of Fenton's presence in London did strengthen the belief that he was actually visiting his family—besides, no one had reason to question him about your father's murder or to doubt his alibi. He was never a suspect.'

'Mr Fenton would appear remarkably adept at concealing his tracks.'

'All the same, after listening to what your father's manservant, who had been at his house in London at the time, had to say when I managed to track him down in Southwark, it appears that Mr Fenton and Henry Barrington called and did not stay more than a few minutes.'

'But long enough to commit the crime. And the servant? Did he see anything suspicious?'

'No, but as they left, Barrington was greatly agitated and muttering, "You should not have done it. There must have been another way." Mr Fenton appeared angry and kept telling him to shut his mouth.'

'Why did the servant not reveal this at the time?'

'Fenton threatened him. He feared for his life and the lives of his entire family.'

'I see. You have done well, Roger.'

'Of course the man had to be bribed to disclose what he knew.'

'You will be reimbursed.'

'No, indeed. It was worth every penny.' Stretching his legs out in front of him, he heaved a laborious sigh. 'Don't forget I was doing it for Elizabeth, too. She suffered as you did when your father was murdered.'

'I know. They were always close. Are you certain your information was correct?'

'I am willing to admit that I had my doubts initially, since the information was divulged following a generous bribe, but, yes, it was definite and serious. I believed it. The man was a loyal servant to your father.'

'Do you think Fenton did it, Roger?'

'I am certain of it. I have learnt much about Mr Fenton in the Republican clubs, where I have been spying quite unblushingly—and talking at length with Mr Watkins, while ostensibly engaged in partaking of the evil drink and giving everyone the impression that I am about to change my politics and become a Republican.'

Marcus smiled slightly. 'And I suppose it did not occur to you that you might be arrested?'

'That was why I came down here as soon as I had what I wanted. But if you want to hear more, for pity's sake give me another glass of your excellent brandy and feed me. I am parched and dying of hunger.'

Immediately Catherine rose. 'Forgive me, Roger, I am forgetting my manners. I shall see to it at once.' She hurried from the room to give orders.

Roger sat back and looked hard at his brother-in-law. 'So, how is Catherine bearing up?'

'As well as she is able, considering the circumstances.'

'And Stapleton? He is here?'

'Yes, but not a word, Roger. It could mean death for us all if it is discovered we are harbouring a fugitive—especially one who was close to Monmouth. Apart from myself and Catherine, Alice and Archie, no one has any idea he is here. I want it to remain that way until I've decided what to do. Are you aware that Lord Jeffreys is on his way to the West Country to dispense the King's justice?'

'I am—and I can only pity the miserable devils awaiting trial.'

'They are no different from you and I, Roger. My own loyalties are at war within me. I have served the King and have done my duty loyally—yet the King is a Catholic and as such threatens the peace of Protestant England. For a long time now these two sides have tormented me and refuse to rub along together. If only it can be resolved one way or the other without further bloodshed.'

'I couldn't agree more, but what is to be done?'

When Roger fell silent and sat savouring his brandy, Marcus stared off into space for some time, drumming his fingers on the table top and thinking at a furious rate. Finally, he said, 'For my part, I think I've known for so long that it was Fenton who killed my father. Yet even now, I find it hard to believe that a man of such diabolical cunning could have allowed himself to be caught.'

'What will you do now?'

'Leave for London.'

Roger stared at him in amazement. 'Is there a reason for this?'

Marcus told him of George's warning and the threat to Catherine, and that because he feared she would be arrested, even though as yet there was no charge against her, he felt she would be safer in London. Roger agreed.

'As you well know, Jeffreys presided over the trials of The Rye House Plotters. The names of all those involved are detested by any royalist as fervid as Lord Jeffreys, and given it was suspected at the time that Henry Barrington was involved in a minor way, yet escaped justice because of insufficient evidence, Jeffreys will remember his name. My advice is that you leave Saxton Court before he gets here.'

'There is just one thing, Roger. Would you mind if Catherine and I imposed on you? The house in Westminster has stood empty these past two years. The servants will have their work cut out making it habitable—in fact, I may decide to sell it.'

'You're more than welcome to stay with us for as long as you like. I intend remaining down here for now—with most of my work force having left to join Monmouth and losing money by the day, I have business to attend to—but I know Elizabeth would love to have you. When do you intend going?'

'As soon as possible, but first I must see Fenton.'

'In gaol? Is that wise? I've heard the gaols are hell holes inhabited by demons and that the prisoners are dying of smallpox.'

Marcus was resolute. 'No matter what the conditions are, Roger, I must see Fenton before Kirke hangs him. I want to hear him confess his guilt, and to do that I must overcome my repugnance I feel at the notion of seeing him again.' He glanced towards the door, seeing that Catherine had returned and must have heard his words. She came towards him and looked at him hard, her eyes very clear.

'You must go—yes, go by all means,' she said slowly. 'I understand why you feel you must…only, please take care. And tell Mr Fenton that I hate him.'

Marcus's mouth curved with irony. 'I think he knows that already.'

'And please be careful of Captain Kirke. Avoid him if you can. I never wish to set eyes on him again.'

'I pray you won't have to.' His tone held an odd note—of tenderness, perhaps, that made Catherine lift her face to his. Marcus drew in a breath. With her hair drawn from her face she looked pale and extremely vulnerable. Something in his chest tightened. Wordlessly he opened his arms, and when she came into them, he could feel her body trembling against his. 'There's nothing to fear, Catherine,' he said gently. 'While ever Harry remains secure, you have no charge to answer and Kirke knows that. He will not come back.'

'How can you be so sure?'

'Because when I've seen Fenton—if his gaolers allow me access to his prison cell—it is my intention that we leave for London immediately. It is clear to me that if we do not leave here, my energy will be spent in tearing myself to bits waiting for Kirke to come to try to arrest you. With Jeffreys on his way, there's no telling what might happen.'

'But what about Harry? We can't leave him here.'

'I don't intend to. I'll think of something.'

She smiled. 'I know you will,' she replied softly. Something caught at her heart, a warming hope that when they were in London and Harry had escaped to Holland, all would be well between them and that they could enjoy each other and become close without restrictions.

* * *

Mid-morning the following day, Marcus rode into Taunton alone. He was too late to speak to Fenton, but not too late to see him hang.

Marcus stood back from the sweaty reek of the crowd to watch the proceedings outside the White Hart Inn. Drummers beat out a dead march, slow and grim. Spectators stood around, quiet, used to the sight of hangings and sickened by them. The day was hot, the air humid and thick with flies. Marcus removed his hat and wiped his forehead. Replacing it, he hoped for a cool breeze. He was morbidly aware of what was to happen. Women and children, some on their fathers' shoulders, craned their necks to see the condemned men.

Suddenly there was a ripple of excitement. Soldiers came, and then the prisoners. A long murmur ran through the crowd, a murmur in which curiosity predominated over pity. There were three of them, their hands bound in front of them. Fenton was the third in line. Marcus stepped back so as to avoid notice. The first man, with white, close-cropped hair and a greasy leather jerkin, looked sick and staggered. The second man, small and disreputable, his eyes wide with terror, his face red and distorted, was a pitiful specimen.

All Marcus's attention became focused on Fenton. He stood straight and seemed surprisingly calm. His hard thin lips were tight, and even on the point of death his arrogance was undiminished. His educated eyes scanned the crowd, as if they searched to gain an advantage.

The hangman placed the noose about the neck of the first man, fixing it tight. Fear choked the breath in his lungs as hemp scorched his flesh. Death came quickly as the neck was grotesquely stretched and cleanly broken. The body swung like a dead weight on a string.

The second man became demented on seeing the first man's reflexive jerk. He began shrieking and threw himself on the

ground. The soldiers of the guard fell on him, the captain of the
guard purple with rage. The crowd roared and surged, and not
until order was restored and the prisoner had been hauled to his
feet and was suspended and jerking beside his fellow rebel, did
everyone realise that the third prisoner had escaped. Immediately pandemonium broke out with soldiers scattering in every
direction, but it was as if Mr Fenton had vanished into thin air.

True to his word, Marcus came up with a solution to the
problem of what to do with Harry. Without a word to Catherine, he enlisted the services of Alice, who, sworn to secrecy,
concocted a black dye for Harry's hair and multicoloured fuzz
that had appeared on his chin, which he had left unshaven during his weeks of hiding. His appearance was completely
changed. What Marcus had in mind was a great risk, but when
he saw Harry with his dark, shoulder-length hair and his youthful face half-covered by a short black beard, wearing new at-
tire, he was confident his plan could work.

Everyone believed the handsome new addition to the household—alias John Oakley, his lordship's new manservant who
had replaced poor Dickon—had arrived from London with Sir
Roger. As soon as he walked into the house, maids paused in
their work to gaze at him with admiration and hopes of future
assignations.

On the morning they were due to depart for London, much
to Marcus's amusement, as he studied her reaction from a dis-
creet distance, Catherine didn't recognise the bearded man as
he went about his duties. There was something about his gait
and the way he carried himself that seemed oddly familiar, but
she was so busy preparing to leave that she thought little of it.
Then, as he was carrying baggage out to the coach, he moved
into the light and she caught the flash of dark blue eyes, and
her own opened wide in astonishment.

'Harry?' she mouthed silently.

Without a word he placed a finger to his lips and went on his way. Immediately Catherine went in search of her husband. Nothing mattered to her at that moment but that Marcus had after all made plans for Harry. Dangerously fascinated by this unexpected, vulnerable side of her enigmatic husband, she knocked on his chamber door. On entering, she found him seated in a chair pulling on his boots.

Marcus looked up when she swept in, noting her high colour and the shining excitement in her eyes. Lowering his head to hide his amusement, he knew only too well what had prompted her to seek him out in his chamber.

'Why, Catherine, you look as if you've seen a ghost.'

'Marcus,' she gasped, her eyes doing a quick flick around the room to make sure he was entirely alone, 'I have just seen Harry—but he looks so different I didn't recognise him immediately. Why didn't you tell me what you intended? Do you not think he will be recognised?'

'Why?' he chuckled. 'If you couldn't see through his disguise, why should anyone else? It's a risk, I know, but I believe he is unlikely to raise suspicion out in the open as my manservant.'

'Oh, Marcus, you are a marvel. It's so kind of you to consider Harry in this way.'

'Kind?' He stood up, his dark eyes mocking her. 'I make no secret of the fact that I want Stapleton off my hands as quickly as possible, and I warn you it was not kindness that made me bring him out of his hiding place. Always remember, Catherine, that I never do anything without a reason, and I always expect something in return.'

Catherine looked at him, and a small, wry smile formed on her lips. 'You always get paid, that's what you mean, isn't it? I know what you expect from me, Marcus, and I have told you that I accept our marriage, that I will not deny you. I have not done so on the two occasions you have come to my bed. It is you that is at fault. Your celibacy is of your own making.'

'Most women in that situation would welcome a cold bed to the unwelcome attention of their husbands.'

'My bed is never cold, Marcus, and neither am I,' she assured him softly, 'as you know.'

A lazy smile tugged at the corner of his mouth. Rubbing his knuckles against her cheek, tenderly he asked, 'Am I to infer from that remark that you actually like having me in your bed?'

Her face turned pink. 'I can imagine the awful damage to your pride if I said no, but, yes, if you really want to know, I do like having you in my bed. I have never forbidden you to touch me. I have always been accessible to you. Little did I realise that you would come to play the reluctant husband. It is no compliment to me. You cannot blame me if I think perhaps that the distance you have placed between us is because you do not find me desirable, that you do not want me anymore.'

Marcus remained unconvinced that what Catherine had once felt for Harry was in the past. He was impatient for the time when the matter of that young man was resolved, when he was out of their lives for good and he could have his wife to himself. His gaze travelled from Catherine's eyes to her lips. 'You are everything a man could ask for in a wife—and more.'

Tilting her head to one side, she smiled mischievously. 'Then I don't suppose,' she said softly, 'that it would do the least bit of good for me to insist that you come to my bed.'

Marcus's lips twitched. 'None whatsoever,' he said lightly, 'unless you are in it.'

'Where else would I be—and you would be most welcome. But now, enough of your seduction, my lord, for since you made Harry your manservant, you will have to get used to seeing him every day. But how will you spirit him out of London?'

'I have connections among the shipping merchants there,

who ply their trade between London and the Continent. There is one who owes me a favour. I am confident he will agree to take Harry on board with no questions asked.'

'I am happy to know that all is not lost. His disguise is perfect. We may get away with it.'

'May?' returned Marcus. 'We shall save him, Catherine.' He cocked one dark eyebrow at her, and she laughed.

'You are right. We shall. I know it,' Catherine echoed in a tone of such ferocious determination that Marcus smiled, delighted to find her showing a touch of her old spirit.

'I did my best—with a little help from Alice.'

'Alice? Do you mean to tell me that she was in on this little subterfuge—and never a word to me?' she remarked with mock indignation. 'Oh, just wait until I see her.'

One corner of his mouth curled up as he glanced at her. 'I couldn't have done it without her. Now, go and get ready. I want to make Wells before nightfall.'

Catherine hurried away to do his bidding, carried away by the new hope that had risen in her with this new turn of events, and to Marcus, his wife's infectious enthusiasm was like a breath of joy.

They left Saxton Court at midday. Since the deprivations of the rebellion had reduced the staff at the house, the demands on Archie and the other male servants had increased. They doubled as gardeners and stable hands, and on this occasion, for Archie and two others, coachmen. A rather apprehensive Harry travelled up front with Archie. Marcus and Catherine were alone in the coach. Alice and two maids followed on behind with most of the baggage.

'I do not wish to delay any longer,' Marcus said as he assisted Catherine up into the spacious conveyance with its domed roof. 'I'm in a hurry to put as much distance as possible between us and Taunton.'

Relieved to be heading for London at last, leaning his head against the upholstery, Marcus had plenty of time to mull over recent events during the journey. He had not seen Captain Kirke since he had come to Saxton Court that day, and nor had he heard what had become of Fenton. Roger had promised to keep an eye on things while he was absent, and also to keep him informed if he should hear anything concerning Fenton.

Settling herself opposite, Catherine bowed her head, hoping to hide her amusement. How she liked him to display such frantic anxiety on her behalf. Across from her, he stretched his legs out and stared out of the window as the coach set off, leaving a whirling cloud of dust in its wake.

They were apprehended from time to time by soldiers in search of rebels, who hardly gave the dark-haired, good-looking young man on the driver's seat a second glance, since he was a member of Lord Reresby's household and therefore beyond suspicion. The roads were deplorable, making the occupants of the coaches feel as if they were inside perpetual motion machines; the inns they stopped at for the night tolerable; and apart from these discomforts, the journey was uneventful.

At first, on finding herself alone with her husband for long periods and delighting at this closeness, Catherine's heart began to beat faster, but the tedium of the time they were confined to the coach, and Harry's constant presence, made Marcus frustrated and irritable. His ill humour, all his grievances, discord and unpleasant memories were reasserted.

To Catherine, his stilted conversation punctuated with long silences became unbearable and insulting. There was nothing lover-like in his look or his tone, and brought instantly down to earth from her dreaming heights, she could not repress a sigh. Marcus was seated a little sideways, his legs negligently stretched out in front of him. Having discarded his waistcoat and neckcloth on account of the heat, his white linen shirt was open at the neck to reveal a firm, strongly muscled throat. A lock of dark hair had fallen forward over his brow.

'Why do you sit with me if you can find nothing interesting to say to me?'

'Because it happens to be more comfortable than sitting on top,' he answered coolly.

'And because the company is better?'

'Infinitely.'

The curtness in his voice stung Catherine to reply with sarcasm, 'I am flattered.'

'Don't be.'

She sighed. 'Marcus, this is difficult for you, I know, with Harry's constant attendance. You really do dislike him, don't you?'

'On the contrary, which makes this more difficult for me. He believes he has right on his side, and I admire him for it. I want to despise him, but I can't.'

'And do you still condemn me for befriending him at his time of need, when I have made my feelings where Harry is concerned plain to you?'

'No. I would have done the same. But your concern for Stapleton, whom you profess now fills such a negligible place in your life, I find irritating to say the least.'

And so a strange sort of existence began for the two of them and they found they had very little to say to each other. Impatient for this interminable journey to be over, Catherine tried hard not to let her disappointment show as Marcus sat with his lean face turned away, absorbed in the passing scenery, as if to find there the answer to the problem that made his finely drawn face look sterner than ever and brought that dark, brooding look into his eyes.

Being constantly in the company of Marcus or Alice, Catherine had scant opportunity to speak to Harry alone, and when she did she was careful what she said about her life with Marcus. She didn't wish to hurt him by what she might say so she always turned the conversation around to other things.

When the journey was almost over and they had stopped to eat at a rambling, ivy-covered inn, seeing that Marcus seemed to want to linger over his ale, Catherine wandered outside to wait, content to sit on a wooden bench and watch the hostlers run forward to take charge of another coach that had pulled into the inn yard. The air was warm and fragrant with the scent of summer flowers, the pale blue sky bright with sunshine. Small fleecy clouds, pursued by a strong breeze, skittered across like playful lambs.

Seeing her standing alone, Harry walked over to her and sat beside her. She looked at him and smiled. 'It won't be long now, Harry. The next stop is London. You must be relieved that the journey is almost over.'

'I am—although the journey would have been more bearable had I been able to speak to you occasionally. Your husband has his eyes strictly upon us at all times.'

'The situation is difficult for him, Harry. He is finding it hard. However, I'm glad he decided to help you. It means a lot to me.'

'I'm grateful for your husband's show of kindness. Where I am concerned he has acted most honourably, when he could easily have handed me over to Kirke. He must love you very much, Catherine.' When Catherine flushed and averted her eyes, he placed his finger gently beneath her chin and turned her face back to his. 'What's wrong? I know there's something. I could always tell. Has he not told you that he loves you? Is that why you're hurting?'

'I never know what Marcus is feeling from one minute to the next. His moods are so varied.'

'Is that why you love him?' Harry was unable to hide the pain in his eyes.

'Yes, I do love him, Harry, and now that I realise it I feel as though I've betrayed you yet again.'

'Don't feel like that. There's no need. I know exactly how you feel,' he said gently. 'I am willing to gamble that if you left him and came with me to Holland, I would not be able to make you forget him. You see, I no longer have any false hope. In the beginning you were put in an impossible situation, and for that you resented him and ran away with me to The Hague to avoid him. I know that I resented him myself for taking you away from me, but now I have got to know him better, I no longer feel that way.'

Catherine laid her hand over his on the bench. 'Oh, Harry, I'm glad. You are my dear friend,' she whispered brokenly, 'and I will love you for ever, but always as my friend—and I thank you for being there for me in the past, and for being all the things you are. My life is with Marcus now, I know that, and no matter what he has done, he is a good man.'

'I know. He's also a proud man. It cannot be easy having me along. I suspect he's not sure of your feelings for him and is unsure as to whether or not you are still in love with me. Have you told him how you feel about him?'

Catherine shook her head. 'No.'

Seeing Marcus emerge from the inn, Harry stood up. Before he left her, he said softly, 'It won't be him who declares his love first.'

Catherine turned away. She knew Harry was right.

Arriving on the outskirts of London, Catherine looked through the window at the passing scenery with little interest. At this time England basked in its summer glory and the countryside had been a delight. The same could not be said of this sprawling metropolis. Out of the hubbub of sound beyond the window came the clear, high-pitched cries of street vendors plying their trades, their sing-song voices echoing inside the coach. Never having been a lover of the city, already Catherine felt stifled, hot and confined and missed the calm and clean fresh air of the country, but she was glad the long journey was almost over.

The coach halted in front of the Danbys' town house in one of the fashionable new squares to the north of St James's Palace, along the road that led to the village of Knightsbridge. Having observed the coach come to a halt in the street and her brother climb out, Elizabeth was already coming down the stairs to the cool dim hall to which they were admitted by a footman. A smile of welcome lifted the corners of her mouth.

'Why,' she remarked, embracing Catherine, 'you look different—rejuvenated. What has happened to you?'

Catherine found herself blushing. Alice was constantly pointing out that her pregnancy was beginning to show in her eyes and the healthy bloom her skin had acquired, as well as her slightly thickening waist line. If Elizabeth could see this, why couldn't Marcus? she thought despondently.

'I am surprised you should say that, Elizabeth, since the journey seemed interminable and being confined to the coach for such long periods must have made me look quite wan. I only hope the London air is as healthy as the Somerset air.'

'I hope so too. I have arranged which room you shall have, and Marcus shall have the one immediately next to yours. There is a connecting door, which you will find convenient.'

'That is thoughtful of you,' Catherine said, glancing directly at her husband, a glint of amusement in her eyes. 'We like to be close.' She was relieved to see that in place of the cool animosity that had marked his mood of late, Marcus's expression had softened somewhat. There was an answering spark in his eyes when they rested on her face, and one corner of his mouth lifted lazily in a smile. Her stomach clenched at the thought that everything might be all right between them now they had reached London.

'Naturally,' Elizabeth said airily, not having the slightest inclination that things were not as they should be between her brother and his wife. 'I'm so glad you decided to come to London, and you can stay with us as long as you like. The house is quiet this afternoon—the children's nurse has taken them into the park to run off some of their energy. It's complete bliss. They'll be back at any time, so we must make the most of it. Come into the salon and I'll have some refreshment brought in. I want to hear all about what is happening in Taunton.'

'You must be missing Roger,' Marcus said, following his sister into the sunlit salon, feeling his spirits beginning to lighten now the journey was over.

'I am, but he has business to take care of—and you know how immersed Roger always is in his work. He appears to have little interest in anything else just now. It's all very worrying with half the workers gone. Taunton is in upheaval, I believe.'

'The whole of the West Country is in upheaval, Elizabeth. It's not the place to be just now, which is why we decided to come to London. However, I do not intend imposing on you longer than is necessary. I shall be taking a look at the house in Westminster tomorrow,' Marcus said.

'You were thinking of selling it, as I recall,' Elizabeth remarked, seating herself beside Catherine on the sofa.

'I was. I'm still undecided. It reminds me too much of what happened there. I'll take Catherine with me—see what she thinks to the place.'

'Well, if you decided not to sell, after two years it will need more than a spring clean and will not be made habitable overnight.'

'I'm sure you're right. I would go and take a look later today, but there is something I have to take care of first.'

Meeting her husband's hard gaze, Catherine knew this had something to do with Harry. Like him, this was one problem she wanted resolved as quickly as possible.

The following afternoon they journeyed to Westminster. Catherine was surprised when Marcus insisted on Harry accompanying them and queried this.

'According to my plan, I think it best that he stays there,' Marcus answered as the coach jostled with the heavy traffic at Charing Cross. 'A friend of mine—a King's man and an honest man—has a ship sailing for Holland on tomorrow's tide and he's agreed to take Harry.'

'Can he be trusted?'

Marcus's lips curved into an ironic smile. 'I would not have approached him if I thought not. The ports are being watched, but the ship and its captain are well known to the authorities and will not be suspect. Stapleton has to present himself to the captain at first light, as John Oakley. He will be able to slip away from the house in Westminster without arousing suspicion. Besides, I'm uneasy having him stay at Elizabeth's. I have no wish to incriminate her in any way.'

'You haven't told her about Harry?'

'No, and I don't like deceiving her.'

'Of course. You are right. I should have thought of that. Still, he will not have long to wait before he can leave. I only hope he makes the crossing without mishap.'

'The sooner he leaves the better.' Marcus smiled sardonically as he regarded his wife. 'And leaves me to my amorous devices.'

At that pronouncement, Catherine's head rose, and she looked her husband squarely in the eye. 'Don't worry. I am sure everything will go in strict accordance to your wishes. Does that make you happy?'

For answer, he leaned towards her and, taking her shoulders, pulled her towards him, placing his lips on hers. 'Happier than you can ever imagine,' he murmured between kisses. 'Enough time has been wasted. When I have you to myself I shall expect nothing less than total and absolute submission.'

'I'll give you all your heart desires,' she whispered softly. 'Willingly.'

The house in Westminster was old. It had been bought by Marcus's grandfather when politicians and noblemen had wanted to live close to Whitehall and the Court. The entrance presented a dismal sight. It stood silent, lonely and neglected, contrasting strongly with its opulent, impressive neighbours. Rampant weeds sprouted from between gaps in the paving stones, and ivy had begun to climb the walls. Catherine stood back and Harry hung back even further as Marcus inserted a heavy key into the lock. He was prepared to find the lock rusty and the key difficult to turn, but it turned smoothly.

'How odd,' Marcus remarked, a puzzled frown creasing his brow. 'The lock has been oiled recently. I wonder who can have done it?'

'Perhaps Elizabeth arranged for it to be done.'

'Apart from removing several of Father's personal possessions and items of value from the house for safe keeping at the time of his death, she told me she hasn't been near the place.'

The door opened without the least resistance, the noise of Marcus's booted feet as he stepped into the hall awaking the sleeping echoes of the old house. He turned and took Catherine's hand.

'Come, shall we go in?'

Strangely reluctant to enter the house, Catherine followed him inside and looked around. For no reason she could name, the house raised the hairs on the back of her neck. Despite the warmth outside, the house was cold. For a moment she stood looking round, vividly aware in some inner part of herself that this was where Marcus's father had met a vicious death. An icy draught coming from an open door made her shiver and she clutched Marcus's hand a little tighter. The dark panelled entrance hall was large, the furniture covered in dust, the wall hangings drab. It was readily apparent that two years had passed without the care and attention of servants in the house. It would need a magic wand to give it new life, but at least it gave no sign of having been damaged by marauders or thieves.

As they went from room to room there were pathetic reminders of the family that had lived there—books, trinkets, a sewing basket. Pressing on, they climbed the stairs to the bedchambers while Harry went to inspect the domestic quarters. Marcus seemed to be avoiding a closed, heavy oak door, leaving it until last. When he finally opened it he stood on the threshold, seeming reluctant to enter. From his side, Catherine saw the room was a small study. It smelled musty and was cold and dank, despite the warmth of the day.

'What is it, Marcus?' she asked, her voice hardly above a whisper.

'This was the room where my father was murdered,' he said tonelessly.

There was a great poignancy in this moment. Suddenly Catherine stiffened as from somewhere within the house a floorboard creaked and what sounded like a footfall from the floor above. They looked at each other.

'Is there someone else in the house?' Catherine asked, her voice barely audible. 'It can't be Harry because we left him downstairs.'

'There shouldn't be, but I'll go and see.'

Left alone, Catherine had the strangest feeling that this silent, desolate house, where Marcus's father had been murdered, was none the less alive with a murky life of its own and that something threatening stalked the darkness. She had an urge to turn and run from it, to close the doors that had opened with such suspicious ease. Her eyes returned to the room, and she wondered where the unfortunate man had died. With hesitant steps she moved in further, her eyes sliding over the open news-sheet on the desk. Trailing her fingers absently over the surface, she cast her eyes down. There was no bloodstain on the carpet, nothing to suggest that a brutal act had been committed there, only a cold silence that seemed to instil itself inside her, to follow her when she backed away and turned to go in search of her husband. She found him on the landing at the top of the stairs.

'There's no one here,' he said, his expression telling her he was not absolutely convinced. 'It must have been a cat or a rat.'

Catherine shivered. 'Or just the house creaking. Is the house haunted, do you think?'

'Not to my knowledge. Why, are you afraid of spirits?'

'Ghosts? They don't pose a threat. Only people do that.'

'Then perhaps we do have a ghost in the house—a living ghost.'

'What do you mean?'

'That someone hides here. There are secret hiding places, which had been constructed in many large old houses in town and country to hide priests and those fleeing persecution in the past. You must have had some of your own at Riverside House.'

'Yes, two that I know of. It is possible, I suppose, that someone is hiding—but who would want to?'

'Some homeless wretch, someone who knows the house is empty.' Some instinct was telling Marcus that he was right. He had been conscious of a presence in the house from the moment he had pushed the door open. He recalled the creaking floorboard, the footfall from up above. He had told Catherine that it was probably a cat or a rat—but was it? There was some mystery here he was determined to get to the bottom of.

'Shall we search?' Catherine asked, her look telling him that she hoped he wouldn't.

'The hiding places could be anywhere—in the attics, the cellars, behind panelling.'

'In that case the search could take a long time. At all events, they need to come out some time for food and water. Do you want to live here, Marcus?'

He looked at her. 'I don't know. I thought I did, but now I'm not sure if I can. Do you like the house?'

It put Catherine in mind of a shrine. 'I can't say,' she answered, not wishing to give offence at this early stage by telling him that she didn't like the house in the least. Time enough to voice her opinion when she was away from this place.

Marcus gave her a rueful smile. 'The atmosphere leaves a lot to be desired when the house is empty like this. But we mustn't be foolish or fanciful. My rational mind tells me there is nothing to fear.'

'I'm sure you are right. It's very fine, very attractive, yet I feel a sadness here—as if the house has lost its soul.'

Marcus glanced towards the study. 'My father loved this house. He was its soul.'

'It means a lot to you, doesn't it, Marcus?'

'A great deal, but I don't know if I could live here. However, I would like it restored to the state in which it was before my father died, and then decide.'

'Your father is dead, Marcus. You cannot recreate the past.' She slipped her arm in his. 'Come. Let's go and find Harry. We can discuss this later with Elizabeth.'

Catherine didn't relish the prospect of saying goodbye to Harry, but it was time, and for the best. No longer would she dream and yearn for the love of her childhood, but embrace a new life with her husband, the man she now loved above any other, and not until they were free of Harry's presence would they be able to emerge from the nightmare that had overtaken them with the Duke of Monmouth's arrival in Somerset and its aftermath. Nevertheless her throat was suddenly stopped with tears as she faced Harry; as she looked at his familiar features, a sweet wave of memories flowed between them.

'I pray that God keeps you safe, Harry,' she said with a genuine ache in her heart. 'I shall miss you. More than I can say.'

'And I you, Catherine, but you are a married woman now—the wife of a good man.' Turning his head, he looked across the hall and met the eyes of the man who had usurped him in Catherine's affections and befriended him. 'Your place is with your husband. I hope he knows how fortunate he is.'

'What will you do when you reach Holland?'

'I have friends there I will stay with. I am impatient to leave England and I shall not return until we have shaken off James's rule. There are troubled times ahead, but already the Protestant wind has begun to blow. With the Duke of Monmouth captured, royalists will look towards Prince William and Princess Mary in Holland. I shall work to that end and serve them as best I can.'

There was a solemn expression on Harry's face that made him look extremely sad. Catherine wanted to take one of his long slender hands and press it to her cheek, but those days were gone—and she was acutely aware of Marcus's presence. He stood in the gloom, his face a brooding mask, his eyes two narrow ebony slits between glowering brows. Motionless save for the steady movement of his breathing, he stood with his shoulders resting against the dark panelling, his arms folded across his chest.

Thinking Catherine's farewell had gone on long enough, feeling a pang of jealousy that was becoming all too familiar every time he watched these two together, Marcus moved closer to put an end to it. He pulled out a leather bag. From within sounded the metallic clink of coins. He handed it to Harry.

'Take this. You will need funds when you reach Holland.'

'Thank you. You are generous, sir. I am in your debt.'

Marcus cleared his throat. 'It is a debt I do not acknowledge.'

'You might not acknowledge it, but I do. You took me in when I needed shelter—knowing you could have died for it. It renewed my faith in my fellow man, and for that I shall be eternally grateful.'

Marcus nodded, his expression thoughtful. 'It is my belief that we cannot truly be happy unless our debts we owe have been paid. Is that not so?'

'Yes.'

'And I am indebted to you. I wronged you when I made Catherine my wife without a thought to what her feelings might be for you, and for that I ask your pardon.'

'You have it, gladly given in return for my life, which you saved, and for the woman Catherine has become. It is difficult for me to acknowledge that she has transferred her affections to someone else, and if I could see that she were not truly happy, then I would not do so. I am glad to be going to Holland, and I am not proud of my eagerness that drove me to take part in the rebellion.'

'No?'

'It was never what I wanted, but I was too much of a fool to realise that rebellion is never a justifiable instrument of policy.'

Marcus nodded, smiling slightly. 'Now you're talking sense.'

'Only those changes made gradually and with care last. I intend to work towards stripping James of his throne by peaceful means. It will come, you will see.'

'I do not doubt it, but until you reach Holland your life is still in danger. You know what you must do. The vessel you must look for is the *Expedience*, the captain's name Daniel Erskine. He will be expecting you. Show yourself at first light and remember you must continue to go by the name of John Oakley until you reach Holland.' His tone was polite, impersonal and businesslike. 'Is there anything further you wish to ask?'

'No, sir.'

'Then I wish you good fortune. Come, Catherine. The time has come for us to leave.'

Catherine allowed her husband to lead her across the hall. In the doorway she paused and looked back, strangely uneasy about leaving Harry alone. Was there another presence in the house secreted away in some hole in the wall, and was it just her imagination when she looked up and thought she saw something melt into the shadows?

It was dark. Harry had been in the house for several hours and was thinking about making his way to the docks when he heard a footfall from up above. Frowning, he picked up a candle and climbed the stairs. Staring into the darkness, he saw an amorphous figure looming towards him. He stepped back in alarm. Then, gathering his wits and suspecting danger, he drew his knife and was ready when the shadowy figure leapt at him, pushing him backwards. Losing his footing, Harry stumbled, but before he crashed down the stairs he thrust at the figure with his knife, feeling a surge of triumph when the blade penetrated flesh and struck bone.

Harry struck the stairs like a rock, half-bouncing, and rolled, ending up on his face on the cold stone flags at the bottom of the stairs, his arms flung out. He could see nothing, feel nothing but the pain inside his head, as the formless shape that had attacked him crept away. He breathed, mechanically, one breath at a time. He didn't quite lose consciousness. His head spun with the effort of trying to raise himself, but his stubborn body wouldn't move.

Chapter Eleven

When Marcus went out to meet with friends, after saying goodnight to Elizabeth and her offspring, Catherine retired early that night. She felt tired, which Alice told her was to do with her pregnancy—and wasn't it high time she informed his lordship that he was going to be a father? she remarked crossly. Catherine sighed and, closing her eyes, relaxed against the pillows.

'I will, Alice, tomorrow, so don't nag. I want to tell him when Harry is safely on his way to France, so that he can truly savour the idea of being a father. At this moment all I want to do is sleep.'

But sleep did not come easily to her that night. It was way after midnight when, with a jolt, she started to wake, ill at ease. She could not stop thinking about her visit to Westminster and Harry. There was something in that house that had instilled fear in her. What was it? She had seen something. It nagged at her mind, but she couldn't for the life of her remember what it was.

Getting out of bed, she paced restlessly back and forth, trawling her mind methodically, going from room to room in that house, the downstairs rooms, and the upstairs, until the study remained prominent. The books, the chair pushed back from the desk as though someone had just risen from it, the disturbed dust on the surface, the open news-sheet and the headlines—something about Sedgemoor and the Duke of Monmouth. Recent news, news of interest to the person who had taken it to the house during the last few days. But who could it be?

Suddenly the truth struck her with awesome finality and she froze, fighting to control the shaking that gripped her body. Fenton! Was it possible that after escaping the gallows, Fenton had somehow found his way to London and was hiding in that house in Westminster—with an unsuspecting Harry? Every shred of intuition told her that she was right and that Harry was in danger.

Panic welled up in her throat and stifled her breath. The emotions and fear for Harry sweeping through her obliterated every other thought in her head. She had to help him. She wanted only one thing now, to go to him without loss of time, to go to him that instant and warn him, to make sure he was all right. With bare feet she sped across the carpet and wrenched open the connecting door. Groping her way in the darkness to the bed, she stared down at her sleeping husband, unaware that he had only just arrived home and climbed into bed—or that he had considered waking her from her slumber and making love to her.

Pressing her hand to her heart, which was pounding as though she had been running hard, with her other hand she shook Marcus's shoulder. 'Marcus, please wake up.'

Trained in the ways of a soldier, Marcus was awake immediately. Peering up at the figure attired in a white nightdress bending over him, he knew her at once.

'Are you awake?'

He cocked an eyebrow. 'Do you want me to be?'

'Please be serious, Marcus. This is terribly important.'

Raising himself, he smiled provocatively as he leaned over and lit a candle, illuminating the room with a soft glow. 'I know of no other woman who would invade the privacy of my bedchamber at this hour,' he murmured, his gaze absorbing the glorious picture she presented. The single candle betrayed her beauty through the flimsy nightdress, showing the slender curves of her body in silhouette. 'However, I am surprised. Why aren't you asleep? It must have been a very potent nightmare to bring you rushing to me. Would you like me to accompany you back to your room? If any demons are still lurking there, then I will dispel them.'

'No, it's nothing like that. I—I couldn't sleep.'

'Indeed. Perhaps it was something you ate for dinner—which is surprising, for it was a well-cooked meal.'

'No, it was nothing like that.'

Taking her hand, he pulled her down on to the bed, where she sat facing him. 'Then dare I presume that you sought me out in my bed because you were missing me?' he asked, coiling a lock of her hair around his finger.

Colour flared in her cheeks. 'No, of course not.'

'I am sorry to hear that. Never the less, now everything is resolved, I think it is time we began living together as man and wife—sleeping together. It is, after all, how heirs are made.'

To Marcus's astonishment, a stunned look crossed Catherine's face and she suddenly turned her head away. Placing his finger beneath her chin, he turned her face back to his. 'What did I say?' he asked.

'Nothing—not really,' she replied. Despite her fear, as Catherine looked into his mesmerising dark eyes and felt his fingers gently trace the curve of her cheek, she felt a sudden quiver run through her, a sudden quickening within, as if something came to life, something awoke that had been asleep for a very long time. She had to fight down the wanton urge to plead with him to take her, to beg him to love her with his heart, his body and his soul. She thought that now would be the perfect time to tell him about the baby, but there simply wasn't the time if they were to help Harry.

'I'm glad you feel so, Marcus, because that is my wish, also. It—it's just that ever since we returned from Westminster I've had the strangest feeling. I can't help worrying about Harry.'

'Why—because he's nursing a broken heart?' Marcus retorted drily, irritated that even now, when he had resolved that particular problem and had her sitting on his bed in her nightdress ripe for seduction, she still insisted on thinking of Harry Stapleton.

'Oh, stop it, Marcus. It's got nothing to do with his heart and more to do with the danger I believe he is in from whoever is in that house.' She spoke in a voice that strove to be natural, but succeeded only in being breathless and very afraid.

Marcus stared at her in surprise, his gaze probing hers and finding fear and distress within the translucent depths. 'You are upset,' he said gently. 'Tell me what this is all about.'

'It's a feeling I have—an instinct. Please don't think I'm mad, Marcus, but I am certain Mr Fenton is in that house.'

'Fenton? Catherine, have you taken leave of your wits? How can it possibly be Fenton?'

'Why not? He escaped being hanged. If he can do that under the oh, so superior nose of Captain Kirke, then he is capable of anything. He has many friends, so someone will have helped him get out of Somerset undetected. He must have found his way to London—it's not impossible. He knew your house was empty—he probably had a key, which would explain the oiled lock. Think about it, Marcus. Where better for a fugitive to hide than in any empty house belonging to an esteemed peer of the realm?'

Marcus looked searchingly into her eyes at the sound of genuine panic in her voice, his mind racing. Was there some truth in what she said? Was Fenton holed up in his house at Westminster? Personally he thought it highly improbable, but Catherine had convinced herself that he was. 'There has to be something more than that.'

'There is, but I was so uneasy when you left me alone to investigate the noise we heard that I thought nothing of it at the time. Lying on the desk in the study I saw an open news-sheet. The headlines were about Sedgemoor and the Duke of Monmouth, so someone must have been there within the last few days—and is still there. If I am right and Fenton is inside that house, then Harry is threatened with deadly danger. We must do something—warn him.'

Still unconvinced, Marcus sighed. 'Considering the publicity the rebellion and Monmouth's capture has attracted, it is hardly surprising that it is spread over every news-sheet in London. And if there is someone hiding in the house, no doubt he will want to keep up with what is happening in the outside world, so there is nothing unusual in the news-sheet.'

Catherine was becoming increasingly frustrated with Marcus's seeming lack of interest in what to her was an immensely important and worrying issue. Seeing his discarded clothes on a chair, she rushed to pick them up and thrust them at his chest. 'Here—get up and get dressed. We have to go to Westminster. For Heaven's sake, please help me to save Harry, Marcus.'

The appeal in her voice went straight to Marcus's heart. 'Very well. I can see you will give me no peace until I've been to Westminster to see for myself. But mark my words, it will be a wasted journey and our time much better spent in bed.'

'Separate beds,' she threatened, 'if you do not oblige me in this one last thing for Harry. If all is well, then we can take him to the ship ourselves to ensure he gets there safely.'

Marcus sighed. 'Very well. But I shall go alone.'

Catherine's green eyes had begun to snap and her jaw

clenched wilfully. 'No, you will not. I'm going with you,' she insisted. Marcus got out of bed and quickly stripped off his nightshirt to reveal his powerful masculine body, the long, muscular form, superbly proportioned with broad shoulders tapering to narrow hips and thighs. Catherine felt her cheeks grow annoyingly hot. She wanted to let her eyes linger, but hastily turned away. 'I'll go and get ready.'

'Oh, no, Catherine. You will stay here. The streets of London are no place for a respectable woman to be at this hour. You will attract attention from lechers, thieves and drunkards, and any other unsavoury characters who roam the byways after dark.'

'What? In the confines of a carriage and with my husband to protect me? I think not, Marcus. 'Tis an excuse and you know it.'

'Have a care, Catherine. I do not expect to have my decision questioned.'

Catherine spun round and met his hard stare. There was an imperious edge to his voice that warned her that he would not tolerate her disobedience. However, she was determined not to be left behind. She tossed her head challengingly. 'I am going with you, Marcus. I insist.'

'You can insist all night if you want, but you'll do what you're damned well told to,' he snapped angrily. 'You're safe here.'

Catherine flinched from the sting of his tone, but she carried on regardless. 'Safe, but restrained like a prisoner. My mind is made up. If you refuse to take me, then I will follow you even if I have to walk every step of the way to Westminster. It's up to you.'

Pulling on his breeches, Marcus tasted bitter defeat as he saw her soft lips tighten and her eyes blaze with jade fire. He watched her march into her room with her head held high, and, facing away from his observant eyes, with one careless, glorious movement she drew her nightdress over her head and flung it on to the bed. She'd had the last word and was bold in her certainty that she had won the round, but Marcus's smile was almost lecherous as he took a moment to observe the soft white flesh exposed to his admiring, lustful gaze, the graceful curve of her spine, the gentle swell of her firm buttocks and long shapely legs.

His smile broadened to reveal teeth that glistened like pearls and his eyes held a devilish light, for he was supremely confident that when they returned, his wife wouldn't take much persuading to share his bed.

It was still dark, with a smattering of stars in the clear sky when they reached Westminster and entered the house. The light from a single candle cast a meagre glow over the lower half of the hall, but up above the darkness was dense. The silence was intense. Catherine's skin crawled at the nape and unconsciously she moved closer to Marcus. Her fear for Harry prodded her forward and then she saw him, lying where he had come to rest at the bottom of the stairs.

'Oh, no,' she moaned.

Marcus hurried towards the inert form. 'Bring the candle close, Catherine.' Going down on one knee, he rolled Harry's limp form over. 'Harry,' he said. The light of the candle showed his face drawn and ashen. His eyes flickered up, devoid of the usual sparkle.

'Harry, what has happened to you?' Catherine gasped.

Seeing Catherine bending over him, Harry smiled with difficulty and tried to allay her fears. 'Catherine, what are you doing here? I—I think I'm all right…'

'Of course you're not.' Collapsing to her knees, she cradled his tousled head close against her breast. 'Did you fall down the stairs?'

'It's all rather confused—and there isn't much to tell. I was pushed, that I do know. I heard someone in the house—and—I went upstairs to investigate. Then the devil attacked me.'

'Who was it? Did you see?' she asked.

He shook his head, swallowing hard. 'Too dark.'

'What are your injuries?' Marcus asked. 'Can you move your legs?'

'I think so. I hit my head when I fell. Help me to sit up, will you?'

With Marcus's assistance he managed to drag himself to a sitting position and lean weakly against the panelling, wincing when sharp pain shot through his head. On examination, Marcus could detect no serious injury.

'Is the person who attacked you still in the house, do you think, Harry?' Catherine queried.

'No. I heard the door close when he left. I did manage to wound him—I don't know how seriously or how far he'll get, but I must leave myself, otherwise the *Expedience* will sail without me.'

'But you can't possibly go like this,' Catherine objected.

'Yes, he can,' Marcus said firmly. 'We'll take him to the docks.'

Catherine gave him a sideways glance and said tartly, 'But he's hurt. We must take him back to Elizabeth's where we can tend him.'

'No, Catherine,' Harry said. 'Your husband is right. I shall be perfectly all right. I have to go. I cannot miss this chance. We must hurry. Please—help me to stand.'

Marcus took his arm and hoisted him to his feet. Harry had to brace himself until his world stopped reeling. Gingerly he tested his limbs by stretching them, and then his youthful features broke into a smile when he looked at Marcus, who was supporting him until he got his balance.

'It would appear you've had a lodger in your absence, Lord

Reresby, living rent free. I think you'll have to change your locks in case he returns.'

Catherine stared at him, wondering how he could joke at a time like this.

'I think it's a little late for that,' Marcus quipped, relieved to know the younger man had not lost his sense of humour.

'It was Fenton,' Catherine whispered. 'I'm sure of it. And if so, then he might have heard what you said to Harry about the ship. It is my belief that you will find him on the *Expedience* posing as John Oakley.'

'It is a possibility I will not discount, Catherine.' He looked at Harry. 'Do you think you can make it to the coach?'

'Aye, if I have to crawl on my hands and knees.'

Marcus took his arm and half-carried him across the hall. Fortunately, by the time they reached the door Harry was walking better and managed to climb into the coach unaided.

Dawn streaked the sky by the time they reached the docks. Ships of every kind, with tall masts and gilded hulls, lay on the black, calm waters of the River Thames in great numbers. The wharves were busy, with a constant procession of loaders and quaymen streaming like ants across the dock. Archie stopped the coach when they came to the *Expedience*. Having had its cargo loaded into the hold, the vessel was almost ready to sail.

Marcus had endured the journey with a minimum of words and emotions, for he no longer had any doubt that Catherine was right about Fenton, and that he would find him on board the *Expedience*. As he was about to climb out of the coach, he suddenly stiffened.

'What is it?' Catherine asked.

'Soldiers—still on the look-out for fleeing rebels.'

Catherine looked and saw two soldiers shoving their way through the crowd. Two more made a slow circuit, glancing about. Another remained on watch, his eyes flicking over the ships that were preparing to leave. No one appeared perturbed by the soldiers' presence—the same could not be said of the occupants in the coach.

Marcus was outwardly calm, but Catherine saw his hand clench slowly into a fist. Harry, less able to control his feelings, bent his head to hide his expression, unable to feel at ease in the presence of the King's soldiers, and for good reason. Marcus glanced at him.

'Don't worry. You've passed notice so far. Once you're on board you'll be safe.' While his tone was not inhospitable, it was clear that he would prefer to be rid of his dangerous cargo as soon as possible.

Leaving his wife and Harry inside the coach, he went on board to find the captain. He found him watching as the last of the water casks were being loaded into the forward hold. Marcus was already acquainted with Captain Erskine, having sailed on the *Expedience* himself when he had journeyed to The Hague in search of his errant wife in April.

'Ah, Lord Reresby, good to see you again,' Captain Erskine said, smiling broadly as he strode across the deck to greet him. 'You're just in time. We're ready to sail. What can I do for you?'

'I've brought your passenger, Captain—John Oakley.'

The captain frowned. 'Then there has to be some mistake. Mr Oakley is already on board. He asked to go straight to his cabin—seemed to be suffering under the effects of some kind of malady. Came aboard an hour ago.'

'That's impossible. Mr Oakley is in my carriage on the wharf. Describe the man you have on board, Captain.'

'Quite tall, brown hair going grey—long face—fiftyish, I'd say.' Captain Erskine saw Marcus stiffen. 'You know him?'

'Indeed I do.'

'Then I'll have him brought up.'

'No, say nothing. Do not announce me.'

Captain Erskine looked surprised at the sharpness of his tone. 'May I ask why?'

'I can assure you, Captain, that the man you have on board is not John Oakley but a fugitive from justice. His name is Fenton, and he is highly dangerous. I know enough about him to put a rope around his neck. He was one of the instigators of Monmouth's rebellion and escaped the noose by seconds in Taunton. He was my bailiff, and I know the power of evil that inhabits the man, and the deadly, consuming hatred he feels for me. I—also have my own reason for wanting to bring the man to book.'

'What's that?'

'He murdered my father.'

The captain nodded slowly, digesting what Marcus had told him. 'I see. My commiserations, Lord Reresby, but if it is revenge you are seeking, you will not commit murder on my ship.'

'I have no intention of murdering anyone. I want Fenton to stand trial and will not cheat the hangman of his neck a second time. Give me a few minutes, Captain, and then summon a couple of the soldiers.'

'And what shall I tell them?'

'That you have a stowaway.'

'Very well, but I ask you to be quick. I want to weigh anchor in the next half-hour. You'll find who you're looking for in the cabin to the right of the companionway.'

Marcus's hand went to the hilt of his sword as he strode cross the deck and climbed down the companionway. When he reached the bottom he paused and looked around the cramped space. Overhead he could hear men moving, but down here it was empty and still, the captain's sector totally deserted. He listened at the cabin door. Nothing. There was nothing he could do but enter and hope for the best. He pushed open the door a crack.

* * *

Inside the coach Catherine waited with feverish impatience for Marcus to return. She nearly panicked when she saw two of the soldiers move close to the ship, unaware that Marcus had told Captain Erskine to summon them. Her fear for her husband prompted her to warn him, regardless of anyone who might try and stop her. To Harry's astonishment she left the coach and went on board. She looked around frantically, searching. Unable to see Marcus, she dashed across the deck towards the companionway.

'If it's the captain you're wanting,' a voice said as Marcus pushed open the door, 'he's up on deck.'

'The captain?' Marcus exclaimed. 'Whatever gave you that idea? No, Fenton, it is not the captain I'm wanting. I've come to see you.' He stepped inside. It was hot, the cabin small and cramped, the atmosphere closed. He could smell blood, fresh blood. He looked at the figure slumped in a chair at the side of a narrow bed, his clothes soiled and crumpled, and looking all of his fifty years and more. His days as a fugitive had taken their toll. At last Marcus was face to face with his enemy, his nemesis, the man who had murdered his father.

Fenton's head jerked up at the sound of Marcus's voice. The sight of the tall man standing, feet planted well apart, in the doorway, brought him to his own feet, a gun in his hand. He swayed and had to hold on to the back of the chair to steady himself. His face was waxen and a blue vein twitched at his temple. It was obvious to Marcus that the man was suffering great discomfort. Harry had said he had injured him—if so, how badly?

'I see you are expecting me, Fenton.'

'Stay where you are,' Fenton hissed. His eyes held a bright, cold gleam. 'I'm sure Lord Reresby's wife does not wish her husband to become a dead hero.'

'Put away the gun, Fenton, and we will see how much of a dead hero I am.'

'Why are you here? Have you brought a pardon from the King?' he asked, his voice heavily laced with sarcasm, for this was the last thing he could expect.

'You should be so lucky, Fenton,' Marcus sneered. 'I'll have you back on the scaffold as fast as your head can spin.' He gripped the hilt of his sword, knuckles white. Self-restraint was nearly impossible, but the position of Fenton's gun and his trembling hand made fruitless any display of bravado.

'Did you think to escape me? I have a score to settle with you—a heavy score, and one I mean to make you pay in full. You're injured, I see,' he said, seeing Fenton's blood-soaked shirt when his jerkin gaped open.

'It looks worse than it is.'

Marcus wasn't convinced. The man was struggling to remain upright. 'In my mind you are guilty beyond doubt of numerous crimes. It was you who assisted Trenchard in raising men to join the rebellion. When my father found incriminating letters and manuscripts proving beyond doubt your part in The Rye House Plot, it was you who murdered him to stop him exposing you. Such ingratitude, after all he did for you.'

'Do not concern yourself with my ability to capture your father's trust. I did it and succeeded with nothing more than my own wits and because he was a sublime fool.'

'His trust in you made him the tool of a villain and brought about his death. Do you admit that it was you who killed him?'

'Aye, since you ask, I killed him. When he found the letters he disposed of my services and threatened to expose me—me and Barrington—and he had to be stopped. We followed him to London. Barrington didn't have the nerve to silence him, so I did it—and burned the papers.' Fenton actually flinched at the cold, ruthless fury in the younger man's eyes as they locked on his.

'I suspected as much. Now you have confirmed what I have suspected for some time, I want your life, and no less. You murdered my father, you insulted my wife. You terrified the people who work for me and dared to invade the peace of my house. You are vile, Fenton, and you cannot treat anything of mine in such a manner without answering to me.'

He had spoken quietly, too quietly for Fenton's nerves. 'So, you mean to kill me.'

'No, but the King's men will. You will hang, Fenton, and when I come to see it I will not pity you. I shall rest a lot easier once you're dead.' Aware that someone had come to stand behind him, he turned slightly to see his wife, her large eyes filled with concern. 'Catherine, what the hell are you trying to do—get yourself killed? I told you to remain in the coach.'

In the face of his angry displeasure, Catherine swallowed audibly, and her voice wavered. 'You were a long time. I was worried about you—and there are soldiers close to the ship.'

'Don't worry. Erskine will have summoned them.' Marcus glanced at her sharply. 'Stapleton is still inside the coach?'

'Yes.'

'So, you have found him,' Fenton gasped, his eyes gloating horribly. 'He took quite a tumble—thought I'd killed him.'

'He is very much alive—with no thanks to you, Mr Fenton,' Catherine remarked coldly. 'He has survived his encounter with you without scars.'

'A resilient young man, that. So, he is here and about to take my place. No doubt you have summoned the soldiers to arrest me, but I shall see to it that I am not taken alone.' Fenton's voice was weak now, for pain had shortened his breath.

On his face was a look of such malice and determination to do Harry harm, that Catherine felt dread and apprehension, combined with misery and hopelessness, deep and palpable. Stepping past her husband, she faced Fenton, staring at the black muzzle of his gun aimed directly at her stomach. For a moment she saw madness in his eyes and feared he would shoot her. She did not want to die, not needlessly like this. Life had grown very dear to her. Suddenly she had everything to live for, beginning with Marcus and their unborn child. But she had to plead for Harry.

'Will you not do one honourable thing to redeem yourself before you die, Mr Fenton?' she said quietly. 'Harry has done you no wrong. He means nothing to you. Please don't use him as an instrument to avenge my husband. He may not be a Republican, but Harry fights for the cause so dear to your own heart. If he reaches Holland he will strive to place Prince William and Princess Mary on England's throne. He is young and will devote himself to that end. Knowing this, can you not show mercy and help him on his way?'

'Why should I grant him any favours?'

'Surely it must gladden your heart knowing he is just one of many who will continue the struggle to depose King James. I beg of you, Mr Fenton, give Harry's predicament decent consideration. I would be grateful to you.' Her voice was devoid of expression, but her eyes were pleading. 'Please, do not expose him.'

With the sharp reflex of a soldier, and the sharp instinct of a man who will protect that which he holds most dear, even with his life, seeing the gun waver menacingly in Fenton's hand, Marcus moved to place himself between his wife and the man who glared at her.

'I warn you, Fenton, if you attempt to harm my wife in any way, I will run you through—soldiers or not.'

Fenton swayed, and before he had recovered, Marcus was on him. Twisting the weapon out of his hand, Marcus knocked him off balance and shoved him back into the chair. Fenton made no attempt to get up. Breathing hard, beads of perspiration glistened on his brow.

Marcus looked down on him with contempt. 'I could kill you now if I chose, but, unlike you, murder has never been one of my favourite pastimes.'

Hearing heavy footsteps climbing down the companionway, Marcus turned when two soldiers appeared in the doorway. Seeing Fenton slumped in the chair, his bloodied shirt exposed, they peered at him suspiciously. It was obvious who was the stowaway.

One of the soldiers, a burly fellow, stepped forward. 'In the name of the King, who are you?'

When Fenton remained silent, white-faced, his eyes burning with rage, Marcus obliged the soldiers. 'His name is Fenton—Jacob Fenton.'

'And who might you be?' the soldier asked tentatively because there was an undeniable authority in Marcus's stance and voice.

'Lord Reresby of Saxton Court in Somerset. Until recently I was an officer in the King's army.'

Respect flared in the soldier's eyes. 'Now there's a turn-up. Fought at Sedgemoor, did you, my lord?'

Marcus nodded.

The stern expression of the gentleman's countenance told the soldier that he was in no mood for cordial conversation, so he turned his attention on Fenton. 'Setting aside the fact that this man is a stowaway, what has he done?'

'Fenton played an important part in Monmouth's rebellion. He was captured and escaped the gallows by the skin of his teeth. He has been a fugitive since then—and, as you can see, he is wounded.'

'Did you do that, sir?'

'No.'

'And might I ask what you are doing on board this vessel?'

'You may. Captain Erskine is a personal friend of mine. My

wife and I came to wish him *bon voyage*. He told us he had a stowaway on board, so I came to investigate. You can imagine my astonishment when I discovered the stowaway to be Mr Fenton. He used to be my bailiff, but what with one thing and another and his unacceptable political beliefs, I was forced to get rid of him.'

'Aye, I can understand that. We'll take him away—to the Tower, where he'll no doubt be interrogated.'

'He'll hang,' the other soldier mumbled. 'No more than he deserves.'

Catherine watched them haul Fenton to his feet and bind his hands in front of him with a kind of horror. She knew the evil that inhabited the man and the deadly consuming hatred that he held for Marcus, a hatred she hoped and prayed he would not appease by exposing Harry. But as the soldiers took hold of him to drag him away and she saw his features contort with pain, unable to stand by and witness suffering of any kind, she took a step towards them.

'Mr Fenton is badly wounded. There is no need for such rough handling.'

As if divining her thoughts, Fenton looked at her directly. His face was as rigid as if it had been carved out of stone, and his eyes gave an impression of extraordinary resignation. 'My regards to your friend,' he hissed, the words for her ears alone. 'Maybe he will succeed where men like me failed.' And then he was gone, stumbling his way up the ladder. Catherine waited tensely, and not until his footsteps could be heard no more did she turn to her husband.

Putting away his sword, Marcus looked at his wife, an array of fleeting emotions crossing his face as he slipped an arm about her waist and drew her close. 'You must prepare yourself for what Fenton might tell them. If he exposes Harry, then I cannot see how I can help him,' he said with inexpressible tenderness.

Catherine tilted her face to his, gripping her floundering emotions with a tight rein of determination. 'You have done your best, Marcus. No one could have done more, but I do not believe Mr Fenton will expose Harry.'

'How can you know that?'

'I don't know how—instinct, perhaps.' She did not reveal Fenton's parting words. *Dear God, let him have meant what he said*, she prayed silently. 'Wait until the soldiers have gone, then have Harry come aboard.'

Fenton's arrest created a great deal of interest, and as everyone crowded round to watch him being taken away by the military, Marcus calmly took Harry on board. Captain Erskine asked no questions and, impatient to set sail, when Lord Reresby and his charming wife had bade the young man farewell, he saw them off his vessel and weighed anchor.

Not until Marcus and Catherine were satisfied that the vessel would not be apprehended and saw it disappear down the Thames, did they return to the coach. Marcus had watched Catherine apprehensively as she had said goodbye to Harry, carefully noting her expressions. Before they climbed inside the coach he took her hand, seeing tears glistening in her eyes.

'Tell me you no longer love him, Catherine.' There was an edge to his voice, but his expression revealed nothing of his thoughts and his dark eyes were carefully guarded.

Brushing aside her tears, she gazed up at his handsome face, her eyes tender. 'If you cast your mind back, you will recall that I have told you on numerous occasions that my love for Harry is in the past. What we had was special to both of us. I am relieved that he is safe and I know he will find someone else to love him in time, but there will always be good memories and no regrets. I am your wife, Marcus, and that is all I shall ever want to be.' Her teary smile was so dazzling that she had no idea how it swelled her husband's heart. 'All this trouble with

Harry and the rebellion has kept us apart for far too long. Now take me home—I've no wish to spoil your pleasure a moment longer.'

'I haven't had you to myself since our marriage, and the idea rather appeals to me.'

'It appeals to me, too.'

'I'm gratified to know that,' he replied. 'And tonight, you will sleep in my bed where you belong.'

A slow smile lighted Catherine's eyes, reflecting her joy. 'I am happy to know you do not mean to avoid me any longer. I thought you didn't want me.'

Marcus's brows drew together in a frown. 'You little fool. Of course I wanted you—and all the more because I had already experienced making love to you. Do you have any idea what torment I endured night after night, sleeping apart from you, knowing you were so close?'

'I wanted you too, Marcus, and from now on things will be so very different. Now, help me inside. It has been a long night and Elizabeth will be waiting for us to explain ourselves— but…' she paused and looked up at him, a serious light in her eyes, '…I don't think I want to go back to that house again, Marcus. I know you are undecided about selling it—but I wish you would.'

'I intend to. We'll buy something else, to the north of the city, where the air is cleaner—something new, close to Elizabeth.'

She smiled, thankful. 'Yes, I'd like that.'

With an enormous burden lifted from his shoulders, Marcus was content to sit and gaze across at his wife as the coach travelled north. Her hands were elegantly folded and resting on the deep pink satin folds of her skirt. Relief that it was over and that his wife was entirely his at last overwhelmed him.

'You are very quiet, Catherine,' Marcus commented softly after travelling in silence for a while, his curiosity aroused. 'It is most unusual in one who normally has so much to say. What are you looking at that occupies your attention?'

'Since you were so engrossed in your thoughts, I have generally behaved as though I were quite invisible. I have been thinking and admiring the scenery.'

'What were you thinking?'

'Oh, nothing in particular.'

Marcus sighed, his face thoughtful. 'Though you can be a troublesome wench, I will condescend to speak to you,' he teased.

A little smile dimpled her cheeks. 'Do not trouble yourself. I am quite happy in my solitude.'

'Are you, by God,' he chuckled. The bright buttons on his coat caught the sun and flashed as he leaned forward and pulled her across to sit beside him. 'That is treasonable talk and deserving of severe punishment. Come now, confess you are more comfortable seated beside me.'

'I will do nothing of the sort,' Catherine said, avoiding his smiling dark eyes. She reached up to straighten her hat, which he had knocked awry. The moment it was back in place he immediately removed it.

'That's better. You have beautiful hair. I like to see it exposed.'

She settled against him, basking in his praise. 'Very well, I shall leave it off and allow you to disarrange my hair—if you don't mind me arriving on your sister's doorstep looking like a gypsy.'

'I like gypsies.'

'You do?'

'Yes. I like their nomadic way of life, and I like people who behave and look like gypsies—which puts me in mind of you, my love.'

Catherine sighed. She liked to hear him call her his love. It gave her a warm glow. Resting her head against his shoulder, she closed her eyes. 'Then I shall be more than happy to be a gypsy wench.' They were silent for a few minutes, content in this new closeness that was developing between them.

Marcus could feel the heat of her reaching out to him, and his heart and body ached for her. 'Despite everything that has happened in these past weeks, my darling, in all that time I never stopped loving you.'

Marcus's pronouncement was so unexpected, and so very welcome, that Catherine gasped and pulled back in his arms the better to see his face. 'You love me?' she repeated with wonder.

The passion in his eyes was compelling and tender. 'Aye, I love you, Catherine. Never doubt it.' There was real agony in his reply. 'You seem surprised.'

'Because,' she murmured brokenly, 'until this moment, I had despaired of ever hearing you say that to me.'

With a groan, Marcus hugged her tightly to him. 'I think I fell in love with you the night I married you and you were so determined to stand against me. You swore to make me a cold and unwilling wife and told me with such ire that your heart was yours to give and yours to withhold.'

'I withhold it no longer, Marcus. I love you, too,' Catherine whispered, shyly laying her trembling hand against his jaw. 'I love you very much.'

As his arms twined round her and he sought her lips with his own, proceeding to kiss her with a tender, arousing passion, tiny shivers of joy raced through her. When he finally drew away, too dazed to move, Catherine gazed up at him, remembering that she had something important to tell him.

'Shall we remain in London, Marcus?'

'For the time being—until the assizes are over and things have settled down in the West Country. Somerset is not the place to be right now.'

'But we will return to Saxton Court, won't we?'

Marcus frowned down at her flushed face. 'What is this? Have you an aversion to London?'

'No, not usually, but—it is not the place I want to bring up our child.'

'When you are with child, Catherine, I shall consider returning to Somerset.'

'Then perhaps you should consider it now, Marcus.'

It took about a full ten seconds before it dawned on Marcus what she was telling him. 'What? What are you saying? You—' He broke off to stare at her incredulously, sitting bolt upright.

'Ah, so I have captured your attention.'

'Catherine, are you with child?'

'I am, Marcus.'

'When? When did it happen?'

'The first time. At The Hague.'

He was incredulous. 'Why—that's going on four months.'

'You—must have known it would happen.'

'The occasion was so taxing that the question of reproduction never crossed my mind.'

She smiled. 'It was the last thing I was thinking about, too.'

'And are you happy?'

'Yes, I am—more so since the baby has become active. It makes me realise there's a little person in there,' she said softly, placing her hands on her abdomen.

'Why didn't you tell me earlier?'

She looked at his unsmiling face with dismay. 'I was waiting for the right moment.'

'And you consider that moment to be now?'

'Yes. Now Harry has gone, everything will be utterly changed. I promise you. Are you not pleased?'

Her words seemed to galvanise him into action. He caught her up in his arms. 'Pleased? This news is most dear to my heart. Silly little fool,' he murmured roughly but fondly. 'You might have told me that you are with child. Although I should have seen it for myself. It's written all over your face. But you must take care, Catherine, and rest. 'Tis a serious, hazardous business to bear a child—and had I known of this last night, I would never have taken you with me.'

She laughed. 'Come now, Marcus, no gloomy thoughts. I will come to no harm, I promise you. You need have no fears for me or our babe. I am strong and healthy and will recover disgustingly fast in order to plague you yet again.'

There was an unnaturally bright glitter in his eyes as his arms tightened around her. 'I shall hold you to that.'

Mr Fenton died of the wound inflicted by Harry Stapleton before he could be brought to trial.

Not until Judge Jeffreys had cleansed the West Country of its rebels and returned to London did Marcus and Catherine return to Saxton Court. The Bloody Assizes had occupied the Lord Chief Justice's time for a mere nine days, during which almost two thousand rebels were dealt with, some receiving death sentences and hundreds more ordered for transportation and countless years of slavery working on the plantations.

All through the autumn executions were in progress. These were most cruel days and those who had taken up arms against King James—men of conscience and brave hearts—discovered there was a high price to pay for treason. What particularly angered and sickened the population of the western counties was the manner in which the putrefying remains of so many were exhibited long after they had been hanged, drawn and quartered. The memory of Judge Jeffreys's scourge would live vividly among the people of the West Country, its countless incidents passed on by word of mouth for generations to come.

Marcus believed that the rebellion laid bare an extremely dangerous threat to society. It was also his belief that both the

King and Judge Jeffreys believed the Bloody Assizes was a necessary and effective part of Government policy to teach the
West Country its duty and all Englishmen the folly of armed
rebellion.

For three years, James carried on with his plans to turn Brit-
ain back to Catholicism, and failed dismally. When John
Churchill and two of his colonels—one of them being Captain
Kirke—along with four hundred of the men under them de-
fected to William, Prince of Orange and Stadtholder of Holland,
he realised that his chances of clinging to office were non-ex-
istent. William succeeded where Monmouth had failed, landing at Torbay on the fifth of November, 1688. Along with many
who had been in exile in Holland, awaiting a time such as this
and eager to return to their homes, was Harry Stapleton and his
bride of twelve months. James fled to France, never to see England again.

The scent of summer, of water and grass and wild flowers,
was trapped under a low sky. It was late afternoon and the col-
ours of the landscape, rampant with growth, deepened. Along the
banks of the lake hosted duck, moorhen and other wildfowl. Marcus had slipped the oars to let the boat drift. With his three-year-
old son Charles rocking the boat in his excitement to reel in his
line and proudly present his father with his first catch, Marcus
tenderly covered the boy's small hands with his own to help him.

Dragging his gaze from the water, and his mind from the victory that was almost within his son's grasp, he gazed at the
shore, where Catherine sat on the grass, their two-month-old
daughter cradled in her arms. As if she sensed that she was
being observed, she looked towards the boat and then smiled
and waved. Charles had captured his prize, and was filled with
a sense of achievement and impatient to show it to his mother,
so Marcus obliged the boy, taking up the oars and rowing to-

vards the shore. Pushing the nose of the boat into the soft mud, hey climbed ashore, Charles gleefully running up the bank holding his fish.

Placing the baby on a blanket, Catherine admired the catch. Charles proceeded to show it to his sister, blissfully ignorant of the fact that she was only two months old and had not yet acquired the taste for fish. Catherine got to her feet, her green eyes smiling happily into those of her husband. Together they looked down at their children.

'Our son is a child of many talents,' Marcus remarked. 'Our lives will never be dull.'

'What a pity we have to eat the fish—his first catch. I think Charles would like to keep it for posterity.'

'I think the stench might change his mind.' Marcus laughed, putting his arm about her shoulders. 'His next will be even bigger, you'll see.'

They stood together on the shoreline, looking out over the lake, each content with their lives and the way things had turned out for them, after such a stormy beginning.

'It seems to me that this moment is a continuation of another moment—over three years ago when I first came to Saxton Court. I feel that I belong here now. Do you remember when we stood upon this same spot and we watched the sunlight dance on the water?'

'As if it were yesterday.' He looked down at her. 'You belong with me, wherever that might be. I love you, Catherine.'

The words echoed in the fullness of her heart, filling her with a tune too sweet to be sung, a coming together of harmony and the ever-surging tide of ecstasy, and that which defied the telling because words were inadequate and simply not enough to capture how she felt. So all she said was, 'I love you too.'

* * * * *

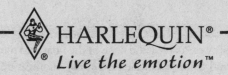

HARLEQUIN®
Live the emotion™

American ROMANCE®
Heart, Home & Happiness

HARLEQUIN®
Blaze™
Red-hot reads.

HARLEQUIN®
EVERLASTING LOVE™
Every great love has a story to tell™

HARLEQUIN® Historical
Historical Romantic Adventure!

HARLEQUIN®
HARLEQUIN ROMANCE®
From the Heart, For the Heart

HARLEQUIN®
INTRIGUE®
Breathtaking Romantic Suspense

Medical Romance™...
love is just a heartbeat away

N**e**xt™
**There's the life you planned.
And there's what comes next.**

HARLEQUIN®
Presents
Seduction and Passion Guaranteed!

HARLEQUIN®
Super Romance®
Exciting, Emotional, Unexpected

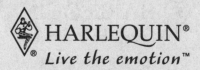

HARLEQUIN®
INTRIGUE®

BREATHTAKING ROMANTIC SUSPENSE

Shared dangers and passions lead to electrifying
romance and heart-stopping suspense!

Every month, you'll meet six new heroes
who are guaranteed to make your spine tingle
and your pulse pound. With them you'll enter
into the exciting world of Harlequin Intrigue—
where your life is on the line
and so is your heart!

THAT'S INTRIGUE—
ROMANTIC SUSPENSE
AT ITS BEST!

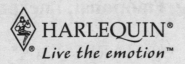

HARLEQUIN®
Live the emotion™

HARLEQUIN®
SuperRomance®

...there's more to the story!

Superromance.
A *big* satisfying read about unforgettable characters. Each month we offer *six* very different stories that range from family drama to adventure and mystery, from highly emotional stories to romantic comedies—and much more! Stories about people you'll believe in and care about. Stories too compelling to put down....

Our authors are among today's *best* romance writers. You'll find familiar names and talented newcomers. Many of them are award winners— and you'll see why!

If you want the biggest and best in romance fiction, you'll get it from Superromance!

Exciting, Emotional, Unexpected...

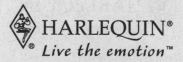

HARLEQUIN®
Live the emotion™

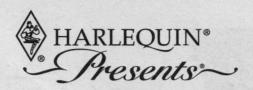

HARLEQUIN®
Presents

The world's bestselling romance series...
The series that brings you your favorite authors,
month after month:

Helen Bianchin...Emma Darcy
Lynne Graham...Penny Jordan
Miranda Lee...Sandra Marton
Anne Mather...Carole Mortimer
Susan Napier...Michelle Reid

and many more uniquely talented authors!

Wealthy, powerful, gorgeous men...
Women who have feelings just like your own...
The stories you love, set in exotic, glamorous locations...

HARLEQUIN®
Presents
Seduction and Passion Guaranteed!